June's expression softened. For a second, her hand lifted, like she was going to touch him, and Clay couldn't decide whether to lean in or jerk away.

She tucked her hands into the pockets of her dress. One corner of her red lips rose.

"Well, I can't say you've won me over completely. But you at least convinced me to hate you a little less."

And good grief, that shouldn't make some kind of warmth build in his chest.

Clay shrugged it off. "Flatter a guy..."

Tipping her head to the side, June smiled.

Slowly, he told her, "I suppose you've got yourself a deal."

He extended his hand.

She regarded it for half a second too long. What? Did he have dirt under his nails or something? She didn't like grease stains and calluses?

Or did she feel the same hum of electricity singing between their bodies that he did?

The
INN ON
SWEETBRIAR
LANE

The INN ON SWEETBRIAR LANE

A Blue Cedar Falls Novel

JEANNIE CHIN

FOREVER

New York Boston

Forever
Hachette Book Group
1290 Avenue of the Americas, New York, NY 10104
read-forever.com
twitter.com/readforeverpub

Kiss Me at Sweetwater Springs was originally published in 2019 as an ebook by Forever.

First edition: September 2021

Forever is an imprint of Grand Central Publishing. The Forever name and logo are trademarks of Hachette Book Group, Inc.

The publisher is not responsible for websites (or their content) that are not owned by the publisher.

The Hachette Speakers Bureau provides a wide range of authors for speaking events. To find out more, go to www.hachettespeakersbureau.com or call (866) 376-6591.

ISBNs: 978-1-5387-5360-6 (mass market); 978-1-5387-5361-3 (ebook)

Printed in the United States of America

CW

10 9 8 7 6 5 4 3 2 1

*For everyone still trying their best, even
after this miserable year.
You're doing great.*

The
INN ON
SWEETBRIAR
LANE

CHAPTER ONE

Three tours overseas might have cost Clay Hawthorne a chunk of bone from his knee and the better part of his soul. But the good thing about coming back stateside after something like that was that not much could surprise a guy.

Or at least that's what he told himself.

Worrying the shiny brass key between his rough fingers, he sized up the building he'd bought. Sight unseen, plucked off some real estate website: 23 Main Street, Blue Cedar Falls, North Carolina.

It was hard to tell in the dimness of twilight, but the foundations of the old storefront looked sound enough. No big cracks in the red brick. The awning would need replacing, and the dusty glass of the big, boarded-up front window might, too.

To either side stood little shops that were in a lot better shape. The bed-and-breakfast across the street just about shone, the fresh coat of paint on it was so bright and new.

They weren't any concern of his, though.

He'd seen a lot of small towns in the year since he'd gotten back. He'd seen even more as a kid, kicking around from one foster home to another. In the end, they were all the same. Charming on the outside, but no amount of white paint could cover up the dingy parts underneath. No doubt in his mind this place would be the same.

Yet there was still an odd prickle of hope in his chest as he approached the big wood door. Solid oak. Strong and true. He fit his key to the lock, held his breath, and pushed inside.

He fumbled for a minute, searching blindly in the dark for a switch. He finally found it and flipped the lights on.

With a groan of protest, a lone flickering fluorescent bulb buzzed to life overhead, and it was all he could do not to turn it right back off again.

Rose-colored walls met him everywhere he looked. All along the top border, salmon flowers had been stamped on with a sponge. Carpet in a different shade of dusty, faded pink spread out beneath his boots. The counter had probably been white at one point, but the peeling paint had just about given up the ghost and decided to go ahead and turn pink, too.

Well, at least now he understood why the place had been such a good deal.

Gritty laughter bubbled up in the back of his throat. "Good grief, Bug. What have we gotten ourselves into now?"

No one replied. No one had in a year and four weeks, and damn if he didn't miss the voice that had always answered all his stupid questions as much today as he did the day it'd been silenced. Forever.

This had been Bug's dream, after all. He'd talked about it when they'd been camped under the stars in the desert and hunkered down in the blistering sun, waiting for orders outside a suspected insurgent hideout. Every time he'd told the story about the bar he was going to go home and build, Bug had added little details. Clay had chuckled and told him *Sure, sure*, skeptical as anything, but he'd liked the stories, no matter how many times he'd heard them.

And the first, most central piece of Bug's plan had been to open his bar right here where he grew up. Blue Cedar Falls, in the western mountains of North Carolina. He'd put it smack-dab in the middle of their quaint little tourist district, too—the part of town where rich people from all over the country swung through for the weekend, never to be seen again, while the regular folks who lived there felt like scenery.

It wouldn't be one of those trendy places with fancy wine lists and cocktails in every color of the rainbow, either.

It'd be a real bar, serving beer and whiskey and maybe scotch if things got out of hand. With leather stools and wood panel-ing and the game playing on a TV in the corner. A jukebox with honest music on it—no auto-tuned crap. With voices and guitars and heartache of the kind anybody could understand.

A bar for people who'd never had a seat at the table.

Bug didn't live to see his dream through. But Clay was here. Alive and breathing, if not entirely whole.

Clenching his jaw against the twinge in his knee, he circled the perimeter of the big, pink storefront to stand in its very center. It had been a knitting shop, or maybe quilting. He didn't know and he didn't care.

He sized the space up with a more careful eye. As a teen in foster care, he'd worked under the table for a handyman for a couple of years, and he knew what he was doing well enough. The carpet he could tear out. A building of this age, ten to one there'd be wood underneath, and wood he could work with. Panels would go up on the walls as easy as could be. He'd need to build the bar itself and put in lighting of some kind. A stage for local acts on Saturday nights. There'd be a couple of high-tops with stools, of course, and a few big tables with benches where real people could drink real drinks and eat real food and forget their troubles, at least for a little while.

A lot of the details were fuzzy, but that didn't matter. He'd figure them out. Already, he could almost smell the spilled beer and hear the rumble of laughter and conversation.

Then he blinked.

And yeah, those walls were still pink. The room was empty and silent as the grave. But not for long.

"Okay, Bug." He rubbed his hands together, then nodded to himself. "Let's do this."

"How can they *do* this?"

June Wu tossed the letter from the hospital aside and dropped her head into her hands.

In the first thirty-two years of her life, she'd never once failed to pay a bill on time. She'd never so much as incurred a library fine.

Now the stack of notices screaming PAST DUE barely fit in the file she secreted them away in.

She took a deep breath and glanced around the lobby of the Sweetbriar Inn. With the exception of what sounded like a jack-hammer firing away outside and the muffled din of her stepfather Ned handling the breakfast crowd down the hall, everything was silent. Confident she was alone, she picked up the letter again and reread the reminder about the anesthesiologist's assistant's out-of-network fee for handing the doctor a tube—or whatever this particular bill was about. The threat to turn the debt over to a collection agency made her throat constrict.

Every time she got one of these notices, all she could see was her mother, ashen and mute and hooked up to wires and machines, doctors everywhere, nurses pushing June aside while she screamed at them to save her mom. Just save her. The sheer panic still sent ice flooding through her veins, and she had to shake herself so as not to give over to it.

Her mom was fine. She was fine. Her family—they'd all be fine.

Just as soon as she got these bills under control.

She was working on getting a payment plan set up with the hospital, but everybody who had so much as laid eyes on her mother seemed to want a piece of her. She was barely treading water, and the sea of medical debt kept rising.

At this rate, she was going to lose the inn.

She crumpled the paper in her hand.

Over her dead body. This inn was her family's lifeblood. Ned had been born here, and his parents had managed it before him. It had weathered tough times in the past. No way the bank would get it under June's watch.

She just needed business to pick up a bit.

She chewed at the inside of her lip. Bookings were all right for now, but ever since the new highway had opened that spring, cutting Blue Cedar Falls off from the usual flow of traffic, tourism had been trending down. Everyone on Main Street had been feeling the pinch. The last meeting of the business association had been two long hours of people going around in circles complaining.

June had binders full of ideas for how to drum up business, but the only one she'd been able to get enough support for had been a relaunch of their classic Pumpkin Festival. Even that had been a nail-biter. People like Patty Boyd—owner of the gallery at the end of the road, current association president and de facto leader of a coalition of pearl-clutching PTA moms—and Dottie Gallagher—the eighty-year-old florist who'd been putting her nose in everyone's business since before the Cold War—seemed determined to keep anything from changing, ever.

Well, June would show them. Autumn was supposed to be their busiest season, but right now, it was looking like a bust.

She was going to fix that. Bold new branding for the festival, a big online ad campaign, and specials going on up and down Main Street would bring people in. She was sure of it.

Plus, there was her ace in the hole.

Speaking of which...

She tucked the latest notice from the hospital in the locked filing cabinet behind the desk before pulling out her phone. She dismissed a couple of notifications she could deal with later—something from her youngest sister Elizabeth and one of the chain emails her mom was so fond of sending, especially while she was still on doctor's orders to relax and take it easy.

She pulled up the text message thread she had going with her other sister, May, and frowned.

May's fast-paced, on-the-go life as a travel writer had always made her hard to get a hold of, but recently it had gotten ridiculous—at least when it came to anything that mattered. Send her a screenshot of a guilty pleasure TV show and she was there with exclamation points and commentary. Ask her if she'd booked her tickets to come down for the festival you were relaunching to try to resuscitate your hometown and keep your family out of the poorhouse?

Crickets.

Just for fun, June sent another, maybe slightly less than gentle nudge, along with an animated gif of a sad puppy staring pleadingly at the screen. It would probably get ignored, too, but no one could say June hadn't tried.

A successful Pumpkin Festival would give this year's numbers a much-needed boost, but if June was going to keep the collection agencies at bay, she needed to think long-term. May coming in and writing a glowing article for her magazine could really expand their reach.

She just had to get her sister back here, was all.

Before she could get too worked up about it, footsteps echoed on the stairs heading down from the second floor. June shoved her phone in the pocket of her dress and put on her best smile as the Andersons from room thirteen headed her way. Rising to her feet, she plucked their folio from the tray beside the computer. "Checking out?" she asked brightly.

Mr. Anderson nodded, his mouth pursed.

Hmm.

June walked them through their bill and ran their card, but she kept an eye on them all the while. Happy guests became repeat guests, or at least positive reviewers, and these were not happy guests.

"Is there anything we could have done to make your stay more pleasant?" June tried.

Mrs. Anderson rubbed her eyes and shook her head. "No, dear. Unless you have any sway with whoever's making that racket outside."

"They were at it half the night, too," her husband added.

At precisely that moment banging sounded through the air, and June winced.

The sale on the old quilt shop across the street had been finalized a few days ago. The Main Street rumor mill had been in a tizzy about it, too, but no one had been able to get the scoop on what was going on over there.

Whatever it was, it was *loud*. The Andersons weren't the first to complain.

"I'm so sorry," June started, but the Andersons waved her off. It wasn't her fault, but that didn't mean she didn't want to fix it. "Let me see what I can do about taking a little something off your bill..."

Their mood seemed to improve after that.

Once they were gone, she sighed. No more guests were scheduled to check out this morning—though with all the noise, she'd been bracing herself for the possibility.

Not that she had time to dwell on it.

Double-checking that the sign inviting guests to ring the bell for service was lined up beside the candy bowl and the vase of fresh flowers she had delivered twice a week, she stepped out from behind the desk.

Immediately, she felt freer.

It wasn't that she minded running the front desk, but too many hours cooped up behind it made her a little batty sometimes. A selfish part of her longed for the days when her mother had happily whiled away the days at her post there, playing mah-jongg online and reading paperback mysteries and gossiping with anyone who came through. With her mom as captain, June had been second mate, following orders and living her life. Carefree, by comparison, though she'd imagined she was stressed at the time.

She sighed. She'd had no idea how good she'd had it back then.

As if to taunt her for that very thought, her mother's laughter echoed down the hall. Shaking her head fondly, June followed the sound to its usual location these days.

The breakfast room of the inn was bustling. Delicious scents of frying bacon and fresh pancakes on the griddle filled the air as warmly as the sound of good conversation and clinking silverware and plates.

The Sweetbriar Inn was known for miles around as one of the best bed-and-breakfasts in the western half of the state. June smiled as she picked up a carafe of coffee and started casually making the rounds of the tables. Half of them were occupied by guests, whom she greeted warmly, asking about their stay and how they were planning to spend their day—crossing her fingers they wouldn't say anything about the odd hours her hammer-happy new neighbor seemed to keep.

The other half were filled with locals who knew full well that the breakfasts served at the Sweetbriar Inn were just as special as their beds. They *definitely* said something about the sounds of construction outside, but none of them seemed to know what was going on, either.

When her carafe was empty, she headed for the kitchen, where her stepdad had ten orders going at once.

"Hey, June-y," Ned said, presenting his stubbly cheek for a kiss.

She gave one to him happily. "You doing all right back here?"

"Just fine." The sweat on his brow and the tired lines around his eyes told a different story, but she wasn't going to call him out right now. Between running the kitchen, tending the grounds, and taking care of her mother, he had his hands as full as she did. As she drew back, he tilted his head toward a set of plates on the counter. "Take those to table three?"

Of course. The sliced scallions on top of the eggs on one of the plates were a dead giveaway. "Sure thing."

Grabbing a tray, she loaded the plates up and headed for the big table in the corner.

"*Finally.*" Her mother smiled at her approach, softening the judgment in her tone.

As was her wont these days, Li Mei Wu sat in the cushy chair at the far end of the dining room. She was dressed in a blue and white floral blouse, a pale green jade pendant hanging from a gold chain draped across her throat. She was sixty, but her chin-length hair was still mostly black, the curls June had put in it that morning holding well. Sunny—the mean, three-legged calico cat she'd taken in—occupied her lap. A half dozen women of a certain age surrounded them.

As soon as her mother had gotten home from the hospital, June had been on the phone trying to line up people to come by and see her. It was the only way she could think of to keep her mother from diving straight into work and setting back her recovery.

She just hadn't realized how out of hand it would get.

A few friends swinging by for a chat now and then had turned into a rotating crew of them showing up for breakfast every morning. If any more of them started coming by, Ned would have to haul in another table. As it was, when they really got going, their cackles gave the jackhammer across the street a run for its money.

Smiling at her mother's friends, June set the tray down and started to pass out plates. Most of these women got the same thing every day, so that was easy enough. She placed the dish with the scallions in front of her mother.

Her mom picked up her fork with her left hand, keeping her once-dominant right arm draped across Sunny's back. With a long-suffering expression, she looked to her friends on either side of her. "Good help is so hard to find these days."

The slight slurring of her words had nothing to do with her subtle Chinese accent and everything to do with the lingering effects of her stroke.

Trying not to react—because her mom *loved* it when she pointed out the places where her recovery needed work—June rolled her eyes, distributing the rest of the plates. "Well, when your boss goes on vacation for nine months..."

"Only because my employee tells me I have to!"

"Your doctor said—"

"Doctor," her mother scoffed. "What do they know? Your

great-aunt Chung never saw a doctor her whole life. When she had stroke, she took Chinese herbs. Better in three weeks."

"My great-aunt Chung died when she was sixty."

"But so healthy until then."

Her mother's best friend, Mrs. Leung, patted her hand. "No point arguing. You can't tell children anything." She made a *tch*ing sound behind her teeth. "My youngest, Zoe? The worst. Never listens."

"You know they say the same thing about you behind your back," Ms. Smith said, smiling at June as she accepted her plate of hash and toast. She pitched her voice higher, mimicking her own kids. "*Mom is so stuck in her ways. It's like she doesn't even know what social media is.*"

"I have all the accounts," June's mother insisted. "Facebook, Twitter." Her eyes sparkled. "Ellen DeGeneres followed me back on Instagram."

"Of course she did, Mom."

Her mom put her hand to her chest. "She doesn't believe me!"

Mrs. Leung tutted. "Like I said, no reasoning with children."

"There's no reasoning with you, either," Ms. Smith scolded. "We could learn a thing or two from our kids if we just listened."

"And they could learn a thing or two from us," Mrs. Leung insisted.

June's mother waved her hand dismissively. "Both sides have points. Need to meet in the middle. That's what I always say."

But Mrs. Leung didn't seem to have any interest in talking about compromise. She looked at June pointedly. "Wait until you have children of your own. Then you understand."

A dull ache panged behind June's ribs.

Right. As if that was going to happen anytime soon.

She smiled as sweetly as she could. "I'll report back to you if I ever do."

Out of the corner of her eye, she caught her mother's slightly lopsided smile falling by a fraction.

If June couldn't handle Mrs. Leung's *advice* about her life, she sure as heck couldn't handle her mother's sympathy about her lack of one.

Guilt tugged at her, but she mumbled something about having to get back to the front desk. She didn't meet anyone else's gaze as she turned away.

Fortunately, no one called after her, though she had no doubt her mom would bring it up again when they were alone. She seemed to think June could handle everything here *and* get out and find her soul mate.

She waved at Ned as she passed the kitchen and headed out into the cooler, clearer, quieter air of the hall. On the way, she made a quick stop in the restroom. She locked the door behind her before dropping her head into her hands.

The thing was that she didn't exactly mind the fact that she had no time or energy for a personal life. Sure, she'd always wanted kids, and yeah, at thirty-two, she wasn't what some of the older ladies would call a spring chicken anymore.

But she had responsibilities. Her mother, Ned, the inn. The never-ending swamp of medical debt and the new highway and their terrible bookings for fall and relaunching the Pumpkin Festival and, well...*everything*.

She couldn't rely on her sisters. Elizabeth was too scatter-brained, and May was never, ever around. Ned was getting up there himself, and he'd taken on the majority of her mother's care, not to mention pulling his usual weight with the breakfast crowd and handling most of the maintenance around the inn. The rest of it was up to June. Always had been. Ever since she'd been eight years old, fatherless and scared and with no option but to roll up her sleeves and get things done.

It was easy for her mom to give her sad looks and harp on her that she should get out and have some fun. For now, this was her life, and it was enough.

Whatever else she wanted for herself...Well, it would just have to wait.

With that, she blew out a breath and stood up straight again. She checked herself over in the mirror to make sure she hadn't smudged or rumpled anything while she was taking a moment to herself. Tucking her hair behind her ear, she plastered on a smile and tugged open the door.

Back in the lobby, the sound of the banging outside was even louder. Scowling, she headed to the window and peeked out.

The old quilt shop stared back at her, as boarded up and impenetrable as it had been the last time she'd tried to peer into it.

Her phone buzzed in her pocket and she pulled it out.

The general store is out of earplugs. Can you see anything?

June huffed a laugh. *Nothing you can't see just as well from where you are.*

Her best friend Bobbi ran the bakery next door, and the two of them had been reliving their Nancy Drew–reading days, trying to suss out the mystery of their new neighbor this week.

What is HAPPENING? And more importantly, when will it stop???

June smiled at her friend's emotive texting. Then the corners of her mouth turned down.

She glanced at the checkout desk, Mr. and Mrs. Anderson's frustration playing again in her mind. She couldn't afford to offer a discount to every guest who complained about the noise. Not for long.

Turning back around, she gazed through the window and across the street once more. She narrowed her eyes at the darkened storefront.

Bobbi's questions were valid.

And it was high time June got some answers.

CHAPTER TWO

Later that afternoon, June looked both ways before crossing Main Street. She nodded in appreciation at the driver who rolled to a stop to let her pass.

Shade from one of the magnolia trees that lined the street provided welcome respite from the first wave of summer heat. Shifting the bundle in her arms to one hand, she swiped her hair off her face and looked up.

To all outward appearances, nothing at Susie's Quilts and More had changed. The windows remained boarded up, and the faded awning displayed the same picture of a star-shaped pink-and-white quilt block. The building had been vacant for a year now, though. The titular Susie had passed away at ninety-three—still sewing until the very end. With her children scattered across the country, it had taken ages to get the estate settled, and by the time the building had hit the market, the freeway's construction was underway. June had worried it would sit empty forever, a gloomy harbinger of what was to come for them all if they didn't act. Finding out it had sold had been a relief.

Right until whoever bought it decided to have a party with some power tools.

Things had finally settled down around lunchtime, but they'd gotten going again by midafternoon—this time with the addition of a blaring hair metal soundtrack. As June approached, what sounded like a buzz saw roared, adding to the, uh, ambience. Hiding her wince, she put on a bright, welcoming smile.

The button for the doorbell lit up when she pressed it, but any chime it made was drowned out by all the noise. Leaning in, her ear toward the door, she hit the bell again. And again.

Finally, the saw cut off, followed a few seconds later by the music. A gruff, indistinct voice muttered something. Heavy, uneven footfalls approached, and she stepped back, standing straight, beaming cheerfully, because she hadn't been eavesdropping—nope, not at all.

The door swung open with a *thwack* against the inside wall. Her eyes fluttered wide.

The man filling the doorway glistened with sweat. Dressed in a smudged gray tank top and faded camo cargo shorts, he rippled with corded muscle. The tanned skin of his arms was etched with faded black ink, and angry red scars slashed one shoulder and calf, making her draw in a harsh breath.

"What?" he growled, and June snapped her gaze up to his face, her cheeks flashing hot.

In their days of speculation and futile sleuthing, June and Bobbi had considered just about every possibility for who or what their new mystery neighbor could be. The only possibility they hadn't considered was "freaking gorgeous." If rugged and dirty were the kinds of things that did it for you.

For June, they did not.

But try telling her heart that as she stared at him, because it was going wild inside her chest.

The man was white, probably in his mid-thirties, with the

kind of sun-touched complexion that said he was too macho to wear sunscreen. Close-cropped, red-brown hair was matted to his head, and a few days' worth of scruff roughened his chiseled jaw.

Piercing green eyes bored into her like an accusation. He lifted a brow expectantly.

Right. Because she was the one who had rung his doorbell. Three times. She was supposed to say something.

All the casual introductions she'd rehearsed, waiting for Elizabeth to come spell her at the front desk, disappeared from her brain. The plan was to come over here, say hello, offer him one of the inn's famous blueberry pies, then charm her way inside and engage him in such riveting conversation that he'd tell her every single thing there was to know about him and his plans and why on earth he felt the need to operate a jackhammer at eight in the bleeping morning. And if maybe, pretty, pretty please, he might consider...you know...*stopping*.

Just as she opened her mouth to do precisely that, movement inside caught her eye. Before she could think better of it, she gasped and darted forward.

"Hey—"

His hot skin seared into her as she rushed past him. She sucked in a breath. It had been much too long since she'd been close enough to a man to feel that kind of heat, much less smell that kind of toe-tingling, clean sweat and pine sort of scent.

Only she couldn't focus on it, much less enjoy it.

As she ran, the rickety old ladder she'd spied propped precariously against the wall slipped another few inches. The bunch of tools balanced on its top step rattled, and a wrench went tumbling. Cradling the bundle in her arm, she lunged for the wrench, narrowly grabbing it before it could hit the ground.

The ladder creaked and slipped, and she moved to brace it with her shoulder—

Only a muscular arm blocked her way. The man raised a brow at her as he easily held the ladder in place. With his free hand, he reached up and snagged the box of tools. He dropped them unceremoniously on the ground with a clatter, then pulled the wrench from her hand and added it to the pile. He didn't release his grip on the ladder—or her gaze—the entire time.

And right. That definitely didn't do it for her, either.

Warmth rose to her cheeks, and she averted her gaze. "You're welcome," she blurted out.

"For what?"

She gestured vaguely at the ladder that had been in the process of toppling.

He rolled his eyes, picked the ladder up single-handedly, and set it down on the floor on its side. Something in the wood definitely cracked. "I had it under control."

Clearly.

Sealing her lips together to keep the dismissive comment in, she glanced around.

At what she saw, she had to purse her mouth even more tightly.

The last time she'd set foot inside the old quilt shop, it had been a handful of weeks after Susie Everly had passed. June had volunteered herself, Bobbi, and a few of their other neighbors on Main Street to help clean out the storefront. The place had been a bit of a mess, honestly, but it had been a familiar one. She'd been sad to pack it all up.

This, though? This was an entirely different kind of mess.

Her first impression was that this man had to be opening up a tool store or something, he had so many of them laid out. The jackhammer that had been driving everyone to distraction was nowhere to be seen, but the table saw, nail gun, and a whole collection of hammers, drills, and goodness even knew what else were in plain sight.

Right above where the rickety old ladder had been propped, a lighting fixture had been removed—none too gently, from the looks of it—leaving a hole with exposed wiring sticking out. Dark wood shiplap paneling lay scattered across the torn-up floor. Some had gone up already in horizontal lines, covering the walls poor Susie had painted herself—and yes, she'd painted them twenty years ago, but it was the principle of the matter. The old lady must be spinning in her grave.

Especially if she could see the neon beer signs where the sewing machines used to be. The ancient jukebox. And was that...

Over in the corner. Was he building a *stage*?

June's head reeled.

This wasn't a tool shop.

This was a bar.

And don't get her wrong—she could enjoy a good night out on the town. In theory. Ella's bistro with the great wine list was more her speed, really, but that wasn't the point. She had nothing against bars in general, but here? On Main Street? In the heart of Blue Cedar Falls's quaint little tourist district?

Run by a guy who used a jackhammer before breakfast?

She sunk her teeth into the inside of her cheek. Panic wasn't going to help. Mentally, she composed fifty texts to Bobbi, explaining everything she'd learned in her reconnaissance mission—with enough all caps and exclamation points to put even Bobbi's messages to shame.

Externally, she smiled and turned to the guy still standing

over her, eyes narrowed, suspicion written all over his chiseled, distractingly handsome face.

She swallowed hard, accidentally glancing down at his muscular biceps. She blinked. Shook the haze of irrational attraction off.

Stick to the plan, she reminded herself. Come over. Give him pie. Engage him in conversation.

Convince him not to drive her guests away with power tools and blaring music.

Right. Easy.

Smiling sweetly, she redirected her gaze back to his. "Where are my manners?" She extended a hand. "I'm June. I run the Sweetbriar Inn across the street."

"Clay," he offered.

That was it. No follow-up questions, no *Nice to meet you*, no additional details.

Her smile threatened to falter, and she dropped her hand. She tried again. "I just wanted to welcome you and introduce myself."

He crossed his arms.

Crap. Maybe she should have had a backup plan, because "engage him in sparkling conversation" was going over like a lead balloon.

She glanced around. "Seems like you've got quite the renovation underway. You doing this all by yourself or—"

"I am." His voice was deep, with the barest hint of a growl to it.

She shifted her weight, fighting not to squirm under the weight of his gaze.

Forget a lead balloon. This was the conversational equivalent of the *Titanic*.

"Well, I was just—"

He shook his head. "I'm gonna stop you right there."

Oh, thank goodness. She'd had no idea where she was going with that.

But before she could rejoice too much, he took a step into her space. His warm spicy scent washed over her again, scrambling her brains. His mouth was a flat, unimpressed line. "I don't care what you were 'just stopping by for,' or what you were 'just wondering,' or however else you were planning to so politely pick my brain. I know you and all your other small-town busybody friends think you can barge in whenever you want—"

A crackle of irritation lit at the base of her spine. Yes, maybe she had come over here to do a little sleuthing, but he made it sound so sinister. A little too indignantly, she insisted, "I'm not a small-town busybody." That was Patty Boyd, thank you very much. "I'm your neighbor."

"Me." He pointed to his alarmingly attractive, increasingly angry-looking face. "Still not caring."

"I was just—"

"Save it, lady."

Okay, now she was getting mad. "Can you let me finish a sentence?"

"Why should I?"

"Because." She cast about. He was actually giving her a second to speak, but her brain was coming up blank. How did she get this man to let down his guard for a second so they could have an actual conversation? She spotted the ladder lying on its side, and she snapped her gaze to his again. "I can help."

That was always a winner. People liked people who could help.

"I don't need any help."

She wanted to throw her hands up in the air.

Instead, she passed him the pie. "Here, hold this."

"What?" He accepted it, but he held it like it might be a bomb.

She bent down to inspect the ladder more closely, and—yup. Standing again, she pointed at it. "This is a display prop."

"It's fine."

"It absolutely is not. Did you climb this thing?"

He gritted his teeth, but he dropped his gaze. "Maybe."

No wonder it had given up the ghost. The man was enormous. Tall and muscular and just…That pesky heat rose on her face again. He was huge, was all.

"You're lucky you didn't break your neck. Susie Everly used to hang quilts from there."

"Well, how was I supposed to know that?"

"You could have asked your neighbor." Her grin was genuine this time. She had her in. Turning to the door, she beckoned him to follow. "Come on."

"Come where?"

She rolled her eyes. "Right across the street. You can borrow my stepfather's ladder."

"You don't have to—"

Tilting her chin up, she looked him in the eyes. "Save it." Wasn't that what he'd told her when he'd cut her off? "Us neighbors around here are not busybodies, but we are a tight-knit group. Welcome to Main Street." She pointed at the covered dish that looked utterly ridiculous in his giant mitts of hands. "I hope you like blueberry pie." Finally, she jerked her thumb to the door once more. "Now do you want to borrow a ladder that can support a grown man or not?"

The grown man in question regarded her with even more suspicion than he'd first shown to her pie. But then he looked to the jumbled pile of tools and the unstable ladder on the floor. She was pretty sure another rung of it gave way under the weight of his gaze.

He muttered a few choice words beneath his breath. Louder, he grumbled, "Fine. Lead the way."

Cracking a smile, she turned and did precisely that.

Forget casual conversation and charm. Food and tools were the way to a man's heart. And she was in the enviable position of being able to offer him both.

If it had been hot in the unair-conditioned, pink-and-rose hellscape Clay had been working in all day, it was roasting out in the street. He mopped his brow with his arm, but it didn't do any good.

How many years had he spent in the desert? Decked out in combat uniforms and hauling a full complement of gear under that infernal sun, he and Bug had complained plenty, sure. But it was like their buddy AJ from Vegas had said—at least it was a dry heat.

The Carolinas were a swamp, and he cursed Bug's ghost all over again for leading him here.

What had he been thinking, listening to a dead man's voice in his ear? He and his bum knee could've headed up to Alaska if they'd wanted to.

But here he was. Up to his neck in a mortgage and a business loan on top of that, following Bug's dream to prove to the people of Blue Cedar Falls that a regular Joe could make it on their precious Main Street. So far, Clay didn't have much to show for his effort except splinters and new calluses, but he'd had worse. Three days he'd been at it now, and he wasn't going to stop until he saw this thing through.

Even if it meant accepting help from some woman he didn't know from Eve.

He eyed her up as she led him across the street. June, she'd said her name was.

Trouble was more like it.

She was beautiful—he had to give her that. Asian, with long inky hair and deep eyes. The flower-printed dress she wore floated off her curves, even in the sticky heat, showing off tanned legs and a hint of cleavage he had a hard time keeping his eyes off. But that didn't matter.

Irritation gnawed at him. The past three days, people had been gawking at his storefront. A few had been bold enough to knock, and he'd even said hello to the first handful, but they kept poking at him.

And Bug had warned him. Small-town southerners were all honey on the surface, but beneath it they were up in everybody's business. According to Bug, the folks on Main Street were the worst offenders of them all. They might have the best ice cream stand and the hippest record store south of the Mason-Dixon, but they were gossipy and snooty, and Clay didn't trust them one bit.

Now there was this June woman. He'd tried to get rid of her the same way he had the others, but she'd taken nosiness to a whole new level, marching into his place like that and then acting like she was doing him a favor.

Chewing on the inside of his lip, he narrowed his eyes.

And sure, that ladder may have been a safety hazard and yes, this June woman might be offering to help him, but he could smell the secret agenda she was hiding. He didn't know what it was, but he had no doubt she'd show her hand in time.

Hopefully he could speed this along and grab her ladder before she could try to convert him to a cult. Or worse, invite him to a Tupperware party.

As June walked, she took it upon herself to become some

sort of a tour guide, prattling on. Nervous, maybe, though she put up a good front. She pointed out all kinds of nonsense Clay didn't have time for, from the variety of trees the town had planted along the street to the precise shade of white—sorry, not white, *eggshell-chiffon*—they'd painted the fences.

What he heard loudest was what she wasn't saying. *You don't fit here. You don't belong.*

Yeah. No kidding.

To make matters worse, his busted knee was giving him grief after going up and down that crappy ladder all day. Stepping onto the curb on the opposite side of the street, he bit down at the crunching sound it made.

But he didn't hide his reaction well enough.

June glanced back at him, concern and curiosity twin forces in her gaze. "You okay?"

"Peachy," he muttered.

She rolled her eyes like she didn't believe him, and that was fine. She didn't have to.

Up close and in the clear light of day, the inn was as shiny and white—he didn't know what shade and he didn't care, thank you very much—as it had looked from across the street. Avoiding the blue-painted front porch with its showy rocking chairs and hanging flower baskets, she took him around back to a gate in the eggshell-chiffon fence. She opened the lock and held the door wide. "After you."

That really shouldn't grate on him, but it did. With a scowl, he headed in.

The back of the property was nice, with a sitting area and a garden and more flowers. Behind a row of hedges, though, some of the shine came off. A wheelbarrow lay on its side next to a pile of stones and dirt. Tools had been left out in a way that wasn't good for them.

"Sorry about the mess," June said breezily. Too breezily.

Huh. So there *was* more to this perfect little tourist trap of an inn than met the eye.

Shocker.

She opened a shed that was about as messy as the rest of the work area. "I'd ask my stepfather to come lend us a hand, but he's prepping rooms for new guests right now."

"Not a problem."

"It's our family inn, you see," she babbled. "Owned and operated for generations."

"Uh-huh."

The folded ladder lay just inside. Surging past her, Clay grabbed it and hefted it over one shoulder. Awkward, but he could handle it.

"Thanks," he said, gruff. "I'll get it back to you in a couple of days."

He turned to go.

Of course she followed. Racing after him, she held the gate, and yeah, okay, that was helpful, but couldn't the woman take a hint? He had this.

"Lots of the businesses around here are like that," she continued, falling into step with him as he hauled the ladder toward the street. "Mom-and-pop kinds of shops."

"Super."

Main Street wasn't the busiest as far as car traffic went, but he had to wait for a couple of trucks to pass, which she took full advantage of.

"It's part of what makes this town so special. You'll learn all about it, of course."

Yeah, no. He kept his trap shut, crossing the street at his first opportunity.

She stuck to his side. "The business association is meeting

next week. I'm sure you'll want to come—it's the best place to make connections, network, really get the vibe of Blue Cedar Falls, you know?"

He grunted in reply because it was more polite than what he wanted to say.

She was so full of horse manure she might as well have stepped right off the farm.

She followed him under the magnolia trees and past another stretch of matching fence to his door, her voice rising in pitch. "I'm sure they'd have some great ideas for how to get set up and start your business." She swallowed, and he narrowed his eyes. That was one heck of a tell. "Make it a good fit for the Main Street community."

Bingo. There it was.

Her real angle for being so "nice."

She was going to all this effort to tell him how great this place was. A less cynical guy might think it was because she was just that good of a neighbor, but he could see right through her.

It had been one of the details Bug had savored the most, nights he'd spun his yarns about what he'd do when he got out of the service. The look on all those Main Street people's faces when they found out what he was doing.

Bug had loved Main Street. In high school he and his friends had hung out here every weekend. They liked the ice cream and the bakery and the guy at the record store who didn't mind them wandering around for ages. Their folks had liked window-shopping during the off-season. Dinner out on a special night.

But none of them had ever really felt like Main Street was meant for *them*. Sure, they were welcome to visit and all. But everything was geared toward tourists. Fancy-schmancy this, artsy-fartsy that.

Bug wanted to put his bar up here *because* he knew it wouldn't fit.

And the people so focused on bringing in the big bucks from out of town? They would hate it.

Bug didn't care. He welcomed the fight.

So Clay did, too.

He set down the ladder in front of the closed door of his new bar and turned around. Crossing his arms over his chest, he glared down at her.

She stopped short, barely avoiding crashing into him, her scent sweet and warm. He almost got distracted for a second by the tingling under his skin as their bodies brushed, but he ignored it.

He didn't pull back.

"Look, I'll say this one time," he all but growled. "I'm not joining a business association. I don't care how perfect your precious little downtown is or what you think would be a good fit. I'm here. I'm building a bar, with loud music and cold beer and whatever color fence I want, and no one's changing my mind. Are we clear?"

Her eyes widened, and she blinked rapidly. "Okay, that's a lot to process."

"It's really not." He turned away, finished with this conversation. He got the door open and lugged the ladder inside.

Only she followed, because of course she did. "Can we just sit down and talk for a minute?"

"There's nothing to talk about." He planted himself in the doorway, blocking her way. This was his property, and she wasn't barging her way inside again. He didn't care if the roof fell on his head. He gestured around. "I bought this building. It's zoned commercial. End of story."

"Would you at least consider discussing hours?" Her voice

ticked up, and a pretty little flush rose on her cheeks. He probably shouldn't find her growing irritation sexy, but what could he do? "Noise levels."

"Definitely not."

"My guests are already complaining."

"Well, I guess you better figure out what to tell them, then. Because this is happening, sweetheart."

Yeah, that "sweetheart" really got her mad. Her nostrils flared, and her little hands curled up into fists at her sides. "Shall I tell them to take it up with the rude jerk across the street?"

"If you want to."

"You can't just open a place with no consideration for the people around you and how your actions are affecting them."

He laughed. "Sure I can." Wasn't that what he'd spent all that time overseas fighting to protect? A twinge fired off in his gut. Sometimes even he didn't know what he'd been fighting for anymore. And it didn't matter. He redirected the lost, hurt feelings that threatened to well up back into the conversation at hand. "What are you going to do? Stop me?"

A flash of real anger lit her eyes. "To protect my business and my family? I'll do whatever I have to." She sucked in a rough breath and let it out slow. When she spoke again, her tone was cool but strained. "But I'd much rather we could settle this civilly. Maybe find some way to compromise."

What a load. He cocked a brow. "Would you now?"

"This is a community. All of us here." She threw her hands out to the sides. "We work together. We sink or swim together."

"I'm pretty sure you'll manage." The way Bug told it, tourists came in by the truckload, crowding everybody else out. During the busy season, locals couldn't even get tables.

"Are you? You waltz in here out of nowhere—"

"That's rich." Clay jerked a thumb over his shoulder. "Because as I recall it, I wasn't the one waltzing in ten minutes ago."

Flush deepening, she stepped closer to him, and his nostrils flared. He couldn't help the way his body responded, his blood heating in a way it hadn't in over a year.

She flexed her jaw and bit out, "I. Was. Trying. To. Be. Neighborly."

He laughed out loud. "Sure."

"I loaned you a ladder and baked you a pie."

"And I thank you for both of them."

"You're welcome," she said, and how was it even possible for that soft, kissable mouth to make those two words hostile?

Why did he want to hear more?

He pushed the instinct down. Screw all of this.

He gripped the doorknob hard enough to crush it. "Now go away."

"Excuse me?" Her brows about rocketed off her face they jumped so high.

"I think I was plenty clear." He took a step back and instantly regretted losing the static buzzing between his body and hers, but it was for the best. He didn't wind this up now, he'd do something he'd regret. Whether that was yelling at her or kissing her, he didn't know.

She shook her head in exasperation, moving as if to follow him. "You have no interest in discussing—"

"Nope."

And with that, he shoved the door closed in her face.

Loud thumping on the other side told him she wasn't done with him, but she could give herself raw knuckles for all he cared. Striding across the room, he flipped on the jukebox and cranked it as loud as it could go. Now that was better.

Chuckling wryly, he lifted his face to the ceiling. "You were right, Bug. This is going to be fun."

CHAPTER THREE

Three days later, Clay wasn't having nearly so much fun.

"Is this some kind of game to you?" he growled.

"Um…" The mousy woman behind the counter at the town hall shrunk before his eyes, and Clay swiped a hand over his face, trying to keep his cool.

"Do you have a manager?"

She nodded in relief and ran off. Clay looked over his shoulder at the people behind him waiting to be helped. It was a middle-aged couple, friendly looking enough. The man smiled from beneath a bushy mustache and shook his head in sympathy.

A couple of minutes later, the woman from behind the counter returned, a guy in a collar shirt and dark slacks in tow. He was young, maybe thirty, but he had a calm to him that gave Clay some faint hope that they could get this all straightened out.

"Hi, I'm Graham. Mindy here told me you were having some trouble?"

Clay scoffed. "That's one way of putting it."

"How can I help?" Graham steered him toward the other end of the counter so Mindy could see to the next folks.

Clay shoved the piece of paper he'd come in with across the counter.

Graham took it and looked it over. "I'm not seeing—"

Clay stabbed a finger at the typed words. "A ninety-day comment period for a liquor license?" His voice rose with every word. "Seriously? What does that even mean?"

"Ah." Graham nodded. "It's to allow time for the public to submit their opinion before the licensing board makes its decision. Standard procedure for controversial requests."

"Internet said it was supposed to take two weeks." Clay wasn't a whiz with computers but he could read.

Graham smiled apologetically and passed the letter back. "Usually, it does, but there were some concerns raised."

"I bet there were."

June showing up the other day with her stupid, delicious pie had been the tip of the busybody iceberg. Bug had told him Main Street types were gossips, but how word got around so fast he had no idea. Before June had come poking her nose in his business, folks had been curious, sure, but after, they got brazen. More ladies with pies had shown up. None as good as June's, though he had to admit the perky blonde who ran the bakery had rustled up some pretty great cookie-brownie things. But that wasn't the point.

It was open season on him and what he planned to do with the space. Everyone wanted to know more about his bar or talk to him about the hours he was keeping or question his taste in music.

None of them had been as fun to chase away as June had been—or gotten his blood as heated arguing—but that was probably for the best.

The real problem was the people who couldn't even be bothered to show their faces. Nasty notes shoved under his door made good kindling, but not much else. Someone had even sent a cop, and fine, okay, he'd lost track of time, and yes, he could see that not everybody appreciated Van Halen at two in the morning. He definitely hadn't cranked it louder at ten a.m. the next day to make up for it.

And now this.

"Mayor Horton's office listens very carefully to its constituents," Graham said.

Enough crap. "So whose rear end do I have to kiss to get this fixed?"

Ninety days wasn't going to sink him. It might take most of that time to get the place rehabbed anyway. But it was the principle of the matter. He was throwing everything he had into this renovation. What was to stop the "concerned constituents" from turning ninety days into six months? Or a year?

"Uh…" Graham blinked a couple of times.

"Come on, we all know what's going on."

"I'm sorry—"

Clay dropped his hand onto the table, barely stopping himself from slamming it there. "Who?"

Graham let out a sigh and rubbed the bridge of his nose. "The Main Street Business Association is…in flux."

The guy with the big mustache over by Mindy muffled a snort.

"Look," Graham said, dropping his hand from his face, "all comments submitted to the town hall are kept confidential." He glanced around before leaning closer over the counter. Lowering his voice, he confided, "But if I wanted to find out who was behind this, I'd talk to Patty Boyd or Dottie Gallagher." He tilted his head back and forth. "Maaaybe June Wu."

Clay ground his teeth together. He grabbed a pencil out of

his pocket and scribbled down the first two names on the back of the letter, but he didn't need the last one.

June's pretty face flashed in front of his vision. The anger in her eyes when he told her what was what, the way she brought up the noise and the hours and the complaints from guests at her inn...

He should have known.

"Hey," Graham said as Clay started to turn away. "I hope you can get this sorted out. Main Street could use a good bar if you ask me."

That wasn't all it could use, but Clay wasn't a proctologist, so there wasn't much he could do about the stick it had where sticks shouldn't be. He'd try his best, though.

He nodded at Graham and took a step back. Before he could stalk out of there, though, a voice stopped him.

"A bar?" mustache guy asked, his southern accent deep and drawling.

Clay paused. "That's right."

"On Main Street."

Clay braced himself for more bullcrap, but the guy's face lit up.

"Now, son, that is something I could drink to."

The woman next to him rolled her eyes, but her expression was fond to the point of indulgent.

"Duke Moore." Mustache guy held out a hand. "This here is my wife, Tracy."

"Nice to make your acquaintance." Clay shook Duke's hand. It was a good grip, the man's hands calloused and work-worn.

"You're new here."

"Sure am."

Duke and Tracy seemed done with their business. Graham had disappeared back into whatever office Mindy had summoned

him from. Duke nodded toward the exit, and Clay walked out
with them.

"Have to say, I'm mighty sorry you're not getting the warm-
est welcome."

"There's been pie," Clay said dryly.

"Pie's not much of a match for red tape." Duke squinted at
him in the midday sun. "You look familiar. I seen you around
somewhere?"

Now that he mentioned it... "Tim's Hardware?"

Clay spent so much time there getting supplies for the work
he was doing fixing up the bar, he was glad they weren't asking
him to pay rent.

Duke beamed. "That's it. You a handy guy?"

"I know my way around."

Duke looked to Tracy, who nodded.

"I like a man who can work with his hands. You got plans
for dinner Sunday night?"

Other than more takeout from the awesome Chinese place
he'd found on Poplar? Hardly.

But he could see where this was going, and he wasn't sure it
was the right direction. He shook his head. "I don't—"

"Well, you have plans now," Duke said. "I insist."

"I'm not—"

"No sense fighting it," Tracy hummed, looking at her
husband in amusement. "He won't take no for an answer."

Clay took a step back. He hadn't come here to this town to
make friends.

This whole past year since he'd gotten out, he'd been
wandering around, never staying anywhere for long. Any time
his buddies from his army days had reached out, he'd brushed
them off. He hadn't been fit for company. Mean and hurt.
Grieving.

He'd burned his bridges with them all.

Because the last time he let anyone close...the last time he made a friend...

Clay tugged at the neckline of his shirt. Like he could still feel Bug's hand there, bloody and shaking as he took his last breath.

He blinked, and the world came back into focus.

Well, suffice it to say, it hadn't turned out so great. For anyone.

Duke's smile faltered by a fraction. Clay was tempted to finish the job, tell him off the same way he had June when she'd gotten too friendly.

"I make a darn good pot roast," Tracy said, drawing his gaze to her. She smiled, so sweet and hopeful it almost hurt.

And crap. Clay may be a mean SOB sometimes, but he didn't kick puppies, for crying out loud.

"I do like pot roast."

Duke clapped him on the back, and yeah, that was taking things too far, but Clay was in it now. "Had a feeling you would." He grabbed the letter from the mayor's office out of Clay's hands and turned it over. Tracy passed him a pen from her purse without having to be asked, and Duke wrote an address right under Patty's and Dottie's names. "Seven o'clock. Don't feel like you have to bring anything, but I do like Coors Light."

"Duly noted."

Duke handed back the paper. He gave Clay a little salute before he and Tracy headed to an SUV parked under a tree a few spots down. Clay waved before making for his own truck.

He settled into the driver's seat. Brows pinching, he reread the address Duke had scribbled down for him. He still wasn't quite sure how he felt about being so aggressively befriended when all he wanted was to be left alone, but even he could recognize the kindness of offering the new guy in town a home-cooked meal.

He narrowed his eyes, shifting his gaze higher.

He could also recognize the not-so-subtle act of war by a bunch of concerned constituents trying to deny a liquor license to a bar. Grinding his teeth together, he tossed the letter aside and fired up his truck.

As it kicked into gear, he pointed it in the direction of Tim's Hardware. Main Street's business association might have painted a target on his back, but he'd had worse.

They weren't going to stop him from building Bug's Bar. Nobody was.

Not Patty Boyd. Not Dottie Gallagher.

And definitely not June Wu.

"You sure you'll be okay for a few hours?" June asked, chewing on her lip.

As he sank into the computer chair behind the front desk, Ned's blue eyes were tired, his white and straw-colored hair rumpled, but his smile was genuine. "June. I've been manning this desk since before you were born."

That didn't exactly set her mind at ease.

The Sweetbriar Inn was a hundred-year-old institution. Ned and his siblings had terrorized the place as children, and yes, they'd worked here, too. But that was before Ned married June's mom and the Wu girls modernized the place.

He was never going to live down that time he'd decided to "update" the computer and managed to not only download a virus but erase the entire month of April from the calendar.

June sighed and leaned in to press a kiss to his temple. "Remember, don't download any attachments."

"I learned my lesson, sweetie."

"And everything is backed up." At least she hoped it was.

He let out a long-suffering sigh. "I'll be fine. And besides"—he looked at her pointedly—"your mother is around here somewhere if I really muck anything up."

June frowned despite herself. "You know she's supposed to be resting."

"Yes, but when do I get to rest?" His crotchetiness perfectly straddled the line between teasing and true complaint. "It's been *months*. If she's not busy, she's making me busy." He waved a hand around. "If it's not putting in a new rock wall in the garden—"

"Which you still have to finish, by the way."

He glared, not missing a beat. "—then it's setting up photo shoots for the cat. The *cat*, June."

"Whatever makes her happy."

"So long as we both shall live." If he'd said the words once, he'd said them a thousand times. "But that woman needs to get back to work, or she's going to drive all of us to an early grave."

He wasn't wrong.

"Once she gets the okay from her doctor, we can ease her back in."

"And until then, she can put her feet up and relax and maybe answer one little technical support question from her stone-age husband, all right?"

He'd backed her into a corner on that one.

"I'll only be gone a few hours," she promised.

"Take your time." He waved her off. "The place will still be standing."

"Pretty hard to blow up a building with a computer."

He cracked his knuckles. "Don't give me a challenge."

Good grief. Now it was really time to go, before she gave him any more ideas.

Clipboard in hand, she headed out. On her way, she exchanged greetings with a couple of guests enjoying the gardens and seating areas around the inn. One of her mom's friends was out walking her dog, and June waved.

Then her gaze landed on the building across the street. Her smile disappeared.

She hadn't seen much of her new neighbor in the past few days, but the entirety of Main Street had been in a flutter about him. After their run-in, she'd told Bobbi, and Bobbi'd told... well, probably every local who wandered into her bakery that day. Everybody had an opinion about the new bar and its owner, and June had more than a few of her own.

The fact of the matter was that Clay had been downright rude. He'd gone out of his way to make his bar sound terrible, then shut her down when she'd tried to engage with him. A flush of anger rose to her cheeks just thinking about his big, muscular frame eclipsing his doorway, the piercing green of his eyes as they'd stared down at her, the curl of those red lips above that chiseled jaw...

And okay, fine, anger hadn't been the only thing making her flush. She wasn't cutting him any slack about being a rude jerk just on account of his being handsome or anything, but her attraction to him had blindsided her. His taunts had riled her up, making her lose her cool in a way she never did, and with every barb they traded, the unexpected flicker of desire inside her only grew.

Which didn't make any sense. She may not have had time for dating of late, but when she had, she'd dated nice men. Pillars of the community in khakis and button-down shirts.

Not burly, unshaven bartenders covered in tattoos.

Huffing out a breath, she turned away.

Rumors had been flying about the business owners on Main Street getting together to keep his bar from opening. She wasn't quite ready to go that far yet, despite her losing her cool and taking his bait the other day. Yes, she would do whatever she had to in order to protect her family and their inn. If he insisted on sabotaging her business, she'd find a way to stop him. But she didn't want it to come to that. New businesses on Main Street had the potential to help everyone. She'd rather have a nice neighborhood tavern than an empty storefront across the street. Infuriating as he was, she wanted to take another shot at convincing him to be reasonable. Once they'd both calmed down.

In the meantime, Dottie Gallagher asking Officer Dwight to pay Clay a visit had gotten results in terms of him respecting noise ordinances. That would have to be good enough for now.

As long as he wasn't actively driving away her guests, June had other fish to fry.

Even though it was still months away, the clock was ticking on early preparations for the new Pumpkin Festival. Her goal for this week was to get her sponsor list nailed down. All the businesses on Main Street had committed—reluctantly, in some cases, but committed all the same. She also had deals in the works with a few bigger companies that had locations in and around Blue Cedar Falls. If she was going to save her family's inn, she needed this festival to be huge, though, bringing in tourists from near and far, and that meant rallying the entire town.

Rehearsing her pitch the whole way over, she headed toward the north end of town. Fewer visitors ventured out this direction. It was more residential, but enough people lived here and worked on Main Street that it was worth a shot.

She had mixed success on her first few stops. Roger's Pharmacy was willing to buy a small ad and Cut & Curl Salon donated a makeover for the big raffle. Blue Cedar Falls Heating and Cooling couldn't justify the expense, though. Disappointing as that was, she couldn't blame them.

Her spirits rose as she turned into Tim's Hardware. Ned always took her there when they were doing renovations or repairs at the inn, and she knew most of the folks who ran the place.

She grabbed a spot in the front of the lot, sliding her tiny car in between two enormous pickup trucks. She squeezed out and headed past the outdoor landscaping area and into the store.

A friendly smile greeted her at the customer service area. Tim's daughter Stephanie was forty-ish and white, with long coppery hair she wore in a braid down her back. As June approached, Stephanie put down the copy of *Popular Mechanics* she'd been paging through and raised a brow. "What's Ned broken now?"

"Oh, only a few customers' hearts," June joked. "I was actually coming by to talk to you about this year's Pumpkin Festival. You have a minute?"

"Sure."

June laid out her pitch, emphasizing the big marketing push they were doing to bring in a crowd. "So what do you say? Can I count on Tim's Hardware? There's still room on the program and the volunteer T-shirts if you want a sponsorship slot."

Stephanie's mouth pinched as she perused the materials June had provided. "I don't know. I'd have to talk it over with my dad. Tourists don't usually have a lot of call for two-by-fours while they're in town."

June's heart sank by a fraction, but she was prepared for this. "We're really trying to get the community involved this year, too. It'd be good advertising." She leaned in conspiratorially. "The big garden center on the other side of town is putting up a booth."

"Are they now?" Stephanie's forehead crinkled.

Those were the magical words. "Let me show you our 'Shop Local' package."

Ten minutes later, she had Stephanie signed on for a giveaway at the local spotlight booth and a buy-in for the ads they were airing in the western Carolinas area. As June got the agreement written up, Stephanie leaned her elbow on the counter.

Lowering her voice, she asked, "So what's the scoop about your new neighbor?"

June didn't snap her pen in half. Was he all anyone wanted to talk about these days?

"What have you heard?" she asked.

"Not much except a lot of gossip about a dive bar that's got Patty Boyd madder'n a hare."

June snickered. "That about sums it up."

"What do you think of it all?"

"Hard to say until we find out more," June said, trying to be diplomatic. "It could be great, or it could be a migraine in the making."

"You met the new owner yet?"

Had she ever.

"Once," June conceded.

"He's been in and out of here every couple of days." Stephanie waggled her brows. "I have to say I do *not* mind the view."

June's cheeks warmed, and she cleared her throat, shuffling her papers. "I guess he's all right."

"All right? You need to get your eyesight checked." She glanced meaningfully to the side then lowered her voice. "Tell me that right there is not ten shades of gorgeous."

Oh, no.

A familiar scent of woodsy pine and something strong and virile wafted toward her. June turned to find Clay standing only a handful of feet away. Cleaned up from the last time she'd seen him, he was dressed casually, in jeans that looked distressed from hard work, as opposed to the influence of the fashion industry. A black T-shirt clung to the muscles of his chest, and those enticing tattoos along his arms looked even better than she remembered. His rust-colored hair was tucked beneath a baseball cap, and thick stubble graced his sharp jaw.

"Hey there, Clay," Stephanie called, a thinly veiled invitation in her tone that rubbed June all kinds of the wrong way, which was ridiculous, because she had no interest in the man.

A genuine smile curled his lips. It reached the bright points of his eyes as he turned toward the sound of his name coming from Stephanie's mouth.

But then his gaze caught on June.

In an instant, the openness to his expression disappeared, like shutters slamming closed. His eyes went hard, and the corners of his mouth twisted down.

"What're *you* doing here?" He didn't spit in her general direction, but he might as well have.

Well hello to him, too.

"Talking to Stephanie about a project we're working on," she said simply, trying not to let him get a rise out of her this time. "You?"

"Buying wood." He scowled and glanced around. "Rescuing kittens from trees, helping little old ladies. You know. The usual."

She'd been so distracted by his appearance that she hadn't really noticed what he was doing. Her eyes widened as she took in why his biceps were bulging so enticingly. He was carrying a gigantic planter, with none other than her mother's friend Ms. Smith trailing behind him.

"June, fancy running into you here," the old woman said, smiling warmly. "I'm finally getting that new bit of landscaping done at the house. Won't this look just perfect on the porch?"

"Uh-huh," June agreed dimly, her gaze still drawn to Clay as he turned toward the door. Her throat went dry when his backside came into view.

"This young man was so kind as to offer to help," Ms. Smith told her. "Isn't that sweet? Says he's bought the old quilt shop. I'm so excited to see what he decides to do with it."

"Right." June had been pretty evasive when she'd spoken to her mother about the banging and noise coming from across the street. She didn't want her mom getting worried about the bar. Of course, she should have realized the senior citizen rumor mill would eventually get wind of it, one way or another.

"Be a dear," Ms. Smith asked, "and give me a hand, too?" She held out her wrinkled palm.

Grabbing her clipboard, June stepped forward and extended her arm. Ms. Smith was pretty spry, as June's mother's friends went, but she had arthritis that flared up from time to time. She leaned into June, and before she knew it, June was following Clay and the giant planter into the parking lot.

Clay scowled at her even harder as they reached Ms. Smith's old Buick, but June refused to let him goad her into losing her cool this time. She ignored him and helped Ms. Smith dig her keys out of her purse. While Clay loaded the planter into the back, June led Ms. Smith to the driver's seat and held the door for her, keeping her steady as she got in.

Ducking his head into the car, Clay asked, "You have someone to help you unload this when you get home?"

"Aren't you a sweetheart for asking. You want to follow me home?" Was she—she wasn't flirting with him, was she? Before he could respond, she waved him off. "Don't worry, one of the neighbor boys'll take care of me."

"I'm sure they will." He matched her teasing tone, but there was relief on his face as he stood and closed the door.

Ms. Smith looked to June with hearts in her eyes. "Such a gentleman." She started the car, and June pushed the door shut. The old lady waved at both of them. "Thank you!"

They stepped away from the car. Ms. Smith backed out before steering toward the road.

Leaving June alone with Clay in the parking lot.

He seemed to realize it at the same time June did. Their gazes met, and any warmth in his flashed to fire.

She wished she knew—which was the real him? The kind man who smiled at little old ladies and helped them carry heavy things to their cars?

Or the angry, surly jerk who couldn't seem to do anything but growl and sneer at her?

Proving exactly which version she was dealing with now, he curled his hands into fists at his sides. "You have got some nerve."

"Excuse me?"

"You know what you did." Growling, he brushed past her, but nope. He'd slammed a door in her face the other day. He wasn't accusing her of some new offense and then running away today.

She chased after him. "Actually, I have no idea."

"Really?" He stopped abruptly, and she almost slammed into him, *again*. The scent of him made her insides go all squirmy, and she had to stop herself from reaching out and putting a hand on that broad chest of his to steady herself.

"Really," she promised, exasperated and flustered.

He laughed. "Right." He shook his head. "From the second I met you, I knew I wasn't going to like you."

Sure, because he was such a peach. "Hey—"

"But at least I respected you dealing with me face-to-face." He was getting up in her space now, too close for comfort, but she refused to cede an inch. So what if the heat his body gave off made her brain spin? "But no. You didn't waste a second, did you? Going over my head and behind my back."

Wait. "What?"

"Well, I'm sick of it," he barreled on, like she hadn't said anything at all. He took another step closer, but a distance formed in his eyes. "Sick of people pulling strings. People who don't care who they hurt."

She wanted to shake him.

She gave in, reaching out and putting a hand on his arm. His skin sizzled, and electricity zipped through her, but she wasn't letting herself get distracted. "What are you talking about?"

His gaze suddenly focused, zeroing in on her. He shook his head as if to clear it. "You and your friends. Holding up my liquor license. I knew you'd go low, but—"

She jerked back. "I'm not holding up your liquor license."

Good grief—was that what Patty and Dottie were doing? She'd heard murmurs about them trying to stop the bar from opening, but she'd figured they'd discuss it at the Main Street Business Association Meeting next week. Not start pulling in favors with Mayor Horton's office.

"They told me at town hall," Clay sneered. "Said you were one of the ringleaders."

That was... actually pretty flattering. Inaccurate, but flattering. She *had* spearheaded the doomed campaign against the highway construction project and taken the lead on relaunching the Pumpkin Festival. But that last one had required calling in all the favors she had out. Whoever he'd talked to had seriously overestimated her pull.

She crossed her arms over her chest and squared her jaw. "Well, they need to get their stories straight."

"So you're saying you didn't try to stop me from opening a bar."

"No." She shifted her weight. "I mean, I considered it, but I was reserving judgment. I like working *with* people, thank you very much—not going behind their backs."

"Sure," he scoffed.

"Why would I lie?"

"I don't know. Why would you?"

He was accusing her of things she wasn't doing again, and she only had so much patience. The heat that flared inside her had started out as attraction, but it was turning into real anger now.

She threw her hands up in the air. "You tell me!"

His eyes went stony.

He pointed an accusing finger at her. "You know, Bug warned me about you people."

"Bug?"

"Hernandez." He shook his head. "Sal. He was from here."

Sal Hernandez, Sal Hernandez... Oh. Oh, she knew that name, why did she—

Realization smacked her in the face. "Wait, wasn't he—"

"Local boy who signed up for the army and never came

back? That's right." Shadows crossed his eyes, real pain marring his features, and the sudden shift in his stance threatened to take her breath away.

Right. Sal—Bug—he'd been a few years younger than her, but June had known him—or at least known of him. The articles about his death overseas had been everywhere when it had happened. A year ago maybe?

"You and Sal...," she started, trying to piece this together.

Clay straightened. Raw grief still haunted his eyes, but he was back in the present with her now. "Were best friends." His jaw flexed, and his voice went rough. "He used to talk about Blue Cedar Falls all the time, over there."

"Over there in..."

"Afghanistan."

June swallowed. This was starting to make sense. "You served with him."

"I did." His jaw flexed, and he looked to the side. None of the anger had left his frame, but some of the fire behind it was starting to wane.

"I'm so sorry."

"Stuff happens," he grumbled.

"I'm still sorry."

"Whatever." He scrubbed a hand over his face, sniffed once, then returned his attention to her. "Building this bar was his dream. He told me it was going to be a fight, but he was ready to take it on, and I am, too." He took a deep breath. "But if you and your uptight, underhanded, backstabbing, busybody—"

"Would you *stop* already?" June cried out.

It came out more forcefully than she had meant it to, but at least it finally got his attention.

His jaw dropped. He picked it up and started to talk again,

but she held up a hand, her palm toward him as she pinched the bridge of her nose.

In her head, she counted down from ten.

She didn't know who this man was. She didn't know why he'd decided to project all his earthly grievances on her. She wasn't going to let him keep doing it. She was going to say her peace. But she was going to do it kindly. Firmly. And without losing her head.

Dropping her hand, she fixed him with the no-nonsense gaze she'd honed on her baby sister Elizabeth every time she broke curfew growing up.

"Thank you for your service," she said. "I am sorry for your loss."

He opened his mouth, and she glared at him until he closed it. That was better.

"I understand that you are angry," she told him, "and I suspect that you have a right to be. But I have done nothing except kindly introduce myself, bake you a pie, loan you a ladder, and ask if maybe you would consider discussing how the noise levels at your bar are affecting my business."

"You—" He stepped forward again, his big body and skin-prickling male scent threatening to derail her, but she shook her head.

"Uh-uh." Nope, no sirree, no thank you. It didn't matter that she could almost literally see the sparks flying between them. She barreled on, her heart pounding against her ribs. She was going to get this out. "And you have been nothing but presumptive and rude and disrespectful to my family and my inn. You asked me if I was going to try to stop you, and I told you I would if I had to, but I prefer it didn't come to that, and I meant it. You want to build a bar in memory of your friend? Great. You'll take a lot of flak from Main Street, but great."

He scoffed. "So now suddenly you're on board?"

"I didn't say that. But I didn't say anything against you, either, and you would have known that if you had stopped to ask. Instead, you attacked." That was what hurt the most. "You could have had an ally. Heck, I might have helped you, if we could have found a way to come together."

Sure, there would have been potentially tough negotiations about his business hours and how loud things got, but there were so many possibilities for partnerships. A bar selling drinks at Pumpkin Festival would have been great. She could have done a special promo with him for guests at her inn. Even locals might have taken advantage during the off-season—who wouldn't love to spend a night out at a neighborhood watering hole and then be able to walk across the street for a good night's sleep?

But no.

"So enjoy doing it all on your own," she spat. "Since that's clearly what you're so intent on doing." She jabbed a finger at him through the air, narrowly missing grazing his body, they were standing so close. "For what it's worth, I hope they hold your license up forever."

A whole new level of scowl curled his lips, but there was injury in his eyes, too. She'd almost feel bad if he hadn't been a royal jerk at every opportunity. As it was, she wasn't taking a word of it back.

Before he could call her one more name, before the heat crackling through the air between them could sear her any further, she turned on her heels and stalked toward her car.

The instant she put a few feet of space between her body and his, her head cleared. She could breathe again.

But as she walked, a sinking feeling gathered in her stomach. She'd come to this side of town today to win over support for the festival that was going to help her save her family's business. Maybe even to make some new friends. She'd succeeded, for the most part.

She'd also made an enemy.

As she slammed the door of her car behind her, she bit the inside of her cheek.

She had a really bad feeling it was an enemy she couldn't afford.

CHAPTER FOUR

❁ ❁ ❁ ❁ ❁ ❁ ❁ ❁ ❁ ❁ ❁ ❁ ❁

Of all the self-righteous"—Clay kicked the door of his pickup shut—"stubborn"—another kick—"know-it-all..."

Muttering some more choice words beneath his breath, he gave the door one last kick, only to have his knee light up with a flare of pain so bright it took his breath away.

Served him right.

Normally, he was above having temper tantrums in public places, but that June woman had gotten under his skin this time.

Where did she get off? Goading him. Telling him she hoped he never got his liquor license at all. Making it sound as if someone like her with her soft hands and batting black lashes would've ever helped someone like him.

Ha.

He knew better than to believe crap like that.

So why couldn't he get her words out of his head?

Resisting the urge to kick his truck again, he growled and hit the lock button on his keys.

She had him all twisted around was the problem. One minute she was thanking him for his service, the next she was telling him to get his head out of his butt. She was smart as a whip and just as biting. He wanted to *shake* her. Or kiss that smug pout off her full, red lips...

And he didn't want to stop with kissing, either. If he wasn't mistaken, he'd seen the same fire in her eyes he felt in the pit of his abdomen every time they'd gotten close to each other.

What would it be like to get his hands on her? Would she be as fierce in bed as she was with a clipboard? Or would she go all soft and pliant in his arms?

He cut off that line of thought before it could go a single step further. He wasn't going to get a chance to find out. He had a bar to build and a whole bunch of buttinskies organizing against him. Whether June was one of them or not didn't matter. Sleeping with the enemy might be fun, but it wouldn't get him any closer to seeing Bug's dream through.

With a cloud of annoyance and sexual frustration hanging over his head, he turned his back on the load of lumber in the bed of the truck. There'd be time to deal with that later. He'd driven straight from the hardware store to his other favorite find in Blue Cedar Falls so far.

From the outside, the Jade Garden looked like any other Chinese takeout place. The inside wasn't revolutionary, either. But his first night in town, he'd gotten the best, most authentic box of beef chow fun he'd had on this continent. He'd been craving it again ever since.

He didn't know about anybody else, but for him, there wasn't a better cure for a foul mood than shoving a pile of dumplings in his face.

The bells on the door chimed as he strode in. The guy behind the register was the same from last time. Tall, built. Clean-shaven with messy hair. He looked like he belonged in one of those Asian boy bands everybody was so excited about these days, not someone who'd be working in a place like this. But who was Clay to judge?

The guy raised a brow as he approached. "Back again?"

Clay grunted in reply and grabbed a paper menu. "You do table service?"

"Of course."

Taking the menu with him, he pulled up a chair at one of the half dozen red-draped, glass-topped tables. A couple of other people were seated, too, but they were closer to the counter, playing with their phones, probably waiting for their takeout orders.

As Clay scanned the menu, the guy came over. He set down a glass of water. His tray held a tiny china cup and a metal teapot, too. "Tea?"

Nice touch for a takeout joint. Clay nodded, and the guy set down both.

"My name's Han, and I'll be taking care of you today," he said, face serious, like this really was some fancy place.

Clay shoved the menu aside. "Fried dumplings and whatever's your favorite."

Han chuckled. "My favorite's not on the menu."

"Surprise me."

"Okay." Taking the menu, he wandered off.

Leaving Clay to stew with his thoughts again.

He pulled a notebook and a pencil out of his pocket. It was an old habit from his days in logistics in the army; he thought better with a pencil in his hand. And there was plenty to do to figure out the next steps for construction at the bar.

Only today he couldn't seem to think at all. June kept creeping back into his head. If she were just hot or aggravating, he could handle it. Both was lethal.

The fact that she might be right only made it worse.

He was still replaying their whole altercation in his head when Han returned. The guy set down a plate of dumplings that smelled like the best kind of grease, then offered Clay an actual cloth napkin with both a fork and a packet of chopsticks. Clay tore open the chopsticks and picked up a dumpling.

Then he put it back down.

"Everybody in this town knows everybody, right?"

Han had been about to walk away, but he turned around. "Present company excluded?"

"Yeah, yeah." Clay waved him off. "You're Han, I'm Clay, now we know each other, too." He pointed his chopsticks toward the big front window. "But everybody else."

"Pretty much."

"You know a lady named June?"

The guy flinched. Interesting. "June Wu?"

"None other."

The point of his jaw sharpened. "What about her?"

"What do you think about her?"

"I try not to think about her, in general."

"You and me both," Clay said under his breath.

Han shook his head. "Not like that." He pulled a face. "I used to date her sister. That'd be weird."

"So you really do know her, then."

Regarding him steadily, Han let out a long breath. "Let me go get your entrée."

He returned a minute later with a plate of what looked like pork with vegetables over noodles, as well as two identical green bottles. He held one out with a question in his gaze. "Tsingtao."

Yeah, Clay could read the English characters on the label. He raised a brow.

"Like Sam Adams but better," Han clarified.

Well, if the guy was offering.

He nodded, and Han uncapped both bottles, then pulled out the chair across from Clay and dropped himself into it. Clay glanced back at the front counter and saw an older Chinese lady had taken over at the register.

"So what did June do to you?" Han asked.

"Is it that obvious?"

"Kind of."

Clay poked at a piece of the pork with his chopsticks. It smelled as awesome as the dumplings, but he couldn't focus on his food.

Clay was the sort of man who kept to himself. All he'd needed this past year was his pickup and the open road. He'd scarcely talked to anyone since his discharge. Heck—since Bug had died. Sure, Duke and Tracy had tried to adopt him like a stray puppy, but they were old enough to be his folks— if they were still alive.

Now this stranger had offered him a beer and an ear, and apparently it was exactly the opening Clay had been waiting for.

"She's this stubborn, self-righteous, know-it-all," he sputtered, just as uncontrolled as when he'd been trying to dent his truck.

His mouth kept going, too, the suppressed anger of the past few days boiling over.

Before he knew it, he'd drained half his beer—which wasn't bad, for all that it was weird—and told Han the whole story. How he'd lost his best friend. How on the anniversary of Bug's death he'd come right here to his hometown to see through his dream of opening a bar, and how everybody and their mother seemed to be giving him crap about it now.

How June Wu kept showing up, trying to "help" and only making him want to kick something.

Maybe she hadn't been the one complaining to town hall and trying to shut him down, but did that matter? She was clearly on their side now. Even if he hadn't gone after her, she probably would have ended up fighting against him sooner or later.

Clay took another swig from the bottle and tried to ignore the twinge of doubt gnawing at him.

"I mean, I have the right to open my bar anyplace I want, right?"

"Sure," Han agreed.

"But...?" he supplied.

"But it is going to be tough getting a place going if you keep pissing everybody off. The kind of bar you're talking about is going to stick out like a sore thumb over there."

Clay scrubbed at his eyes. "Not you, too."

"I'm not saying you shouldn't follow your dreams. I'm just saying that those Wu girls..." Han shook his head.

"What?"

"Look. I knew May better than June, but the two of them were cut from the same cloth. Opinionated, stubborn."

"Tell me about it."

"Brilliant. Persuasive." His Adam's apple bobbed. "Beautiful."

Yeah. Clay had noticed that, too.

"But as much as it kills me to admit it, they also tended to know what they were talking about."

"So I should give up?"

"Of course not." Han reached over and grabbed a dumpling right off Clay's plate and took a bite. He chewed it thoughtfully. "But you might want to think about listening to her. At least a little bit."

Clay downed the rest of his beer in one gulp. If the food here weren't so good, he'd storm out right now.

Listen to her? That was his answer?

They were so far past that.

They'd had not one but two fights in public now. He still felt like he was in the right about them both, but he could see how *maybe* he might have jumped to conclusions.

The doubt that had started as a tiny twinge grew until it was pressing on the inside of his chest.

When June told him she might have helped him if he'd asked...could she have really meant it?

And was there any way he could bring it up now without looking like a complete and total jerk?

Clay shook his head. "I can't."

"It's your funeral." Han's gaze drifted off into some middle distance. "But I'll tell you this. The last time I talked to May, I let my pride get the best of me. I told her she was wrong about something when she and I both knew she was right, and I'm never going to stop regretting it."

"Okay..." This was getting way too deep.

Han looked at him again. "Those Wu girls...June and May—Elizabeth, too. They're the most frustrating women on the planet. But they're also smart and determined. Take it from a guy who learned the hard way. You do not want to be their enemy. Not when you have a chance to be their friend."

With that, he took his beer and stood.

"That's it?" Clay asked. "Your advice is to be her friend?"

"My advice is to do whatever you want..But you'll save yourself a lot of time and grief if you can figure out a way to do it *with* her, instead of despite her." Han gestured at the table. "Take your time here. I'll come by with your bill in a minute."

Han headed back to the register, leaving Clay alone with a pile of noodles, one less dumpling than he'd started with, and about three times more food for thought than he wanted to chew.

"This is getting ridiculous." June's friend Bobbi Moore ran her hands through her long, blond hair dramatically.

June frowned in sympathy, her elbows braced against the front desk of the inn. "Do you have any idea what you're going to do?"

"If I did, would I be here complaining to you?"

True.

Bobbi had a delightful habit of coming by with some of the unsold pastries after she closed up the bakery in the afternoon. If they had time, she and Bobbi would chat and drink a fresh pot of lobby coffee, and it was honestly one of the nicest parts of June's day.

Especially recently, when she'd desperately needed the distraction.

Unconsciously, her gaze flitted to the front window. The sight of the bar being renovated across the street taunted her.

A pit of angry resentment burned deep in her chest every time she thought about the previous day's run-in with Clay at Tim's Hardware. How dare he accuse her of things she didn't do, or call her names like that.

But underneath all the anger, a thread of anxiety twisted itself into knots inside her, too. Calling him out had felt like cleansing fire, but had it been the right thing to do? He was a vet who'd suffered a terrible loss. He deserved some empathy and patience.

She also didn't put it past him to retaliate.

She and her family couldn't afford him driving a single customer away. This morning's mail had brought another notice from another billing department at the hospital. She'd barely managed to hide it from Ned as he'd been passing by the front desk.

Between the declining business at the inn, the Pumpkin Festival, the mountain of medical debt, and the utter wildcard that was her infuriating, frustrating, obnoxiously attractive new neighbor, her whole life felt like it was shadowed by a cloud of impending doom.

So she was more than happy to focus on someone else's problems for a change.

Sighing dramatically, Bobbi poked at the remains of her chocolate croissant. "What if Caitlin and I just run away and join the circus or something?"

As if. Bobbi could be flighty, but she and her girlfriend were two of the most deeply rooted people June knew.

Tapping her chin, June pretended to consider the idea seriously. "What would your act be?"

"I don't know. We could learn the trapeze maybe?"

"You hate heights."

"Okay, yeah, not the trapeze." Bobbi shrugged. "Who says we need an act anyway? I can cook. I mean, the circus must need breakfast, right?"

"Definitely."

"And Caitlin's handy. She could put up tents."

"She could."

"This is good. I'm liking this plan."

June raised a brow. "Do you want me to start poking holes in it or should I just smile and offer to help pack?"

"Neither. I know it's stupid." Bobbi deflated. She popped another bite of croissant in her mouth and chewed morosely.

Reaching across the desk, June patted Bobbi's hand. "You'll figure it out."

"Easy for you to say. You're not the idiot who's been putting off coming out to her parents for a decade and a half."

"You're not an idiot."

June and Bobbi had been friends since junior high, and June had been there through the tough teen years when Bobbi had started to realize that the hot quarterback of the football team held absolutely zero interest for her.

But that the captain of the cheerleading squad did.

Bobbi came to terms with her sexuality over time, and she ended up coming out to a handful of close friends. She'd had good relationships and bad.

Through it all, she'd kept her orientation a secret from her parents, though. Mr. and Mrs. Moore were good people, but they were also...traditional. June was pretty sure they would accept Bobbi and keep loving her exactly the way they had her entire life, but she couldn't blame Bobbi for being nervous about their reaction.

At this point, though, her friend was right. It was getting ridiculous.

Caitlin was amazing, and she made Bobbi happy. After a year and a half of dating, their relationship had been getting more and more serious. Bobbi had a ring and everything. She was ready to take it to the next level.

Right after she told her mom and dad that she was gay.

"We could elope?" Bobbi tried.

"You absolutely could." June smiled ruefully. "But would you really be okay with your parents not being there?"

"No."

"Well there you are."

"It's just gotten too much! I don't think they've even met Caitlin."

"She's in construction. Surely she's run into your folks at Tim's Hardware."

Bobbi rolled her eyes. "Passing each other in the grout aisle is not the same as me introducing them."

"Just saying."

Bobbi barreled on. "What am I supposed to do? Tell them I'm a lesbian and oh by the way here's my superhot girlfriend, I'm about to propose, hope you'll come to our wedding and not disown me?"

Slanting her mouth to the side, June had to admit, "That might be a little overwhelming."

"Eloping it is, then." Bobbi gulped down the last of her coffee. "I'm going to go shop for airplane tickets."

And June had been trying so hard to be a good listener and a good friend and not try to fix everything for Bobbi, but Bobbi was just spinning now.

If she didn't want June to help solve her problem, she would have picked a different friend to commiserate with. She knew what she was getting coming here.

"Look," June finally said. "Maybe it's time to look at this from a different angle."

"You think so?" Bobbi jerked her head up, all ears.

That was the approval June needed to plow ahead. "I mean, yes, you've put this off for kind of a long time, but that doesn't mean you have to do all of it at once."

"True."

"What if you focus on introducing them to Caitlin first?"

"Caitlin is pretty amazing."

June nodded. "How could they not love her?"

"But it would be super weird to invite them over to meet one random friend who happens to be a girl."

"Then don't invite them over to meet one friend." Eureka—

June had it now. "Invite them over to meet a bunch of them. A dinner party, maybe?"

Bobbi tilted her head to the side. "I do love a good dinner party."

"Who doesn't? Then Caitlin can just happen to be there. You introduce them. They'll adore her so much, when you get up the nerve to tell them who she really is to you, it'll be easier, because they'll know you're in love with someone great."

Hope glimmered in Bobbi's eyes. "You really think that would work?"

"I mean, there's no guarantee. But it's worth a shot. If nothing else, it would get you started."

Bobbi reached for her hand. "Promise me you'll come."

June smiled. "Of course."

"Phew!" Bobbi pretended to wipe her brow.

June glanced at the time.

Bobbi took the cue and closed up the box on the other couple of pastries she'd brought. "Guess I'd better get home and start planning the menu."

"Nothing fancy," June encouraged her, though she knew it was pointless.

Bobbi grinned. "Maybe a little fancy."

"Let me know what I can bring."

"Just yourself—and maybe a bottle of something strong, in case it all ends in disaster."

"Or to celebrate with when it goes perfectly well."

"That's my June." Bobbi headed toward the door. "Always planning for every possible outcome."

June did like to be prepared.

But there was something about the way Bobbi said it that made her pause. Did she plan too much?

Obviously, the answer was yes—but in a bad way?

She was still pondering it as Bobbi said goodbye. Her friend let herself out, and June sat back in her seat and wiggled the mouse on the front desk computer to see if she'd missed anything.

The bell over the door chimed. Assuming Bobbi had forgotten something, she barely glanced up.

Then she registered what she'd seen.

She rose from her chair and squared her jaw.

Because striding toward her, a guarded look in his piercing green eyes, was Clay. He was as handsome as ever. Maybe even more so because for once he didn't particularly look like he wanted to murder her, but she knew better than to trust that now.

She floundered for a second, all the anger he'd brought forward in her yesterday rearing up. She was ready to tell him to head right back out that door he'd just come in.

But before she could get a word out, he marched straight to the desk, his mouth a determined line. His inexplicably delicious scent washed over her, and she cursed herself for liking it.

He set down a familiar round metal tin. "I brought your pie plate."

"Oh." She wanted to pinch herself. Not only was that non-murderous. It was downright polite. "Thank you. I think."

Stepping back to a respectable—if slightly, irrationally disappointing—distance from the desk, Clay took off his ball cap and worried the brim in his hands.

"I'm returning your ladder, too."

Of course. Why else would he have been stopping over?

She had no idea. And yet she somehow still felt the tiniest bit let down.

Too brightly, she responded, "Great." She reached for the

phone. "I can call my stepfather and he can open up the shed for you."

His level gaze met hers, pinning her in place. "Actually, do you have a minute?"

Why? So he could yell at her some more?

Something about his demeanor was different this afternoon, though. She considered him for a moment. She might regret this in about five minutes, but she nodded warily.

"Good," he said. "Because I have something I need to talk to you about."

CHAPTER FIVE

With begrudging respect, Clay looked around the lobby of the Sweetbriar Inn while June put up her BACK IN 15 MINUTES sign and locked her computer.

The place was more or less what he would have expected from the outside. It was…nice. Not so pretentious as to be off-putting, with couches and tables that looked clean and comfortable. The couple of paintings on the wall had price tags under them—high but not ridiculous—and descriptions about the local artists who had painted them. Fresh flowers sat on the desk and in vases scattered around.

Clay would never stay in a place like this. But if he *had* to, he supposed this one in particular wouldn't be too bad.

June finished up whatever else it was she felt she had to do before stepping away from her post, then she followed him through the front door. With a grunt, he picked up the ladder and headed around to where June had let him in the last time.

The back area had been cleaned up a little since then, but seeing how perfect the inside of the inn looked only made it more obvious that not everything was getting done out here. He didn't comment as they got the ladder stowed away in the shed again.

He turned to June, who stood there in the summer sun, staring at him expectantly. Her arms were crossed over her chest, her red nails stark against her smooth skin. Brows arched, she chewed at her bottom lip.

Anxious. Waiting for him to say whatever he'd asked her to come out and talk to her about, and yeah—he guessed he couldn't blame her. Every time it had been just the two of them, he'd let himself get worked up. His anger had sparked her anger, electric tension crackling between them.

But that wasn't how it was going to go today.

Late last night, as he'd worked on *quietly* refinishing the floors of the bar, he'd replayed their arguments in his head. Instead of stewing over all the ways she'd pissed him off, though, he'd forced himself to consider his new buddy Han's advice.

He freaking hated to admit it, but the guy might have been right.

So here he was, literal hat in hand.

He cleared his throat. "So it seems to me we may have gotten off on the wrong foot."

"You think?"

He fought to keep the growl out of his voice. "I'm trying to be nice here."

"I know, I know. Sorry. Continue." She didn't exactly sound happy about so graciously allowing him to try to not be a tool.

Whatever. He huffed out a breath and smacked his hat against his good leg. "Look. When I first got here, I had some preconceived notions. Bug told me how Main Street worked, and I..." What was the word that shrink the VA had tried to shove at him used to use? "... projected some of it onto you."

Yeah, June had nosed around his place. She'd insinuated he needed the busybody council to help him make his bar a "better fit," and she'd tried to give him crap about the hours and the noise.

That didn't mean she was single-handedly trying to ruin him.

At the very least, she had plenty of help. Clay had spent the morning chasing down the other couple of people Graham had named as likely suspects at town hall, and *wow*. They made June Wu look like a saint. Patty Boyd had refused to even talk to him. The instant he'd told her who he was, she'd sneered and gone back to rearranging pictures at her overpriced art gallery.

Meanwhile, Dottie Gallagher had refused to *stop* talking, telling him seventy years of Main Street history and making it crystal clear he had no part in its future, as far as she was concerned.

Neither of them had fired him up the way June had, but even he had to admit that his intense reaction to June might have had more to do with chemistry than it did with the substance of their arguments.

As if to prove it, June tightened the way her arms were crossed, and he had to jerk his gaze up before he got caught staring at what the motion did to the neckline of her dress.

"Anyway," he ground out, "I guess what I'm trying to say is that I'm"—he swallowed, his throat rough—"sorry."

"For?"

Was she really going to make him do this? His temper threatened to flare, but he forced it down. "I'm sorry I jumped to conclusions."

"And?"

And? He clenched his jaw and cracked his knuckles. "And accused you of screwing me over at town hall."

"And?"

Good grief. "Look—"

She dropped her hands to her sides, her red lips parting and her eyes ablaze. She took a step toward him. "Are you sorry for yelling at me for no reason or not?"

"I just said I was." And he was getting wound up again. Fresh oxygen hit the spark that always seemed to light between them—either out of anger or attraction, he didn't even know anymore.

He swiped a hand across his brow. Maybe it'd been a mistake coming over here, but June, Han—they were both right. His go-it-alone approach wasn't working anymore. He couldn't expect to get a business off the ground by picking fights with everyone he met.

He needed help. And infuriating as June was, she was the closest thing he had to someone who could provide it.

"Yesterday"—he dropped his hand from his face—"you said that if things had gone differently—"

"You mean if you hadn't been a presumptuous jerk?"

"Yeah, yeah." He waved her interruption off. They'd already covered that. "If that hadn't happened." He curled and uncurled the brim of his hat in his hands. Looking up, he met her fiery gaze.

Forget his pride. Forget the reaction this woman brought out in him. He had to get through this.

"You said you might have been willing to help me. With the bar." His throat grated, but he kept his tone even. "I'm wondering how that would work."

She stared at him for a minute that seemed to go on forever. Maybe she was going to tell him to take a hike. He deserved it.

Finally, she let out a rough breath.

"I don't know, exactly." She crossed her arms again, but some of the defensiveness in her posture eased. "Depends what you're trying to do with the bar and what kind of help you want."

Ugh. He'd already opened his yap and told his whole sob story to Han the day before. He didn't want to get into it again.

How else could he explain what he was trying to accomplish here, though?

Han had told him to listen to June. But the more he thought about it, the more he had to face the fact that he probably had to open up to her some, too.

That kind of talking didn't come easy to him. After this last miserable year of driving around alone, nursing his wounds, talking at all didn't seem to come easy.

Shaking his head, he scrubbed at his face. Good grief, it was a scorcher.

"Can I?" He gestured at the seats in the shade. They were probably for guests, but no one was using them now.

"I guess."

He trucked on over and flopped down into one. His knee thanked him as he stretched out his legs. It was still hot, the air heavy and sticky, but at least under the tree it was bearable.

He gazed up at the big blue sky above.

For a minute, he could imagine he was somewhere else entirely. In another life, one where he knew what he was fighting for and everything made sense. It was half a world away and a half dozen years ago, but in that instant it felt so close that he could touch it.

A low chuckle rumbled in his throat. "It's funny. You can go all the way to the other side of the world, and the sky still looks the same."

It was never this hazy in the desert, but that didn't matter.

His unit had been assigned to plenty of other places, too. He and Bug had stared up from the sand and from rooftops in Germany and from an island in the middle of the Pacific.

Seeing all that vastness out there really put things in perspective. No matter where you were.

"Yeah?" June tentatively perched on the edge of a chair kitty-corner from his.

"Yeah." He turned his head to look at her.

There was something brittle about her. She'd seemed so strong and fierce, standing up to him when he couldn't keep his mouth shut or his anger to himself. But right now, when she didn't feel like she needed to fight him, she held herself too carefully.

Like she was trying to stop herself from falling apart.

Did everyone else see those mismatched edges of her? Or did they just see the perfect inn and the eggshell-chiffon paint on the fences she was always talking about?

He blinked, and his vision cleared, or maybe she shifted her position. Either way, the brittleness disappeared.

But the impression it had left on him didn't.

He swallowed past the stone that was trying to lodge itself in his throat.

"I told you the other day about my friend, Bug." He shook his head. "Sal."

"Heck of a nickname."

Clay chuckled, the memory of how Bug had gotten the name clear as day in his head. "First day of basic, he was standing in the wrong place while folks were moving equipment. Drill sergeant cursed him out. Said two feet to the right and he would've been squished like a bug." He shrugged. "The name stuck."

"Cute."

"Nah, he was an ugly SOB."

Didn't stop the girls from falling all over him. Nights they ended up on leave, they'd go out on the town, and Bug could have his pick.

Clay had done all right for himself, too, back then. But he had to work for it. That or find a girl who liked the strong, silent type.

He chewed on his words for a minute. For all that June had prattled on at him plenty that first day they'd met, she gave him the time and space to gather his thoughts now.

Finally, he sucked in a breath. "There's this thing that happens when you're stationed overseas for long enough. You get this kind of homesickness." Even a guy like him who'd never really had a home and didn't want one. "You find ways to deal with the endless deployments, the orders that don't make sense. The food you don't like and the languages you don't speak." The enemies you couldn't see—never knowing if they'd be hiding behind the next market stall or if they'd already rigged a bomb to blow and fled the scene.

June's mouth pulled to the side, empathetic in a way that should probably tick him off, but the way she was really listening somehow made him want to open up more. "Sounds tough."

"Yeah." Understatement of the year. "Me—I always thought I'd be a lifer." He clenched his teeth together, a sharp, phantom pain flaring in his knee. "But Bug..." He sighed, looking up at the sky once more. "Bug always thought that he'd come back."

"I'm really sorry he didn't."

"You and me both." He said a silent prayer in his head, then looked to June. Her attentive gaze somehow spurred him on. He pointed down at the solid earth beneath them. "The place he always swore he'd come back to was right here. Blue Cedar Falls."

No matter how much he complained about it, Blue Cedar Falls would always be home for Bug. But Bug's family was long gone—his dad absent from birth, his mom dead. His sister Lisa raising her kid out in Charlotte now. There was no trace of his people left here.

Which made it even more important that Clay stand his ground.

"Someday, after he got out, he was going to come home, and he was going to open a bar on Main Street. A 'real bar,' he'd say. The kind of place regular folks could go and unwind. Cold beer and greasy food and country music." Clay's voice broke, but he pulled it together. "He talked about it all the time. Described it so vivid it was like you could see it in your mind."

"Sounds like it means a lot to you," June said quietly.

She had no idea.

"So that's what I'm trying to do. I'm not trying to ruin this town." Not like old Dottie Gallagher had seemed to think. "Or drive away your guests."

June chuckled and shook her head. "You've got a funny way of showing it."

And now it was his turn to shut his yap, for all that he wanted to defend himself. But lashing out at her without thinking it through or giving her a chance to speak was how he'd ended up in this crappy position in the first place.

After a minute, June allowed, "I think it's really great that you're trying to honor your friend's memory like this."

He could hear another shoe getting picked up and held in the air. "But...?"

"But you have managed to alienate a lot of people in one week."

Irritation prickled at the rear of Clay's throat. His first instinct was to say *Good*. He hadn't come here to make friends.

He swallowed the impulse down.

June was right, and he could be brave enough to admit it. He'd been shooting himself in the foot this entire time.

"I know." It rankled something fierce, but he looked her right in the eye. "Will you help me fix it?"

She regarded him for a long moment. "What's in it for me?"

Crap.

He winced. "Don't suppose you're looking for free beer and pretzels, huh?"

"Hate to break it to you, considering you're opening a new business here, but Blue Cedar Falls has been having a tough time of it since they finished building the highway this spring." Her throat bobbed. "My family, our inn—we ... we've had a rough year." Something vulnerable flashed in her eyes, but then it was gone. She gazed at him pointedly. "We can't afford to lose a single booking. Or keep giving unhappy guests discounts on account of all the noise across the street, for example."

Ugh, here they went. "I'll turn the jukebox down," he grumbled.

But she just raised a brow.

"And see if I get some soundproofing put in." He hadn't finished installing the paneling yet. It'd be a pain in the rear, but he could get it done.

"And ... ?"

Was this how she handled every argument?

He flexed his jaw. "And try to keep patrons quiet after midnight." At her unimpressed look, he tried, "Eleven?"

"I was going to say nine."

She had to be kidding him.

"I'll see what I can do," he ground out.

One corner of her mouth twitched up. "I also have some featured business spots open in our Pumpkin Festival promotions."

Good grief. "And how much are those going to run me?"

Her smile grew. She had him, and she knew it, and why did she have to look so pretty when she was being smug?

"I think you'll find the buy-in is quite reasonable."

"This is extortion, you know."

She shrugged. "This is business."

He cursed Bug all over again for bringing him to this town. "So that's it? I keep the noise down and buy an ad for some Oktoberfest—"

"Pumpkin Festival."

"Whatever." He waved her off. "Just so we're clear, I do that and you'll get them to stop holding up my liquor license?"

The force of her laughter caught him off guard.

"Oh gracious no," she said.

He leaned forward in his seat. "Now hold on one—"

"Sorry, sorry. It's just funny to think that I would have that kind of sway."

"Hilarious," he said dryly.

What was he even doing here if she couldn't help him?

"What I can do is get you on the agenda at the Main Street Business Association meeting coming up on Tuesday."

"What good is that going to do me?" He was in danger of getting hot under the collar again.

She regarded him with skepticism. Either she didn't know she was playing with fire or he'd already yelled at her enough times, and now she didn't care. "How did it go, trying to talk to Patty and Dottie about this?"

He grimaced, and she laughed again, but it was softer this time.

Almost fond?

No. Definitely not.

"You heard?" he grumbled.

"No, but your face gives it all away." Dark eyes sparkling, she leaned forward. "Why? Should I have? Are my sources holding out on me?"

"It could have gone better," he admitted.

And there was that smile again. "Why am I not shocked?"

"I didn't fly off the handle or anything."

Her brows rose. He could almost hear her *Oh really?*

"I didn't," he insisted.

"Then me getting you on the agenda is the second chance to make a first impression that I'd say you need." She stood, so he did, too.

They were a little farther apart than they'd ended up the last couple of times, and he planted his feet, intent on keeping things that way. It didn't help. The way she was looking at him was so much gentler. Instead of a crackle of heat under his skin at being close to her, it was more of a warm buzz of awareness surrounding them.

It wasn't any less potent—especially when she stared up at him with respect in her gaze instead of outrage.

"Think about how you want to make your case," she told him.

Her expression softened further. For a second, her hand lifted, like she was going to touch him, and he couldn't decide whether to lean in or jerk away.

She tucked her hands into the pockets of her dress. One corner of her red lips rose.

"Today," she said. "Coming here, apologizing. Really talking to me about what you're trying to do across the street." She gestured with her elbow in that direction. "Well, I can't say you've won me over completely. But you at least convinced me to hate you a little less."

And good grief, that shouldn't make some kind of warmth build in his chest.

He shrugged it off. "Flatter a guy..."

She was undeterred. "Do the same with them, and who knows."

"Maybe I can get them to hate me less, too?"

Tipping her head to the side, she smiled. "Maybe you can convince the 'backstabbing busybodies' to give you—and your bar—a second chance."

Huh.

He wasn't sure if he could get a bunch of art dealers and florists to come over to his side. But without June's help, he didn't see how he was going to get a better chance to try.

Slowly, he told her, "I suppose you've got yourself a deal."

He extended his hand.

She regarded it for half a second too long. What? Did he have dirt under his nails or something? She didn't like grease stains and calluses?

Or did she feel the same hum of electricity singing between their bodies that he did?

Whatever it was, she squared her shoulders. "Deal."

With that, she put her palm in his. He closed his fingers, and her skin was hot and smooth and so perfect he felt a jolt of desire rocket straight through his spine. Her gaze jerked up to meet his, her soft mouth parting.

Unwanted thoughts shot through his brain. Pulling her in. Kissing her.

Doing a whole lot more than just kissing.

"Well, then I guess I'll see you Tuesday." She pulled her hand away.

Somehow, he let her go, but her touch was seared into his palm. He flexed his fingers.

He forced himself to take a step back.

He wasn't sure how much he liked this deal. But as with everything about building Bug's Bar, he was in it now.

With a grimace, he agreed, "I guess you will."

CHAPTER SIX

So what's the word on the street?" June asked, slotting herself in beside Bobbi at the back of the room. "Folks willing to hear Clay out?"

Bobbi wobbled a hand back and forth, her mouth pulling to the side. "Hard to say."

Not quite the result June was hoping for. She checked the clock on the wall over the door of the town hall's community room. Ten minutes to go. Worrying the strap of her purse, she surveyed the crowd.

More or less the usual crew had shown up for the monthly meeting of the Main Street Business Association. Bobbi and June were stationed near the snacks, the handful of other thirty-somethings in the group clustered around them. Riley, who helped manage the bookshop. Ella from the wine bar and James who ran the new board game café that had opened the previous fall. Mackenzie, who worked for the record store that had somehow managed to stay in business through all this upheaval.

Then there were the other factions.

Current president Patty Boyd was the ringleader of the pearl-clutching PTA moms, of course. June didn't have anything against them. She hoped to be a mom herself someday. But her own mother—loving and invested in her daughters' lives as she had always been—had constantly regarded those types with a tut-tutting sound in the back of her throat.

Such helicopters, she would complain. *Let your children stand up for themselves!*

Ha. Patty, Nancy, Sandy, and the rest of them would have looked down their nose at June's mother just as hard. They involved themselves in everything, and anytime anything failed to go their way, they'd put their hands over their hearts, and gasp, *But think about the children!*

June mentally rolled her eyes.

Yeah, she wasn't shocked that Clay had struck out with them his first time around.

Finally, the over-sixty crowd filled the first two rows of seats. Dottie Gallagher was the most vocal of them, but none of them were shy about speaking their minds. Her mother's friend, Mrs. Leung, whose family ran the Chinese takeout place that stood just barely on the end of the Main Street strip, was an occasional voice of reason with them. But in the end, most of them came from families that had lived here since before the Depression. None of them were ever going anywhere, and nothing should ever change from how it was when they were born. Computers were passing fads. Italian food was "ethnic." A cup of coffee should cost a nickel.

And more importantly: There had never been a bar on Main Street. So why on earth did they need one now?

The sinking feeling in the pit of June's stomach was about to take her clear through the floor.

She'd fulfilled her part of the bargain, though. Presuming Clay's bar ever got up and running, he'd work with her on keeping his business from detracting from hers, and he'd support her efforts to revitalize the Pumpkin Festival. In return, she'd gotten him a ten-minute slot to argue his case to the people standing in his way.

Even that hadn't been easy. It had taken all her powers of persuasion—not to mention the promise of a few free breakfasts at the Sweetbriar Inn—to so much as get him on the agenda.

She still wasn't convinced he'd be able to win them over, either.

But there'd been something in his eyes when he'd come over the other day to apologize. Hearing him talk about his friend and his time overseas had pulled at her heart in ways she never would have expected, considering their rocky start.

He deserved to have Patty, Dottie, and the rest of them hear him out.

Convincing this crew to support a bar on Main Street would be a Herculean task, but if he opened up to them the way he'd opened up to her...If he emphasized the compromises they had made about noise levels and hours of operations...

Well. Hopefully, at least he had a chance.

As the seconds ticked past, June watched the door in nervous anticipation, barely picking at the fabulous little lemon cookies Bobbi had brought.

Finally, a familiar figure darkened the door.

June had to give Clay some credit. He'd skipped the ball cap and combed his hair to one side. The jeans he wore were clearly working jeans—she had a sense that he would never own anything that wasn't in some way functional. But they were clean and well-fitting, and the black and green plaid shirt he wore was buttoned and tucked in. Even his boots had been shined.

With his sleeves rolled to his elbows, his tattoos were on display. There was no hiding that he was a far sight from the typical Main Street aesthetic. But he'd tried.

A hush fell over the room as he walked in. Every head turned his way.

Absently setting down her plate, June swallowed hard.

People wordlessly got out of her way as she walked toward Clay. Patty Boyd gave her a dirty look, but that wasn't exactly anything new.

"Clay." She greeted him warmly.

His broad shoulders and big presence filled the room. His green eyes met hers, something like relief filling them.

"June."

"I'm so glad you came."

She was. And not just because it would have made her look bad if he hadn't showed. The flutters he set off in her chest had only grown since she'd seen the less grouchy side of him.

He chuckled dryly. "Yeah, sure."

She rolled her eyes. "Come on, let me introduce you around."

Conversation slowly resumed as she took him around the room. They only had a few minutes before the meeting started, so she didn't linger anywhere. Most of Patty's pals turned up their noses, so at least saying hello to them was quick. One of the grannies tried to engage him in a more extended discussion about politics that seemed doomed to go exactly nowhere, but June made an excuse to keep moving. Over by the snack table, she introduced him to her friends. Bobbi knew what was going on, but most of the others shot her looks of confusion. She mentally begged them not to ask for details about how this unlikely alliance had come to be. The story was too long to get into now, and she wasn't sure either of them came out of it smelling like roses.

For his part, Clay kept his greetings to everyone gruff and terse. That probably wasn't doing himself any favors, but at least he wasn't digging any holes he would have to fill later, so she supposed it could have been worse.

"You know what you're going to say?" she asked him quietly as she helped herself to another cookie.

"Sort of?"

She bit back a sigh. "Please tell me you at least wrote something down."

"Uhhh…"

Crap. So much for her advice about taking some time to think about how he wanted to make his case.

As Patty headed to the front of the room to call the meeting to order, all June could do was hope Clay was really, really good on his feet.

What fresh hell had Bug led Clay into now?

Clay stood next to June as Patty Boyd took the podium at the front of the town hall meeting room. She brushed the longer strands of blond hair at the front of her head out of her face and straightened her blazer. Glancing out across the couple dozen people, she tapped the mic. In a quick, sharp southern accent, she said, "If everyone could have a seat, we can get started."

Conversation died down. A bunch of senior citizens were already sitting near the front left. Some women who all looked like they shopped at the same store as Patty up there filed in on the other side. June tipped her head toward the chairs in the back. Clay shook his head. If he sat down, he'd be antsy and fidgety. Better to stand.

June frowned but let him be. Patty glared at him. Whatever. He wiped his palms on his jeans.

It wasn't as if he was nervous, exactly. There was just this itch under his skin.

All he wanted to do was open a bar and serve beer. It wasn't complicated. So why did he keep having to explain it to everyone?

Patty launched into whatever agenda these people had. Another middle-aged lady got up and talked about the budget, and then another reminded everybody about what color flowers they were putting in the planters the following month.

"June?" Patty called.

June took a step forward.

"Any updates about the Pumpkin Festival?"

The request was met with a few snide murmurs from various parts of the room. Clay glanced around.

June's smile was tight, but she kept her voice bright. "Half a dozen new businesses have signed on for the online ad buy, and booths are almost sold out. Plenty of room for more donations to the raffle, though."

"Lovely," Patty said, dismissive, and Clay frowned. "So be sure to talk to June if you want part of *that*."

Rolling her eyes, Bobbi elbowed June, but June kept her gaze forward, her expression sunny. There was a steely determination beneath it, though, that Clay couldn't get out of his head.

Finally, after another half dozen committee reports and points of parliamentary procedure, and who even knew what else, Patty looked at the paper in front of her and grimaced. "All right, y'all, the last item up for discussion today is a proposal from a Mr. Clay Hawthorne about his new, uh, establishment."

Great.

All eyes turned to him. The itching under his skin intensified, but he kept it together. As he stalked toward the front, his big boots thudding on the linoleum, whispers floated through the air.

Well, let them talk.

Patty made a big show of getting out of his way. Good for her. He didn't need a mic or a podium, so he stood in front of it. Still standing toward the back, June gave him an encouraging smile. How on earth did he get to a place where the woman he'd assumed was leading the pack against him had become the friendliest face in the room?

You are such a jerk, Bug, he muttered in his head.

Then he nodded. "Good afternoon. Thanks for the, uh, introduction."

One of June's other friends snickered.

Clay barreled on, "As some of you may know, I bought the old quilt shop. I'm turning it into a bar. Cold beer, good food, live music." He cleared his throat. Here went nothing. "What most of you probably don't know is that I was sent here by a local boy. Sal Hernandez."

A murmur passed through the crowd. Even Patty blinked in surprise.

Clay glanced at June, and she nodded.

He barreled on. "Me and Bug—we called him that. We met overseas in the army. Building a bar here was his dream, and I'm seeing it through."

He stumbled for a second.

What else was there to say? He wasn't going to go into his whole sob story the way he had the other day with June or Han. Not in front of all these people. No matter what he was trying to convince them about.

Straight to the point, then.

He took a deep breath. "Some folks here don't like the idea,

I know. Think it won't be good for business, but Bug disagreed, and I do, too. Everyone needs to let off some steam sometimes, and there's nothing like a decent bar in this town. People will come from all over. You expand your options, and that's good for everybody, if you ask me."

"Excuse me." One of the Patty-types raised her hand and stood at the same time. She clearly wasn't waiting to be called on. "There's already a bar on Main Street."

"He isn't talking about *wine bars*, Sandy," a little old lady in the front piped up.

An old man beside her asked Clay, "Are you, son?"

"Uh. No."

"I don't think there should be any bars of any kind on Main Street," a middle-aged lady said. "This is a family-friendly destination."

"Think of the children," another agreed.

In the back, June covered her face with her hands, but Clay couldn't dwell too long on what that meant.

An older lady laughed. "Any family traveling with children needs a drink at the end of the day."

"Aren't any families coming right now anyway," a man in an actual tweed suit grumbled.

"My bookings for fall are down twenty percent."

"It's that highway," an older man said.

Clay furrowed his brows. "Uh…"

"He's right," the person who'd first brought up the wine bar said. "Until we get Blue Cedar Falls back on the map, it doesn't matter what new businesses we allow to open. We need traffic, we need people."

"We need an exit on that freeway," Patty chimed in. "June?"

All heads turned toward the back.

June had lowered her hand from her face, but her cheeks

were turning a vivid red. "Don't look at me. The committee protesting the freeway disbanded months ago."

"Well, maybe we should start it up again," someone else said.

General voices of agreement sounded.

June held up a hand. "The highway's been built. There's nothing we can do about that now."

Bobbi nodded. "So what do we do with what we've got?"

Clay lost track of the conversation for a bit after that. The middle-aged ladies and the old people seemed to have a whole bunch of different opinions on the matter—half of them dating back twenty years as far as he could tell.

"Look," he tried to break in.

"Turning this into a dry town might be the answer," Ms. Think of the Children suggested.

"Wait—"

An old lady stood up. "Over my dead body."

"Well, that won't take long," someone else said.

"Hey—"

"Um…" Clay took a step back.

Patty cleared her throat. "Ladies and gentlemen. Can we come to order?"

But things were well out of hand.

He turned to her, even though she was the last person he expected to help him—well, the last person after the women who wanted the whole town to go Prohibition style. "You planning to try to get any kind of control over these people?"

"They'll tire themselves out eventually." She glanced at the time. "Your ten minutes are up anyway."

Yeah, he didn't think so.

Stepping forward, he addressed the room once more. "Hey." A few people looked up from their squabbling. He opened his mouth, the inner drill sergeant inside him ready to come out. He clenched his hands into fists.

"Clay," came a quiet voice at his side.

Startled, he turned.

When had June gotten over here? Last he'd looked, she'd been yammering with someone about whatever committee had been trying to stop a freaking freeway of all things, but out of the blue, she had rematerialized a foot away.

"Look," he started.

"I know, I know. I'm sorry." She tipped her head toward the door. "You wanna get out of here?"

And there wasn't a lick of innuendo in the invitation, but the animal part of his brain heard it all the same.

She must've, too. "I mean...," she stammered.

"Yeah, yeah, I know what you mean."

He held out his hand, gesturing for her to lead the way. As they left, the arguments inside were really getting going. The last thing he heard was one of the grannies telling one of the middle-aged ladies to stick her intolerant, teetotaling opinions where the sun didn't shine, and who knew. Maybe that particular granny'd served in the same unit he had, she cursed so creatively.

"Wow," he whistled.

"They aren't usually that bad." June wrung her hands.

"Uh-huh."

"I swear." The guilty expression on her face made him not so sure.

They emerged into a courtyard outside the town hall. After the air-conditioning, the heat outside smacked into him like a damp ten-ton wall. He tugged at the collar of his shirt.

Idiot. Dressing up, combing his hair. And for what?

He rounded on June. "I'm not putting on a monkey act like that again."

She chewed on her lip. "Look..."

"They couldn't agree on whether or not the sky is blue."

"They can be herded along..."

"Seriously?"

"We've gotten all kinds of things done. You heard about the new plans for the Pumpkin Festival—"

Yeah. He'd heard that for sure.

He didn't want to let the betrayal churning around in the pit of his stomach be real. But he wasn't going to swallow a load of horse manure like this, either. June had made it sound like if he just explained what he was trying to do, he could convince them to get out of his way. For a bit there he'd almost let himself believe it, but grim reality was sinking in.

Even June was having a hard time getting those people to take her and her ridiculous Pumpkin Festival seriously. How well did that bode for him?

"They're never going to approve of a bar." He kicked at the curb, like that would help anything. Then again, harder. "Don't even know why I bothered." He turned his face skyward. "Don't know what Bug saw in this place."

Whenever Bug had talked about it, he'd made Blue Cedar Falls seem magical, but so far it was full of people who wouldn't leave him alone or people who wouldn't give him a chance, and he was sick of it. If it weren't for Bug, he'd be in Alaska now, maybe Montana. Someplace where he could have gotten a plot of land all to himself. Wouldn't have needed anybody's approval for anything.

Wouldn't have needed anybody at all.

Then June's hand was on his arm.

He whipped around, his skin on fire from her touch. He was

ready to lash out, angry at himself and at Bug and at the Main Street Business Association and at June, too, for letting him think that they might help.

But June's touch was soft, her eyes big and guileless. "I do."

"What?"

"I do," she repeated. "I know what Bug saw in this place. Why he thought it was worth fighting for."

"Care to enlighten me?"

She pulled her hand away. Part of him was glad, and part of him wanted to pull it back.

She lifted her chin. "Actually, yeah. I would."

"I'm all ears."

"Uh-uh." She shook her head. "You have to see it with your own eyes."

"I think I've seen everything."

"You've seen an outsider's perspective on it. Let me give you the insider one." A new inspiration lit her eyes. "I know the business association folks are making life difficult—"

"'Difficult'? Try a living h—"

"But they're fighting for something, too. In an annoying, stubborn, circular-firing-squad way, I know. But they are. Let me show you what they think they're trying to preserve." Her throat bobbed. "Let me show you what I love about this place. Let me show you why I want to help it grow. No matter how hard it seems, sometimes."

He was ready to tell her no thanks. Her babbling monologue about her perfect town had given him a migraine the first time they'd met. Why would her touring him around be any better?

But just as he was about to shut her down, he paused. The warmth in her gaze made sparks flare low in his abdomen.

He didn't want her as an enemy—he'd learned that much

already. And they were too different for him to think they could ever be friends.

But maybe he owed it to himself to find out exactly what it would be like to see things from her side.

And besides.

What exactly did he have to lose?

CHAPTER SEVEN

Hansen's is one of the oldest bookstores in the state," June said with pride as they passed its summer-themed beach-read window display. She looked up at Clay, trying to gauge his reaction.

He wasn't frowning or grumbling or telling her that bookstores were for nerds, so that was something, at least.

They'd been strolling the shaded sidewalk along Main Street for the better part of an hour now, walking and talking and talking and walking.

Well, to be honest, she'd been doing the vast, vast majority of the talking. Clay had been a quiet presence at her side, not yelling at her or shutting her down, but not exactly enthusiastic, either.

Doubt began to creep into her heart. Was this a total waste of time?

She just hadn't been able to stand the simmering defeat in his posture after the business association meeting. He'd been ready to give up on his plans, on the frustrating, impossible people she knew and loved. On this town.

So here they were, with her showing him around, trying to convince him that this place was worth fighting for.

After he didn't so much as crack a smile as she showed him around the inside of the bookstore, she started to despair. They stepped back outside, and the late afternoon heat slapped her. She swabbed at the dampness on her neck, the heavy curtain of her hair sticking to the hot skin. Her dress was breezy and easy for summer, but the longer they were out, the more oppressive it felt.

Clay seemed equally uncomfortable. He'd opened up his shirt more as they'd walked. She glanced at the golden skin at his collar, the exposed ink on his forearms. She swallowed, the sight of him with a sheen of sweat affecting her in ways she still didn't know what to do with. Needing a distraction, she cast about for the next thing to show him on the tour.

Across the street, she spied Sprinkles, and she sighed with relief.

Then she looked at Clay with narrowed eyes. "Please tell me you like ice cream."

He seemed personally offended. "*Everybody* likes ice cream."

Oh thank goodness.

They crossed the street to where a small line of people waited their turn to order at the window. June frowned. A sticky summer day like this, with their usual tourist crowd, the line would have been around the block.

It was nice to not have to wait, but it was a terrible sign.

She put on a bright face, though. "This is one of my favorite places on Main Street," she told Clay.

He rolled his eyes, but a smile flirted with his lips. "You're as bad as Hadley."

"Who?"

The smile turned more rueful. "Bug's niece. Four years old. Every single thing in the world is her favorite these days."

Before she could think about it too hard, June mock-slapped Clay's arm. She had to work to keep her voice even, her tone teasing; his biceps were rock hard in the most appealing way. "I'm not that bad."

"You're worse." If the casual physical contact distracted him as much as it did her, he didn't let on. Doing a terrible impression of her, he said, "Look at my favorite bookstore! My favorite restaurant! My favorite record store!"

"Hey—that record store is a gem."

It was also just about the only thing on this street that had piqued his interest in any way.

"Of course it is," he agreed, "but it kind of loses its impact when it's followed by my favorite bench! My favorite leaf!"

"Look, if you've seen prettier ginkgo leaves than the ones on the tree in that green space—"

"It's the principle of the matter." He shook his head. "You talk as if everything in this town is the best in the world."

"How do you know it's not?"

"Seen a lot of the world, sweetheart. Have you?"

She frowned. Not really, but she didn't need to. "Blue Cedar Falls has everything I need."

"Sure."

Her annoyance with his underwhelmed reaction to her tour brewed over. "Stop doing that."

"Doing what?"

"Humoring me." It was better than him constantly picking fights with her, but it was almost as insulting.

He shifted his gaze to the menu as they inched closer to the window. "Look, I've been trying to be patient. Keep my jerkwad comments to myself. You want me to stop humoring you, too? What am I gonna have left?"

"Ha-ha."

"I'm serious."

"Me, too." She was trying not to get worked up, but she felt strongly about this. "You act like I'm full of it, but I really, honestly do think this town is that great."

He looked at her, his mouth pulling to the side. He seemed to be considering her. "You really do, don't you?"

"That's what I've been trying to tell you."

Finally, without irony, he shrugged. "Must be nice."

"What?"

"To be that attached to a place. You don't see that often."

She eyed him with suspicion for a second, waiting for him to take it back or give away how he was actually, quietly making fun of her. When he didn't, she let out a breath.

Blue Cedar Falls was objectively the greatest place on earth.

But that wasn't all there was to it. The town was special to her on a personal level, too.

"I wasn't actually born here, you know," she admitted.

"Oh?"

"My mom and dad—my bio dad—they lived in Astoria. Queens. New York."

"I'm familiar."

Not everybody around here was. "Me and my sisters, May and Elizabeth, were born there." June fiddled with her fingers in front of her. "My dad had a lot of...issues."

A terrible temper for one.

Some of June's first memories had been of going toe to toe with him. Defending her sisters. Poor Elizabeth had been a baby; she didn't remember any of it. But that hadn't spared her.

Their father had been set off by anything. You never knew if you were about to step in something. If forgetting your manners would earn laughs or a slap across the face.

She'd tried so hard to keep him happy. Make him proud, even. But it had never been enough.

When her mother finally kicked him out, he hurled insults and accusations, but he didn't ask for custody. June watched him pack his bags and leave, rejection and relief swirling in her gut. Along with them came the heavy weight of responsibility. To fight for herself and her family. To take care of them—always.

June took another step forward. They were almost to the front of the line. She should probably wrap this up.

"After he and my mother split, she took my sisters and followed a job offer down here."

It was one of the bravest things June could imagine. A young, immigrant woman with three girls, traveling south all alone without a friend in the world.

The Chinese American community in New York had been supportive and strong.

Down here, the Wu girls had been entirely on their own.

"We stuck out like sore thumbs."

Blue Cedar Falls was diverse, and the Latinx community in particular had grown over the years. But June had been the only Asian American in her elementary school class at the time.

Her English had been excellent, but the home and neighborhood she'd grown up in had been largely Chinese-speaking, and she'd had an accent back then. Her clothes had been different, her food different.

Her first day of school, she'd never been more self-conscious in her life.

But then a girl with blond pigtails had sat down next to her at lunch, introduced herself as Bobbi, and asked if June liked unicorns.

And they'd been best friends ever since.

"It didn't matter, was the thing," June said, her throat going tight.

Sure, she and her sisters got made fun of from time to time. Her sister May in particular had a tough time with a crew of mean girls who'd made her life difficult.

Those jerks had been the exception, not the rule, though.

"We were welcomed with so much warmth."

They'd been invited to churches, potlucks, social clubs, Brownies and Girl Scouts, you name it. They'd found a home.

After her mother met Ned and left her career in teaching behind to help run the Sweetbriar Inn...

Their family never looked back. *June* never looked back.

There was a reason she was working so hard to save both the town and the inn.

"Everything I ever needed, I found here," she told him. "If I ramble on too much about how I love the bookshop, it's because that's where I went as a kid and discovered my favorite stories. Fran's Diner is where my stepfather took me to get a hamburger and fries when he was trying to get to know us kids." She flung a hand in the direction of the greenspace. "My favorite bench is where me and my friends would sit, and that beautiful ginkgo tree was where I had my first kiss."

She blushed, snapping her mouth shut. What on earth had possessed her to tell him that?

Big, strong, rough around the edges, seen everything Clay didn't need to hear about her awkward first kiss with a gangly teenage boy a decade and a half ago.

But Clay didn't know how awkward it had been. Heat flared inside her as he dropped his gaze to her lips. She licked them despite herself, and his pupils darkened.

"Next?" a voice called out. Then, more sharply, "Hey, June— you gonna order or not?"

June snapped out of her haze. The blazing heat on her cheeks grew to an inferno as Jimmy Jenkins smirked at her from the ice cream stand window. She stepped forward.

"Yeah, sorry—" She glanced at the menu to see what this week's special flavor was. "Small vanilla raspberry twist in a sugar cone, please."

Clay filled the window beside her. "And a banana split with everything."

His big hand appeared on the window ledge, and good grief, he was standing so close. His scent threatened to overwhelm her.

He slid a twenty dollar bill over to Jimmy. Jimmy looked between the two of them, brows raised, and June mentally cursed.

First she'd convinced the business association to put Clay on the agenda. Now she'd not only presumably been seen wandering all over Main Street with him, but Jimmy was going to tell everyone they'd been canoodling while grabbing ice cream.

June wanted to smack herself. She hadn't dated in so long. The rumor mill was going to have a field day with this.

As Jimmy handed Clay his change, June put some distance between them.

She was attracted to him, sure, and now that they were starting to get to know each other, she was even starting to like him, but this wasn't a date.

Even if it were, it wouldn't be anybody's business but their own.

They waited for their ice cream in charged silence. June accepted her cone and took it to one of the picnic benches in the shade. Clay joined her with a colossal sundae, gazing at her in defiance as if challenging her to make some sort of comment. Declining to take the bait, she concentrated on her cone, the ice cream already beginning to drip in the heat. She automatically went to stick out her tongue and lick the sticky sweetness from the base.

She caught herself. She glanced at Clay. His gaze was too intent on her.

Crap.

What was she supposed to do, though?

Willing away her self-consciousness, she stared right back and went ahead and licked fast, broad stripes all up the length of the cone, smoothing out the ridges on the soft serve. Dark heat burned in Clay's eyes, but she carried on.

Electricity hummed in the space between them. Suddenly the heat was less oppressive, more...sultry.

"Taste good?" Clay asked, voice low and rough. Was that how he would sound in the bedroom?

June clenched down deep inside and nodded. Staring at him was like staring at the sun. She couldn't do it any longer.

Looking away, she ate another bite of ice cream off the top and refused to think about how she looked, her mouth open around the creamy point.

"How about yours?" she asked. She dared a glance at him.

As if he'd been waiting for that very opportunity, he chose that moment to pop a glistening, red cherry into his mouth. "Delicious."

"Great."

She couldn't concentrate enough to keep going with any kind of substantive conversation, so she ate her ice cream and surreptitiously watched him eating his. Tension filled the air around them, but the awkwardness of two people sitting together and not talking to each other never materialized. It was...strangely comfortable.

Finally, she tossed the last bite of her cone into her mouth.

She sucked the bit of melted ice cream off her fingers, her cheeks on fire, then dabbed at them with a napkin. Considering how large Clay's treat had been, he'd made quick work of it. He shoveled down the last few chunks of banana and ice cream before sitting back.

June cleared her throat. There was more of Main Street to explore with him, of course. She could spend days showing off all the nooks and crannies and delights waiting to be discovered by visitors.

Would any of it sway Clay?

Had sharing as much as she had so far made any difference at all?

"Well?" she asked, unable to keep the challenge from her tone. "You warming up to Main Street?"

"It's cute, I guess," he said begrudgingly.

It was a heck of a lot more than that. "This is what your friend loved. This is what I'm trying to save." She rolled her eyes fondly. "This is what all those folks in the Main Street Business Association think they're trying to preserve, every time they fight you."

"I still don't see how me building a bar is going to affect them one bit."

And June was stuck in the middle, understanding both sides. "I'm not saying they're right, but you have to admit"—she waved a hand around—"the kind of bar you're talking about would be a pretty big change."

"A good change."

Maybe, maybe not.

As if he could sense her hesitation, he frowned. Standing, he grabbed the dish from his sundae and tipped his head toward the street. "I think it's time maybe I show you what I'm trying to build."

* * *

Twenty minutes later, June sat in the passenger's seat of Clay's pickup, Blue Cedar Falls growing distant in the rearview mirror. He'd refused to tell her where he was taking her, and that should probably make her nervous, but it didn't.

Glancing at his strong, rugged profile, she bit down on the inside of her cheek.

She barely knew this man. He could be taking her heaven knew where. He could have all kinds of bad intentions.

She dismissed the idea out of hand.

Even though she disagreed with him on...everything, so far, she trusted him somehow.

Clay followed the back roads with a confident assurance. The silence between them didn't feel uncomfortable, and she settled in, taking in the view of the mountains against the clear blue sky, the bright green summer leaves on the trees. Wildflowers blooming in the grass along the side of the road.

When the speed limit dropped, she watched Clay, curious if this was their destination. Lincoln was the next town over, and one she didn't have much occasion to visit. Sure enough, he turned down its central drag. It wasn't as cute or quaint as Main Street in Blue Cedar Falls, with mismatched storefronts and a real hodgepodge of businesses. He kept driving to the end of the strip before finding a place to park.

"Come on." He got out, and she followed him into a little bodega market with its door open.

A fan blasted just inside. There wasn't air-conditioning, but without the brutal sun it wasn't so bad.

"Clay," an older Latina woman greeted him.

"Hey, Maria, how's it going?"

"Good, good." The two talked for a minute.

June looked around. The place was small but well stocked. If you swapped the yucca and mangoes for bok choy and lychee, it could have been one of the tiny Asian groceries back in New York.

Clay picked up a couple of good-looking mangoes and some tortilla chips and paid for them. He said goodbye to the shop-keeper, who also bid a warm farewell to June. Waving shyly, June scurried to keep up with Clay.

"Where—"

Before she could finish the question, he opened the next door. Stepping inside, June frowned. "What—"

"When, why, and how," Clay mused.

June rolled her eyes.

It took a second for her vision to adjust to the dimness inside after the bright sun. Slowly, the interior resolved into a wood-paneled bar, rows of half-full liquor bottles arrayed against a mirror, the logos for a handful of domestic beers displayed on the tap. A jukebox sat silent by the wall, and old ceiling fans spun lazily above. Baseball highlights played on a single TV in the corner. Smoking indoors had been outlawed ages ago, but she could almost see the aftereffects of it lingering like an invisible haze.

A dark-skinned man in a tank top stood behind the bar, slowly rubbing a cloth over its surface. A few barstools were occupied, and a middle-aged white couple sat at one of the tables scattered about.

The bartender nodded at Clay, and Clay nodded back. "The usual?"

"Yeah, man. And make it two."

"I don't—"

"Humor me." Clay chose a table in the far corner of the room.

June sat beside him, perching on the edge of her seat. Self-consciousness stole over her.

She'd dressed this morning for a meeting of the Main Street Business Association—not a walking tour of Blue Cedar Falls in the summer heat and definitely not for a drink at a hole-in-the-wall bar. Her dress stood out among the T-shirts and cutoffs.

Some raised eyebrows glanced her way. But unlike Jimmy at Sprinkles, the people here didn't gawk or insinuate. Once they'd gotten a gander, most of them went back to minding their own business.

Clay, for his part, made himself comfortable. He pulled out a pocketknife, wiped it on a handkerchief, and then sliced off a big chunk of mango. He scored it and bent it, making cubes of the ripe, orange fruit stand on end. He offered it to June.

She hesitated.

"Oh, go on," Clay encouraged her.

It did look good. She accepted it gingerly. She waited as Clay performed the same surgery on another section of the mango. The bartender appeared at their side with a pile of paper napkins and two dewy glasses of light beer. Clay thanked him, and June did likewise, grabbing a couple of the napkins.

Thus armed, she leaned forward and took a bite of mango. Its cool, sweet tartness exploded over her tongue.

Clay was utterly unashamed as he did likewise. Something tingled inside June, watching him bury his mouth in ripe fruit. Wetness clung to his lips, and she swallowed hard.

"Good?" Clay asked.

June's throat was tight. "Yeah."

She finished her section of the mango and set down the peel before wiping her hands. Clay opened the bag of chips and started in on his beer.

June picked hers up and gave it a sniff. Beer wasn't usually her drink of choice. She took a careful sip anyway. It didn't do much for her, but it wasn't as bitter as some could be, so she'd muddle through.

She waited on Clay, expecting some sort of explanation. He kept his gaze on the TV in the corner, though, slowly munching on fruit and chips and sipping on beer. She tried to relax, but she couldn't.

She glanced around again, trying to sort this all out. Clay had started this adventure by telling her he wanted to show her what he was trying to build. So far, this didn't exactly seem unique.

She finally broke. "Look, Clay—"

"Shh."

Her mouth snapped shut, and her brows rose.

"Shh," he said again. "Listen."

She managed to refrain from asking *What?*, but barely.

Just as her impatience began to rise again, he addressed her. "You hear that?"

"I—"

"Quiet. Not silence, but quiet. Nobody chattering." He gazed at her pointedly. "No one scurrying around or getting in your business. No activity to do, no perfect scene to appreciate."

"Okay…"

"It's life. Regular life with regular folks. Good beer." He gestured at his half-empty glass. "Good food. Good company."

"But nobody is talking to you."

"Exactly. But I'm not alone."

"What am I missing?"

He huffed out a breath. "The point. But I guess that's to be expected. Your Main Street—it's cute. But it's not real. This is."

"I don't know about that."

"Look." Clay sighed and shot his gaze upward. "Bug and his friends used to come here when he was on leave, because there wasn't anything like this on Main Street." He looked at her and tapped a finger against the table. "The folks in your business association act like a bar is going to scare everyone away, or that 'the children' are going to end up scarred because they see a grown man drink beer. But they're not paying attention to all the people they're turning away."

"So this is what you want to build?" She could understand the community aspect. The population that wasn't being catered to and that Main Street could better serve, but there was something missing here. Some spark.

"Not too far from it. The jukebox would be going, and the TV would be bigger, and I'd serve food instead of making you go get your snacks next door. It'd get livelier at night, especially if a band comes in, but this place does, too."

That could be fun, but it also brought back her old concerns. "You're not setting me at ease about me not getting noise complaints at my inn."

"I'd keep it under control."

Would he, though?

"I don't want to agree with Patty and Dottie here, but I'm still trying to figure out how that works on Main Street," she told him bluntly. Attracting more locals would be great, but her only way out of debt was more tourists coming in from out of town, and out-of-towners chose Main Street because of what it was. Cute. Charming. Quaint.

That was why she'd been putting so much of her time and energy into drumming up the Pumpkin Festival. It epitomized the qualities of Blue Cedar Falls that had once made it a tourist destination for the western Carolinas.

"A good bar would make Main Street better," he argued. "It brings in exactly what all your perfect ice cream shops and bistros and gingko trees can't replace."

"And what's that?"

"Normal life. Real folks."

Her frustration mounted. "Why do you keep saying that? What makes you think the people on Main Street aren't real?" She reached for him before she could stop herself, grabbing his hand. His skin was hot and rough, but she grasped on to him all the same. "What about me doesn't feel real?"

Clay's Adam's apple bobbed, and his eyes darkened. He pulled his hand away. "Of course you're real. You're too much of a pain in the butt not to be."

"Look—"

He shook his head. "I'm not saying you or your side of town isn't real. But it's too perfect. Things that perfect... they don't exist."

"Of course they do. They just take a little work."

Blood, sweat, and tears kind of work. But it was worth it. Creating something beautiful like that... giving guests a perfect experience... enchanting them enough to make them want to come back time and time again...

There hadn't been many special touches like that in her life in New York. But in Blue Cedar Falls, she'd come to understand their importance. Throwing themselves into the work of enhancing the Sweetbriar Inn and growing Main Street had been key to her mother and sisters building a better life for themselves, here with Ned and all the people who'd welcomed them in.

It was worth it.

For his part, Clay sat there, chewing on a chip. "Y'know, it's funny. That whole time you were talking about how great it was, growing up here, how good everybody was to you after your dad screwed you over—"

June flinched. "I didn't say—"

He waved her off. "After your mom kicked him out, whatever."

The broody, stormy look in his eyes kept her from opening her mouth again to protest.

He considered for a long moment, his gaze going to some point in the distance. "I lost my folks, too. Both of them."

Oh. "I'm so sorry."

"Doesn't matter." The set to his jaw said it absolutely did. "Car accident. Gone in a second—or at least that's what they said."

"Clay..."

"Didn't have anybody else, so I got placed in a foster home in a town not too different from this." He gestured around. "It had its 'good' parts and its 'bad.' Always seemed to me that the good parts were too good to be true, but maybe that's because I was in the part that was bad."

Something behind her ribs squeezed.

"I didn't last there long, or in the next place or the next. I was a little turd when my parents left me behind, and half the people who were willing to take me in were looking for a check to cash. Plenty of other kids who were less trouble waiting for homes."

"That's awful."

"It is what it is." Some of the haze in his troubled eyes parted. "But what I figured out fast is that what matters is finding a place where you feel like you belong. Could be a corner of whatever room you're sharing, could be a teacher's office at whatever school you're in for the moment during lunch." His gaze met hers. "Could be a great Chinese takeout joint or no-nonsense bar. You find your place where you fit. The rest of it isn't important."

He said it with such conviction.

And really, in the end, his story was a whole lot sadder than hers. It had left him bitter and prickly and quick to anger. But was the lesson all that different? She'd gotten lucky and ended up in Blue Cedar Falls, with a mom and stepdad and sisters who loved her, and neighbors and friends who became a second family to her.

She'd found her people and her place. They just happened to be right here.

"I wish you'd had more than that," she finally settled on. "I wish the family and the town you ended up in could have given you everything that this one gave me."

"I found enough," he told her. "My unit in the army—they were the brothers I never had. Bug. He was home for a real long time." Pain creased his brow, but he kept his voice steady. "And there was no place he felt more at home than a good dive bar. Anywhere in the world. With any kind of people."

"So that's what you've set out to make."

"It sure is," he agreed. He waved a hand at the bar they were in right now. "Doesn't need to be fancy. All it needs is to feel right to the right people."

Chewing the inside of her lip, June ran a fingertip through the condensation on the side of her still mostly full glass.

She agreed with most of what Clay was saying, in principle.

But he was making it too simple. He was discounting so much of what she'd learned, practically growing up behind the desk at the inn. Refining it into a place that people chose and loved. That *she* loved.

She considered her words carefully.

Lifting her beer to her lips, she took a measured sip.

"Wanting a place to be authentic is one thing"—she held up a finger when he started to interrupt—"a great thing. Building a community is the most important piece of the puzzle, and restaurants and bars live and die by their regulars, even in a tourist town like Blue Cedar Falls."

"You think I don't know that?"

"I think you know a heck of a lot." Maybe more than she'd given him credit for when he first showed up. "But I've been living here and doing this for almost my entire life. I know Blue Cedar Falls, and I know the hospitality business."

He visibly bristled, his fingers flexing and releasing. But maybe he really meant it the other day at the inn when he apologized and conceded that he couldn't do this on his own. Despite his agitation, he kept his mouth shut and listened.

"If you want to thrive there," she told him. "If you want to still be around in a year, much less a couple of decades, you need to consider both the new business you could be bringing in *and* what already exists where you're trying to build."

"That wasn't part of Bug's plan."

"But maybe it should be a part of yours." She let out a long exhalation, giving her next words careful thought. "You said Bug was ready for a fight when he started this whole thing, but is that really how you want to spend your entire time here? Fighting?"

"Maybe," he said, but there was a hint of a pout to it.

"A neighborhood watering hole like this is fine. It's good." She glanced around again at the nondescript decor and the dour faces of the people drinking. "But if you want to create a place where people will feel at home? A place that doesn't just fill a void but really adds to the community? It's got to be tailored to the area where you're building it. It's got to be more."

Like that, she had it. The missing piece.

"You want to fulfill your friend's dream? Then I think you need to go bigger. You need to stop just doing everything to spite everyone around you. Stop being limited by what you think he would have wanted." This could work. "You need to consider yourself and what you want, what your patrons will want. And yeah, you have to think about what will fit in on Main Street, too."

All the ideas she'd had about ways their businesses could help each other returned to her with a vengeance. A spark of hope lit inside her as she imagined what he could build.

"But you do that…" Her voice lifted, and her heart went right along with it. "You dig deep and you put in the work. And I think you could have something special."

Something that might help save them all.

CHAPTER EIGHT

❖ ❖ ❖ ❖ ❖ ❖ ❖ ❖ ❖ ❖ ❖

Uncle Clay, watch me!"

"Go for it." Clay grinned as Bug's niece Hadley started dancing like a jumping bean on a trampoline on the other side of the video chat. "Wow!"

"She's been like this all day," her mom, Lisa, said from behind the camera.

Clay winced. "Well, at least she'll sleep good tonight?"

"Man, I hope so."

"Wanna prop up the phone and go grab another cup of coffee?"

"There is not enough coffee in the world."

He took a swig from his own cup. It was dark and rich and bitter. So basically, perfect.

He scowled.

The tour June had given him the other afternoon might have been ridiculous, but he had to admit it had also been useful. He still didn't believe that any place on earth could be as perfect as she claimed Blue Cedar Falls was.

But the coffee from Gracie's Café over on the corner of Larch was pretty freaking delicious, and he probably never would have wandered over there if June hadn't practically forced him to. The stuff he made out of the old percolator he'd found at the secondhand shop next to the hardware store just didn't compare.

The sandwich he'd picked up at the bakery was pretty good, too.

He downed the last of the coffee, annoyed by how much he enjoyed it.

June's speech about how everything had to be special this and special that echoed in his ears. His entire life, good enough had been good enough. Food was fuel, coffee was rocket fuel, and that was that.

As if she could tell his attention was wandering, Hadley chose that moment to charge at the camera with an ear-splitting scream. Clay yelped right back, and she squealed with delight.

"Hey Had, wanna tell me more about those pony books you've been reading with your mom?"

"They're not *ponies*, Uncle Clay, they're *unicorns*."

"Right, right, what was I thinking?"

His slip didn't deter her at all. She launched into summarizing the most recent adventure the unicorns had been on, and Clay sat back, nodding and smiling and putting on his best surprised face at every twist in the convoluted plot.

"And you'll never guess what!"

He leaned forward. "What?"

"Mommy got me a *new* unicorn book."

"Oh, wow."

Lisa interrupted, "Why don't you go get it so you can show it to Uncle Clay?"

"Okay!"

Hadley ran off. Lisa flipped the camera around so he could see her face.

"Hey," she said.

"Oh, hey."

"So how are things going?"

This was the way the two of them got to catch up with each other. He loved watching Hadley's antics, but he'd been friends with Bug's sister ever since that first Christmas they got leave. Clay'd been squirrelly about what he was going to do with the time off, and Bug had seen right through him. He'd dragged Clay to Lisa and her ex's house in Charlotte, and he'd been part of the family ever since.

Sometimes, when he wasn't fantasizing about moving to Alaska, he wished he'd ignored Bug's stupid dream and gotten a place down the road from Lisa and Hadley. It'd be good to be able to see them more often. He could take Hadley on adventures to the junkyard. Show her how to fix a car engine and put up drywall. Give her poor mom a break.

Right. As if it would be all sunshine and tools and toddler tea parties.

He'd had good reasons for keeping to himself. He wasn't fit for human company most days. War and loss and all the shrapnel in his knee had changed him.

And let's be honest. He hadn't exactly been a ray of sunshine before his best friend bled out in his arms.

He gritted his teeth and tried to push that haunting image out of his mind.

Focusing on what Lisa was saying about her job as an art teacher and all the goings on at Hadley's preschool, he nodded.

Hadley yelled something from the background, and Lisa looked over her shoulder. "Try under your bed."

"She can't find the book?"

Lisa whispered, "I can neither confirm nor deny knowing she left it in her backpack when I sent her off to go get it."

"Clever."

"That's me. Twenty-something years old and still occasionally able to outsmart a preschooler." With a tired smile, she sighed. "And how about you? Blue Cedar Falls everything Bug told you it would be?"

He grunted. "It's...fine."

With a wry grin, she spurred him on, "Do tell."

At this point, honestly, he was so turned around he didn't even know what he thought of the place. June's tour of all of her favorite things had opened his eyes a little to the stuff Bug loved, but that hot mess of a business association had proven all the bad stuff Bug had said was true, too. Main Street was full of people who didn't know their heads from their hindquarters. June might think that if he "came up with a vision" for his bar he could get them on board, but he wasn't so optimistic.

"Not quite what I was expecting," he finally settled on.

"It never is," Lisa said, shaking her head, a twinkle in her eye. "I told you."

"You left a few things out."

She'd mostly just rambled on about how much fun she and Bug had had there as a kid. Sure, she'd echoed Bug's warnings—and the warnings of every freaking person he'd met since he'd gotten here, it seemed—that opening a bar on Main Street would be tough, but could she have been a little more explicit about how?

As if she could hear his thoughts, she asked, "And how's the bar coming along?"

He glanced around at the chaos surrounding him. He let out a sigh of his own.

He'd finished a chunk of the renovations, but the stuff June had said about how the bar could be "more" than he'd planned...it kept creeping into his thoughts.

The vision Bug had given him was clear. A dive bar where locals could hang out and laugh at tourists while drinking beer and listening to music. Wood paneling. Jukebox. No frills, no fuss.

Who needed more than that?

Sure, the chunky wooden tables he'd seen at the wine bar were all right. Maybe he could get something more like that, as opposed to the basic unfinished tables he'd been planning to have Tim order for him. And there was this thing a few other restaurants on the strip did with big carved signs hanging from their awnings he was thinking about.

But only because he liked them. Bug would have liked them. It had nothing to do with the nonsense June had been spouting.

"It's coming along," he answered.

"Well, if you ever decide you need any help with it, you know I'm happy to draw you up some sketches."

She'd made the offer before, and he'd turned her down. It hadn't seemed necessary, and he didn't want her wasting her time.

"I'm good," he assured her.

Maybe she could hear that he wasn't as dismissive this time around. "It can help to see things all put together visually, you know. If you ever change your mind…"

"You'll be the first person I call."

The only person he called. Heck, pretty much the only reason he bothered to own a phone.

Her face softened. "And you're making friends? Getting out there and meeting people?"

Ugh. "Yes, Mom."

And the weird part was…he wasn't even lying? Sure, he was still a cranky old recluse, but he and Han talked every time he gave in and went to get dumplings from the Jade Garden.

He'd gotten to know other people, too, both at that bar he'd taken June to and at the hardware store and just around town. Supper at Duke and Tracy's had been…not a disaster, despite the fact that he was crap at small talk. Now they were insisting he come to some dinner party at their daughter's house, meet some people his own age. He had no interest; he was fine on his own, thank you very much. But every time he'd tried to beg off, they'd refused to listen.

Wasn't that southern hospitality for you, though? A guy on his own—no one was going to let him be lonely, no matter how hard he tried.

And of course there was June. No way he'd call her a friend, but she was…something. A chronic pain in his rear end, mostly, but something.

"Try to sound a little less excited, would you?"

"New places are hard."

She pulled her mouth to one side. "I wish I could take some time off and come down, show you around a bit. I don't have that many close friends left out there, but I could introduce you to a few people—"

He shook his head, waving her off. He didn't need any help making friends. At the rate he was going with the people he did meet, ten to one odds he'd just alienate anybody she did try to connect him with. "I'm managing."

Her brows furrowed, but before she could give him any more grief on the subject, banging sounded in the distance. Hadley squealed, and adrenaline shot through Clay. Had she fallen or dragged down a dresser on top of herself or—

The little girl bounded into view, so okay, no, she was fine. And besides, that wasn't a squeal of pain. It was pure, unbridled four-year-old glee.

"Uh—"

Lisa cursed beneath her breath. Over her shoulder, Clay spied Hadley pulling open the front door.

And in barreled three way too familiar faces.

"Sorry, Clay, I lost track of time," Lisa said.

Clay's throat tried to close. "What are they doing there?"

It was fuzzy in the background of the video, but a dark gaze snapped to his. "Wait—is that Clay Hawthorne?"

"Surprise?" Lisa said weakly.

Hadley rambled, "I was showing Uncle Clay my new dance moves and my unicorn books, but I couldn't find—"

"Well, I'll be." The owner of the voice approached.

And yup. That was definitely Owen Tucker.

Instinct told Clay to turn his phone off now, but he knew when he was beat.

Tuck turned to Lisa. "We've been trying to get ahold of this a-hole for months, and you knew where he was this whole time?"

"Mommy, what's a 'a-hole'?" Hadley asked.

Lisa covered her eyes and shook her head.

"Sorry," Tuck said.

"Me, too." Lisa looked at Clay.

Clay let out a breath. "It's fine, Lisa."

He'd known this day would have to come eventually.

When he'd gotten out of the service, Bug had just died, and he'd still been trying to figure out how to walk again with the pile of scrap metal buried in his knee. He'd been angry and lost and so alone—and that was how he'd wanted it. Nobody deserved to be inflicted with his crappy company, and he didn't have the energy to play nice.

So he'd driven around, camping and hunting and staying in cheap motels when the weather didn't suit. He hadn't really known what he was doing, honestly.

It'd been bad. Real bad.

Lisa's messages with cute pictures of Hadley had been impossible to ignore, but everybody else…The guys from his unit…When they'd kept calling him, asking where he was and if they could catch up with him, now that they were out, too…

He hadn't wanted them to see him like that. So he'd ignored them.

By the time he was starting to realize what a jerk he'd been, refusing to so much as reply to a text message, enough time had passed that he hadn't known where to start. So he'd put it off and put it off.

A low, dark anger had settled in his chest when he thought of the friends he'd lost through his own stubborn pride. But what was he supposed to do?

Wait for them to find him, apparently.

He managed a half smile, even as nerves churned in his gut. "Hey, Tuck."

Lisa moved out of the way, letting Tuck have her phone. His big, ugly mug filled the screen.

"So you are still alive," Tuck said.

"More or less."

Tuck swung the phone around. "Look guys, it's Clay."

The other two figures who had been in the background resolved into AJ and Riz, which shouldn't have been any surprise. The three of them had been as tight as Bug and Clay had been, back in the day.

Instead of pissed, they grinned and waved.

Tuck turned the camera to face him again.

Clay chuckled despite himself. Relief filled him, because the smile that spread across Tuck's face was too real to be an act.

"Holy crap, man, it's good to see you," Tuck said.

"Yeah." Clay's voice went rough. "You, too." He cleared his throat. "Sorry, I—uh—"

Hadley climbed Tuck's back until she was in frame. "Uncle Clay's been having a real tough time," she recited.

And okay, Clay was going to have to talk to Lisa about that, because Hadley was definitely quoting her mom directly.

"Is that right, pumpkin?" Tuck asked.

Hadley nodded solemnly, then slid down off Tuck's back.

Clay rolled his eyes and put on his best bravado. "You know I hate it when you call me 'pumpkin,' sugarplum."

Tuck narrowed his eyes. "Oh, is that how it's gonna be?"

"You know it."

Tuck gazed at him for a second. Clay squared his jaw and returned his stare. He wasn't going to talk about his feelings or what a jerk he'd been the past year.

And Tuck proved exactly what a good friend he was. Because he didn't push at all. "So what the heck have you been up to, pumpkin?"

Clay exhaled, and a spasm of a laugh went right on out with the air. "Not much. You?"

"Not much, either. Just road-tripping around the country with these a-holes."

"Language," Lisa yelled from the background.

Hadley started screaming "a-hole" at the top of her lungs.

Clay and Tuck both laughed.

Tuck continued, "Aiming to see every state we can get to by land by the end of the year. Been to about half of 'em so far."

"How long you staying with Lisa?" Clay asked.

"Week or two. See how long it takes until our welcome wears out."

"Mind your mouth or it'll be more like an hour or two," Lisa called.

"That's good," Clay said, ignoring her. Charlotte was only a couple of hours away. He should really get out there and see her himself someday. Give Hadley a big old bear hug and squeeze her until she squealed. "Real good."

Tuck raised a brow. "You ever give us your address, and maybe someday we'll come visit you."

Clay popped his knuckles. He could rattle it off right now. He had no doubt Tuck, AJ, and Riz would come beat down his door.

But tearing off the Band-Aid and talking to them on the phone was one thing. Showing them his injuries and the pit of isolation he'd been wallowing in for all this time…that was something else.

"Yeah," he managed to choke out. "Yeah, maybe someday."

It wasn't enough. It wasn't what they wanted—or even, maybe, what he did. But it was more than he could have offered them a year before, when he'd assumed he'd never see them again.

For now, it was the best he could do.

CHAPTER NINE

❖ ❖ ❖ ❖ ❖ ❖ ❖ ❖ ❖ ❖ ❖

W hat's this?"

June's youngest sister Elizabeth crinkled her brow.

June's heart leaped into her throat. She plucked the piece of paper Elizabeth had grabbed off the printer right out of her hand. "Nothing."

"It's from the hospital."

"Follow-up stuff," June said dismissively, and technically that wasn't a lie.

Goodness knew the hospital spent more time following up on the Wu family's unpaid bills than they ever had on its matriarch.

She stuffed the latest version of the payment plan they'd been hammering out in her purse and silently scolded herself. She and the bean-counting leeches at the hospital had finally settled on an agreement that looked like it might work. Plenty of time to pay off the debt, reasonable monthly payments. Assuming business stayed more or less where it was, she'd be okay. One more read-through and she would be ready to sign, return, and get this boulder of anxiety off her chest. No one in her family would have to know what a mess they'd landed in.

Unless of course she was a total idiot and left the thing on the printer. Getting distracted by Bobbi's panicked texts about last-minute preparations for their big meet-the-parents dinner party was no excuse.

She had to do better. Be better.

Elizabeth rolled her eyes and plopped down into the chair behind the inn's front desk. She was in one of her usual bohemian outfits—a big flowy skirt, probably hand-dyed by some indigenous farmer somewhere, and a thrift store T-shirt. Her long, black hair with its purple highlights was swept into a loose bun at the nape of her neck.

June fought not to frown. It wasn't how June chose to dress when she was working the desk, but at least there weren't any swear words on her sister's shirt like there probably would have been when she was sixteen and driving their mother out of her gourd.

"Fine," Elizabeth huffed, wiggling the mouse on the computer. "Keep your secrets."

The payment plan did its best to burn a hole in the bottom of June's bag. "I'm not keeping secrets."

June hated lying.

"Uh-huh. Sure."

"Don't be like that."

"Like what? A petulant child? Isn't that what you and Mom always call me?"

"Elizabeth."

"Whatever." Elizabeth waved her off.

If she was trying not to be petulant she was doing a really terrible job of it.

"Look—"

Elizabeth huffed and rolled her eyes. "I know the score, okay? You call me when you need me and you leave me out of all the big-picture stuff. I'm used to it enough by now."

Were they really going to have this argument again?

"You're the one who moved out."

At eighteen years old—basically the second she could.

"You're never going to let that go, are you?" Elizabeth asked.

June pinched the bridge of her nose. "I'm sorry. That wasn't fair."

But the truth of the matter was that no—June wasn't ever going to let it go completely. Nearly a decade had passed. She'd forgiven as much as she could, but forgetting your last sister abandoning you was a pretty tall order.

As tetchy as Elizabeth was being about feeling left out now, back then she'd been pretty clear about exactly how involved she wanted to be with the big-picture stuff when it came to running the inn.

About how much responsibility she thought she owed to the family and its business.

Sure, Elizabeth had come around some as she'd gotten older and realized how hard it was to make a living as an artist. She'd never abandoned them completely; she'd always worked shifts when they needed her. But she'd made her choices about her larger goals a long, long time ago. She hadn't wanted to do the hard work of managing the inn, and that was fine. No one was asking her to.

But that also meant she didn't get to act all offended over a piece of paper June didn't want her to see.

Elizabeth sighed, "Whatever. I didn't mean to pick a fight, either."

"I know."

They were getting dangerously close to talking about their feelings.

Fortunately, June's phone buzzed in her pocket. She used it as an excuse to pull away. Elizabeth seemed just as relieved.

The latest message from Bobbi flashed across the screen of June's phone.

Help, they're here.

June glanced at the time. Crap. Bobbi's house wasn't far away, but she was supposed to be there already and she hadn't even left.

Sorry, got held up. Leaving now!

"Look," June said, tapping send.

"I know, you've got to go."

June tossed her phone in her purse. "I'll probably be home before nine, but if I'm not—"

"I'll close things down and put the sign up, I know, I know."

Anything that happened after the front desk closed Ned could handle.

"Thanks again for taking the shift," June said, trying to be diplomatic. Appreciative, even.

Elizabeth turned back to the computer and waved her off.

June resisted the urge to call any additional reminders at her sister. She'd taken on the role of their mother a lot, especially in the past few months, but she was still self-possessed enough to catch herself before she got quite *that* overbearing.

Most of the time.

With one last backward glance, she slung her bag over her arm, grabbed the salad she'd prepared, and headed out the door.

On the drive over to Bobbi's her phone buzzed at least three more times, but she ignored it.

The day of her friend's big dinner party had finally arrived. Bobbi had obsessed about the menu, the guest list, the place settings—everything. June had provided a supportive sounding board through it all, only drawing a line when Bobbi debated repainting her living room because "yellow would be more friendly, wouldn't it?"

Eventually, the plans had been settled. An even dozen people had RSVPed—just enough of a crowd that Caitlin wouldn't be conspicuous, but not so much of one that she'd get lost in the hubbub, either.

Everything was going to be perfect.

Or if it wasn't, at least a corner of the Band-Aid would get ripped off, and that had to count for something, right?

June parked on the street outside Bobbi's tiny house on a corner lot in a cute, residential part of town just north of Main Street. Bobbi's parents' giant truck sat behind Bobbi's tiny hatchback in the driveway, but nobody else was there yet. June let out a rough breath. Bobbi's parents being early was inconvenient. It would make Bobbi even more on edge, and it meant she and Bobbi would have to talk in veiled terms.

Still, she put on a cheerful smile as she got to the door. "Knock, knock," she called out before letting herself in.

"Where. Have. You. Been?" Bobbi basically attacked her the second she was in the door, grabbing her by the arm and steering her right back outside.

"Breathe," June started.

"Easy for you to say," Bobbi muttered. Over her shoulder, she called, "I'm just going to show June the patio."

"Oh hi, June!" Bobbi's mom poked her head out of the kitchen. Her signature blond perm was extra poufy today.

"Hi!" June managed to call before Bobbi pulled the door closed between them.

"An hour!" Bobbi dragged June along the path toward the back. "They're *an hour* early."

"To be fair, that's actually pretty restrained for your mom."

"I had plans." Bobbi waved a hand around dramatically. "I

was going to rehearse what I was going to say and string more lights and buy plane tickets to Hawaii so my girlfriend and I can elope."

They turned the corner, and the entire yard was lit with crisscrossing strands of fairy lights.

"Outside of rehearsing, you should do absolutely none of those things."

Bobbi stopped, whipping around to face June. Her blue eyes were wide and maybe slightly crossed. "I can't do this."

"You absolutely can."

"How?"

June put her salad down on a folding table draped in a brightly colored cloth, lit with yet more little lights glowing inside an empty wine bottle. She put her hands on Bobbi's shoulders. "It's just dinner, remember? No pressure. No big reveals. Just a chance for them to meet Caitlin and for Caitlin to meet them."

"They invited extra people, June. To my house."

Yikes. June did her best to keep her calm face on. "It's okay. You cooked enough for an army."

"They're going to run roughshod over me. I'm never going to tell them. I'm going to elope. That's it, I'm going to elope."

"No, you're not."

"I am." Bobbi pulled out her phone. "I'm buying the plane tickets to Hawaii right now."

June plucked the phone out of her hands and set it next to the salad. "Bobbi. *Breathe.*"

Bobbi sucked in an exaggerated lungful, then let it go. "This isn't helping."

"Do it again. Like, a hundred more times."

Bobbi was usually so breezy and easy. But when it came to

her family and her relationships, she could wind herself up so tightly she was bound to explode.

June reeled Bobbi in and wrestled her into a squeezing hug. Slowly, Bobbi relaxed into it. When she pulled back, her eyes were slightly less deranged.

"What if they don't like her?" she asked in a small voice.

"Then they have terrible taste, because she is awesome."

A small smile appeared on Bobbi's face. "She really is, isn't she?"

"Yup."

"Will you help me string more lights?"

"I will not." It was going to be a safety issue for the electric grid soon. June looked around, searching for something else to focus her friend's attention on. Two glass drink dispensers and a few jugs of liquor and mixers caught her eye. "But I will help you mix some cocktails."

"That is an excellent suggestion."

They worked together, measuring and pouring and adding ice. As evening fell, the heat of the day relented, a welcome breeze beginning to cool the air. By the time they each had a glass of boozy blueberry lemonade in hand, life was looking positively rosy.

They clinked glasses and took a sip. Yum.

Bobbi breathed out a sigh. "You really think things are going to go okay tonight?"

"I really do," June promised. "And besides—look at it this way. What's the worst that can happen?"

As if on cue, Mrs. Moore picked that moment to open the back door. She stepped out with a tray of delicious-smelling barbecue.

"I was wondering what you girls were up to out here," she said, setting the tray down. She gestured over her shoulder.

"Your first guest just arrived. Clay, this is my daughter Bobbi and her friend June."

June jerked her head up. Two narrowed green eyes zeroed in on her.

June's heart thumped into overdrive.

Of course.

Bobbi's worst-case scenario was still to be determined.

But June's had just walked in the door.

"And then I told him he could shove his fence post right up his—"

"Duke!" Tracy gave her husband a scolding look, but her mouth was smiling an awful lot for someone who actually disapproved.

"What?" Duke played dumb, looking to Clay and Han for approval. "I was going to say he could shove it right up into the ground."

Tracy swatted his arm. "You are such a—"

"Uh-huh, go ahead and finish that sentence."

Clay chuckled and lifted his beer to his mouth.

He was about an hour into this backyard dinner party, and he was finally loosening up. It had been a while since he'd been around so many people, though he should probably get used to that, considering he was opening a bar. Most of the folks were at least familiar, despite the fact that he'd only lived here for a couple of weeks now. In some cases, that was a good thing. Han walking in the door a few minutes after Clay had been pure relief.

In other cases, it was ... less good.

Frowning, he glanced across the yard.

Small towns were always connected in weird ways. Everybody knew everybody. But if he'd known that Duke and Tracy's party was being hosted at their daughter's house, and that their daughter would happen to be Bobbi the Main Street bakery owner who happened to be best friends with June Wu...

Well. He didn't know if he could have managed to beg off without Duke and Tracy giving him the stink eye for the rest of his life. But he sure might have tried a little harder.

It didn't help that June had upped her game in the looks department. She was always attractive, but apparently prim-and-proper daytime June was only a part of the story.

Nighttime dinner party June was a chapter he wasn't going to be able to get out of his head. The difference was subtle, but it was driving him to distraction. Her long hair was up, the back of her neck begging to be kissed. Her dress was black instead of covered in flowers, and the neckline was lower, the skirt shorter. She'd done something with her makeup, too. He didn't know what it was, but the pout of her lips heated his blood.

Of course, she picked that moment to look over in his direction.

He averted his gaze quick, taking another deep pull on his beer.

Han caught his eye, his brow raised in question. Clay shrugged and pretended it was nothing.

Duke and Tracy continued verbally poking at each other, and Clay tried to focus on that. In his periphery, though, he couldn't help but notice June conspiring with Bobbi. Another woman about their age stood beside them, her skin a deep ebony, her dreads tied up in a ponytail on top of her head.

June patted Bobbi on the shoulder. The other woman did the same, only the touch was...different.

Then the whole group headed his way.

Clay frowned, instinctively distrustful of three women

marching toward him with *plans* in their eyes. But they paid him no mind as they inserted themselves into the group.

Bobbi sidled up to her father.

"Hey there, pumpkin," Duke said.

"Having a good time?" Bobbi asked, addressing the group as a whole, but her attention was clearly on her parents.

Huh.

"Sure," Clay said.

Han nodded, and Duke agreed.

"Everything's perfect, honey," Tracy said.

"Oh, good. You need anything? More drinks? Apps?" Bobbi's tone was light, but she was talking awfully fast and high-pitched for someone who was really at ease.

June fiddled with her nails and looked at her friend meaningfully. The other woman with them seemed to be visibly restraining herself from face-palming.

Tracy smiled and waved a hand dismissively. "You know you don't need to host us. We're good. Relax."

"Right, sure. Um."

"Mr. and Mrs. Moore," June finally took over. "Have you met Caitlin?"

The other woman smiled.

Duke tilted his head to the side, then held out his hand. "Can't say I've had the pleasure."

"Hi," Caitlin said, accepting the handshake with what looked like a firm grip. "I've heard a lot about you."

"Is that so?" Tracy asked, reaching out to shake Caitlin's hand, too. She side-eyed Bobbi.

Bobbi nodded. "Yeah, Mama, remember I was telling you about my new friend? The one I met at the hiking meetup?"

"Oh yes," Tracy said, but she wasn't that convincing.

"Hiking, eh?" Duke asked.

"Yes, sir," Caitlin replied. She looked at Bobbi and smiled. "We try to get out every week."

"How nice," Tracy said.

"Caitlin's actually in construction," Bobbi offered.

"You've probably seen her around Tim's Hardware," June added.

"Maybe I have." Duke's expression shifted to one that was more considering. "Good field. Tough one for a woman."

"Good thing I'm a tough woman." Caitlin's smile radiated confidence.

Duke laughed and held out his bottle of beer. Caitlin clinked her own against it.

Caitlin and Duke settled into making polite small talk about construction. Bobbi hung on their words, and June watched the whole proceeding with an intensity that was plain weird. Clay glanced at Han, and even he seemed to be acting like there was something at stake here.

After a few minutes of talking shop, Tracy lost patience with it all. "Oh," she interrupted. Clay followed her gaze to a tall guy with dark hair who'd just arrived. "There's Henry. Bobbi, come on, he's the one I was talking to you about earlier."

"Mom—"

"Hush, it's bad manners for the host not to greet her guest." Tracy grabbed Bobbi by the arm and basically hauled her away.

Bobbi looked back at Caitlin with wide eyes. Caitlin shook her head.

With a sigh and a shrug, Duke excused himself to follow Tracy and Bobbi across the yard. Clay was half tempted to head that way, too. But even though Tracy and Duke may have been the ones to invite him here, that didn't mean he had to be a barnacle on their side all night.

Caitlin pinched the bridge of her nose, shaking her head.

June sighed. "Well, that could have gone better."

"Could've gone worse, too," Han offered.

Dropping her hand, Caitlin raised a brow. "How?"

"What could have gone better?" Clay asked.

All eyes turned to him.

"Uh," Han said.

June pinched her lips. The appraising way she stared at him made something uncomfortable flip around in his gut.

Finally, Caitlin put him out of his misery. "That was me 'meeting the parents.'"

Clay scrunched up his face. "You mean—" He stopped as Caitlin gave him a withering stare and June cringed. "Oh." Suddenly all of the awkwardness clicked. "*Oh.*"

"Yeah, 'oh,'" Caitlin said.

"I mean, good for you," Clay scrambled. Crud, that judging look June had given him really made him feel like dirt now. What did she think—that he wasn't going to be okay with her buddy batting for the other team? Except "good for you" really wasn't the right sentiment. He stammered. "Um. Yeah, that wasn't awesome."

Han chuckled and tipped back his beer. "No kidding."

"To be fair," June piped in, "Bobbi's parents don't even know she's gay."

Clay's face was getting a workout as he fought to keep all his reactions tamped down. "Oh."

"Exactly," Caitlin said.

"Come on." Han finished off his beer and started walking toward the house. "Bobbi's gonna need more alcohol by the time she's done."

Clay glanced across the yard to where Bobbi stood, bracketed by her parents, her mother gabbing away at the guy she'd been so eager for her daughter to meet. Bobbi looked like she wanted to sink into the ground.

"That she will," Caitlin agreed.

She followed Han. June hesitated. She tipped her head toward the house. "You coming?"

Yeah, no way Clay could go barge into Duke and Tracy's conversation now. "Sure, why not."

And that was how he found himself sitting at the breakfast bar in Bobbi's kitchen with a fresh bottle of beer, June beside him, her cheeks flushed even though she swore she was only on her second cocktail of the night. Caitlin was opening a bottle of berry-flavored wine, when Bobbi threw open the door and skittered into the room like it was all she could do not to scream.

Caitlin poured a glass of the wine and held it out. Bobbi took it without a word and gulped it down like she was doing a keg stand at an army party.

"Uh—" Clay started.

June elbowed him in the side.

He batted her away. "Ow."

Caitlin glared at them both.

"Sorry," they said in unison.

Bobbi set down her glass with a thunk. "Arghgh," she groaned and shoved her head into Caitlin's shoulder. Caitlin glanced around at the drawn curtains before curling an arm around Bobbi. Bobbi went soft, leaning into her. "I'm so sorry."

"It's fine. This was always going to be a process, baby."

"I'm the one who should be sorry," June said tersely. She fiddled with her glass. "This whole meet-the-parents thing was my idea."

"It wasn't a terrible one." Han shrugged. "You know, in theory."

Bobbi stood up. She and Caitlin automatically put a careful foot of space between them. She tugged at her hair in frustration. "Do you know why my mom was so insistent on me going over and talking to Henry? Do you?"

"Um..." June winced.

"To set me up with him." Bobbi flung an arm out to the side. "That's how oblivious my parents are. They tried to set me up with a guy in the middle of me introducing them to my girlfriend. Can my life get any worse?"

"Always," Caitlin assured her, pouring her another glass.

"I'll drink to that," Han said.

Everyone raised their drinks. And yeah, okay. Clay could get behind that kind of toast.

They tapped bottles and glasses and downed more alcohol, and for one second, Clay had this spinning sensation in his head. Like he was back on base with Bug and Tuck and AJ and Riz and all the rest of the guys, shooting the breeze and drinking beer, and he fit, there with them.

His vision cleared. This wasn't any army base, and these weren't his brothers-in-arms, and he didn't fit. He never would.

As if to prove it, June turned full Pollyanna on Bobbi and Caitlin. "I'm sure it'll all work out somehow. At least your parents have met Caitlin now."

Caitlin pursed her lips. "True."

"You really think that's going to help?" Bobbi asked.

June shrugged. "I think it's a start. And that's definitely something."

"I guess..." Bobbi didn't sound so sure.

"Look," June said, gathering steam again, and oh boy. She'd gotten that gleam in her eyes around him before, and he wished he was wearing a hat so he could hold on to it.

"Your parents are good people. I know they might be a little traditional, but they love you so much. They're going to be on your side."

Bobbi frowned. "I hope so."

"I know so." June sounded so certain. "That's what parents do. They support their kids, and I really believe yours will support you, once you give them the chance."

Clay barely stopped himself from laughing. What came out was a snort. June shot him a murderous look.

"What?" she asked.

"Nothing, nothing." He did *not* want to put his nose in this.

But could she really be that naive?

Duke and Tracy were good folks, and she was probably right that they would come around, but "all parents support their kids"? Did she really have that perfect of a family that she could believe this crap coming out of her mouth?

June turned toward him, and it made him way too aware of how close they were sitting. Her warm knee grazed his, and heat shot up his spine, and that definitely did not have *anything* to do with the fact she was getting that pissy look on her face again that always did it for him.

"Seriously—you have something to contribute?" June invited him.

Oh, he was in so much trouble now. Han caught his gaze and shook his head vigorously. Caitlin crossed her arms.

But Bobbi was all ears, and June was goading him *again*.

He let out a low breath. "Look, I hope you're right. Everything is going to be fine, and you're all going to be at Pride next year as some big happy family."

"But?" June said, and the set of her jaw was his kryptonite.

"But don't just sit there being all sunshine and roses about it. If this goes pear-shaped, what's your plan?"

Han face-palmed, and Caitlin stood up straighter, flashing him a glance of warning.

But Bobbi blinked owlishly. "What do you mean?"

Clay swallowed a gulp of his beer. "I mean, hope for the best, plan for the worst." He gestured at June, stopping just short of touching the bare skin of her arm. "June's right. Parents are supposed to support you, and I hope yours do. But I've known plenty of 'parents' who certainly didn't."

How many people had he met in the service who'd been kicked out of their families' homes, or had parents who shoved them around?

How many foster homes had he bounced in and out of? And yeah, maybe he'd deserved it with his crappy attitude, but that hadn't made it any easier to take. Watching door after door get slammed shut in his face hadn't filled him with support and love.

He clenched his hand into a fist beneath the table. "All parents support their kids" his rear end.

Those folks who'd passed him around hadn't popped kids out by accident, either. They'd taken him in by choice.

They'd sent him packing again by choice, too.

"I'm just saying." He took another swig of his beer to wash down the acid creeping up his throat. "Always have a backup plan."

He'd kept his own stupid sob story to himself, but some of the bitterness must have leaked into his voice. Caitlin's face softened, and she uncrossed her arms. Han tilted his head to the side.

For once, June didn't start arguing with him or try to tell him why families were all great and amazing and full of puppies and rainbows. Instead, she pursed her lips together, giving him this look like she could see way too deeply into him.

For a second, he felt like maybe she really could.

Then Bobbi let out a sigh. "I mean, there's always eloping in Hawaii."

Caitlin smiled and playfully tapped her arm with her fist. "That's my girl."

Like that, the heaviness slipped away. Clay sat back on his stool. He met June's gaze, and she was still looking at him with too much meaning in her eyes.

Making it his turn to ask, "What?"

She stared at him for another second. Then she shook her head. "Nothing."

Right.

Static buzzed between them, even though they were done debating whether or not you could rely on your folks for unconditional support, apparently. Bobbi started talking more about her secret elopement plans, and Caitlin and Han and eventually even June joined in. It was silly, and everyone was a little tipsy.

Clay relaxed more, just listening. He might not fit here, and he might be the jerk who always had to bring up the fact that things might go sideways at any minute.

But sitting here with a bunch of other people about his age, not in a literal war zone...

It was pretty okay.

Even if the way he and June kept accidentally brushing elbows and knees was slowly driving him insane.

Caitlin addressed Clay, just as he'd started to zone out. "So you're the guy opening a dive bar on Main Street?"

Clay returned his attention to the present. June sat up straighter beside him.

"I sure am."

"Sounds awesome."

"Glad *you* think so."

He shot a pointed glance at June, who rolled her eyes. "I hope it's awesome," she said. She took a sip of her drink. "I just worry it won't be."

"How come?" Caitlin asked.

June huffed. "Mostly because this guy"—she pointed at him with her thumb, but she ended up poking him in the biceps with it—"told me to my face that I would hate it."

"You probably will," he agreed.

Caitlin laughed out loud. "You don't pull any punches, do you?"

"Not if I can help it."

"I'm starting to like you."

"Likewise." Clay held up his bottle, and she tapped her own against it.

"Main Street could use some shaking up," Caitlin said.

June pointed at Caitlin. "Now there we agree. And I don't think a bar is a bad idea, necessarily. So long as it's the right bar." Then she looked to Clay, one eyebrow cocked. "You give any more thought to what we talked about last time?"

He suppressed his groan. "A little."

He'd tried not to, for the most part, but her voice in the back of his head had kept hounding him, asking if he was thinking big enough, if he was doing enough to make his bar "special."

And he got her point, okay? Main Street was special. In her eyes, his plan for a bar was not.

A part of him was even starting to think that she was right, at least to some extent.

His bar was basic by design, while everything else on Main Street was fancy this and eggshell-chiffon that.

But Bug's dream of a down-home dive bar was special to *him*.

How did he make her—or the rest of the Main Street Busy-body Association—see that?

How did he reconcile what June wanted him to build with what he'd come to this town to do?

He wasn't any closer to figuring it out when Caitlin said, "Well, any bar that serves alcohol sounds like the right kind of bar to me. When you open, you be sure to let me know."

"That I can do."

Caitlin tipped her beer back. Lowering it again, she tapped her finger against the glass. "You know, I get a contractor discount at a couple of places around town. You need any plumbing or lighting?"

Huh. "Now that you mention it, I have been meaning to get some new lights. The ones the shop came with are crap." He furrowed his brow. "You sure you don't mind?"

"Not at all." She pointed her bottle to the side. "June uses it all the time."

June rolled her eyes. "I wouldn't say *all* the time."

"Uh-huh."

"I like to keep the inn updated is all." She scrunched up her face. "It's funny you should bring it up actually, because I've been meaning to replace the broken fixture near room fifteen."

"I've got to stop by the showroom on Route 8 on Thursday anyway." Caitlin glanced between the two of them. "That work for you?"

Clay blinked. Okay, he probably should have seen that coming, but he hadn't. He'd been signing up for new lights for the bar. Not a field trip with June.

His budget was stretched pretty thin, though. A contractor discount would probably be worth the company and the un-solicited opinions.

June met his gaze. She shrugged, leaving it up to him.

He ground his teeth together for a second before conceding, "Thursday's good by me."

"Thursday it is, then," June agreed.

As she turned back to whatever conversation Bobbi and Han were having, her leg brushed his beneath the counter, sending a ripple of heat through him. She didn't let it linger—though was it just him, or did she not jerk it away as fast as she would have a couple of days ago? She wasn't looking at him, but her cheeks flushed a deeper shade of red.

Something turned over low in the pit of his abdomen, and his skin prickled.

He took another deep pull at his beer.

Too bad he couldn't decide if her reaction to him and his reaction to her made him even less excited about spending extra time together...or more.

CHAPTER TEN

 ❀ ❀ ❀ ❀ ❀ ❀ ❀ ❀ ❀ ❀ ❀ ❀ ❀

Any additional questions, Ms. Wu?"

June stepped out of the finance office of the Pine View Medical Center with a spring in her step. She may not have been treated there by a physician—thank goodness, she couldn't afford another co-pay—but she'd never felt so healed.

Tucking her copy of the finalized payment plan agreement into her bag, she turned back and beamed. "Not that I can think of right now, though you know I'll be in touch if I come up with anything."

"I have no doubt," Mr. Gutierrez said, laughing. He looked as relieved as she felt.

June hadn't exactly made his life easy these past few weeks, but it had been worth it. All her mother's medical debt from her stroke had been rolled into one giant package and then broken up into manageable chunks. The Wu-Millers would be paying it off for the rest of time, but that was okay. June's budgeting skills were meticulous. As long as she could keep business at the inn steady, things were going to be all right.

No collection agencies would come knocking down her door. Her mom and Ned and May and Elizabeth would never have to know how close they'd come to losing everything.

She'd handled it. Exactly the way she'd promised everyone she would.

"Thank you again for working with us on this."

"It's what we do." Mr. Gutierrez smiled. "Now you just concentrate on helping your mother get well."

"Happily."

Her mother's health had always been the most important part of these negotiations. June would be delighted to focus on it instead of running around in circles with medical billing departments.

Except as she made her way to the parking lot, some of the euphoria of finally having the debt settled began to wear off. Keeping up with the repayment schedule she had agreed to relied on the inn continuing to bring in guests. Business was still down, thanks to the new freeway.

But she was going to tackle that, too. The new bigger, better Pumpkin Festival would bring in tons of tourists. Her sister May hadn't confirmed her travel plans yet, but she'd promised she was working on it. She'd come in and do her magic. Between the articles May would write and the word of mouth from the Pumpkin Festival, things would pick up. And with that success under her belt, June would have more support for her other plans to revitalize the area, expand their marketing, and find new ways to drum up business.

Everything was going to be okay. She just had to keep working.

Right after she went light fixture shopping with Clay.

Shaking her head, she started up her car and pointed it toward the showroom where they were scheduled to meet Caitlin. She wasn't entirely sure how she'd gotten roped into running this particular errand *with* Clay. One minute she was mentioning needing a new fixture to replace one that had gotten damaged

by a family staying at the inn who had apparently decided that
Ultimate Frisbee was an indoor sport. The next, Caitlin was
naming a time and a place to meet. It made sense. Of course
Caitlin wouldn't want to make extra trips to help them both use
her discount separately.

The weird thing was that she actually . . . wasn't dreading it?

Her first couple of interactions with Clay had left her angry
and indignant. He was stubborn and combative, always jumping to conclusions and assuming the worst about her. He had a
knack for pushing her buttons and making her temper flare.

He was also quiet. Reflective. Honest to a fault.

Hanging out with him at Bobbi's dinner party had been an
eye-opener. Maybe it was that she'd had a little more to drink
than usual, or maybe it was seeing him get along so well with
her other friends. Maybe it had been the warm hum of their
bodies slotted in around Bobbi's breakfast nook. Whatever it
was, it had given her a chance to see him in a different light.

They still had plenty they disagreed about. But maybe they
also had more in common than she would have thought.

She hadn't quite finished mulling it over as she pulled into
the showroom's parking lot. No sign of Caitlin's Jeep or Clay's
rusty old truck yet, but June was running a couple of minutes
early. She found a spot and got out.

She only made it about two steps toward the sidewalk before
the rumble of an engine had her looking over her shoulder.

Clay's truck trundled into the space next to hers, a song
she liked blaring on the radio. She smiled despite herself. She
should probably be annoyed about the noise, but no guests
could complain to her here, and the freedom of finally having
her family's finances straightened out made her feel light in a
way she hadn't for who even knew how long.

He killed the engine and joined her. He was freshly showered, his hair damp. He hadn't bothered to shave, though, which was just as well. The more times she looked at his face, the more she liked the reddish-brown scruff.

The more she liked those incisive eyes and the sun-kissed lines around them. The strong shape of his shoulders and his trim waist and rough hands.

She swallowed against the warmth gathering inside her and the upward tick of her pulse.

He came to a stop a respectable couple of feet away from her, but it felt like less. His gaze raked her up and down, and tingles raced along her skin.

Then he lifted his brows. "You headed to a contractor supply store or the opera?"

A ripple of irritation moved through her, but she wasn't going to let it sour her good mood.

"If I were going to the opera, I'd be wearing gloves." Not to mention a floor-length gown as opposed to a simple green and white polka dot wrap dress, but that wasn't the point.

"What was I thinking?" he scoffed.

Tart replies rose to her mind. Only she didn't let them out.

It felt like things had changed between them, these last few times they'd met. Falling into their initial pattern of riling each other up would be easy enough, but for some reason, today, she didn't want to go back to sniping and egging each other on. It was a rush, sometimes, arguing with him. It got her pulse hammering in a way that was about more than the simmering conflict between them.

But she liked this, too. The quiet. The calm.

Before she'd fully decided to speak, she opened her mouth. "Can we just—just for today, Clay. Can we...not?"

He frowned and shifted his weight. "Not what?"

"You know." She gestured uselessly with her hands, trying

to indicate the space that surrounded them. "Can we try to be nice?"

Slowly, staring at her levelly, he said, "I'm always nice."

She laughed, the sound coming out of nowhere.

And he smiled. Had she ever really seen him do that before? It lit his eyes and made barely visible dimples appear at the corners of his mouth.

"Fine, be like that," she said, but there wasn't any heat in it.

He was nice, and she was nice.

Maybe they could even both manage to stay that way long enough to look at some lights.

They were halfway to the door when June's purse buzzed. She fished her phone out. A message from Caitlin flashed across the screen.

Sorry, running a little late—be there in 15.

She showed the text to Clay, but he squinted and held out his hand, so she let him grab her phone to read it. Their fingers brushed, and she ignored the crackle of static. When he passed it back, she stuffed it in her purse.

Inside, Todd Lubock from June's high school class was manning the register. He was talking to another contractor clearly straight off a job site, his black T-shirt and heavy work jeans both streaked with plaster.

"Hey, June," Todd called. "Clay."

Clay saluted. "Hiya, Todd."

June waved as well, then looked at Clay. "You two know each other?"

"Ran into each other at Tim's Hardware and got talking."

"Of course."

She shook her head. It amazed her how the man could be so grumpy and quick to anger every time the two of them bumped heads, but he was friendly enough otherwise to be on a first-name basis with half the town already. Heck, he'd made such fast friends with Bobbi's parents that they'd invited him to Bobbi's party, even.

That probably shouldn't bother her. But for some reason, it kind of did.

"Well, I'm going to—" She pointed to the corner of the showroom where they stocked the fixtures she'd gotten last time. Realistically, all she had to do was have Todd look up the part for her, but she'd taken the time to come all the way out here, she had might as well at least look around.

"Sure." Clay wandered off in another direction.

She kept half an eye on him as she browsed. He didn't seem to have all that much of a plan, strolling through a bunch of outdoor lighting supplies before hitting the section that was geared toward businesses and restaurants.

She found the item she needed and made a note of the part number. Nothing else really caught her eye.

Meanwhile, Clay had managed to head off into a display full of bathroom vanities.

Which was none of her business. None at all.

But they were here together, and she didn't exactly have anything else to do.

And honestly, the guy looked lost.

She did her best not to sneak up on him as she approached, but he still was startled when she asked, "Find what you were looking for?"

"Should put a bell on you," he muttered. Scowling, he looked back at the display he'd been staring at. "Not really."

And there was something to the way he said it. On the surface, his tone was defensive. But they'd agreed to be nice today.

Maybe he really, actually was lost.

She tried to keep her voice soft. "Do you know what you're looking for?"

His mouth drew further down into a deep frown. "Lights."

"Okay…"

It struck her that this might be an opportunity.

Last week, when he'd taken her to the next town over to show her Bug's preferred kind of bar, she'd been concerned—both for him and for her. He'd shrugged off her advice about trying to find a vision for the place that went beyond Bug's plan to drop a dive bar into the middle of Main Street. But she still believed that if he could find a way to cater to both the locals who needed to unwind and the out-of-towners who liked charming and quaint, he could really have something special on his hands.

Testing the waters, she offered, "Do you mind if I show you some things?"

"Don't put yourself out," he grumbled.

"I won't. Promise."

He gave her an appraising look. Then he shrugged and waved a hand as if to tell her to be his guest.

"I'm no interior designer," she told him, though she'd muddled through pretty decently. With her mother's help and Elizabeth's artistic eye, she'd overseen a whole host of renovations at the inn, and if she had to say so herself, they'd turned out well. "But the way I see it, it's about the overall look you want for the place."

"I want it to look like a bar."

"But what kind of bar? The details matter. How do you want people to feel when they walk in?"

"I don't know." He threw his arms out to the side. "Thirsty."

Good grief. "How about welcomed? Relaxed? Happy?" She shook her head. "You know part of why Dottie and Patty are so against you building this bar is because all you told anyone about it was that it was going to piss people off."

"Was I wrong?"

She shot him a dirty look. Then she led him back to the restaurant section.

"I know it probably seems superficial to you, but the way you present your bar says a lot about who you are and what you're offering." She pointed at some green-shaded pendant lights. "These say one thing." Then another set with big, stylized bare bulbs. "These say something else."

"And what does that one say?" he asked, pointing at a lamp that was shaped like a woman's leg.

"That you watched *A Christmas Story* too many times as a kid," she said.

He let out a grunt of frustration. "I don't want the place to be dark, is all. Can't I just buy light bulbs?"

"You can." She kept her tone even. She was not going to pick a fight. She was going to elect to believe that he wasn't trying to pick one, either, debatable as that was starting to seem. "But the choices you make matter. To me, to what you're trying to build. To the people you need to convince to stop holding up your liquor license. And not making a choice *is* a choice."

He muttered something under his breath that sounded a lot like "eggshell chiffon" and a creative string of curse words. Then he raked a hand through his hair and exhaled hard. "Okay, fine. But you keep telling me that all these different hunks of glass say different things, only I don't speak the language."

And was he . . . was that . . .

All at once it hit her that he wasn't just *not* antagonizing her. He was asking for help.

And that was something she knew how to give.

Considering the display before them carefully, she went back to where they'd started. "The green ones hanging down? They're sort of vintage. Funky."

"Like hipster beards funky?"

"Exactly." She grinned. He was catching on fast. She pointed to the ones next to them with the big bare bulbs. "This says every single thing will be served in a mason jar."

Clay laughed, and she felt it down in her toes.

On a roll now, she moved to a set of white frosted glass shades with a square shape. "These say modern and clean." Another pair had been tinted a more yellow hue. "These are more classic. Homier."

He reached up to point at a clear glass dome etched with little flowers. "That says old lady who painted her quilt store seven shades of pink."

"So you'll take a dozen of them?"

"Ha-ha."

Somehow, he'd ended up right next to her. She shivered, and yes, the air-conditioning in the showroom was turned up too high, but that wasn't it at all. Without putting any space between them, she gestured to the next row. Her arm brushed his and she fought not to flush.

Indicating some amber shades with ironwork along the edges, she told him quietly, "These say masculine, creative. Thoughtful."

"And what about those?" He pointed to a group of big oval pendant lights in the same glass.

She looked back at him, and any remaining bit of space separating them had disappeared. His lips were almost by her ear, his breath warm against her skin, and she quivered inside. She flicked her gaze up, meeting his.

"I don't know. What do you think they say?"

His clear green eyes bore into her. For the briefest instant, they darted to her mouth.

He took a single step away.

Looking up at the lights, he nodded. "I think they say 'Bug's Bar.'"

"Good grief, Bug." Clay stared at his reflection in the mirror. "We are so screwed."

In the harsh fluorescent light of the bathroom in the apartment above the bar, his skin looked pale, his hair all over the place. He needed a shave.

An ugly laugh shook him. He could hear June's voice in his head telling him it was the cheap bulbs in the ceiling that were the problem. They were what the apartment had come with, and with all the renovations he'd been doing downstairs, he hadn't had the energy to fix anything up here.

Not making a choice is still a choice.

She was so annoying.

Annoying and beautiful and *right*, was the worst part of all.

From the moment he got kicked out of the service with his bum knee and the ghost of his dead best friend on his shoulder, he'd been avoiding making any choices at all. He'd roamed around the country at random for a miserable year. Even when he'd finally gotten his head out of his rear end, it had been the anniversary of Bug's death that had moved him along.

Bug's plan. Bug's idea. Bug's fight.

Bug's vision to build the bar of his dreams, right here in his own hometown.

But the more Clay got to know Blue Cedar Falls—the more he got to know June, the blurrier that vision became.

He wanted to make a haven for people like him and Bug and the other guys from their unit. Regular folks who'd appreciate wood paneling and a jukebox and a lone TV in the corner. Cheap beer and good, greasy food.

He might not have a full handle on Bug's vision anymore, but he knew it wasn't about lighting fixtures. It was about community.

Well, Clay had definitely landed himself in one of those.

Now he was being pulled in all these directions. June had come around some, hadn't she? She was trying to help him. She'd shown him glimpses of a different vision for the bar. One that would make Bug smile, but one that was particular to a time and a place.

This time. This place.

This town in the middle of nowhere, where he'd been welcomed with pie and invitations to dinner parties and con- tractor discounts and a bunch of bickering busybodies standing in the way of what he was here to build.

A bunch of bickering busybodies that June still believed he could win over to his side.

This town had gotten under his skin.

June had gotten under his skin.

He was so turned around he could hardly see straight.

Dropping his gaze, he turned on the tap. He washed his hands, then splashed cold water on his face, but it didn't help. He dried off and stalked back out into the bare living room. Down the stairs and out into the main area of what was going to be Bug's Bar, heaven help him.

Only it was going to be his bar, too. It was going to be this town's.

In the corner sat the truckload of stuff he'd bought at the lighting store. Even with Caitlin's discount, it had cost him a pretty penny, but June's little interior design pep talk had con- vinced him that it would be worth it. The fixtures and all the bits that went with them were matte bronze and iron, warm yellows and oranges, and he liked them. Bug would have liked them, too, and June had looked at him with so much encouragement in her gaze, it had cracked something inside of him.

He didn't want to fight her anymore.

Problem was, that meant having a fight with himself he'd been putting off for a year.

He had decisions to make. He had to commit.

He needed a plan.

With a growl, he pulled out his phone. Before he could talk himself out of it, he started up the video call app.

After two rings that seemed to take two hours, Lisa's face appeared on the screen, stark lines between her brows. "Clay, are you okay?"

"Yeah, yeah," he promised.

And he was.

Conviction suddenly filled him. This was the right choice, and it was right because it was *his*.

"What's going on?" Lisa asked.

"Did you really mean it? When you offered to draw up some sketches for the bar?"

And just like that, the lines of concern on her face disappeared. She smiled, big and wide, and the last layer of his wariness crumbled. "Of course."

"You're the best," he sighed.

It took a while. But in fits and starts, he tried to put into words exactly what it was he had in mind.

CHAPTER ELEVEN

A rush of nervous anticipation prickled June's skin as she knocked on Clay's door a few days later. She hadn't heard from him since they'd gone to the lighting store together. His text inviting her to swing by had been an unexpected—but welcome—surprise.

He answered the door a minute later, filling the gap with his big frame. This time though, instead of barking at her, he greeted her with a smile.

She wiggled her fingers in greeting. "Hi."

"Hey." He stood there for a long moment, his eyes raking her up and down.

Static hummed in the space between them. Her pulse roared, but she couldn't move. Not toward him and not away, and she didn't know which direction she wanted to go anyway.

Then he seemed to come out of his trance.

"Hey," he said again. He cleared his voice and shifted his weight. He moved aside, inviting her in. "So I had some things I wanted to show you."

"Oh, wow." As she followed him inside, she glanced around, marveling at how much work he'd accomplished these last few days. Any last vestiges of Susie's Quilts and More were gone.

Dark shiplap paneling lined the walls, and the floors shone. The lights they'd picked out together looked even better than she'd imagined—homey and classy all at the same time. Leading her toward a folding table in the corner, he shoved a few piles of hardware and tools aside.

"This is just a first concept, okay?" He said the words as if he was reciting something someone else had told him to say.

She stared at him in confusion. "Okay."

In his other hand, he held a few folded pieces of cardboard. Putting his body between her and the table, he opened the display boards up. She craned her neck, trying to see around him, but she couldn't understand what he was showing her.

He stepped away, and it wasn't all that much clearer.

"Um . . ." She inched closer.

"It's the bar," he finally said, the words coming out too fast, like he'd been holding them in. "Bug's Bar. It's what I think it could be."

"Oh." Suddenly, everything resolved in her vision. It all made sense. "*Oh*."

The printouts he'd pinned to the cardboard were drawings— nice ones, too. She lost any hesitation and walked right up to them, leaning in to see the details. Now that she knew what she was looking for, she could see the interior of the storefront they were standing in at that very moment. There was the horizontal paneling and the new fixtures.

And there was so much more.

The rest of the things Clay had bought at the lighting store had been sketched in. The bar would be installed right beside where she was now, the jukebox on the other side of the room. A TV on the wall and mirrors and a pool table and pieces of art. A stage with drawn-back curtains that could also serve as extra seating when he didn't have a band. Tables, where people sat and ate or drank while servers in blue T-shirts and white half aprons bustled around them. The tables were draped in a matching shade of blue, and it was...

It was...

"Clay," she said, turning around. Her mouth worked around the words she was trying to get out. "It's..."

He swallowed, his Adam's apple bobbing. He cracked his knuckles and raised his brows. "Yeah?"

She smiled. Too soft, too fond for this man who had been nothing but difficult with her all this time.

Only that wasn't really true, was it? He'd started out by antagonizing her, and sure, they were shockingly good at riling each other up. But bit by bit, he'd closed the gap between them. He'd come over with olive branches and ideas, offers to share his perspective with her and to listen to what she had to say.

He'd met her in the middle, in so many ways.

And that was exactly what he was doing now.

"It's perfect," she finally managed to get out.

It really was. Clay was all over the sketches, the rough edges of his personality clear in the stark lines and minimalist decor. But so was his winsome folksiness that had made him so many friends. His charm was irresistible, when he chose to turn it on.

This was the bar he'd vowed to build. Only it was *better*.

There was a softness to it and a sense of design that was never part of the original, angry, confrontational pitch he had given her that very first time they'd met.

It wasn't quite the brand of Main Street polish that most of the other businesses around here aspired to, but it wasn't a giant middle finger held up against it, either.

Heck, with a handful of tweaks and the right marketing, it could be a new highlight for the area. A check mark on the travel sites that might make a whole new group of potential visitors take a second look, and where else would they stay during their visit but at the Sweetbriar Inn?

Even more ideas for tie-ins between the bar and the inn flooded her mind. Locals would come to the bar for drinks. With the right promo, would they come back for Ned's pancakes the next morning?

Then there was the fact that her sister May would love this place. June could practically see the little breakout box on the glossy paper of the travel magazine May worked for. DECORATED VETERAN OPENS UPSCALE BAR: OWNER CLAY HAWTHORNE MAKES LOCALS AND TRAVELERS ALIKE FEEL AT HOME.

She turned to face him, that tiny spark of hope she'd been nurturing growing inside her. "Seriously, Clay. It's great."

"You really think so?" he asked, a grin lighting his eyes.

She nodded with genuine enthusiasm. They could talk about the ideas she had in mind for making it even better later. For now, she savored the victory. This was a win-win-win—for him, for her family's inn, for the entire town of Blue Cedar Falls. "Absolutely."

"My friend drew them up. She's got a real eye for this kind of stuff."

"And you have a vision. It shows."

He stepped closer, and she swayed forward, too, drawn to him and the barely contained, practically vibrating energy coming off him. It was electrifying. *He* was electrifying—how else could she explain the crackling heat arching through the air?

He leaned in, his gaze impossibly deep. "Bug sent me on this mission, but I—I got lost in it. I was so angry. I forgot that this place was supposed to be for me, too. For everybody. That it could make people happy to come here." He licked his lips. "You—June. You helped me remember that."

Her heart fluttered so hard she swore it would grow wings. "Clay…"

"I mean it. I thought you were some stuck-up busybody, but you were trying to help me."

"Charm a girl, would you?"

"You're darn right I would." His voice dipped low, the gravel in it as rough as she imagined his hands would be. His warm, spiced scent surrounded her. She couldn't breathe, could scarcely think. "I'm making choices now, June. Big ones."

"Right," she managed.

The intensity in his gaze burned her. "I want this bar to last. I want everybody from every part of this town to come. The guys from the hardware store and the ones who've never felt welcome on Main Street before, but that's not all. I want Bobbi and Han and those birdbrains from the business association, the grandmas and the housewives. Everyone." A new flame lit deep within his eyes. "You. I want you to be able to come here and have one of those stupid umbrella drinks—"

"They're not stupid—"

"And dance all night, and—"

"Clay," she breathed.

"Yeah?"

"I love that idea."

When had he drifted so close? She could practically touch him now. She was breathing his air. Their faces were just inches apart. She could see the specks in his eyes, smell the warm, heady male scent of him, and her body was on fire.

"I want…" Clay licked his lips. He darted his gaze down to her mouth, and her breasts ached; deep between her legs, she was a swelter.

"Yes," she said. And it was reckless. That simple word.

She should be more careful. She should be focusing on other things. Her family and her town and her business.

But he was looking at her like he wanted to eat her alive, and the chemistry that had been brewing between them on the long road from fighting to resentment to getting to know each other and vulnerability and helping each other and this...this wonderful thing they might be able to build together...

"Yes?" he breathed.

All her reservations fell away.

"Yes."

She grabbed him by the collar of his shirt and yanked him in.

And that was all the by-your-leave Clay needed.

He crushed his mouth to hers with a dominance and a power that made her burst into flames, every last thought in her head melting at once. He was melting, too, crowding into her, and she drank him in.

He tasted like sin and beer and the heat of a Carolina summer. His rough lips and scruffy jaw attacked her. Every bite and scrape felt so good she could scream.

She opened to him, finally giving in to this *thing* that had been developing between them since the first moment they laid eyes on each other.

With all that coiled strength of his, he steered her back and into the table. The display board with his designs toppled, the whole thing shaking as her rear hit the table's edge. He lifted her onto it, and she went willingly, opening her legs. He stepped right into them, towering over her and kissing her until there wasn't any air in her lungs, but she didn't care.

Even when he tore away from her mouth, she fought to drag him back.

His bright eyes were thin rings of green around pupils gone dark with lust. "June," he gritted out.

His gaze was searching, his hands still moving on her skin. Questions hung in the air between them, but she didn't want to think anymore. It had been too long since she'd felt a man's touch like this. The connection between them was too strong and giving into it felt so good.

"Please—" She reached for him, gripping the nape of his neck, letting her fingers twist in his hair.

He gripped her arm, not stopping her, but holding her still. "You're playing with fire," he warned.

"I don't care."

He huffed out a breath. His eyes closed for a moment. When he opened them again, they were filled with resolve. "Upstairs," he growled.

He pulled away and grabbed her by the hand, practically hauling her into the back room, then up a flight of stairs. She scarcely had time to recognize her surroundings—a bare apartment, beige walls and wood floors and an old couch, and then, through a doorway, thank the heavens, a bed.

Claiming her mouth again, he walked her through the mostly empty space. When they reached the bed with its plain white sheets, he pressed her down onto it, and she held on, dragging him right along with her. His weight settled over her, as delicious as she'd imagined. His fingertips pushing up the skirt of her dress were just as calloused and confident as they had been in her fantasies. His hot scent was just as sweet.

When he slipped past the fabric of her underwear to touch her wet, wanting places, she gasped. She was soaked, ready, needy in a way she hadn't known she could be. All this time alone, she'd barely thought about sex, but suddenly her body came flaring to life.

He kissed her mouth and touched her over and over until she shuddered to pieces, gasping for air.

She collapsed onto the bed, and he hovered above her, a smug smile on his lips.

"So does that mean you're on my side about getting that liquor license now?"

That brought her back into her right mind. She swatted at him, but he was grinning, and so was she, and this was *fun*.

Had sex ever been fun before?

"You are such a jerk," she told him, but in the same breath, she pounced.

Rolling him onto his back, she tore at the waistband of his shorts. From there, it was a fight to see who could get naked first, and she was pretty sure both of them won. All his hard muscle felt like stone and heat against her palms. She kissed his jaw and his collarbones and his sinful, red lips, rubbing herself against him until she could scarcely breathe.

"Condom?" she panted.

He swore beneath his breath and rolled to the side. He rooted around the top drawer of a beat up nightstand until he came up with a single packet. She grabbed it from him. Not expired, thank goodness. She'd have to get more before the next time—

Assuming there was a next time.

She couldn't think about the future now. She tore the thing open and rolled it onto him. He grasped her by the arms and bore her down into the bed. Pushing her legs apart, he settled into the valley between them like he belonged there. It felt like he did.

His gaze met hers. She nodded.

Staring deeply into her eyes, he pushed into her.

She gasped, and he let out a groan that sounded like dying and living and everything she'd wanted but had never been able to say out loud. He filled her so deeply she ached with it. Choking on the sounds that wanted to erupt from her, she pulled him down to meet her mouth.

They kissed and moved together in a frenzied rhythm. Sweat poured off her. The impossible heat and weight and strength of him blanketed her as he drove into her again and again. Every stroke set off fireworks deep inside. She pushed into his thrusts. It didn't matter that he was already buried in her body. She wanted closer, rougher, faster, more. She clawed at him and wrapped her legs around him. He slipped a hand into the molten space between them, putting his thumb where they were joined.

She screamed as her pleasure peaked again, pulsing around his thickness. He groaned her name and shoved himself into her a half dozen more times before shuddering and going still.

Slowly, she floated back down, her vision clearing even as her body pulsed. Clay dragged his mouth to hers, and they kissed, slow and wet and soft.

She wrapped her arms around him, holding on tight. Savoring the feeling of him, in her and on her and all around her.

Loose from fantastic sex and more relaxed than she'd been in she didn't even know how long, she fought to stay in the present.

But she couldn't help thinking:

What on earth had she gotten herself into now?

CHAPTER TWELVE

Wow.

Clay lay there afterward, sprawled out naked on his bed, gazing up at the ceiling fan spinning round and round. About ninety percent of his brain had been turned into mush.

The other ten percent was setting off every alarm bell in the station, but for once he refused to listen.

How was he supposed to feel anything but relaxed? June's head was pillowed on his shoulder, her soft hand pressed against his heart. They'd pulled the sheets up to their chests, but that didn't make the swells of her breasts any less enticing. The feel of her bare skin against his kept his blood hot, his whole body in a state of simmering arousal.

He combed his fingers through the silken strands of her jet-black hair. After such a long time hardly touching anybody, having a beautiful woman in his arms was almost too much. He wasn't harboring any illusions about what he and June were doing here, but he was enjoying it while it lasted.

Eventually, June grew restless against his side, though.

Letting out a breath, she started tracing little lines across his chest. "So. That was...unexpected."

Clay laughed. "That's one way to put it."

Weren't there other ways too, though?

Since day one, the chemistry between them had been off the charts. Really, it was a wonder they'd kept their hands off each other as long as they had.

Probably a good thing, too. There was something to be said for hate sex, and make no mistake—about three weeks ago, that's exactly the kind of sex they would have been having. But this?

This was something else.

Before he could follow that thought too far, June rose onto one elbow. She waited until he met her gaze before asking, "So how committed are you to the color scheme you showed me downstairs?"

"Are you kidding me, woman?" With a lurch, he sat up, too.

June grinned, and heaven help him if he wasn't grinning right along with her. This woman. She was annoying and frustrating and infuriating and so beautiful he wanted to kiss the smile right off her face.

So that's what he did.

Bearing her back down into the mattress, he covered her mouth with his, tasting her tongue and the soft curve of her lips. She returned his kiss with the same enthusiasm, and for a minute they got lost in it.

Or at least he thought they did.

"What?" she asked, as soon as he let her up for air. With a teasing grin on her face, she told him, "Picking your color story is really important for setting the whole tone of a place."

He laughed fully this time, resting his forehead against hers for a breath before kissing her again and growling against her mouth. "So is this how it's going to be? You soften me up with sex then try to talk me into changing my mind about my bar?"

"Well, I'm certainly not going to stop telling you what I think just because we're having sex." The pleasure of her fingernails scratching gently at his scalp softened her words. It was all he could do not to purr and push into her magical hands.

"Heaven forbid."

"So yeah, then, I guess. That is how it's going to be." She slid her palm to rest at the place where his shoulder met his neck. He pulled up a fraction. She stared at him with strength in her eyes. But right behind them, uncertainty flickered. "Unless..."

Unless what? He wanted to stop with the sex?

Heck no.

He didn't have any idea what they were doing together here, but he liked it. The arguing and the butting heads and the confessions she somehow dragged out of him. The kissing and the feel of her soft body pressed against the whole length of his.

But how much could he commit to, in good conscience? He had no interest in letting her out of his bed anytime soon, but he couldn't let her go getting any ideas, either.

He'd come out of the service patched up with a Band-Aid he'd torn right off and a therapist whose number he'd lost after the first appointment. He was basically one of those prescription medications they advertised with three screens worth of disclaimers and warning signs, and he didn't have the time or the will to read them all out to her.

"June," he said, too serious. "I can't promise you..."

Before he could try to put into words all the things she couldn't rely on him for, she shook her head and waved him off.

"Oh, please. With business being the way it is and everything with my family…"

He frowned. "Are they okay?"

"They're fine. They're just…a lot sometimes." Reaching up, she ran her fingers through his hair. "My mom's had some health issues." Dropping her hand, she shrugged. "Nothing we can't handle, but it's just me and my stepdad. My sister helps sometimes, but that's a whole other issue."

"Okay…"

"I'm just saying." She sighed, gesturing between the two of them. "It's not like I can commit to much of anything here, either."

And that was a relief. They were on the same page.

So why did he feel like a sinkhole had formed in his chest?

He forced a smile. "Great."

"Great." If she didn't look as enthusiastic about them agreeing this was a no-strings kind of situation as she sounded, well, he was going to ignore that for now. She screwed up her face, putting on that look of challenge that got him every time. "Now about that color palette downstairs…"

He was all too happy for the distraction. "Woman," he warned again.

But they were back on track, now. He pushed her into the mattress with his whole weight.

"What?" she laughed, reeling him in, her hands linking behind his neck and pulling him close.

His body responded, that low simmer of arousal flaring into a blaze again. "I'll show you what."

He kissed her, deep and hot.

"I know you're just distracting me," she gasped as he released her mouth to suck wet marks along the column of her throat.

"Is it working?" He pushed the sheet off her breasts and put his mouth there, too.

She dug her nails into his arm. "Would you respect me less if I said yes?"

"Nope."

Letting her nipple slip out from between his teeth, he licked and bit a trail leading lower still. When he fit his shoulders between them, she parted her legs. Holding her dark gaze, he lowered his mouth.

And that was all the talking they did about color stories for a while.

June's pillow was snoring.

She came awake slowly, annoyed by the sound and the intense heat, fully prepared to turn the pillow over, roll onto her side, and drift right back off to sleep.

Then reality crashed over her, and she sat up with a start.

With a strangled yelp, she yanked the sheets up to cover her bare breasts. Beside her, her "pillow" snuffled and muttered something unintelligible before settling.

Right. Because her pillow was actually six feet and several inches of burly, muscled, tattooed man. She darted a glance at the clock beside the bed. Five a.m.

This was bad.

Panic and doom clanged around inside her. She'd come over here yesterday expecting to spend half an hour, and she'd spent the entire night. She'd texted Ned at some point, but she'd told him she'd be back to handle anything that happened overnight.

But then Clay had started kissing her neck again, and well . . .

She sighed out long and slow, letting her gaze sweep over his body. His tanned skin gleamed against the white sheets in the predawn light. The dips and ridges of his muscles called to her, flashbacks of his mouth between her legs and on her breasts, the weight of him and the feel of him tempting her all over again.

Sleeping with Clay—that hadn't been a bad thing. A risky, wild, reckless thing, maybe, but not bad.

Who was she kidding? It had been *amazing*.

That still didn't change that she'd been a complete flake last night. How many times had she given Elizabeth grief for exactly this kind of nonsense? Not communicating, expecting other people to pick up her slack, getting caught up in her own selfish adventures.

It wouldn't happen again. Not the sex—based on the brief conversation she and Clay had had between rounds last night, she was fully confident that they were both *extremely* interested in the sex part happening again. But she'd do a better job at keeping it from interfering with her responsibilities.

She'd keep her head on straight and her focus where it was supposed to be. On her family, her business, her town.

And so what if Clay's quiet, "I can't promise you…" had made something pang inside her? She could be practical. Neither of them had space in their lives for anything but casual right now. Knowing that they were on the exact same page was a relief.

Or at least that's what she'd tell herself.

Resolved to keep her feelings under wraps and her mind on work, she crept out of the bed, trying not to disturb Clay. He was a sound sleeper, at least she could say that much for him.

She tiptoed around the room, gathering her clothes and dressing quietly. On Clay's nightstand, she found a couple of notebooks and a pencil. She flipped to a blank page, tore it out, and scribbled a note to tell him that she'd needed to get back to the inn. She left it on the side of the bed where hopefully he couldn't miss it.

She cast one last look at him. Something squeezed inside her chest. He really was unfairly handsome. In sleep, he was even more gorgeous, his face soft in a way it never was when he was awake.

He looked peaceful.

No matter what happened between them next, she was glad she'd gotten to see him like that. Not troubled, not angry, not sad or lost or defensive.

She hoped she got to see him like that again. Soon.

For now, though, she really had to go.

Touching her lips and pushing a kiss through the air toward him, she turned on her heels. She headed out of his apartment at top speed, past the unpacked boxes and bare walls, down the stairs and out through the rear entrance to the bar.

Outside, the cool, still morning air greeted her, and she breathed it in. In the east, the sun just kissed the horizon, turning the sky gold at the edges, bright blue beginning to creep toward the puffy wisps of clouds.

Main Street was quiet, the stretch between the bar and the inn deserted. The lights were on in the bakery next to the inn. Bobbi was always there early, getting pastries in the oven. June scurried past its windows fast, praying her friend wouldn't spot her. She had no doubt she'd tell her about this unexpected twist in her love life soon, but she really didn't know how she was going to explain herself yet.

She snuck into the little apartment in the back of the inn where her family lived. Everything seemed quiet. Maybe—just maybe—she'd actually managed to get away with this.

Heart racing, she slipped off her shoes and crept down the hall.

Then the light in the living room flicked on.

Crap.

Seated in her favorite chair near the window, Sunny arranged imperiously in her lap, her mother raised a brow.

June's whole body flushed. She was thirty-two years old, but one judgmental glance from her mom and she felt like she was in high school, coming in after curfew. Not that she'd ever really done that, but still. This must be how it would have felt.

She held her hands up in front of herself. "Mom, this isn't what it looks like."

"Really?" Her mom's appraising gaze skimmed her up and down. "Because it looks like you're wearing your same clothes from yesterday. And you have a hickey."

She pointed at her own neck, and if it was possible, June's face flashed even hotter. "Mom—"

Her mother patted Sunny's side and gave her a little shove. The cat glared at June before consenting to hop down to the floor. June's mom rose to stand, grabbing her cane in her stronger hand and leaning into it heavily.

"You don't have to explain."

"I just—"

"June." Her mom leveled her with the kind of look that *really* made her feel like she was back in high school again. "You trying to tell me you didn't spend the night with somebody?"

She was considering it.

She blew out a breath. She was a grown woman. Yes, she lived in her childhood bedroom and worked for her family's business. But that didn't make her a kid.

"No."

She stood there, braced for a lecture, her entire body ready to be indignant about the whole thing.

But her mother smiled. "Good."

"Good?" June blinked in disbelief. "Me spending the night at Clay's is 'good'?"

Her mother's eyes widened, and June wanted to slap herself. Had she really just volunteered even more information about her evening out?

"I mean, he's a handsome boy." Her mom gestured at her own arm and shoulder as if to convey big, muscular biceps. "Very nice—"

"*Mom.*" June was going to melt into the floor in mortification.

"Like I don't have eyes." Her mom shook her head, mercifully bringing the conversation back to June sneaking in instead of Clay's physique. "You never have any fun. It's been too long since you went on a date. Seeing you go out makes me happy."

Happy?

"Uh…"

Her mom's expression softened. "You work so hard, June. Running the inn. Taking care of all of us." She crossed the room. Her right hand trembled a little as she reached up to brush June's cheek. Then she gave it a little pinch. "Take care of yourself, too, sometimes, okay?"

Letting go, she pulled away.

June stared at her in confusion. It was June's job to keep things running around here—it always had been, ever since her dad had left and June had become second-in-command. Her mom had relied on her through those tough first few years. Everybody relied on her.

She'd screwed up tonight. She'd stayed out late and fallen

asleep with a naked man, and now her mother was *congratulating* her on it?

"Wait—" she started.

"Just call next time," her mother admonished briskly, and okay, yeah, that was more like her. "Or text after ten."

"Sure," June said faintly.

"Oh, and little boy in room seven flushed Batman down the toilet."

June face-palmed. "Right. I'll handle it."

"I know you will," her mother said. A little of the softness in her voice returned. "You always do." With that, she made her way to her and Ned's bedroom, Sunny limping along behind her, the mean old cat giving June the stink eye.

When she was sure her mother wasn't looking, June scowled at Sunny right back.

The master bedroom's door closed, and June sagged. Rolling her eyes at herself, she shook her head.

Realistically, if a dirty look from a cat and plumber duty was the worst she got for being completely irresponsible and spending the night with Clay, she couldn't complain.

Even as she grabbed the plunger and the toolbox from the utility closet, she felt...lighter than she had of late.

Her mom's comments about how she should take better care of herself still seemed weird, but it was nice to have her hard work be appreciated, she supposed. The last nine months, scrambling to deal with the inn and worrying about her mother and handling the bills...they had taken their toll on June.

Maybe her mom was right. It had been too long since she'd had fun or gone on a date. Whatever she was doing with Clay couldn't be anything serious—no matter how intense their connection had felt or how incredible he'd been in bed.

No matter how much she'd begun to respect him, now that they'd finally figured out how to talk to each other instead of yelling.

But if she could keep her head on straight, and not drop the ball on everything else she had to handle...Maybe this was something she could have. Something just for her.

At least for a little while.

CHAPTER THIRTEEN

The next day, Clay literally whistled while he worked.

What a sap.

All morning, he'd been walking around with a spring in his step. Who cared that he'd had to follow his coffee with an ibuprofen chaser to calm the ache in his bum knee? Over-exerting himself making love to a beautiful woman was the best aggravation to his injury he'd ever had.

His blood heated at the memory of laying June out on his bed. Touching her and feeling her clench and moan, pressing into her body and losing himself in the wet heat of her over and over...

Sure, it would've been even better if June had stuck around for another round in the morning. He'd have made her pancakes. Kissed the taste of syrup off her lips and maybe tried to talk her into taking a shower with him.

All the stuff he'd never done with the women he'd slept with in the service. One-night stands after an evening on the town with Bug, Tuck, AJ, and Riz had usually ended with him being the one sneaking out.

A low prickle of unease rolled around in his gut. He'd had his reasons for pulling vanishing acts back then, and they hadn't been great ones. At the time, he'd been in the market for a little fun and some stress relief—nothing more. Forging a real connection with a woman hadn't been anywhere on his agenda.

June's reasons for ducking out...They were different. He hadn't been a one-night stand for her. They'd agreed to that much before they'd fallen asleep. More importantly, they'd gotten to know each other before they'd ended up in bed together.

He'd see her again. Soon. He hoped.

Struggling to keep his focus on work, he finished putting in some of the shelves behind the bar. When he was done, he stepped away to admire the results. Not bad.

The new plans Lisa had drawn up for him were going to be a pain to see through, but it'd be worth it. This bar was going to be the stuff of Bug's dreams. A place Clay would be proud of. And a place that this ridiculous little town would embrace, too—even if he had to go and make his case to every single one of the biddies who were holding him up.

Satisfied with his work, he took a few minutes to clean up, then headed upstairs to comb his hair and put on some decent clothes.

He paused for a second with his sock drawer open. A piece of paper wedged in the back caught his eye. He tugged it out and stared at it with a frown.

He wasn't sure why he'd kept the list of exercises that physical therapist quack at the VA had given him. That kind of stuff didn't work, and he was more of a grin and bear it kind of guy. But just for fun, as he brushed his teeth, he tried standing there and lifting and lowering his bum leg a dozen times.

Probably useless, but who knew? For some reason, he was feeling optimistic today.

Once he was presentable, he headed out. Main Street was sweltering, and he mopped his brow as he walked.

The blast of cold air when he tugged open the door to the Jade Garden made him sigh out loud.

"Hot one out there?" Han asked, looking up from the menu he was doodling on.

"You know it."

"The usual?"

"Know what? Let's go nuts." Clay rifled past the stack of regular menus for the clipboard in the back. It was Han's "secret" menu—fancy stuff Han had developed himself. Could never go wrong there. He made a show of closing his eyes, twirling his finger in the air, then plunking it down on a random spot on the paper.

Jeez, what had gotten into him? Forget a spring in his step and whistling while he worked. He was being downright chipper. If it was somebody else talking to him like this, he'd be annoyed to no end.

He just couldn't seem to stop, though.

He opened his eyes and leaned in. His finger had landed on "Seafood." He rattled off the name of the dish, and Han punched a few keys on the old-fashioned register.

As Clay dug around for a twenty, Han gave him a sideways smile. "Someone's in a good mood today."

"Musta got up on the right side of the bed this morning."

Han smirked. "Sure it isn't more about whose side of the bed you got up on?"

"Uh…"

Crud.

"Relax, your secret's safe."

Clay squinted. "Which secret is that exactly?"

He and June had reached some basic agreements about what

they were doing together. Namely, that neither of them wanted to stop, and neither of them were in a position to make any heavy commitments.

What they were telling other people? That wasn't something they'd touched on at all.

It didn't matter to him. He hardly knew anybody in town; he certainly didn't care what they thought about him. Even if he did, June was a smart, beautiful woman, and he was happy to be with her.

Women could be funny about that kind of thing, though. He got it. They were judged no matter what they did, either for being too loose or too uptight. June cared about what people thought of her—a lot. Probably too much, but that was another issue all together.

This was a ball he would have left in her court.

Han rolled his eyes and handed him his change, most of which Clay dropped in the tip jar. "June's mom told my mom who thought I couldn't hear her telling one of their other old lady friends."

"Oh."

"Small town." Han shrugged. "Word gets around fast."

"Okay, well, uh…"

"I'm happy for you. As long as you're both happy?" Han raised one brow.

"Yeah. Sure." Clay hesitated.

What red-blooded male wouldn't be happy after a night like that?

It felt like Han was probing at something deeper, though. Han was the closest thing he had to a friend in this town, and he had all kinds of history with the Wu family.

Clay wasn't much for math, but even he could add those things together and wind up with a pile of complications.

"I mean—" he started.

Han shook his head. "None of my business, unless you want to talk about it. June's my friend and you're my friend. And I have outstanding taste in friends, so it makes sense you'd like each other, too. If you're both good, then I'm good."

Slowly, Clay nodded. "I'm good."

Han gestured at the table where Clay usually ate. "You staying or grabbing to go?"

"I'll stay."

Clay took a seat and watched the news scroll by on the TV in the corner. Han seemed to be working both the register and the kitchen at the moment. When Clay's lunch was ready, Han brought it out and sat down with him to shoot the breeze for a while, but inevitably the phone rang, and Han was hopping again, getting more takeout orders going. Clay was glad to see the place doing a good business, but he wouldn't have minded Han hanging out longer.

He shook his head at himself, digging back into the flipping fantastic pile of shrimp he'd ended up with.

Ever since he'd gotten out of the military, he'd preferred his own company. Now look at him. A month in this town, and he had a lunch buddy and a lady friend.

Wonders would never cease.

More people came in as he finished up. He waved to Han, who called "Good luck!" at him from the register.

Not sure why he'd need it, but sure.

He ambled his way toward the bar, turning over his conversation with Han in his head. The way Han had casually brought up him and June sleeping together—and the way he'd heard about it through the Blue Cedar Falls grapevine—made him uneasy for reasons he couldn't exactly explain. He was still fine with it being common knowledge.

But the idea of June getting blindsided left him with this anxious twitch in the back of his brain. Did she know her mother was blabbing what they were doing together all over town? Did she even realize her mom knew?

He stood at the corner, ready to cross the street to the bar. A couple of trucks rumbled by. He glanced over his shoulder at the inn behind him.

"Screw it."

June had been the one to duck out this morning. She'd left a note, of course, telling him she had to get home to the inn, but that didn't change the fact that he'd been the one to wake up to an empty bed.

He'd planned to give her a little space, but he wanted to see her, had an itch under his skin telling him he needed to. Making sure she knew that word had spread about them was all the rationale he needed to tip the scales.

He turned and headed up the perfectly swept walk, the clean, painted steps. He nodded at the couple of guests sitting in the rocking chairs on the porch and headed inside.

Only to find the lobby empty. He frowned at the "BACK IN FIFTEEN MINUTES" sign that stood on the counter. A house phone stood next to it, inviting guests to ring an extension if they needed help immediately.

Clay wasn't in that much of a rush, but he didn't feel right standing around here, either, especially considering he didn't even know if June would be the one to eventually come back.

Before he could overthink his next move, June's voice rang out from somewhere behind the desk. The yelp of pain broke him out of his dithering, fast.

"June?" he barked. He shoved past the desk and through a door that stood ajar on the other side of it.

The office he found there reminded him of the shed out back where June had taken him to loan him that ladder. It wasn't a mess or anything, but it wasn't the public face of the Sweetbriar Inn, either, with cords running across the floor and stacks of paperwork scattered around the place. A cat calendar on the wall was nine months out of date.

He didn't have time to really consider any of it.

June cursed again in the distance, and he crossed the room to the partly open door on the other side. He yanked it wide.

And came screeching to a halt.

He...didn't know what he'd been expecting to find, but it wasn't this.

Clearly, he'd stumbled on the Wu family's private residence. Forget not quite matching the design aesthetic of the Sweetbriar Inn. The apartment in front of him was...

Carefully controlled chaos, he finally decided.

The space was cramped, with stuff everywhere. Nothing was dirty. Heck, he barely saw a speck of dust. But that didn't matter. Stacks of magazines were piled up around the couch. A knitting project had been abandoned on the coffee table, along with a half-finished jigsaw puzzle. Books and pictures and weird figurines were crammed onto the shelves, half of the decor Asian-looking and half of it old-school country, like the crap his first foster parents had liked. The pictures on the wall were the same mix. A Thomas Kinkade painting of a barn hung right next to a black and white tiger with Chinese symbols stamped around the edges.

It was a mess. But somehow it worked. It looked...homey. If your idea of a home was cluttered jumble of cultures, that was.

He liked it, honestly.

Then his gaze swept to the side, and he remembered why he was there.

The living room opened onto a kitchen. June stood at the sink, water running, while all four burners on the stove blazed. Something sizzled, and steam poured off another pot. The contents of at least one of them was burning.

Another woman, about June's height and age, was trying to manage whatever the heck was going on there. She was dressed in a flowing, floor-length skirt and a white T-shirt that looked like it was from some concert tour or something. Her long, black hair had purple streaks in it.

Huh.

An older Asian woman hovered over both of them, speaking fast in what seemed like a mix of Chinese and English, her tone scolding.

"I'm fine, Mom," June told her, waving her away.

"Sit down," the other girl said.

"Ned!" the old woman protested.

A white man with gray hair and a lot of lines around his eyes shook his head from the small table in the corner. He didn't so much as look up from his paper. "They said they're fine, Li."

No one seemed to notice Clay, which was unobservant to the point of reckless. Leaving all these doors open and the desk unmanned. That'd get you killed on the other side of the world. Or at least dressed down if you were an unlucky enough SOB to have your commanding officer catch you like that.

Clay's instincts told him to march right in and do the dressing down himself. June and her family weren't safe like this. He should be protecting them.

He crushed the doorknob in his hand. This wasn't the army,

and Blue Cedar Falls wasn't a war zone, and he was the furthest thing possible from their commanding officer.

He should go. He never should have barged in in the first place. This was private.

Suddenly absolutely sure that he'd stepped in it, he backed away, tugging the door behind him, but it creaked—loud.

Four heads jerked around to gawk at him. Five, if you counted the cat Clay suddenly noticed sitting on the table next to the old guy.

Well, at least it was good to know they weren't *that* unobservant.

"Uh," he started.

"Clay." June shut the water off, muttering under her breath. She grabbed a towel and wrapped it around her hand. Her pale cheeks glowed red.

It occurred to him that the contrasts between the lobby and the rest of the inn didn't end at stacks of unfiled paperwork or mismatched knickknacks on overcrowded shelves. They extended to the people themselves. To June.

He caught on the little details that separated the backstage June he found before him now from front-desk June or even dinner-party June. She wasn't wearing lipstick, and her hair was in a ponytail. Instead of her usual dress, she wore an oversized T-shirt and leggings that hugged those long, long legs of her.

She was *stunning*.

And based on her still-deepening blush, she hadn't meant for him to see her like this.

"I—uh—" He swallowed. "Sorry, I heard you and it sounded like you were hurt."

June pulled her towel-wrapped hand closer to her chest. "I'm fine."

The young woman at the stove rolled her eyes, pushing the

purple strands of hair behind her ear, revealing rows of little stud earrings there. "June's always fine."

"Elizabeth," June and her mom both scolded in unison.

June sighed. "It's nothing. Just grabbed the wrong end of a pan."

Ouch.

"Okay." Clay shifted his weight.

"How's that lunch coming along?" the man at the table asked.

"Charred," Elizabeth muttered.

"It'll be ready in a minute," June promised.

"You both get out of the way." June's mom wrestled her way past them.

June allowed herself to be moved, which was about the first time Clay'd ever seen her let anyone tell her what to do. Elizabeth acted put upon, but she retreated to the table to sit next to the old man, who patted her hand absently.

"I had it," Elizabeth said.

"I know, I know," her mom said, "but I know how your stepfather like it."

"That she does," the old man said, an amused lilt to his tone, and okay, yeah, Clay really needed to get out of here.

"I'll just—" He moved to go, but June shook her head and came over to him.

She was so beautiful he forgot he was supposed to be leaving as soon as she stood in front of him. She looked fresh and soft. Younger. Maybe a little vulnerable, even.

Then she smiled at him, and if he'd dared to forget, he was instantly reminded that he'd had her in his bed the night before, naked and gorgeous and shouting his name.

He stepped closer instinctively.

But not too close. The eyes of her mom and stepdad and sister bored into him.

"What's up?" June asked.

He smiled back at her, trying to be soft and unselfconscious and failing miserably. "Nothing. Nothing that can't wait, anyway, I just..."

He glanced over her shoulder, and her family all looked away, but they sure weren't subtle about it.

June followed his gaze and scowled. "Come on."

She tipped her head to the side, telling him to follow her.

Only she didn't lead him to the lobby of the inn. She took him down a short hallway and into what had to be her bedroom.

He darted his gaze around.

The small room wasn't quite as neat as he would have expected, considering, but it was unmistakably hers. Shelves lined the pale purple walls, with books and framed photos arranged beside stray earbuds and a couple of random charging cables. The twin bed had been made, but the quilt on it was old and soft, a raggedy pink teddy bear set against the pillow.

June closed the door behind them and turned to him.

Just like that, the tension in her body faded away, and he felt himself echoing that softer stance. She moved forward, and he stepped into her.

He scooped her up before he could think about it, pulling her into his chest. She fit in his arms so perfectly—why hadn't they been doing this all along?

She laughed as she wrapped her arms around him, too. She tipped her head up, revealing that soft mouth. He kissed her and smiled against her lips.

Seriously. He was such a sap.

"Hey," he muttered.

"Hey, yourself." She seemed happy to see him. Not annoyed or like she thought he was smothering her, even after she'd snuck out in the middle of the night. "To what do I owe this pleasure?"

He'd had reasons for coming here. Good, urgent ones that mattered. But in that moment, all he could think of to say was, "I wanted to see you."

Her grin deepened, and she curled her fingers in the hairs at the nape of his neck. "Good. Because I wanted to see you, too."

A sultry darkness bloomed in her eyes. When he kissed her this time, it was wetter and warmer, his body reminding him exactly what delicious places this could lead.

Then he heard the rest of her family bickering outside.

June pulled away and thunked her head against his chest. "Sorry."

"Don't be." He rubbed her arms. Yeah, he'd love to keep kissing her, and then kiss her naked, and then do other things with her naked. But this wasn't exactly the ideal setting.

"They're . . ." She waved a hand toward the other side of the closed door.

"Family," he finished for her. He hated the hint of bitter wistfulness that crept into his tone.

He hadn't had a family in decades. He didn't think one was ever going to be in his future, as messed up and solitary as he was, and he was fine with that.

Seeing other people's in all their snippy glory made him feel things, though.

Laughing, she stood up straight. "That's for sure."

There was still an uncertainty to her, like maybe she wasn't quite comfortable letting him see the behind-the-scenes chaos of her life.

Glancing at the door behind him, and then at the room around them, she sucked her bottom lip between her teeth. "I swear we're not usually such slobs. Nobody really comes back here except us. And Mrs. Leung. And Ned's poker buddies, but some of them literally live in barns—"

"June."

A fierce instinct rose up in him. He knew they weren't doing anything serious here, but he wanted to be worthy of seeing her unguarded. Rumpled and imperfect and dealing with her mom and her sister and her stepfather and whatever else she did in her daily life.

He wanted to know what lay behind all those perfect eggshell chiffon fences she liked to put up.

He wanted her to want him to see.

Gently brushing a stray lock of hair behind her ear, he caressed her cheek. "I like it," he said quietly.

"It's a mess."

"It's your home."

And that was all that mattered to him.

After a few too many beats of silence, he dropped his gaze. She was still cradling her hand. He frowned.

"Can I?"

"It's fine."

He raised a brow.

With a sigh, she held out her hand for inspection.

Accepting that as the permission it was, he carefully peeled away the towel she'd wrapped around the burn. The palm of her hand was an angry red, but it wasn't blistering or anything. With all the gentleness he had in him, he put his fingertips to the edges of the injury, turning her hand slightly to make sure it was okay.

"Think I'll live?" she asked quietly.

"Pretty sure." He looked up at her. "It'll sting like heck for a while, though. You have any aloe?"

She nodded toward the door. "I'll go—"

"Tell me where to find it."

Letting out a breath, she bit down on her lip again. "Bathroom next door. Medicine cabinet."

"Be right back."

The little bottle was exactly where she'd said it would be. He grabbed it and a roll of gauze from the shelf above it. He resisted the urge to snoop, even when he spotted a few orange pill bottles. She'd trusted him in this space, and he was going to respect that, meticulously.

When he returned, he found her sitting on the edge of her bed. The teddy bear was no longer in sight, and he smiled to himself as he closed the door.

"What?" she asked.

"Nothing."

He sat beside her and held out his hands. She placed her palm in his with a wince. As delicately as he could, he applied the gel to her skin. Bit by bit, she relaxed into his hold, letting him take care of her, and he liked that. Probably too much.

Once he'd gotten her hand wrapped in gauze, he brought her fingertips to his lips and gave them a soft kiss. He let her go.

"Thank you," she said, pulling her hand back into her lap.

"You're welcome."

And there was something about being here with her. Their thighs brushing, on her bed, in *her* space, twenty feet from her family—a place he was pretty sure that not too many people got to enter. His fingers still tingling from dressing her wound. It felt intimate. Like she trusted him.

Which made him feel like even more of a jerk as he remembered what had kickstarted him into coming over here in the first place.

Crap.

"So, uh, I thought you should know." He scratched the back of his head and looked to the corner of the room. "This." Glancing at her, he flicked a finger between the two of them. "You and me."

Furrows appeared between her brows. "Yeah?"

"You didn't want to keep it too much of a secret did you?"

The corners of her mouth tilted further down. "I hadn't really given it much thought."

"Well. Turns out the cat's out of the bag. If you wanted it in there in the first place." At her expression of confusion, he clarified, "Seems like your mom told someone who told someone who…"

Understanding widened her eyes. "Oh."

"Yeah."

"Oh. Well." A whole set of emotions slid across her face, one after another. Eventually she settled on a chuckle of a sigh and a shrug. "I suppose it was bound to get out eventually."

"Small towns," Clay said, echoing Han.

"Exactly." June sucked in a breath, then let it out, resolute. "It doesn't bother me. Unless it bothers you…?"

"Not a bit."

"Okay, then." With that, she leaned in to kiss him. "I guess that settles that."

A smile stole across his face. He supposed it did.

And this decision didn't mean anything. He didn't expect more from her, just because they weren't going to hide the fact that they were seeing each other.

That didn't stop a lightness from filling his chest. He liked the idea of people knowing he was with her, in a growly, macho way he wasn't sure he was proud of, but he wasn't going to fight it.

Instead, he concentrated on kissing her again, only it was tough what with all the sappy smiling.

Who would have imagined it? A handful of weeks in this impossible town, and despite his worst efforts, he had the prettiest girl he'd ever seen in his arms.

Now all he needed was a liquor license so he could open his flipping bar.

CHAPTER FOURTEEN

Mindy took one look at Clay striding into her office at town hall and squeaked, "I'll go get Graham." Without another word, she scurried toward the back offices.

"What did you do to her?" June asked flatly.

Crap. Clay rubbed the side of his neck. "More or less the same thing I did to you the first time we met?"

June dropped her face into her palm.

"I know, I know." Clay gazed up at the heavens. It had only been a month and a half or so, but it felt like another lifetime when he'd barreled in here, itching for a fight and picking one with everyone who gave him reason to.

Plenty of people had, mind you. Maybe not June and maybe not Mindy, but the Dottie Gallaghers and Patty Boyds of Blue Cedar Falls had proven that Bug wasn't just blowing smoke, warning him about the buttinskies who would give him grief. He didn't feel bad about being gruff with them.

The other folks whose throats he'd jumped down?

Yeah, okay, those he felt kind of guilty about.

Mindy came back. "Graham will be right out." She positioned her chair as far away from where Clay and June stood at the counter as possible. She managed a small smile while still avoiding eye contact. "Hey, June."

"Hey." June poked an elbow into Clay's ribs.

"Ow." He looked down and met her raised brows. Ugh. "Hey, uh, Mindy?"

"Yes?"

Clay sucked in a deep breath. This never got any easier, but at least he'd gotten plenty of practice at it this week. "I feel like I owe you an apology. For last time."

"Is that so?" She chanced a glance up.

"It is," Clay said firmly. "I was angry and I took it out on you, and that wasn't fair."

Mindy gave him an appraising stare. Then with a self-satisfied nod, she returned to her computer. "Apology accepted."

Phew.

"Was that so hard?" June needled him.

This woman.

Before she could give him any more grief, Graham emerged from the back office, a more genuine smile on his face. "Good morning, folks."

"Morning, Graham," June replied.

"Morning, June. How's it going?"

"Not too terrible. You?"

"Other than your sister throwing one of her hand-dyed skirts in with the rest of the laundry?" He tugged down the collar of his dress shirt to reveal an undershirt that was suspiciously pink.

"I told you she was a terrible roommate," June said fondly. She glanced at Clay. "Graham and Elizabeth share a place over on the north end of town."

"Oh." Clay tilted his head to the side. "Like..." He darted his gaze back and forth.

"Just friends," Graham promised, but there was something in his voice that made Clay wonder. The sympathetic gaze June shot him only deepened Clay's suspicion. Whatever he was or wasn't doing with June's sister, Graham clapped his hands together, clearly ready to move on. "So what can I do for you folks today?"

Clay passed the piece of paper he'd brought with him across the counter. "Here to apply for a liquor license."

Graham accepted the new application and smiled. "Had a feeling you might be." He looked to Mindy. "How many calls have we had come in out of the blue this week, expressing support for a new bar on Main Street?"

"Dozens." Mindy rolled her eyes. "Plus one, and I quote, 'retraction of my objection, with reservations.'"

"Well, Dottie Gallagher never has been easy to please," June said.

"No, she has not," Graham agreed.

But that hadn't kept Clay from sucking up his pride and giving it a try.

All week long, he'd been running around town, making roughly equal numbers of deals and amends with all the biddies who'd stood in his way.

His apology tour had been the result of a long, partly naked late-night brainstorming session with June for how to make sure he could get his bar up and running before he spent any more money rehabbing it. They'd both agreed that trying to take on the whole Main Street Busybody Association again would be pointless, but they didn't need everyone on their side. Just enough people for town hall to stop standing in his way.

So off he'd gone, in a stupid collared shirt again, armed with Lisa's designs and June's talking points. In individual meetings with one business owner after another, he'd made his case for what Bug's Bar could be. How it would attract more locals to Main Street and bring in tourists looking for "a more relaxed experience." None of it was untrue, but all of it seemed like an awful lot of boot-licking.

In the end, most of the folks he talked to were willing to give him a shot. He owed a lot of free beers to people, but that was all right. Dottie Gallagher's "reservations" included the right to call the cops on him any time his patrons got too loud. He still hadn't gotten Patty Boyd on his side, but her buddy Nancy had turned in exchange for a gig for her husband's band—heaven help them all.

Now all he could do was hope it had been enough.

"So," Clay asked, "are we good to go then?"

Putting him out of his misery, Graham cracked a smile. "I spoke to Mayor Horton about it this morning, and yes. I'd say we are."

With that, he reached under the counter for a stamp pad and a pen. Clay held his breath as the guy signed and dated and put a big fat imprint of the town's seal in the corner.

"Mindy, you mind running a copy of this for me?"

"No problem, boss."

When she returned with it, Graham passed the duplicate over to Clay. "License should be in the mail in about two weeks."

"About time," Clay grumbled, but as he stared at the piece of paper with his name on it and Bug's Bar at the top, that seal stamped at the bottom, he couldn't ignore the bit of something that got in his eye. He swabbed at it and sniffed. "Thank you," he told Graham. "Seriously."

"No problem, man. Congratulations."

"You should come on down, once we're open. Late September is my guess."

"Before the Pumpkin Festival," June inserted.

"Both of you." Clay looked to Mindy, too. "First round's on me, you hear?"

One corner of Mindy's lips curled up. "I never did turn down free drinks."

June threaded her hand through the crook of his elbow, and it calmed something inside him. He smiled at Graham and Mindy again, then led June out into the sunshine.

"You did it." She beamed, squeezing his arm and leaning into him.

"We did." He turned to her, and it took his breath away, she was so beautiful. "Thank you."

She rose onto her toes, and he dipped down to kiss her.

As they headed to his truck, he cast a glance at the sky.

Here we go, Bug.

This was real now. The boot-licking work was done.

But the blood, sweat, tears, and splinters in your knuckles work?

That had just begun.

June swore, her work never ended.

"Go already, would you?" Ned prodded her, folding napkins behind the front desk.

"I'm going, I'm going." June checked her purse, then cast about for the flyers she was supposed to bring. Ah, there they were. "Could you hand me—"

Ned grabbed the papers from the printer and passed them to her.

"Thanks." She gave them a quick once-over, then carefully slotted them into her giant tote bag next to her water bottle and a couple of tins of food.

Today was Blue Cedar Falls's annual Labor Day celebration.

Technically, June had the day off, but it wasn't as if she was going to let the chance to promote either the inn or the Pumpkin Festival slip past. She already had a stack of pamphlets for the inn to leave at the tourism bureau's setup, plus these hot-off-the-presses announcements about the line-up for the Pumpkin Festival.

She bit her lip. Had Clay thought to get something made up for Bug's Bar? It would be opening soon, and this could be a good chance for him to spread the word. Maybe she should text him and ask if he wanted her to whip up a flyer for him.

She started to reach for her phone, but Ned cleared his throat.

"Have fun," he told her pointedly, nudging her toward the door again. "That's an order now, you hear?" He tipped his head in the direction of the dining room. "And it's coming from the top."

June rolled her eyes. "Tell Mom to relax. I'm fine."

Yes, she'd been busy, but that was nothing new. She'd been busy since she was eight years old. Had to keep the plates spinning and all. The additional responsibilities she'd taken on since her mother's stroke had only added to the high-wire act. But it was fine.

Besides—if anything, she'd been taking more time off than usual of late. Having the payment plan set up with the hospital had relieved so much of her stress.

And having somewhere to go in the evenings…

A little thrill leaped through her chest as she glanced out the window toward Clay's bar.

Nearly three weeks had passed since she and Clay had fallen into bed together, and they had been some of the best weeks of her life. It wasn't always easy, managing all her responsibilities and sneaking in time with him, but she'd been making it work. Despite her worries, the inn had remained standing, and her family had remained more or less solvent. She'd even remembered to text if she stayed out past ten.

Which she did. Regularly.

The explosive chemistry between her and Clay hadn't fizzled one bit, even with repeated experiments. Sex with Clay was fun and athletic and sometimes desperate in a way she hadn't known sex could be. The more she got of him, the more she wanted.

And it wasn't just about the sex, either. They were taking things easy, not putting any pressure on what they were to each other, but when you spent enough time in a man's bed, you got to talking, too.

Beneath that gruff exterior that had put her off so much when they'd first met, Clay was wickedly funny. He was a man of few words sometimes, but every single one of them counted.

She'd had plenty of friends in her life. Great friends. But there was something about having Clay's undivided attention on her, his body close to hers, with his piercing gaze and steady hands. He had no expectations or preconceived notions about her. He challenged her and he still argued with her when they disagreed. But it was with a new respect that ran both ways between them.

Being with him, talking to him, kissing him…It made her feel free.

It was probably dangerous. Too much too fast, considering they were keeping things casual.

But she couldn't help it. As infuriating as she'd found him originally, she just plain *liked* him now.

So she probably shouldn't leave him waiting in the park all afternoon.

Whatever. He was a grown man, and if he wanted flyers for his bar, he could have printed them himself.

With a last blown kiss at her stepfather, she bustled out the door.

By the time she got to Pine Meadows Park, things were just getting underway. Labor Day kicked off the autumn tourist season in the Carolina mountains. Cooler temperatures and gorgeous fall colors brought all sorts of folks out, from families on weekend adventures to young couples looking for a getaway to quilting circle retreats—though there had been fewer of the latter since Susie's Quilts and More had closed, of course. Blue Cedar Falls wouldn't be getting those groups back anytime soon, but that was all right. Bug's Bar would be its own draw. Turnout today seemed to be off to a good start. As she wove through the crowd, June said hi to a half dozen guests from the Sweetbriar Inn, as well a decent portion of the town.

Stands for vendors ran the length of the park, with crafters selling their wares and restaurateurs offering all kinds of delicious treats. A local band played live jazz over by the gazebo, and a handful of performers dressed up like princesses and superheroes wandered the paths, collecting crowds of delighted children in their wake.

In the grass, beneath the shade of big old poplars and pines, people had spread out blankets for picnics. Families and friends were coming together in scores.

It was the kind of day that made June extra proud to live in this town, among this community, and her heart rose, watching it all unfold.

Nodding to herself, she made her way to the tourism bureau's stand to set out her flyers and pamphlets. The Pumpkin Festival the following month would be even bigger and better, she hoped, with even more out-of-towners looking for a comfortable place to stay.

Of course, who would be staffing the booth but Patty Boyd.

"Afternoon," June greeted her.

"Uh-huh." Patty put on one of those nasty public-facing smiles—the kind that outwardly said she was happy to see you, when clearly she wasn't. June returned it with a similar level of enthusiasm.

Ever since Clay had gotten his liquor license sorted out—with Patty as one of the last objectors—the woman had been especially chilly, which was fine. It wasn't as if June particularly liked pretending to enjoy making small talk with her anyway.

She laid out her pamphlets and flyers as fast as she could.

With that task accomplished, June scanned the crowd until she spotted Bobbi over by the baker's stand, giving what June assumed were some final instructions to the fresh-faced high school kid who was helping her out today. Relieved, June made a beeline toward her friend.

"Call me if anything goes wrong, okay?" Bobbi reminded her helper.

"Will do," the kid promised.

June resisted the impulse to grab Bobbi and literally drag her away. The bakery was Bobbi's baby, but she needed to let go every now and then and trust the people who were there to help her with it.

"She'll be fine," June told her, taking Bobbi's hand.

Bobbi rolled her eyes. "And how many times did Ned have to tell you to take a hike?"

"Shh." Three, but who was counting? In the past it probably would have been more like a dozen, so. Progress.

Bobbi left with her willingly—no dragging required—but she cast a few dubious glances back over her shoulder. "I just really hope things go well today. The bakery's been pretty slow this month."

Business had been slow all over town. But this was June's afternoon off, and Bobbi's break. They didn't need to dwell on income projections right now.

"Does Caitlin already have a spot staked out?" June asked.

Bobbi finally turned forward, her face brightening. "Yeah, she said she was over by the fountain."

"Lead the way."

Sure enough, they found Caitlin exactly where she'd promised to be, a big pink and white check blanket spread out to claim their spot. Han and his best friend Devin sat to one side of her. June's mouth watered as she watched Han pull a few baskets of bao out of a box.

She shifted her gaze to the other side.

And then her mouth started watering for a different reason entirely.

Clay sat opposite Han, his short hair gleaming in the bits of dappled sun shining down through the trees. In profile, his jaw was so sharp June could cut herself on it. His worn T-shirt clung to his muscles, his bare forearms huge and golden, and it *did* things to June, just looking at him.

As if he could feel her gaze on him, he chose that moment to turn around. His eyes lit up, and his sinful mouth curled into a smile that made her glow inside.

"Hey," he said, shoving over and patting the blanket beside him.

Instinctively, June glanced at the rest of their friends, then mentally slapped herself. What she was doing with Clay wasn't a secret.

She was just a private person, and it had been so long since she had dated. Being out with a guy—especially a guy so different from the clean-cut men she'd been with in the past— was going to take a little getting used to, was all.

Trying to hide her self-consciousness, she settled in beside Clay, then reached into her bag for a tin of sandwiches Ned had packed for her and some of her mom's famous almond cookies. June had tried to tell her that she didn't need to make anything, that she should be *resting*, but her mother had insisted.

Clay pounced on the cookies, and she resisted swatting his hand away. He made an exaggerated moan as he bit into one. "Haven't had these in ages."

"June's mom should open a Chinese bakery," Han agreed. "You know, if it wouldn't make our families mortal enemies."

June shook her head. "The Leungs can keep the restaurant business."

"Except breakfast," Caitlin said. "Nobody can beat Sweetbriar Inn for that."

"Hey!" Bobbi elbowed Caitlin, offended on behalf of her bakery.

Caitlin held up her hands. "I said what I said. Pastries are awesome, but if there isn't bacon involved, it isn't breakfast."

"Ever try bacon pastries?" Clay suggested.

"Maple bacon doughnuts were a hit last fall," Bobbi conceded.

"Make those again, baby," Caitlin told her, "and I take back everything I said."

"I don't know." Bobbi nudged Caitlin playfully, and Caitlin grinned.

"Well, fancy running into you all," a woman's voice said from above.

They looked up. Standing at the edge of their blanket were Bobbi's parents.

Bobbi sprung upright, putting distance between herself and Caitlin. Caitlin frowned, but then tried to hide it behind a smile.

"Oh, hey, Mom, Dad."

"Don't worry," her dad said, his big mustache twitching as he smiled. "The grown-ups aren't crashing your party. We're meeting Evelyn and Maurice." He pointed toward the other end of the park.

Tracy agreed. "Just wanted to say hi. Beautiful day."

"Sure is," Clay said.

Mrs. Moore's smile widened as she glanced between him and Bobbi. "Oh Clay, I didn't see you there. So glad to see you're fitting in with this crew."

They made small talk for a bit, Bobbi barely hiding her impatience before they finally wandered off.

As soon as they were gone, Bobbi swayed into Caitlin, thunking her head against her shoulder for a fraction of a second before lifting it back up. Caitlin looked down at her indulgently and patted her hand.

"I thought they'd never leave," Bobbi groaned.

"That's probably why they stayed." Han shrugged. "Nothing drives my mom like knowing she's annoying me."

June chuckled. Her mom ran on the same fuel, when she was at full strength. Clay went quiet as they complained about their parents, chewing on another almond cookie. June rested her foot against his leg in silent comfort, and he put his hand on her ankle.

He didn't talk much about having lost his parents young, and he'd never let on that it bothered him, but listening to people griping about their families couldn't be easy. Across the blanket from him, Devin was looking unusually stoic as well.

Time to change the subject.

"Any progress on Operation: Get Bobbi Out of the Closet?" June asked at the next break in conversation.

"No," Bobbi pouted. "If anything it's gotten worse." She

glared pointedly at Clay. "Did you notice the way my mom was trying to shove you and me together?"

Clay pulled his hand away from June's calf, his brows pinching together. "Uh . . ."

"They finally gave up on setting me up with Henry. I bet you twenty bucks you're their next target."

Clay's mouth opened and closed a few times.

June tried to squash down the weird feeling that rose into her chest at the idea of Clay with her best friend—even though she knew full well it was the last thing Bobbi wanted. Clay didn't exactly seem interested in the prospect, either.

Oblivious to the way the whole idea had taken June off guard, Bobbi flopped backward on the grass dramatically, arms out to the side and long, blond hair going everywhere. "I just want to be able to snuggle my girlfriend in public. Is that so much to ask?"

Caitlin smiled sadly. "It's really not, baby."

The moment felt private, even though they were keeping a careful distance from each other. June looked away, uncomfortable.

Her gaze landed on Clay. He was so handsome, there in the bright, early fall sun, it almost took her breath away.

How lucky was she that she had a guy she *could* snuggle with in public? And she wasn't even taking advantage of it. Sometimes, June wished she could let loose a little, but it didn't come naturally to her. Keeping up appearances was literally part of her job.

So what if she was dating a guy who was a little rough around the edges? Would the world really fall apart or think less of her because of it?

Did it matter?

Before she could get it sorted out in her head, Caitlin turned to Clay. "So I hear you got some guys from O'Shea's coming out to do your kitchen next week?"

Clay relaxed, probably happy to be talking shop instead of relationships. "Yeah. Thanks for the recommendation."

"No problem. They're good guys."

"Seemed like it."

Han's friend Devin joined them in discussing the nitty-gritties of the next phase of Clay's renovation. June tuned out a bit, half paying attention and half people watching. Absently, she reached for a slice of watermelon from a container in the middle of the group and took a bite.

Juice ran down her arm, and she bit back a curse. She looked around for a napkin, but there weren't any.

Right, duh, because she'd promised to bring them. She reached for her bag, only to find it empty.

"Crap," she muttered, starting to stand and trying valiantly not to get stains on her dress. Apparently her whole system of keeping all the plates in the air wasn't going as great as she'd thought. "I forgot—"

"Napkins?" Clay said, lurching to his feet. "On it."

"I can—"

He waved a hand. "Sit. I got it."

Before she could say anything, he was off toward one of the stands nearby. She watched him go, her brows scrunching together.

"Clay and Ju-une, sitting in a tree," Bobbi quietly sang. Everybody laughed.

"Oh, shush." June mocked swatting at her, but seriously, her hands really were sticky.

She met Bobbi's eyes, and while her best friend was teasing her, her gaze was genuinely happy. June looked away, warmth squirming around inside her. She was both pleased and embarrassed at the same time, and even she knew that didn't make sense.

Clay returned a minute later, having charmed someone out of an entire roll of paper towels. He tore off a couple and handed them to her before setting the rest of the roll in the middle of the blanket.

"Thanks," she told him. That warmth inside her only grew.

When he patted her leg this time, she didn't shy away. With her now clean hands, she grabbed his. Holding on to him, she rose onto her knees and planted a quick kiss on his cheek. Bobbi let out a little whistle, and June shot her a playful glare as she sat herself back down.

Smug, Clay reached for another cookie, and she didn't even think about giving him a hard time about it.

She gazed at him appraisingly.

This wasn't the first time he'd insisted on doing something for her. From bandaging the burn on her hand, to making her midnight snacks if she so much as mentioned feeling peckish, to this…It was all small stuff, relatively speaking, but when was the last time anyone had ignored her protestations that she had it, she could do it, she was on top of everything, and just taken care of her?

A light flutter dashed around her chest.

Maybe she didn't have all the plates spinning all the time right now.

But Clay reaching up and giving one a little twist every now and then…

It made all the difference in the world.

CHAPTER FIFTEEN

❀ ❀ ❀ ❀ ❀ ❀ ❀ ❀ ❀ ❀ ❀ ❀

O kay, I think we're about set."

Clay looked up from his work to find Marty hovering in the doorway. He was the lead guy for the crew who'd spent the past week renovating the quilt shop's back room into a professional kitchen.

Nodding, Clay took one last swipe with the sanding block at the corner of the sign that was going to go out front, kind of like the ones on a bunch of the other restaurants on Main Street. Imagine that. Him—being a team player with this group.

But it did look cool, and he'd carved it himself, using the logo Lisa had drawn up for him of a beetle drinking out of a pint glass. BUG'S BAR was spelled out in big block letters above and below it.

Perfect.

Leaning the sign against the wall, he rose to his feet. His knee creaked, but maybe not quite as bad as usual. Who knew—maybe those useless exercises were helping.

Just like Caitlin had promised, the contractors had done good work, finishing on time and up to code and everything. As Marty gave him the tour, Clay inspected the fixtures and joints, ran the water and checked that the electrical all seemed to work.

"Happy?" Marty asked.

"Looks good." Clay glanced around one last time before raising a brow. "Suppose you want to get paid?"

"I mean, it'd be nice."

Satisfied, Clay headed to the little office across the hall and grabbed his checkbook. He scribbled out a check for the balance and handed it over. It was hard to let the piece of paper go, but he managed. He opened his wallet and forked over a few bills—enough for each member of the crew.

This bar better work out, or he didn't know what he was going to do. Riding up to Alaska or Montana had been appealing at one point, but recently, it had lost its allure.

Doing it with a pile of business loans riding around on his back only made the idea grimmer.

"Pleasure doing business with you." Marty shoved the payment in his pocket and held out his hand. Clay shook it. On the way to the door, Marty gestured around. "Can't wait till this place is up and running."

"Me, neither."

"Text me about the opening, okay? We'll come out for it. Tell our friends, you know."

"That'd be great." Clay smiled. Always good to make a connection.

Who knew—maybe even a friend.

After Marty left, Clay closed the door behind him and turned around. The bar felt eerily quiet. Having a half dozen people banging around, hauling in equipment and running electric and gas made a lot of noise. On the one hand, Clay was happy for the silence. On the other . . .

He supposed he was going soft, but he was going to miss the

company. He shook his head at himself. Funny how he could go it alone for so long and then get used to being surrounded by people so fast.

He huffed out a breath.

Well, it wouldn't be quiet here for long, at least. Forget that June would be over as soon as she could sneak away; he had no doubt she'd been watching the contractors leave from across the street and was dying to see the place finished. He couldn't wait to show it to her, either.

But soon, he'd have company of a whole other kind. Less than a month remained until the doors on this place were supposed to open. If everything went according to plan, he'd make it with a week or two to spare before the big Pumpkin Festival June was so excited about. He'd do a big grand opening— invite everyone from town. Then use the time between the opening and the Pumpkin Festival to iron out any kinks.

He wandered back over to where the sign he'd been working on stood. With a muffled grunt, he crouched down on the ground again and picked up the sandpaper. He went over the same handful of edges another time, just to be sure, but the thing was as good as it was going to get. There wasn't any reason to keep screwing around with it.

He ran his fingertip along the edges of Bug's name once more anyway. His throat tightened.

"Wish you could see it, bud," he muttered.

He wished a lot of things.

Shaking his head at himself, he stood with a grunt and dusted himself off. He grabbed the Shop-Vac and got to work cleaning up some of the mess of sawdust and shavings he'd made.

When he turned the thing off, its roar took a second to die down. But out on the street, some idiot revved their engine. Clay rolled his eyes and shook his head.

Then he stood up straighter.

Maybe it was a couple of idiots, actually. Instead of receding into the distance, the racket only got louder. June and the Busybody Association crowd weren't going to like that.

Frowning, Clay glanced at the still boarded-up window—he really had to get on that. Unable to see out the front and too curious at this point, he strode to the door and tugged it open.

Just in time to see *three* idiots riding their Harleys in a big circle spanning the whole breadth of Main Street before coming to a halt right in front of the bar.

Three very familiar idiots, in fact.

Clay stood there for a minute, dumbstruck.

How on earth?

One by one, the three killed the engines on their bikes.

Tuck was the first to take off his helmet. His dark hair was longer than it had been in Afghanistan, but then again, whose wasn't? He had a chin strap of a beard and his skin was almost as tanned as it had been in the desert. His well-worn boots thudded on the pavement as he dismounted. Beads of sweat gathered at his temples—he had to be roasting in those riding leathers, but he looked as cool and as confident as ever.

AJ and Riz followed Tuck's lead. AJ was working on the start of an Afro under that helmet. Catching sight of Clay, he flashed a smile that gleamed bright white against his brown skin.

"There he is," AJ crowed.

Clay had to grip the doorframe to keep from bolting.

Which was stupid. These were his buddies, some of the best friends he'd ever had.

But he'd been such a dick for so long. The fact that they hadn't seen each other in the past year was one hundred percent Clay's fault. Heck, they'd tried to get in touch with him how many times? Just last week, Tuck had texted him, and while Clay hadn't ignored him completely, he'd been busy at the time, so he'd put him off.

And now here they were, almost literally knocking down his door.

He wasn't any more ready than he'd been before.

Could he ever be?

Clay had been drummed out of the army with a bum knee and Bug's blood soaked into the creases of his knuckles, left to die by some head-up-his-butt commanding officer.

For a while there, he almost wished he'd gone ahead and bled out, too.

He'd survived, but what was left of him? He heard Bug's voice in his head, and he talked to him, too. Not as often as he used to, but still. The shrapnel in his knee might be bugging him a little less of late, but it had left him slow and cranky, and he knew it. He had all these scars.

Tuck, AJ, Riz...

He hadn't wanted them to see him like this.

But they had eyes. There wasn't any more avoiding it now.

Heart hammering against his ribs, he stood his ground. "Well, look who the cat dragged in."

Tuck laughed, deep and full-throated, his southern accent as thick as glue. "You son of a..."

Then he was crossing the strip of shaded sidewalk.

He threw his arms around Clay.

And something inside Clay's chest went quiet and still. After a long moment, he hugged Tuck in return.

Tuck drew back. His dark eyes took Clay in, and Clay didn't have any reason to hide anymore, so he didn't flinch. "So how've you been?"

"You know," Clay grumbled. He waved a hand dismissively, but he couldn't quite keep his voice even. "Same old, same old."

"Sand in your boots and MREs?"

Clay barked out a laugh. "Okay, so maybe not quite the same." He narrowed his eyes. "How'd you find me?"

"You should be nicer to Lisa," AJ chastened him. Tuck moved out of the way, and AJ held out his hand. Clay slapped their palms together, then the backs, before bumping the tops and the bottoms of their fists.

Just like old times.

Kind of.

AJ stepped aside and Riz moved forward.

"Don't hold it against her," Riz said. "She was just looking out for you."

"Sure."

Riz hugged Clay, too, but it was one of those loose bro-hugs, only the sides of their torsos touching, and that was fine. "You stink," Clay told him.

They all did.

"You know you love it." Riz grabbed Clay by the neck, trying to pull his face down into his armpit, and heaven help him from these idiots.

Clay shoved Riz off, and Riz let him. The guy had lost some bulk since the last time Clay saw him, but he remained wiry and strong. His jet-black hair hung in his eyes, like one of those K-pop stars Lisa was so obsessed with—even if he was Filipino.

Tuck, AJ, and Riz formed a loose circle around the door Clay still hovered in.

"So." Tuck raised a brow. "Can we come in or what?"

Clay only hesitated for a second. Nothing in his life was as settled as he'd told himself he wanted it to be before he saw these guys again. He'd mentally resigned himself to the fact that it never would be, and he could just fade off into oblivion in their memories. It had happened enough times before. It wasn't as if he'd ever heard from any of those foster parents who had kicked him out.

Only these guys hadn't forgotten about him. They hadn't let him disappear from their lives at all. They'd sought him out, despite his protests about how he wanted to be alone. They'd come to see what he was building, here in Bug's hometown.

And Clay was suddenly so grateful for that he could hardly stand it.

"Of course," he said, his voice rough.

He stepped aside, holding the door for them. As they strode in, he glanced across the street. If June was watching, wow, was he going to have some questions to answer about him leading three burly bikers into his bar, but whatever. They could laugh about it together later.

Hopefully.

Somehow, leading these particular friends into the unfinished bar was different from having Marty and his crew of contractors in the space. They'd been here to do a job, and they'd had no expectations. Tuck, AJ, and Riz knew he was seeing out Bug's legacy here.

Clay crushed down the restlessness buzzing around in his gut. "Make yourselves at home."

"Oh, we will," Riz said, thumping Clay's shoulder as he passed.

The guys were so big, they took up all the space in that huge front room as they fanned out, looking around.

Clay got a grip and started showing them what he was up to, pointing out the work he'd done and the stuff that was still on his list. The guys followed him around, nodding and egging him on.

After he showed them the new kitchen and the in-process remodel on the bathroom, they filed out into the front room again. Tuck stopped, tilting his head to the side as he looked at the sign Clay had left next to the Shop-Vac on the ground.

The place got quiet.

"That what you're naming it?" AJ asked, his voice as tight as Clay's throat felt.

Clay crossed his arms. "Yup."

Tuck looked at him with eyes that said all kinds of things Clay didn't know if he was ready to hear.

But that was the thing about these types of friends. The kind who knew exactly what sort of nightmare you'd been through, but had the decency not to make you talk about it.

Returning his gaze to the sign, Tuck nodded. "He would've liked it. Bug."

They were all silent for a moment. It was the first time they'd said his name out loud, and his ghost felt so close he could have walked right out of the walls.

Clay's voice threatened to break. He dropped his arms and cracked his knuckles. "You think?"

"I know," AJ promised.

Something popped inside Clay's chest, and that didn't make sense. He'd been following Bug's dream this entire time. Of course Bug would've liked it.

But he'd changed that vision of what Bug wanted along the way. He'd made it his own. June had had a big hand in shaping it, too. He'd made it part himself and part her and part Blue Cedar Falls, and he didn't know where any of the lines between the different parts even were anymore.

The corners of his eyes stung, but he wasn't going to indulge any emotional crap. He didn't have time for that. None of these guys did.

As if he could tell that Clay was close to cracking, Tuck clapped him on the shoulder. "Now come on. Apparently this dump isn't open yet. So you gotta tell us where the next best place is to get a drink."

Clay swiped the back of his wrist over his eyes and laughed. "Sure, sure."

And just like that, it was all settled. Tuck, AJ, and Riz were here, and Clay was letting them stay. They liked his bar and they approved of what he'd done to honor Bug's memory, and what else mattered?

Nothing. He was done pushing them away.

"I know just the place," Clay told them.

And then he led the way.

CHAPTER SIXTEEN

June gave her phone a dirty look. She'd texted Clay half an hour ago to check and see if she was good to come over and see the new kitchen. Usually he replied within minutes with an enthusiastic yes. The day's business at the inn was all sorted, and Ned had everything under control.

She peered through the window at the soon-to-be bar across the street. Nothing out of the ordinary appeared to be going on, though there were still those three motorcycles parked out front.

And hadn't the town gossips been having a field day with that? Dottie Gallagher and at least half a dozen others had found reasons to casually swing by and ask June if she knew anything about them. Right. Because June didn't have anything better to do than stare out the front window of the lobby and keep track of her neighbors.

Okay, fine, once upon a time, maybe she had made a bit of a hobby of doing precisely that, but she was busy these days. Running an inn and organizing a festival and carrying on a . . . whatever she had with Clay was a full-time job.

The motorcyclists were probably some road-trippers passing through. They weren't exactly the demographic Main Street usually served, but widening their audience had been one of her goals, so she welcomed them, and hoped everyone else on Main Street would do the same.

Finally, the silence had gone on too long. Clay was probably elbow deep in some messy project and hadn't thought to keep his phone on him. He'd never seemed upset by her dropping in unannounced before.

She'd just pop over for a minute. If he was busy, she'd leave him alone.

Just in case, she snuck into the kitchen and grabbed a couple of the custard buns her mother had made that morning. Clay loved any kind of baked good, but her mother's Chinese recipes always seemed to put a special smile on his face. No way he could give her grief about showing up with these in hand.

Thus armed, she headed out and across the street. She knocked on the front door as usual, but no one answered.

Weird.

Well, he could be in the back. Or upstairs.

As usual, the door was unlocked, so she let herself in, calling out as she did, but there was no reply. She crossed the dimly lit space, careful not to trip over the paint cans and tools scattered about.

Down the hall, she peeked into the kitchen and smiled. It looked great. She couldn't wait to see what Clay came up with for the menu. She had a ton of ideas waiting on her Pinterest boards if he needed inspiration. She was thinking sort of a home-brewed, local new-American-meets-pub-grub kind of vibe, but who knew what direction he'd want to go in.

No signs of life greeted her as she popped her head into the other rooms. The light in the stairwell was off, too.

Then she noticed the back door was open. She moved toward

it. Strange voices drifted through the air, deep and gruff and laughing. A whiff of smoke hit her.

She pushed past the screen and out into the night air.

Only to find Clay sitting in a beaten-up lawn chair, surrounded by three men she'd never seen before. She blinked repeatedly, trying to make sense of it.

Because Clay was...laughing.

Not just chuckles and wry amusement, either. Maybe it was the beer in his hand—or the dozen crushed cans scattered around them, but he looked loose and easy and barely recognizable, even.

The other guys were in a similar state. They were a motley crew, one white, one Black, one Asian—all built and all way too attractive. All definitely at least a decent portion of the way to drunk.

Between them, a fire burned in a metal bucket right on the grass.

A strange nostalgia made June swallow.

Back when her mother first got together with Ned, he tried to win June and her sisters over with a fiasco of a camping trip. He'd known they were from New York, but he'd clearly underestimated what would be involved in taking three kids who had barely left Queens out into the woods. There had been bugs and trees and no place to pee. June had tried to put on a happy face, because she could see what this meant to Ned and her mother, but May and Elizabeth had been ruthless.

Right until it came time to make a campfire. There had been something magical about those flickering flames, the scent of roasted marshmallows, and Ned's low, steady voice telling stories in the dark.

It was the first time she realized Ned was really all in with her mother. It was the first time she saw the future of her family.

There were other, better camping trips to come, but those hours spent around the campfire were always the highlight of them.

She was pulled out of her reminiscing when the three men around Clay erupted into laughter at something he'd said.

June's pulse galloped. She stood there, unnoticed in the darkness, wavering. Maybe she should go. Clearly, Clay was busy.

But this new version of him was too enticing. Sheer curiosity practically pulled her through the doorway.

She wouldn't intrude or anything. She'd say hi for a minute and then let them be. But she couldn't see him there, relaxed and smiling, and walk away.

At the top of the steps, she cleared her throat.

Four sets of eyes all swiveled around to look at her. The Asian guy somehow managed not to fall out of his chair, but it was a close thing. She covered her mouth to keep from laughing.

Clay's smile ignited, burning bright as the sun. "June!"

He lumbered to his feet, skirting around the fire and over to her.

"Hey," she greeted him. She held out the plate of baked goods, because they always smoothed everything over. "Just thought I'd drop these off."

"Well, who's this?" one of the guys asked in a low southern drawl.

"Guys, this is June." Clay wrapped an arm around her shoulders and pressed a sloppy kiss to her temple. He waved at the men seated around the fire. "June, these are the guys."

"The guys"? Since when did Clay have "guys"?

June wiggled her fingers at them, unsure. "Hi."

The scent of beer was strong on Clay's breath. It was disarming to see how much less guarded he was.

She gazed at him in wonder as he introduced his companions by name. Tuck, a mountain of a man with tan skin and a beard. The Black man beside him was AJ, the Asian one on the other side of the fire Riz. She said hi to each of them in turn.

She tried to pull away, still intent on not interrupting. "I'll leave you to—"

"Uh-uh." Tuck shook his head. "No way. Clay, you dog, you got a *girl*?"

June's cheeks flushed hot.

"Darn right," Clay told them, pulling her in closer.

The guys whistled, and her embarrassment only grew.

But deep down, was it terrible to say she was also sort of pleased?

"Oh, we gotta know more about this." Riz stood and got another chair from a pile of them folded up by the side of the building. June vaguely remembered them from the one quilting class she'd tried at the shop on a dare. He plunked the extra chair down next to where Clay had been sitting and gestured toward it with a flourish.

June shook her head. "I don't want to interrupt—"

Though wow, she was dying to. Waiting until tomorrow to find out who these guys were would be torture.

"It's fine." Clay frowned. "Unless you don't want—this probably wasn't what you expected—"

She squeezed his hand. She searched his slightly hazy eyes. "Sure. I can stay for a bit."

He lit up. Leaning in, he kissed her, wet and full on the mouth. She put her hands on his chest, not pushing him away, but more reminding herself they had an audience.

In the end, she didn't need the reminder. More whistling and hoots and hollers erupted from Clay's friends. She gave him a gentle push away, her face on fire, and he took the hint.

Holding her hand, he led her over to the chair Riz had set out for her. He pushed his even closer. She sat, perching on the edge, nervous in a way that was almost exciting.

Tuck grabbed two beers from a cooler over by the side, cracked one, and handed it to her. It wasn't her favorite, but she accepted it and took a gulp.

Clay sprawled out beside her, his arm over the back of her chair, and she marveled at him again.

Here she'd thought she had him all figured out, but really, had she even scratched the surface?

Sure, she'd known deep waters ran beneath his tightly controlled exterior. She'd seen the anger he could be driven to, the passion he sometimes let loose, and the grief that shadowed his eyes. Occasionally, there'd been flashes of a lighter side. They'd shared moments of real intimacy, and in his bed, in the glowy haze after making love, he could be soft and sweet.

Seeing him playful and goofy like this was something else entirely. Something that intrigued her.

She waved a hand between Clay and the other guys. "So how exactly do you all know each other?"

"Oh, we go way back," Tuck said.

"You see." Riz smirked. "Clay here used to be an exotic dancer—"

Clay flipped him off, and AJ howled.

"We were in the service together," Clay explained.

"At the Gentleman's Lounge," Riz insisted.

Tuck tossed an empty beer car at him, which Riz batted away. "Ow, man, what the—?"

"We met Clay in Afghanistan," AJ told her. "He was on his first tour."

"He was so cute." Tuck grinned. "Fresh-faced and following orders."

"Ha," Clay said dryly.

AJ raised his beer. "Remember that time Riz hid your clothes while you were in the shower?"

"Remember it?" Clay laughed, loose and easy. "Pretty sure I still got sand in my crack from chasing him down."

Riz shook his head fondly. "Bug punched me in the face for that one."

"Little guy." Tuck sighed. "Had a temper on him, that one did."

"Tell me about it." Clay's voice went rough, and he drained his beer and tossed it aside. He let June go just long enough to grab another.

She watched him, her brow crinkled. He was a grown man, drinking with friends he presumably hadn't seen in a while, here in his own yard where he didn't have to drive. He could imbibe as much as he wanted to, but maybe he could slow down a little.

Nervously, she took another few sips of her own beer.

Tuck shook his head. "Man, I miss that bastard."

"We all do," AJ said quietly.

"Right." Clay drank deeply, his throat bobbing with every swallow.

She reached out for him and put her hand on his knee, silently trying to show her support.

Did he know she was here for him? That he could talk to her about how he was feeling?

He rested his palm over hers, interlacing their fingers, and she hoped to heaven he did.

Especially when Tuck flexed his jaw, the sharp point of it cast in shadow by the fire's flickering light. "That last mission—"

"I know, I know," Clay cut him off.

"But we didn't," AJ told him.

June froze.

The air had suddenly become thick and charged. This wasn't a casual bit of reminiscing between old friends.

Tuck sat up straighter. Even Riz, who seemed like the joker of the crew, went still, the smile sliding off his face.

"We didn't know what you were walking into, Clay," Tuck said. "I swear."

"Not until after." AJ's dark eyes flashed black.

June looked between the four men. Clay flexed his jaw, a distance appearing in his gaze.

And she already knew part of this story, but there were missing pieces of it she'd never heard. Guilt tugged at her. She probably shouldn't be hearing them now, here, with his friends when they had all been drinking, but it felt like they needed to hash it out.

She looked at Clay, her heart squeezing, and she yearned to know more. To better understand all the pain he'd hinted at but rarely explained. To better understand *him*.

Carefully, she asked, "What? What happened?"

Everyone was silent for a minute. Then, quietly, utterly serious, Riz said, "POS commanding officer sent Clay and Bug and half the unit into an ambush."

"Didn't tell them what they needed to know," Tuck added.

Clay dropped his empty beer to the ground and stepped on it, crushing the metal into the dirt. "Then left us to die afterward."

"Oh my God."

"Bug...," AJ said.

"Bug bled out in the sand," Clay spat.

Tuck nodded. "Had to med-evac Clay and the other guys out." He flexed his fist against the arm of the folding chair. "Didn't know if he was going to make it."

"We would've had your back," AJ said. "If we'd known, we would have charged right in there after you."

Clay shook his head. "Wasn't your call."

"Doesn't matter," Tuck growled. "We should've—"

"You did exactly what you were supposed to do." Clay's mouth was a straight, white line.

AJ sat forward on his chair. "Clay—"

"You did the job. I did the job and Bug did the job. We all knew what we were signing up for. We all knew we might go home in bags."

"But neither of you deserved—" Tuck started.

"Don't any of us get what we deserve," Clay ground out.

His tone brooked no further argument. June squeezed his hand, but he didn't respond.

How could he be so matter-of-fact about such terrible things? So much of the anger he'd been carrying around with him when they'd first met began to make a new kind of sense. He'd lived through an ordeal she could scarcely imagine. Anyone would be scarred by that.

The four men gazed into the fire for a long minute.

Clay breathed out, and it felt like the whole world did, too. "Wasn't your fault," he told everyone.

Riz gazed at him with appraising eyes. "And it wasn't yours, either."

Clay didn't have a thing to say to that.

After another pause that seemed to stretch on and on, AJ said, "Lisa sends her love."

Clay's laugh was forced and raw. "Yeah, I'm sure."

"Hadley does, too," Tuck added.

"Bug's sister and niece," AJ clarified, and that was fine. June hadn't been worried.

Not with the dark look on Clay's face.

Firm, Tuck said, "They don't blame you, either."

"Right." Clay shifted in his chair.

June kept her hand on his leg, as if that could do any good. Pain radiated off Clay in waves. She'd known he'd gotten hurt. Both in body and in spirit, but to see him like this made her ache inside.

Had he kept these feelings of guilt and grief and resentment inside for all this time?

It seemed like cheating, getting to know him this way, but even as empathy tugged at the insides of her chest, a kind of gratitude filled her, too.

She was glad to know this man who felt things so deeply, though he wouldn't normally show it. Every bit of him that was revealed made her heart grow. Already, she'd been getting too attached to him for whatever sort of casual fling they'd been pretending to have.

This was taking that to a whole new level, though.

One that scared her with how intense it felt.

But when he made to move his hand away, she met his gaze. She gripped him tighter.

Who knew what was going to happen between them in the future. But for now? Tonight? No way she was going to let him go.

The flames in the center of the group crackled and popped. Tuck stood and used a stick to poke at the charred logs. Sparks flew into the air before fluttering to the ground.

"Hey," Riz said after Tuck had sat back down. "Remember that time Clay ball-tapped that jerk Jiminez right before Hewett came in?"

Clay barked out a laugh that seemed to take even him by surprise. AJ slapped his knee, and Tuck snorted his beer.

"Dang," AJ howled, "the look on his face trying not to double over."

"He returned the favor later." Clay swiped at his eyes. "Kidney punch practically in front of that corporal that was visiting."

Riz clapped his hands. "Oh, yeah, that was a good one, too."

As they dissolved into laughter, the heaviness of the evening faded away.

They traded a few more stories June didn't understand, but she didn't mind. She listened and followed along where she could, but mostly let the conversation flow over her. She kept her gaze on Clay and his expression, her heart almost too full to fit inside her chest.

"So June," Riz said after a while. "You gonna tell us about what this dude's been up to here in NC?"

"Because he hasn't told us a thing," AJ said, egging her on.

She glanced at Clay, who looked back at her, one brow raised. She considered for a second.

She didn't want to betray any confidences. Their relationship— whatever it was—was clearly off-limits. His angry reaction to her when they'd first met didn't seem like the right kind of comedic material, either.

But she knew what was.

She downed the rest of her beer in a few long pulls, swallowing while trying to hide her reaction to the bitter taste. Then she smiled and leaned forward.

"Well, there was this one time he gave a business presentation to a bunch of PTA moms and grandmothers and bombed so hard he left a crater."

"Hey!" Clay protested, but he was smiling.

Tuck caught her eye. He lifted his drink to her. "Girl, you might just be all right."

* * *

"The guys weren't kidding," Clay blabbered. The room was spinning around him, but that was fine, totally great, no problem. "You're all right, June Wu."

June wasn't quite steady on her feet, but she kept an arm wrapped around his waist, and thank goodness, because otherwise he might have gone tumbling over. "Thanks, I think."

"No, no seriously." He batted at her hair as she guided him down the hall. "You're nice and you smell pretty."

"Okay, buddy."

He lowered his voice dramatically. "And that thing you do with your tongue—"

"Oh-*kay*. Upstairs. Now." She blushed—or at least he thought she did. Her face was already weirdly hot. She'd only had like two beers, but she said it was an Asian thing, and Riz had backed her up, so it must be true.

"Yes, ma'am." He saluted and almost knocked himself off balance.

"Never could hold his liquor," Riz slurred.

"And you guys go to bed."

"Working on it." Tuck shut the door behind them all. He was staggering pretty good, too.

AJ looked fine, but Clay knew better. That man could be drunk as a skunk and you never knew. He just got quieter and quieter the more he had to drink.

"You guys make yourselves comfortable," Clay told them.

"I could sleep right here." Riz sagged into the ground.

"Good grief." June leaned Clay up against the wall next to the stairs and went to help Riz.

The guys were crashing in sleeping bags on the floor of

the bar for the night. Clay felt kind of crappy about that, but if he'd known they were coming maybe he could have gotten them a better setup. As it was, they swore they were cool with it. They'd been sleeping rough this whole trip, out under the stars half the time.

Clay sat down on the bottom step and time went hazy for a second.

The next thing he knew, June was back and tugging at his hand, trying to haul him up. He staggered to his feet, slinging an arm around her neck. She grumbled but bore his weight, and she was so great.

"How did I end up with somebody so great?" he asked, his legs wobbly as he climbed the stairs. His bum knee protested, but he wasn't feeling much pain.

"Must be your charm," June said dryly.

"Nah." Clay shook his head, and wow, that was a bad idea. His slumped into the wall when his balance disappeared. He looked up at June. "Bug was the charming one."

Clay was the lug who hung around with him. Clay'd always half thought Bug would notice sometime and tell Clay to get lost. Go find a better best friend. Only he never did. He stayed true to the end.

Man, Clay missed him.

His ghost was close tonight. They'd talked about the selfish jerk too much. Had to go and die and hadn't had the decency to take Clay along with him.

"You can be pretty charming, when you want to," June told him, helping him get going again.

"You think?"

"Yeah," she said quietly. Like maybe she wasn't sure she wanted to admit that. "I do."

They reached the top of the steps and he lumbered forward

mostly of his own power. When he got to his bed, he flopped onto it.

June stood in front of him and struggled with the laces to his boot. He lurched upward to try to help her, but his body didn't seem to work.

He was so drunk. What had he been thinking?

But what else was he supposed to have done? The guys showing up out of nowhere and being their same old selves. They'd acted like nothing had happened. Everything was the same except Bug was gone.

At least they'd accepted June.

June who was so pretty and smart, and she dressed so nice and smelled so good, and he was going to wake up in the morning and smell like the bottom of a barrel.

"What are you doing with me?" he asked, and he wasn't supposed to say that kind of stuff out loud.

She stopped messing around with his boot. "What do you mean?"

"I mean." He didn't have the words. He flopped a hand at him and a hand at her. "You know what I mean. You're me and I'm you." No. Crap. "I mean—"

Giving up on his bootlaces, she climbed up onto the bed. She put a hand on the side of his face, and her fingers were freaking magic on his skin. From the first moment, that's what they had been. When he hadn't been touched in ages and he'd been stewing in all that anger and grief, and she'd touched him gently. She'd kissed him and let him put himself inside her, and he didn't deserve any of it.

"Clay…"

"Doesn't matter," he started to say.

She kissed his lips, firm but lingering. When she pulled away, her eyes were soft. "I'm with you because I want to be."

It was the nicest thing anybody had ever said to him.

He put a hand over hers, keeping it pressed to his cheek. "You mean that?"

Eyes shining, she nodded. "I do."

She pulled her hand out from under his and started to move away, but he caught her.

He'd blame it on the alcohol later. He never asked this kind of thing. No one ever stayed with him, not from day one. His parents died on him and left him in a shattered car, alone in the world. Everyone else...They left him to go to another foster home or they left him in a pool of blood in the desert.

But she'd just told him she wanted to be with him.

"Stay," he ground out. "Can you—?"

He was being so selfish. She had an inn to run, and her family expected her to do everything, it seemed. She always had to go. He never got to hold her long enough.

She gazed at him for what felt like ages. She was going to say no.

But instead, she pulled her phone out of who even knew where. She tapped a bunch of stuff with her thumbs. Then she set it aside.

Pulling away from him, she got up, but it was only to turn out the lights, and then she was there. Crawling into his bed with him, and he was so happy. He wrapped her up tight in his arms and closed his eyes. Her sweet scent surrounded him, and yeah, he was drunk and she wasn't sober and there were three old grumpy vets sleeping on the floor downstairs, and it didn't matter.

For the first time since his parents had died, he felt like he was home.

CHAPTER SEVENTEEN

❋ ❋ ❋ ❋ ❋ ❋ ❋ ❋ ❋ ❋ ❋

Good. Don't be back before noon.

June stared in bewilderment at the text her mother had sent in reply to June letting them know she'd overslept and was running late getting home before the breakfast rush.

Her first instinct was to ignore it, of course. Standing at the top of the stairs heading down from Clay's apartment, she was already dressed and ready to dash across the street. She hadn't missed breakfast hour at the inn since her mother's stroke. Someone needed to man the desk, and Ned always needed help with topping off coffees and ringing up bills.

As if her mother could hear June's protest, June's phone took that opportunity to buzz again. June tapped on the photo that came in. A selfie her mom had clearly taken of herself behind the desk, Sunny the cat draped luxuriously across the computer's keyboard appeared on the screen.

June's stomach did a series of complicated flip-flops.

I'll be right over.

June's mom was on doctor's orders to rest. Sure, maybe June had taken that to an extreme. She hadn't allowed her mother to lift a finger in the nearly nine months since her stroke, and both her mother and Ned had begun to chafe at the restrictions.

Her mom had taken up baking, and she was always doing something or other on the tablet they'd gotten to help keep her occupied during her recovery, and yes, June had started letting her mom and stepdad be on call during off-hours more, now that she was spending so much time with Clay.

But this was something else entirely.

The doctors had been clear. Stress aggravated conditions like her mother's. She wasn't going to set back her mother's recovery or risk her ending up in the hospital again because June had forgotten to set an alarm.

She started typing furiously, telling her mother to go lie down, but before she could get the message finished, her phone buzzed one more time.

This message was from Ned.

Let her, June. Seriously. I mean it.

June paused.

That wasn't like Ned. He'd voiced concerns here and there, of course, but overall, he let June take care of everything these past nine months. Him telling her to stand down was out of character.

Behind her, floorboards creaked. She turned to find Clay standing in the doorway to the bedroom, his hair mussed, dark rings under his eyes, a little unsteady on his feet and green around his gills, but it didn't matter.

Heaven help her, she was in so far over her head with this man.

Last night, hanging out with him and his friends had cemented the situation for her. His loose smile and the rough laughter that accompanied every one of the embarrassing stories she and his buddies had told about him had softened any last, remaining restraints left on her heart.

Then there was the way he'd looked at her after she'd

dragged him upstairs and put him to bed. He'd been unguarded in a way she'd never witnessed before, and it had pulled at her emotions even further.

He'd looked at her like she was a miracle, and he was lucky to have her. No one had ever looked at her that way before. When he'd asked her why she was with him, she'd had nothing but the truth.

She was with him because she wanted to be. Whatever on earth they were doing together, it made her happy. She felt light and free in ways she hadn't, possibly ever.

Like she could let go and enjoy herself.

Enjoy *him*.

"What's going on?" Clay asked, voice rough. He ran a hand through his messy hair.

June glanced at her phone again. Downstairs, she heard the guys stirring, too.

Clay frowned. "You gotta run?"

"Bacon," someone groaned in the distance.

June furrowed her brows and looked down the stairs. Riz stood there, clearly in just as bad shape as Clay. He didn't have a shirt on, and his shorts looked like they might be inside out.

"I need bacon," Riz repeated. "Where in this town can I get bacon, Clay?"

"Hold your horses," Clay shouted. He winced and grasped his head like his brain hurt. Quieter, to June, he said, "We have a tradition. After a night like that, we hit a diner or wherever. Eat as much grease as we can. Best hangover cure there is."

That sounded like a terrible idea.

"June," Riz whined. "Tell Clay to come downstairs and find me bacon."

Clay ignored him. "You could come with? I mean." He scrubbed a hand over his face. "But if you gotta go…"

"No, I just—"

Her mom and Ned were grown adults. If they wanted June to let them handle the inn for the morning, was she really such a terrible person for letting them?

An anxious voice in the back of her head said *yes*, but she pushed it aside.

She dashed off a quick *OK* to her stepdad and her mom.

Then she turned to Clay and smiled. "Bacon sounds great."

Which was about when Riz threw up on the stairs.

Twenty minutes and a gallon of bleach later, June slid into a circular booth at Fran's Diner. Clay took his spot beside her, while the other guys filled in the rest of the table.

Fran herself took one look at them and her brows hit her hairline. "I'll go get you all a carafe."

"Bless you," Tuck grumbled.

He and AJ weren't quite as hungover as Clay and Riz, but they'd swallowed down ibuprofen and water just as eagerly on their way out the door.

"So what's good?" AJ asked.

"Everything," June replied.

It was a bit of a sore point, actually. Everyone knew the Sweetbriar Inn served the best breakfast in town, but Fran's Diner over on the other end of town was a close contender. Fran and Ned had a playful rivalry about it going on some twenty years.

June suppressed a wince. Fran was going to give her stepdad so much grief about June showing up here on her unexpected morning off.

But even June could concede that Fran's place had some

advantages. Fran's husband Vince didn't skimp on the grease. He might not make pancakes as fluffy as Ned's, but the man sure did know how to fry up some bacon.

Plus, there was the matter of June not exactly wanting to waltz a quartet of hungover ex-soldiers past her mom.

She mentally rolled her eyes at herself. Her mom didn't need to see this with her own eyes, but this was a small town. Word would get back to her quickly enough.

Whatever. Her mom was the one who insisted June not come home until noon.

Fran returned with the promised carafe and deftly poured everyone a cup. AJ put his hand over his mug. "Water for me, please."

"Oh, right." Tuck pulled a face at him. "Forgot you're on some health kick."

"Health kicks involve a twelve-pack of beer?" Clay asked.

"It was light beer," AJ said.

"Sure."

Fran got out her pen and pad. "Y'all know what you're having?"

They placed their orders in turn; AJ had his bacon with a fruit cup, which made about as much sense as saying light beer was healthy, but who was June to judge?

As soon as Fran was gone, the guys—excepting AJ—gulped down coffee like it was the elixir of life itself. June couldn't pretend she wasn't pretty desperately in need of caffeine, either. As they waited for their food, the same stream of ribbing and storytelling from the night before started up again.

Turned out, Clay and his buddies were just as funny when they were sober, even if their stories didn't tend quite so much to the absurd.

"Well, look what the cat drug in," came a saccharine voice from the open corner of the booth.

June stopped mid-laughter, glancing up.

And of course. Good flipping grief, of course.

June was in yesterday's clothes, her dress wrinkled from sleeping in it, her hair in a low ponytail. Most of her makeup had worn off or smudged, and she was pretty sure she smelled like beer. She never left the house like this.

Naturally she would run into the person who would judge her the most for it.

"Patty," June managed. "How nice to see you."

"You, too, June." Patty Boyd put her hand on the corner of the booth as if she owned it. June suddenly missed the woman simply being chilly these past few weeks. This overfamiliarity was way worse. "It's so funny, for a minute there I swore you were Elizabeth, but then I took a closer look and realized." She laughed, but it was humorless.

June knew what Patty was implying. If one of the Wu girls was going to end up at Fran's after a rough night, it was Elizabeth. That girl's decision-making skills had been a work in progress for a long time.

But only June was allowed to be frustrated by that. Anybody who wanted to insinuate anything else about her baby sister could take a long walk off a short pier.

Anybody who wanted to insinuate anything about June could do the same. Self-conscious as she might be, she was happy. Last night was the most fun she'd had in she didn't even know how long, and this morning was just as good, Riz's puke and all.

Clay put his hand on her knee under the table, silently supporting her. His touch fueled her confidence.

Didn't she get to let her hair down now and then? Be a thirty-something woman, just living her life?

June straightened her spine and put on a sweet smile. "Beauty does run in the family."

"So does keeping…interesting company, apparently." Patty flitted her gaze across the table.

June stiffened. Clay scowled, but Tuck, AJ, and Riz didn't seem to care. And why should they?

Why did June?

Before June could think of a good response, Patty raised a brow. "Reminds me of the time Elizabeth ended up here the night after prom."

Right. After Elizabeth and all her artsy friends had painted an unauthorized mural on the side of the high school. Thank goodness for Ned's smooth talking or Officer Dwight might have actually taken her in for that one.

Clay cut in. "I do dance a mean Electric Slide."

The guys laughed, and Riz did a little shimmy in his seat. "You sure do."

Patty redirected her attention. "And how are you this morning, Mr. Hawthorne?"

What, so she was talking to him now?

"Dandy," Clay said into his coffee mug.

Patty stared at him with disdain. Well, there went any thoughts that she might be being friendly.

Which was a good reminder for them all. Clay might have won over enough of Main Street for him to get his liquor license and start planning the grand opening of his bar, but Patty was still on her own side.

Clay and his friends were clearly annoyed but unashamed, and June tried her best to be, too. Patty doing her best impersonation of a cat with yellow feathers sticking out of its mouth made it tough, though.

It was all too easy to imagine how Patty might spin this.

Everyone on Main Street had been in a flutter about the motor-cycles parked outside Clay's building. Patty would find plenty of receptive ears to spread the word that Clay and June had been out with three bikers this morning. She'd probably throw in something judgy about how that was the kind of crowd the new bar would attract.

A migraine started to form behind June's temples, just imagining how worked up folks would be by the next Main Street Business Association meeting.

She was going to have to do some damage control. Remind everyone that Clay had a plan. He'd promised to respect existing businesses and their patrons.

A different kind of defensiveness rose inside her as she glanced around at his friends. Tuck, AJ, and Riz might be a little rough around the edges, but they were good people. Main Street business owners had been resisting change for so long. New folks coming through could be exactly what Blue Cedar Falls needed.

"Well, I won't keep you," Patty simpered.

Tuck smiled tightly. "Much appreciated, ma'am."

Patty frowned and put a hand to her chest, as if offended anyone wouldn't want her hanging over their table all morning.

In a huff, she stalked away. June had to give the guys credit—at least they let her get to the other side of the restaurant before they started snickering.

"Man," Riz laughed. "Bug wasn't kidding about some of the folks running this place, was he?"

"Not one bit," Clay confirmed. "Full of busybodies." But then he paused. He put a hand over June's. "But he wasn't kidding about the good stuff, either. Blue Cedar Falls is full of some pretty great folks, too."

June turned her palm over, grasping his. "Flatterer."

"But is the ice cream as good as he said?" Tuck asked.

"Better," Clay promised.

But there was something else shining behind his sea glass–green eyes. June and ice cream weren't the only things he liked about Blue Cedar Falls.

She'd spent so much time trying to convince him that this was the best small town in the world, and that it was worth fighting for. Despite Patty Boyd, it was worth putting down roots here, worth figuring the town out so he could build a bar and a business that would last.

Did he actually believe her now?

"Who cares," Riz groaned. "All I want to know is where the bacon is."

"Coming right up," Fran said, arriving with a tray piled high with the stuff.

Riz gazed up at her in awe. "You are my favorite person in the world."

"That's what all the boys say." Smirking, Fran started passing out plates.

Clay gave June's hand a squeeze before letting her go.

As he and his friends started shoving bacon in their mouths, she considered him, nibbling determinedly on a crisp slice of her own.

Patty might still have the power to make June self-conscious about herself, or about her sister's antics from a decade ago.

But June refused to let her make her second-guess her attachment to Clay. He'd come too far, both as a person and as a citizen of Blue Cedar Falls.

June was going to help him make Bug's Bar a smashing success.

No matter what the Patty Boyds of the world might have to say.

CHAPTER EIGHTEEN

W hat, you gettin' slow now you're retired?" AJ got up in Clay's face, dribbling the ball to the side without even looking at it.

"I'm not retired." He feinted one way, then darted the other to swipe the ball, and *oof* but his knee was going to be mad at him about this tomorrow—didn't matter how many stupid PT exercises he'd been trying out. "I'm a businessman."

What was he supposed to do, though? It was the third day of the guys' visit, and they'd helped him finish the bathroom reno and install new glass in the front window of the bar, not to mention helped him polish off an entire delivery truck's worth of beer, he was pretty sure. They wanted to blow off some steam, and suggested a pickup game at the park, and Clay wasn't going to let on how much that was going to kick his butt.

Not wanting them to see how messed up he was, both physically and mentally, was what had kept him from talking to them for all this time. He'd been an idiot, holding them at such a distance.

Didn't mean he didn't still have some of his pride.

Tuck moved to block him, so Clay passed to Riz, who

charged across the court and nailed a jump shot right over AJ's head. Riz whooped, and Clay pumped his fist before trudging over to where Tuck was ready to toss the ball back into bounds.

Tuck took one look at him and swiped at the sweat on his brow. "Anybody else need a water break?"

Clay narrowed his eyes at him, but Riz nodded.

All four of them headed to the bench at the side of the court where they'd left the cooler. AJ passed out drinks while Clay sat down with a wince. He side-eyed Tuck.

The guy was onto him, and it chafed. Clay didn't need to be babied. He could keep up.

Mostly.

As Clay stewed, Riz chugged his water, then pressed the dripping, cold bottle to the back of AJ's neck. AJ yelped and shot up. He chased Riz, who ran around the court, egging him on and talking crap.

Clay shook his head. He put the bottom of his own cold bottle against his knee. It felt terrible and also pretty great.

"Good to see some things never change," Clay mused, watching AJ tackle Riz to the ground and shove his face into the dirt.

"Yeah." Tuck hummed. "*Some* things."

Clay took a pull on his drink to stop himself from shooting back with something stupid. He swallowed, then restrained himself to a quiet, "You got a point to make?"

"Not really. Just a lot has changed."

"That happens when you play ball stateside instead of on base."

"You know that's not what I mean."

"Do I?"

Tuck's jaw flexed, his gaze on AJ and Riz still affectionately trying to kill each other, but his attention was all on Clay. "There's the way you're babying that knee for one thing."

"None of your concern."

Tuck shook his head. "Someday, maybe you'll see that *you* are one of my concerns, Clay."

"Don't know why."

Turning to look at him full on, Tuck scowled. "Because you're my friend, idiot. No matter how much you try to pretend you're not."

Ouch. That hit too close to home. "Hey—"

Tuck held up a hand. "I'm not trying to start anything. But a guy doesn't return your calls for the better part of a year, and you start getting a hint."

"Well, that sure explains you showing up at my door," Clay grumbled, but there wasn't any heat to it.

"A hint," Tuck continued, "that you need to take some action."

"Whatever."

Something uncomfortable squirmed around in Clay's chest. He hadn't expected to get called out like this. Maybe when they first arrived, sure, but not three days later.

"We're brothers," Tuck told him, voice low. "After the things we went through, nothing can change that." His jaw flexed. "Not your busted knee, not Bug dying, not you running away from everyone and everything, you were so hurt about all of it."

He might as well have punched Clay in the chest. His mouth opened and closed, but what was he supposed to say in response?

"We missed you," Tuck said. "We were worried about you."

Clay turned his gaze toward the distance. He'd been so busy pushing them all away so he wouldn't have to think about everything that he'd lost, he hadn't really given himself time or space to think about what it cost him.

He'd spent a year roaming around, angry and alone, but he could have spent it surrounded by his friends.

Finally, he grumbled, "I missed you idiots, too."

"We know."

Self-righteous, self-assured jerk.

Clay shoved his shoulder into Tuck's, and Tuck shoved right back. Riz and AJ seemed to take that as their cue to wander over.

Freaking setup.

Clay pointed at his own cheek, talking to Riz as he said, "You got a little something..."

Riz rubbed at the dirt on the side of his face with the bottom hem of his shirt.

"What you ladies talking about?" AJ asked.

"Nothing," Tuck said. "Just how some things change and some don't."

Riz smirked. "That mean it's open season on Clay's bar and his girl?"

Clay did a double take. "What the—"

"Because seriously," AJ agreed, "those are some changes I did not see coming."

"What about them?" Clay asked.

"'What about them?'" Riz repeated, pitching his voice to sound like Clay's, which it absolutely did not, thank you very much. "I mean, that bar."

"It is *swank*," AJ said.

"It is not."

Tuck tilted his head side to side. "It kind of is."

Clay whipped back to him, stung. "You were the one who said Bug would've loved it."

"He would've," AJ allowed. "But you do have like ten boxes of cloth napkins in the storeroom."

Clay's head started to hurt. Yeah, he did. Not just cloth napkins, either, but "cerulean" cloth napkins. June had helped him pick them out herself.

He was keeping both those facts to himself. "What? They're more environmentally friendly."

"Since when do you care about that?" Tuck asked.

Clay's temper rose. "You see any other planets for us to live on?"

"Whoa, whoa." AJ lifted his hands in front of his chest. "I'm with you." He looked around at the other guys. "But you have to admit. That wouldn't have been your first priority when you and Bug were dreaming the place up."

"It's good business," Clay said begrudgingly. "The kind of customers they get around here. They care about that stuff."

June cared about that stuff, and she'd made him care about it, too, and was that so bad?

"Look, man." Riz shrugged. "Follow your dream. I just wanna make sure it's *your* dream."

Clay glanced at each of them in turn. This was starting to feel more and more like a setup, or worse an intervention. It made him both kind of pissed and grateful at the same time.

Because he knew what this was about. "You mean and not just June's."

"She seems like a great girl," Tuck told him.

"Smoking hot," Riz agreed.

AJ nodded. "We're happy for you."

"But?"

Tuck thought about it for a second before saying, "But half the things you tell us about the bar are her ideas, or things you saw somewhere else on Main Street. If you're on board with it all, then go ahead and tell us it's none of our business. But if you're not..."

"We're just looking out for you, dude." Riz smiled.

Clay regarded his friends, replaying the last few days in his head. June had come over a couple of times, and they'd all seemed to get along like a house on fire. It had warmed his heart, honestly. June was a classy girl. How many times had he worried she'd be horrified if she knew what he and his life were like before he came to Blue Cedar Falls? The way she'd taken it all in stride had set something at ease inside him.

But the guys weren't wrong. June's insistence that he get to know Main Street and its patrons had led him to tweak a bunch of his plans. He was pretty sure those tweaks had made the bar better.

His and Bug's dream…it was still intact. It was still theirs.

It just looked a little different, was all. His buddies hadn't been here through those tough first months of getting set up and getting to know this ridiculous, beautiful, demanding little town. They hadn't felt the warmth of the way June had looked at him. The way she'd encouraged him to dig down deep and make Bug's dream even better.

If they had, they'd understand.

Right?

"I trust everything was to your satisfaction." With a flourish, June handed the departing guests a copy of their folio.

"Just lovely," the woman in the couple assured her.

June pointed at the slip of paper she'd left protruding ever so slightly. "Leave a review and enter to win a free night on your next stay."

"Thanks." The woman's gentleman companion slipped the whole kit and caboodle into the front of his bag and turned to the door.

"We hope to see you again soon!" June called after them.

The woman waved. As the door swung shut behind them, June sagged.

They weren't going to leave a review. They might be back and they might not, and none of that was the end of the world.

Or at least that was what she kept trying to tell herself.

"You sell too hard."

Sighing, June turned to find her mom at the far end of the lobby, taking pictures of the freaking cat again. And apparently observing June's interactions with the guests.

Great.

"Thanks, Mom, I'll take that under advisement."

Her mom rearranged the Sweetbriar Inn monogrammed towel around Sunny and snapped another shot. "Customers don't like it when you tell them what to do. Much more likely to return if they think it's their choice."

"Obviously it's their choice. I'm just putting the idea in their head."

Her mother pursed her lips. "If you say so."

"She's right, you know," Elizabeth said, wandering in from down the hall.

What was this, gang up on June day?

She was already in a prickly mood. Clay had been busy with his friends the past few days. She hadn't thought she'd mind. After all, she had so much to do. If anything, the extra time at home represented a great chance to get caught up on book-keeping for the inn and finalizing promotions for the Pumpkin Festival.

To her surprise, though, things at the inn were…running smoothly. Ned, Elizabeth, and her mom had everything in hand. Things with the Pumpkin Festival were in good shape, too, with her army of volunteers—and maybe a handful of conscripts—doing their jobs with only minimal supervision.

Which was great. Amazing. Fantastic, really.

So why did she have this weird, anxious, restless feeling rolling around in her gut? She was so used to everybody needing her to take care of everything that standing back and watching a well-oiled machine just *run* was...weird.

Then there was the fact she missed Clay. She missed his big arms wrapped around her, the feeling of his strong body against hers and the heat of his kisses.

She also missed talking to him. Telling him the little nothings of her day, complaining about her family and her guests, gushing about some fabulous treat Bobbi had brought over or sharing some silly thing she saw online.

She liked Tuck, AJ, and Riz. She'd enjoyed their visit, and more importantly, she'd enjoyed seeing the light they brought to Clay's eyes.

But seriously. She couldn't wait to have him all to herself for an evening.

Ignoring her agitation with it all, June asked her sister, "Everything squared away in room ten?"

"Yup. Though the next guy who walks in here with Axe body spray in his suitcase is having it confiscated." Elizabeth flopped down on one of the chairs near their mom.

June scrunched up her face. Yeah, there was a reason she'd conned her sister into cleaning up that mess. "I'm sure it was a defective bottle."

How else could that much of the stuff sunk into the fibers of the carpet?

"Don't care. It's gross, and I never want to smell it again."

"I can make a sign," their mother offered. "Extra fee for anyone with too much cologne."

June shuddered, imagining what reviewers would have to say about that. "No sign."

"I'll make it when she's at her boyfriend's," their mother stage-whispered.

She rolled her eyes, even if deep down she felt a prickle of warmth. "He's not my boyfriend."

"I'll help," Elizabeth promised.

"You are both the worst."

Elizabeth picked up one of the magazines meant for the guests and started paging through it. "How is Mr. Tall, Hot, and Surly, anyway?"

"Clay's fine."

"Clay has visitors," their mother said. "That's why June's in such a bad mood."

"I am not in a bad mood," June snapped, and yeah, okay, she heard it, too.

"Yikes," Elizabeth whispered. "When are they leaving?"

"Tomorrow," their mother said.

Elizabeth dragged a hand across her brow in theatric relief. "Phew."

June counted back from ten in her head. More evenly, she said, "I am not in a bad mood, and even if I were, it would have nothing to do with Clay. I'm just busy."

To prove it, she sat down behind the desk and opened the ledger.

As her mom and sister kept chatting, June listened with half an ear, but most of her attention was on the numbers.

Bookings for this month had been okay, if not stellar. The first check she'd written to the hospital as part of their payment plan had slipped by unnoticed, though she winced at how little it left over. Thank goodness the Pumpkin Festival was coming up soon. They had a mostly sold out house that weekend, and they could really use the infusion of cash.

It was what happened after that that was costing her sleep.

"Hey," she said idly, "anybody hear from May recently?"

Her middle sister had never sent her the itinerary for her trip. June hated having things like that up in the air.

"She liked my last photo on Facebook," her mom contributed, completely unhelpfully.

"Which one?" Elizabeth asked without looking up.

"The one where I framed it so it looked like Sunny was touching the mountain." Her mom made a cooing noise at the cat, who gave June a long-suffering look. "She takes direction very well."

Elizabeth grinned. "That was a good one."

June fought not to roll her eyes. Cat photography made her mom happy, and that was all that mattered. "That's great, Mom."

"You my only daughter who doesn't follow Sunny, you know."

Sure, because that was the real measure of her devotion. "I don't need to follow an account. I can see the cat with my own eyes."

"You just don't appreciate art," her mom said.

"Of course I do." June gestured at the walls where the inn displayed works by local painters. "Did I or did I not scoop Patty Boyd to get these watercolors in here this month?"

She was still pretty smug about that.

"Eh." Her mother tilted her head from side to side. "Would be better if they had cats in them."

"She's not wrong," Elizabeth said.

June was so done with this. Was anyone working in this lobby besides her? "Have *you* heard from May?"

"Sure. We've been binging this period drama you'd hate." Elizabeth's eyes gleamed. "You should join us sometime."

"I don't have time for a show I'd hate."

"I'll text you next time we start," Elizabeth promised.

"Just . . . tell her to call me, would you?"

"Pfft." Elizabeth shook her head. "May never calls anyone."

"She calls me," their mother said. "Once a month, like clockwork."

"Then why were we talking about pictures of the stupid cat?"

"Shh!" Her mother covered Sunny's ears. "She can hear you, you know."

June resisted the urge to thunk her head on the desk. "Mother. Next time you talk to May, will you please tell her to call me? Or ask her when she's arriving for Pumpkin Festival yourself."

"May's coming in for Pumpkin Festival?" Elizabeth asked.

June's heart did a little dip. "I think so. She said she would."

"Cool."

June turned to their mom. "She told you that, too, didn't she?"

"She said she'd try." She shrugged. "You know how her job is. Very busy."

Yeah. June knew.

May wasn't her only hope for the life of Blue Cedar Falls or the Sweetbriar Inn. Not by a long shot.

But June really, really hoped that she would come.

"Well." Elizabeth put down the magazine—on the wrong table, but June would fix it later—and stood. "Unless you have anything else you need me for, I'm out."

"Already?" June asked. She tried not to be disappointed by that.

Nodding, Elizabeth tapped at something on her phone. "Graham's doing an 'Instant Pot experiment' at the apartment, so someone should be standing by with the fire extinguisher."

June and her mom both cringed in unison. Elizabeth's long-term platonic roommate was a good enough cook, but when he went off-script things got dangerous.

"Plus," Elizabeth continued, "I have three different art classes to prep for at the community center tomorrow."

"Kids or seniors?" June asked.

"Both."

More cringing.

"You should definitely get home," their mother agreed.

"You can still come over after?" June asked, and her heart didn't leap into her throat—nope, not at all.

Elizabeth shot her a conspiratorial look. "Why? So you and your *boyfriend* can canoodle? Absolutely."

"He's not my boyfriend," June insisted. It was an automatic response at this point, and she was immune to her sister's teasing.

Mostly.

"Whatever." Elizabeth rolled her eyes. "I can be here for the evening shift."

She didn't know when Clay's friends planned to leave, but knowing she'd have free time at some point in the day was better than having none. "Thanks."

"No problem."

With that, Elizabeth kissed their mom on the cheek and headed out. June settled in behind the desk to do some more accounting. After a few minutes, her mom wandered off with her tablet and the cat.

June watched them go, smiling fondly.

Finally free from interruptions, she turned back to her work. Only it was still tough to concentrate.

Even though she knew it was ridiculous, her gaze kept drifting to the window. Her thoughts to Clay. What was he up to right now? Was he thinking about her as much as she was thinking about him? Did he get the same breathless feeling she did, imagining having some time to be alone together again?

She rolled her eyes at herself. Probably not. But she couldn't seem to keep her anticipation in check. She missed him—so much so that, for once in her life, work wasn't a viable distraction.

And that gave her pause. She'd always been so fixated on taking care of her family and the inn. Losing her focus had never been an option. Everyone relied on her.

But with Clay, it was like all her priorities were shifting. She still cared deeply about her responsibilities. Her family.

She just cared about Clay, too.

Worry and anticipation swirled around in her gut. They'd sworn repeatedly that what they were doing together was casual. But after spending a few torturous days apart, she was starting to wonder if the way she felt about him was really casual at all.

CHAPTER NINETEEN

Late the following afternoon, Clay stood outside the bar.

"Think you guys got everything?" he asked, his tone as dry as the desert they'd served in, once upon a time.

His buddies traveled light, he could say that for them. A couple saddlebags apiece strapped to their Harleys, each packed with not much more than a sleeping bag and a few changes of clothes. It wasn't that different from how he'd traveled, the year after he got out, too. He just had the back of a pickup to spread out his crap in, if he wanted to.

"Pretty sure." Tuck smirked and thumped Clay on the shoulder. Squeezing, he raised a brow. "You haven't changed your mind? We could still get you a bike if you want to come with?"

Riz slung one leg over the side of his Harley. "Or he can ride on the back of mine." He blew Clay a kiss, and Clay shook his head.

"Not this time."

He could imagine it some other time, though. Heading out on the road again. With these guys beside him, it'd be a different kind of a journey. A happier one.

A shorter one.

Because that was the funny thing. He'd wandered around the country for a year, and he hadn't ever minded it. Now, though? Setting out with no destination sounded all right for a little while. But keeping on going forever, no end date in mind, no plans to come back home?

He couldn't imagine it.

He looked past Riz putting on his helmet and AJ finishing cramming a tattered paperback into his saddlebag, at the deep blue sky above. At the magnolia trees and even the stupid eggshell-chiffon fences he'd begrudgingly come to sort of like. At the Sweetbriar Inn across the street.

Blue Cedar Falls had been a dot on the map when he first got here. A fairy tale that Bug had told him, full of both rainbows and dragons. But it was more now. He'd bought his property and begun to build something he hoped would stand the test of time. He'd put down roots, heaven help him.

This place, these people...they'd gotten their hooks in him. Even if he were to take off with his buddies on a road trip, he'd be back.

"Suit yourself." Tuck gave him one last, quick hug before striding to his own ride.

AJ gestured behind Clay, at the bar with the logo gleaming in the new front window. "Wish we could see this place when you've got it up and running."

Clay cocked a brow. "Even if it's swank?"

"Hey." Tuck held out his hands in front of himself. "As long as it's yours, we're here for it."

"Fair enough," Clay said. His throat went dry. "Just means you'll have to come back."

Tuck smiled, slow and genuine. "Suppose we might be able to arrange that."

"Heck, yeah," Riz echoed, the sound muffled through his helmet, but Clay got the point.

"Don't be strangers, then," Clay told them.

After he'd ghosted them for a year, it was a heck of a thing to say, but good friends proved they were good friends by letting that kind of thing slide sometimes.

As he watched, the guys took a minute to finish checking their gear. Tuck and AJ put on their helmets. One by one, they fired up their engines, filling the air with the sound of their roar.

Clay gave them a curt salute. Tuck nodded, gave the signal with his hand, and they peeled out. Clay kept his gaze on them until they disappeared from sight.

Then he bit down on a whole bunch of choice curse words as he limped inside.

Ignoring everything else, he made a lurching, grumbling beeline to the freezer in the bar's kitchen. Nothing else was working yet, but with the guys there, he'd been going through ice, and he was going to go through even more, now.

He filled a shop towel with cubes, then bundled it up and took it with him to the front room.

There hadn't been any more pickup games of basketball after Tuck had caught him babying his knee. Clay had stopped trying to hide the extent of his injury, too. For the most part.

But the fact of the matter was that he'd been pushing it this week, keeping up with the guys and working on the renovations with them. Now he was paying the price. In the past he would've ignored the pain and carried on, but he was trying to take care of himself or something. So. Ice.

He collapsed into one of the folding chairs set up in the front room and placed the makeshift cold pack on his knee. The shock of the ice against his skin felt like burning for a few seconds, but as he got used to it, the relief set in. He leaned back in the chair.

He really was going to miss the guys, but having this place to himself again was pretty all right, too.

But in another sign of how much had changed in the past few months, barely five minutes passed before he realized that "all to himself" wasn't quite how he wanted it, either.

Grunting, he dug his phone out of his pocket and pulled up his text chain with June. He'd seen her a couple of times here and there but never for long enough. Never alone.

His blood flashed hot at the realization of exactly how long it had been since they'd gotten some private time together. His shorts felt too tight, and even the ice on his leg couldn't stop it.

Before he could think too much into his reaction, he fired off a quick, *Guys left early. You busy?*

The reply came almost instantly. *Elizabeth's taking over for me after dinner. OK?*

After dinner? He groaned aloud. It was only a few hours, but even waiting that long sounded like torture. For a second he considered opening up his pants and sending her a picture, demonstrating exactly how little patience he had right now, but he knew better.

You're killing me, he sent instead. Followed by, *Fine*.

Because he was a grown man. He couldn't wait to get his hands on her, but he would.

Passing time while he finished icing his knee, he skimmed through the handful of messages they'd exchanged over the past few days. Just quick things. Checking in and saying good night. Talking about his plans for the bar's opening. She had *ideas*. He chuckled to himself. Didn't she always?

Something made him pause. His friends' comments about

how much his plans for the bar had changed kept coming back to him. They'd worried June was taking over, and he'd tried to explain to them that it wasn't like that.

But she really did have a lot of ideas. She'd never over-stepped, but she'd had a hand in guiding every decision about the place. Her input had helped make his ideas better. Every now and then, he had to stop and wonder if maybe that was because his ideas weren't good enough for her in the first place, though. His buddies' comments had watered the seeds of doubt.

He valued June's input. He wanted to make her happy.

He had to stand by his convictions, too, though. This bar was for him and Bug and all the people Bug would've loved to come here with, back in the day. It could be for the rest of Main Street, too, but he wasn't going to forget his reasons for being here.

Blanking the screen of his phone, he set the thing aside. He stretched his leg out straight and winced openly at the crunching sound it made.

June would be here later tonight. He could talk to her about the bar and the opening and everything else then.

Or…

He could just ignore it all and try to get her naked.

He huffed out a breath. Yeah. That sounded like a pretty good plan, too.

Where on earth was Elizabeth?

June's sister had texted an hour ago to let her know that a toddler with a paintbrush had necessitated a quick trip back to her place to change before she could come over, and that was fine. June was completely patient and calm, and holy crap, if Elizabeth didn't get here soon so June could head to Clay's, she was going to tear out her hair.

As she tidied the front desk for the thirty-second time, her phone buzzed in her pocket. She frowned at the blocked number, but she didn't think too much about it. Swinging her hair away from her ear, she answered, "Hello?"

A bored male voice asked, "Am I speaking with a… 'Limey Wu'?"

June immediately came to a halt. The mangled mispronunciation of her mother's name was never a good sign.

Nor was someone calling her personal number and asking for her mother.

"This is her daughter, June."

"I'm calling on behalf of Pine View Medical Center's billing department."

All the blood drained out of June's face.

Gripping the phone more tightly, she looked around. She lowered her voice and sank down into the computer chair. "Yes, I'm an authorized contact on that account."

The person on the phone led her through a few verification steps. Her pulse ratcheted higher with each one.

Finally, he got to the point. "All right, Ms. Wu. I'm contacting you to let you know that a portion of your mother's bill is now ninety days past due and will be forwarded to a collection agency if it is not paid in full by the end of the month."

June sat up like a rocket. "What—"

The man kept rambling about terms and requirements and penalties.

"But I thought we had a payment plan set up."

"Yes, ma'am, for a portion of the balance, however, out-of-network providers may not be included in—"

"Right." June swallowed and clenched her fists.

She listened in stony silence as the man continued telling her exactly what they owed and what the consequences would be for their credit if the bill went into collection, but nothing was sinking in.

She'd thought she'd gotten everything figured out. She'd gone through all the hoops and taken the steps she was supposed to. Things were going to be tight, especially with business falling off this autumn, but she had a plan.

Turned out, her plan was a sieve.

"Would you like me to transfer you to make a payment at this time?"

June managed not to laugh out loud. With what money? They weren't destitute or anything, but she'd stretched things to the limit, fitting the installment payments into their budget.

"No." Her voice cracked. "No, I'll have to call back another time."

"Very well." For a brief second, a flicker of humanity flared to life in the man's tone. "Take care of yourself and your mother, ma'am."

That was all June had done. That was all she was trying to do.

And she was failing.

She said a perfunctory goodbye and hung up the phone. She stared into blank space, losing time for untold minutes.

What was she going to do?

A terrified, hysterical laugh bubbled in her throat.

Before it could find its way out, the door to the family's apartment opened behind her, forcing her to pull herself together. Her mom poked out her head, and June stood, blinking furiously and working hard to put on a good smile.

Her mother couldn't know what a mess they were in. June had held her hand, there in the hospital, while tubes and wires clung to every bit of her. June had told her she would take care of everything. All her mother had to do was focus on getting better.

Her mother walking and talking—even if it was with a cane—her speech and her hand almost fully back under her control...it was a miracle. June wouldn't do anything differently. She'd sacrifice anything to keep her mom alive and well.

And she'd do everything in her power to keep her mom from ever understanding how much the sacrifice had cost.

"Elizabeth still not here yet?" her mom asked, casual, like everything was normal.

Meanwhile, June had worked herself into such an anxious state she'd almost forgotten she was waiting for her sister to come over so she could head to Clay's.

June shook her head. "She's just running a little late."

"'A little late.'" Her mom smiled, both exasperated and fond. "Where have I heard that before?"

"It's fine."

"Go, go." Her mom made a little shooing motion. "I can handle things until she gets here."

"You don't have to—"

Her mom raised a brow. "You never want to keep your gentleman caller waiting. Besides"—she gestured at the computer—"I have new high score to beat."

Before June could protest any further, her mom stole the desk chair practically out from under her and plunked herself down in it. She started up the online mah-jongg game she'd been obsessed with ever since she'd started taking shifts at the front desk again, and for a second, June saw double. It was so like life had been in the before time. Before her mom had her stroke and everything got so complicated.

June stared at her, lost. Her mom ignored her.

June could start a fight. She could insist her mom rest.

She could go into the back office and try to sort this disaster out. See if she could liquidate something or try to sell her car or get a loan to pay a loan or ... or ...

Or she could go see Clay, exactly like she was supposed to.

The idea of a few minutes to forget this new headache pulled at her with almost irresistible force. She wouldn't burden Clay with the struggles she was facing, but she didn't have to. He always took her mind off things, and if she didn't stop thinking about how she was going to pay these surprise bills, she was going to spiral into a full-blown panic attack.

Right. Going to Clay's. That was the answer. The rest she could figure out later.

In a rush of emotion, she leaned over and put a hand on her mother's shoulder. She pressed a fierce kiss to her temple.

Her mother batted her away, but it was fond. "You're ruining my game."

Why did that make her choke up?

She shook her head, straightening up and blinking the mist from her eyes. "I'll be home in time for breakfast service."

Two minutes later, she burst through the door of Clay's bar. She called his name, but then her voice got stuck in her throat.

Because there he was, standing at the very back of the space, his shirt off, his feet bare. She swallowed, taking in his shadowed jaw, the lines of muscles on his chest and arms, the hint of a V at his hips leading down, down, down. Her breathing sped up, and her pulse hammered, her skin prickling with awareness.

His gaze was just as hungry as he undressed her with his eyes. "June ..." But then something in him shifted. Some of the heat faded. "June?"

She choked on the fears and failures she'd been trying to ignore. "I'm fine."

He arched a brow. "Wanna try that again?"

No, no she didn't. But he was standing there, open and waiting and unwilling to accept her attempts to play this down, and really...

She was a mess.

"I'm not fine." How good did it feel to admit that? To feel safe to tell that to a person in her life?

"We should—" He swallowed.

They should what? Talk?

"We really should."

Instead of saying a word, she rushed him.

It had been a week since she'd had more than a fleeting kiss, and she didn't want to relive the last nine months of fear and anxiety she'd been drowning in since her mother's stroke. She wanted to lose herself.

Maybe he felt the same.

He met her halfway, pulling her into his arms, and hot need surged inside her. His skin felt like magic against her fingertips. He groaned as their bodies collided. He crushed his mouth to hers, and she opened for him without hesitation. Sweeping her tongue against his, she let him in. He tasted like sin and sex and every possible kind of temptation, and it was exactly what she needed. She felt held and safe inside his arms. She didn't have to think about anything. She didn't have to fix everything. Her worries fled her mind, chased out by the ache of desire.

"Later," he managed between kisses. "Later, we'll talk."

Her stomach did a little dip, but she nodded. "Later."

Clutching her tightly, he backed up into the hallway leading toward the stairs. When they reached the base of them, she got lost for a moment in the taste and feel of him, her palms roving over miles of hot, hard muscle.

Fortunately, he was goal-oriented.

Still kissing her, he turned her around and guided her up the stairs. He kept one hand on the railing, and he winced with the first step.

"What—" she started.

"Bum knee," he told her, voice gravel. "Been acting up."

She put her hand on his face. "Then take it slow."

His gaze met hers, searching, and she stood there, inches away from him, her chest heaving with the force of her breaths. Did he really think she'd mind him not being able to carry her up the stairs bridal style? She'd seen his scars. She didn't care.

"Okay," he said slowly.

Hand in hand, they climbed.

At the top, he stopped her. He reeled her in. She tasted gratitude and wonder in his kiss. The flame that had flickered between them roared right back to life.

Now that they were on level ground again, he didn't seem to struggle at all as he walked her toward his bedroom. The backs of her knees hit the edge of his mattress, and he kissed down her jaw, over her collarbone. With questing hands, he tugged at the tie of her dress, then pulled it off her. She shed her under-things and scrabbled at his shorts and boxers. Clothing hit the floor, one piece after another, and his mouth and hands were everywhere, but she needed more, she needed *everything*.

He pulled away from her and stared down at her. Unnamable emotion boiled in his gaze, and she wanted to look away, but how could she?

This man blanked her mind to everything. He made her feel seen and wanted. Like maybe she was enough, just existing here before him. She didn't have to do, say, or manage anything and he beheld her like she was a miracle. It took her breath away.

Before the moment could get too intense, though, he pulled her back into his arms. Kissing her hard and deep, he bore her down onto the bed. He climbed up after her, but he hissed, and she choked on a laugh. This stubborn, stubborn, ridiculous, proud, wonderful man.

She flipped them, brooking no argument. Straddling him, she devoured any protests he might have given her, reveling in the heat and breadth of him. His hands roamed her body, rough and perfect, and when he touched where she was ready and aching for him, she groaned.

He flung a hand out to the side and tore open the nightstand drawer.

The condom wrapper crinkled. He exhaled a rough breath as he rolled it on. Sheathed, he lined himself up.

And then he was there, exactly where she needed him. One hand in her hair and the other at her hip, he tugged her down. Her every nerve ignited as he filled her. She shoved a hand into the space beneath her body, touching herself where they were joined, and there was nothing in her world except him.

Even though she was on top, he guided her motions. His eyes were rough and wild, like he couldn't control himself, and she was so far past control. She let him have everything he wanted, because it was exactly what she wanted, too.

When she came, she screamed his name. He jerked her body down onto his and pulsed his own release inside her, and she closed her eyes.

She'd needed this so badly.

As she slumped over him, boneless, she breathed in deep.

If only this were all she needed in this world. If only there were nothing else she had to worry about or do.

With a sigh, she rose off him and moved to lie prone on the

bed. He dealt with the condom, and then dropped himself onto the space beside her.

"So." He was still breathless from pleasure, but there was wonder in his voice. "I missed you, too."

She blinked open her eyes to take in his handsome face, that piercing gaze that seemed to see into her and accept her.

A delirious thought materialized out of nowhere. And it was stupid. Irresponsible and impossible. She had so much to do, so many people who depended on her.

But before she could stop herself, she blurted out, "Let's play hooky tomorrow."

"Excuse you?" Confused lines appeared between Clay's brows.

"Hooky." Her heart fluttered around like a hummingbird's in her throat. "You know, you skip school, and—"

"No, no, I know what playing hooky is." With a grunt of effort, he rose onto one elbow. "I just didn't think you did."

"Of course I do." She'd never *done* it, of course. But she understood the concept. And the more she thought about it, the better the idea sounded. She'd ignored her problems for half an hour already and look how much better she was feeling. Imagine what an entire day would do.

Giddy, she rolled over onto her side. "Come on. My mom keeps telling me I work too hard. She'll cover for me." Guilt twinged inside of her, but a smile spread across Clay's face. His enthusiasm made it almost easy to push her reservations aside. "You and the guys got so much done while they were here."

She'd barely had a chance to take it all in, she was in such a rush to tear off Clay's clothes, but what little she'd seen of the progress downstairs looked great.

"I am ahead of schedule," he mused.

She reached out and interlaced their fingers. Her pulse kept hammering. Their relationship was casual. She shouldn't draw attention to the ways it was growing beyond those bounds, but she couldn't help it. "And it has been a while since we've gotten to hang out. You know. Alone."

But instead of acting put off by her forwardness, he shifted close and pressed his mouth to hers with a grin. "Twist my arm."

She could barely kiss him, she was smiling so hard.

This was such a departure from her usual way of handling things, which was to knuckle down and charge straight on through. A dozen voices in the back of her head said that was what she should be doing now. It wasn't as if she'd forgotten about the threats to send her bills to a collection agency, or that the future of tourism for the entire town was riding on the success of the Pumpkin Festival.

She just couldn't seem to bring herself to worry about it right now. Not with Clay tugging her in and deepening the kiss.

All the work she had to do would still be waiting for her.

Her conviction grew. She'd been pushing herself to the limit ever since her mother's stroke. Pushing any further might only break her. What she really needed wasn't to work harder.

It was a day off. Bright blue skies. Sunshine.

And Clay.

CHAPTER TWENTY

ust a little farther," June promised.

Clay shook his head and chuckled. She'd been promising that for half a mile now. He glanced over at her fondly. Despite the fact that they were forty-five minutes into a rocky hike down a gorge on a hot September day, she didn't so much sweat as...glisten. Instead of one of her usual dresses, she wore a tank top under an unbuttoned white camp shirt and tan shorts, and he'd never seen so much of her legs except when she was naked.

Clay fought not to get distracted by that as he mopped his brow.

When she'd brought up the idea of playing hooky for a day, he hadn't exactly known what to expect. He'd hoped for a lazy morning in bed, and he'd gotten that—had he ever. But as soon as they'd more or less recovered from the second round, June had been hopping in the shower and rattling off her whole list of things she wanted to do today. All he'd been able to do was stand back and stare, smiling despite himself. Leave it to her to have a bullet-pointed agenda for a rare day off. He probably would've just cracked open a beer and turned on ESPN.

Proving yet again what a sap he turned into around this

woman, her enthusiasm wrapped him up in her embrace, though, and he happily allowed himself to be hauled along in her wake. There was something different about her energy. Sure, she was still planning every detail of every stop they'd need to make, but she was excited about it all. After how stressed she'd seemed last night, it was a welcome change.

He didn't want to go presuming things, but a part of him hoped that he was the reason for the shift. He liked the idea of being able to help her forget her troubles. Relax, even.

"You holding up okay?" June asked. She glanced at his knee, then bit her lip.

"Yeah, mostly." One of her fifteen errands before they set out on this adventure had been to stop at the inn and grab her mom and stepdad's old hiking poles. His pride had reared up reflexively, but instead of cajoling him into using them or acting like she was babying him, she'd told him how much more stable they made *her* feel.

And really, if she was going to be using them, then it'd practically be rude for Clay not to give them a shot, too. Begrudgingly, he had to admit that they did help.

Bringing along the hiking poles was one of a dozen ways she'd subtly taken care of him today. She'd slowed him down on the stairs last night, too. Insisted on climbing on top of him when they got naked, and heaven knew he couldn't argue against that.

He still wasn't sure he loved her knowing how creaky and messed up his body was. But with every wall he lowered, every bit of his faulty inner workings he revealed to her, she never flinched.

He couldn't say he understood the reasons for her acceptance. But for the moment, he'd take it and run.

Or trudge, as the case may be.

"Okay," she said after a few more minutes, "don't laugh."

"No promises."

"But this..." She paused for dramatic effect as they turned a corner on the trail. "Is my favorite view of Blue Cedar Falls."

He looked up, away from the loose rocks and roots along the trail that had been trying to trip him all morning.

And okay. Yeah. Even he wasn't going to give her a hard time about this.

The path into the gorge had been pretty enough, taking them through piney old forests and down big stone steps looking out over rushing water far below. The trail had gradually been smoothing out for the last quarter mile or so. They were facing the way they'd come now, giving them a spectacular view of the Blue Cedar Falls.

"Wow." The falls themselves weren't all that dramatic, relatively speaking, but the white water rushing off the stone cliff above and down into the river sent spray shooting into the sky. Rainbow halos practically sparkled in the air, and the cedars growing along the path really did look blue. Above them, the sun shone with a blinding glare, scarcely a cloud to be seen.

"Better than the leaf?" June leaned into his side, and he shifted his grip on the hiking pole to haul her in even closer.

"Better than the ice cream," he confirmed.

"High praise." Her smile gleamed almost as brightly as the sun.

They stood there together for a little while. The silence probably should have been awkward, but that was one of the things he'd come to appreciate about June. She could talk a donkey's ear off when she wanted to, but she could let the silence be, too.

When he'd looked his fill, he pressed a kiss to her temple and gestured at the picnic fixings in his pack. "So should we..."

She shook her head. "There's another spot—just a few more minutes."

The cookies she'd snuck into the bottom of her own pack were screaming his name, but he could be civilized and wait. "Sure."

They took off again. It was an easy hike along the river and then back into the woods for a bit. The trail was narrower this time, almost disappearing at a few points, but she insisted she knew where she was going, and it wasn't as if he didn't have a compass and GPS, so he didn't see any reason to protest.

The trees thinned out. She led him through a gap between two big rocks that was so narrow he almost had to take his pack off to squeeze through.

"Ta-da!"

On the other side were even more big rocks, and past that a swimming hole with water so clear he could see straight to the bottom. A tiny waterfall fed into it from the far end, and the water had a gentle current leading to a creek that must flow back to the river. Sunlight filtered through the cedar branches above, providing just the right amount of shade while leaving it plenty bright.

"This is Ned's family's secret swimming hole, just so you know." June headed for the edge of one of the big flat rocks and set down her hiking poles. She dropped off her pack with a grunt before turning to him. "So if you tell anybody about it, I will have to kill you."

He mimed sealing his lips and tossing the key over his shoulder.

She started setting out the picnic she'd packed. By her standards, it was pretty chill. Some sandwiches from Bobbi's bakery, fruit and veggies raided from the Wu family kitchen, plus that container of her mom's cookies she was still pretending she hadn't brought. Clay'd packed some stuff, too—napkins, drinks. They spread them out on a blanket near the edge of the rock. Once it was all good to go, Clay plunked himself down and dug in.

Other than the heat—he was never going to get used to that, especially considering it was supposed to be fall now—it was a perfect day. He washed down a bite of awesome turkey, bacon, and pesto on ciabatta and glanced around. "So how did your stepdad find this place?"

"His family's from here," June said. "Pretty sure they've been coming here since he was a kid. Maybe longer."

"And they've kept it secret all that time?"

June shrugged. "Never seen anybody else here."

"Surprised you haven't put it on the tourist brochures."

A half smile curled her lips as she finished chewing a chunk of orange melon. "Ned gave me the same warning I gave you." She sucked a bit of juice from her fingers, either utterly oblivious to how tempting she looked or utterly unconcerned with how it affected Clay. "I know I can get pretty intense about bringing in business, but there are some parts of Blue Cedar Falls that are just for those of us who live here."

Clay hummed. "Funny. Bug always used to get grumpy about the parts of it where locals didn't feel welcome."

Understanding lit her face. "Like Main Street."

"Like Main Street."

"Well, hopefully we're changing that." She nudged his leg with hers, and he liked that "we" part a little too much. After all the doubts his army buddies had put in his head about his plans for Bug's Bar changing since he'd gotten here, it was good to be reminded that he and June were in this together now.

At least for the most part.

"How would your stepdad feel," Clay started, "knowing you brought an outsider like me here?"

June didn't so much as hesitate. "You're not an outsider anymore."

His throat tightened. He liked that idea an awful lot, too. "No?"

"I mean, Patty and Dottie might not agree." She rolled her eyes. "But I've been here for twenty something years, and they still think of me as new, so take that with a shaker of salt. As far as I'm concerned, you're one of us now. I don't think Ned would judge me for it."

It was funny—for all that June talked about her mom and sisters, she rarely brought up her stepdad except as keeper of the tools.

"You two close?" he asked, curious.

"I guess." Her mouth pulled to the side, and she reached for the veggies. She bit into a slice of cucumber and chewed on it for a second longer than seemed necessary. "He's like…a fun uncle more than a dad, if that makes any sense."

Clay had never really had either, but he nodded. "Sure. He and your mom got married…?"

"When I was in high school. They were together for a while before that, though." A soft smile stole across her lips. "Right before he popped the question was actually the first time he took us here. Think he might have been trying to seal the deal."

"Smart."

Voice warm with memory, she agreed, "Yeah." Her gaze drifted off into the distance. "He's a good guy. Loves my mom. Helps me take care of her."

Interesting, how she talked as if she still saw that as primarily her job, not her stepdad's.

"How'd he take to three teenage girls being part of the package?"

"I mean, technically, it was only two teenagers. Elizabeth was a preteen."

"Details, details."

"Important ones." She turned her neck to look at him. "Meant Ned got to experience every single one of her adolescent growing pains. The fact that he didn't wash his hands of all of us after the things she put them through..." She cringed.

Clay furrowed his brow. Huh. "Did you actually think he might?"

"No." She shook her head, smile wry. "From day one, we were family. He never gave us any reason to doubt it. Even if Elizabeth did give him gray hairs."

A raw pang fired off behind Clay's chest. His throat grated. "Lucky."

"Yeah." Her expression remained thoughtful and soft. "We were."

"I had that once." The words seemed to appear out of nowhere, taking him by surprise almost.

Her gaze darted to his, her expression open. "Yeah?"

"Yeah." He hadn't exactly meant to open up about his own experiences, but since she'd been the first to share, it didn't feel that hard to, either.

Funny how he'd started out this relationship by oversharing when his anger got the best of him. Now he was doing it because she was easy to talk to. Because she seemed to care.

"Must've been my second foster family." It definitely was, but speaking in vague terms made it hurt less. "The Thompsons. Kept me for almost an entire year. Treated me decently, gave me my own room and everything."

"What happened?"

"I was an idiot." He set down his sandwich and picked up a napkin instead. He twisted it in his fingers absently. "Got into a fight at school. Then didn't tell them about getting suspended and just roamed around town. Police picked me up." The napkin was a wadded-up ball at this point. He was half tempted to hurl it into the pond, but he wasn't quite that stupid. "They called the foster folks in, and…"

He could still see their faces, was the thing. They were so disappointed.

Clay shoved the napkin ball into his pack. "The Thompsons said it was some official something something—that they had to turn me back over to the foster system, but I think that was them being kind."

He'd screwed up. They'd kicked him out. Story of his life.

The warmth of June's hand on his took him by surprise. "That's awful, Clay."

"It is what it is."

She waited until he looked at her. Her eyes were so deep and open, he could have fallen right into them. "It stinks."

He choked on a laugh. "Yeah. Yeah, it really does, you know?"

"No one should be treated like that." There was a fierceness to her words that reached into his chest. "No one."

And heaven help him. She actually believed that. For once, her Pollyannaism didn't rub him the wrong way. He wanted to believe it, too.

What was it about this woman? She had this ability to make him consider points of view he never would have dared to a handful of months ago. She'd taken him from angry and hurting to picnicking and laughing and talking about ancient history as if it were all okay. As if *he* was okay.

As if he was enough for her.

He didn't dare imagine that was true, but she took one more look at him and threw her arms around him. He held her close, breathing in the sweet scent of her.

When she pulled away, her eyes were shining. "My bio dad. After the divorce, he walked away from us, you know."

Everything in him went silent. His heart scarcely dared to beat, and he wasn't quite sure he was breathing. Naked vulnerability was written all across her face. "June..."

"My mom kicked him out—with good reason. He was." She swallowed and licked her lips. Her gaze went everywhere before returning to his. What he saw in her eyes broke his heart. "He was awful. Mean to my mother, mean to us. You never knew what was going to set him off. He had this temper..."

Something uncomfortable opened up in his gut. He had a temper, too, and he'd let it get the best of him around her. He regretted it so badly. He reached for her hands, and she let him take them in his. He rubbed his thumbs across her knuckles in quiet apology, but this wasn't about him.

Her voice took on a far-off quality. She seemed to be staring past him. "I got these ideas in my head. Like if I just were better at this, or if I just took care of that. I'd win his approval. But it was never enough."

"June." He gripped her hands in his more tightly. "You have to know—"

Her gaze snapped back into focus. She let out a soft, sad laugh and turned her palms over inside his. "I know. It was messed up."

"One hundred percent fubar."

She laughed again. "Anyway, when my mom left him, it was a relief, honestly. I was happy to see him go, only..."

"Yeah?"

"Only he just...went." Pain simmered in her eyes. "No

argument. No custody battle or anything. So." She pulled away by a fraction and looked away. "I know it's not the same, but I guess I know what it feels like, at least a little bit. Having someone turn their back on you like that."

"Hey." He caught her face in his hand, pulling her gaze to his. "Don't act like that doesn't stink, too. He was your dad."

The guy was meant to protect her and take care of her. A low fire burned in Clay's gut. If he ever met the guy in an alley, he'd like to tell him what a huge mistake he'd made.

June was incredible. She was smart and beautiful and she cared more than anyone he'd ever met. She did so much for everyone around her.

"But I got Ned in exchange, eventually." She swabbed at her eyes and shrugged, putting on a smile.

"Sounds like you're better off."

"I am." She said it without a bit of doubt. "I mean, it was tough there for a while. Back when we were still in New York, after my dad left. Before we moved down here. It was only the four of us. I had to take care of my sisters. My mom, too." She shook her head. "The divorce messed her up."

"There you go again," he blurted out, and man, he had to watch his mouth. But it was out there now.

"What?" Lines appeared between her brows.

He couldn't keep it in. A tension had been ratcheting up inside him all this time that she'd been talking. Because he'd been connecting the dots over the past couple of months, and she'd just added the final couple of numbers. The picture he'd made stared back at him. He didn't like it one bit.

"Has it always been your job to take care of everyone?" he asked.

She frowned, like the question honestly took her by surprise. "I mean..."

"Just—" He hesitated for a second. He didn't want to overstep. But didn't she see it? "Does anybody ever take care of *you*?"

She glanced down at their joined hands. For a long minute, she was silent. Then quietly, she asked, "Does this count?"

His tongue was suddenly too thick for his mouth. He wanted to pull his hands away; his palms were sweating. But more, he wanted to pull her in and feed her ice cream or something. He wanted to never, ever let her go.

And he wanted her to have someone better. Someone who'd take care of her the way she deserved.

For now, though, she had him. He wasn't going to screw it up.

"If you want it to," he said quietly.

She looked up at him, and her expression was so hopeful it was like she'd reached into his chest and squeezed. He leaned forward, and she leaned in to meet him. He kissed her, soft and tender, feeling things he had no right feeling, but he was so far gone.

After a long minute, he released her. She bit her lip and looked up at him through her lashes, and temptation tugged at him to kiss her even deeper. One thing could lead to another as easy as could be.

Only that didn't quite seem right. Somehow, it felt more intimate to just be here, sitting in the sunshine in the middle of nowhere with this beautiful girl he didn't deserve but who seemed to enjoy his company anyway.

An hour later, June put the lid on the empty container of cookies she'd brought and tucked it in her bag. Clay had spread himself out on the blanket like a starfish, still smacking his lips and rubbing his complete lack of a belly.

She should probably get to work cleaning up the rest of the picnic, but she didn't want to.

So she didn't. With bubbles of pure freedom forming and popping inside her chest, she lay down beside him and gazed up at the puffy white clouds in the clear blue sky. If she closed her eyes, she could almost imagine floating right on up to join them, and how wild was that?

Letting go and relaxing had always been a struggle for her. There was always so much to do. People depended on her. But there was something about spending time with Clay that made it easy to take it slow for once. Instead of weighed down by responsibility, she felt light as air.

And sure, she knew a crash was coming. As soon as she got back to town, she'd have to dig into the new bills from the hospital. Between that, the normal day-to-day functioning of the inn, and the Pumpkin Festival, her to-do list was a mile long.

For some reason, the idea of getting back to it didn't fill her with dread, though.

Grinning, she kicked off her shoes and let the soles of her feet rest against the cool rock. She'd needed this day off so badly. Already, she felt recharged.

"What?" Clay asked her.

"Hmm?" She turned her neck to find him gazing at her with a warm smile on his face.

"Nothing. You look really happy, is all."

Huh. "I guess I am."

She rolled over onto her tummy and braced herself with an elbow beside Clay's head. Dipping down, she kissed him nice and slow. He put a hand on her waist, just rubbing his palm up and down her side, and heavens above, she was never going to get used to the way he lit her up inside.

Heat poured off his body as they kissed. Everything about him felt soft in a way she so rarely got to see, and it only took the heady, electric feeling inside her to new heights. Her skin buzzed, and her brain continued to soar into a new and carefree place.

With a grunt, Clay turned onto his side, facing her more fully. Their legs tangled, and warmth bloomed between her thighs.

It was blooming everywhere else, though, too. Clay's hair was damp with sweat, and he hated the heat.

And she had brought him here for a reason...

She pulled away. He tried to tug her back, but she rose to her feet.

Tingles shot across her skin as she shrugged off her camp shirt. She tucked her fingers under the hem of the tank top she'd worn underneath. Clay's eyes went wide, darkness flooding them. She tugged the tank top off and let it fall to the ground. Her shorts went next, leaving her in plain cotton underwear and a sports bra.

For a second, she was tempted to climb right back on top of Clay and finish what they'd started. Instead, she winked at him, breathless anticipation in her lungs. "C'mon."

"Wait—what?"

She was already moving toward the edge of the rock. She looked over her shoulder at him. "It's called a secret *swimming* hole for a reason, Clay."

She jumped feetfirst into the clear, calm water below. It wasn't much of a drop, and it was only ten feet deep or so, but it didn't matter. Beneath the surface, everything was cool and quiet, and she stayed submerged as long as she could hold her breath.

The muted sound of impact and a cloud of bubbles burst through the water to her side. Clay surged upward, and she kicked her feet to rise and meet him.

He greeted her with another deep kiss and wonder in his eyes, the sun gleaming off the bare skin of his chest as he pulled her in close. "What's gotten into you, June Wu?"

An immature voice in her head said *You*, and she giggled against his mouth. It wasn't funny, though. They'd had sex, yes—he'd literally been inside her this morning, but the way she felt went so far past the physical.

She brushed his wet hair from his face and wrapped her legs around his hips. "Like you said. I'm just happy."

"Good," he murmured. A flicker of uncertainty colored his eyes. "Yesterday...I was worried. You seemed..."

Right. For a second, the terrified, overwhelmed feelings she'd been battling flashed through her, but she shoved them aside. "I got some bad news. Just money stuff."

Ha. Just money.

She refused to let her worries ruin this stolen pocket of time. But Clay wasn't ready to let it go. "Everything okay?"

"It will be." For once, she could almost believe that, even.

"You sure?" His gaze searched hers. "If there's anything I can do..."

"You're doing it," she promised.

And then she kissed him again, deeper this time. She gave in to the heat of his body pressed against hers in the water, his strength holding her up. There was nothing else she needed to think about or worry about or do.

Safe in Clay's arms, she surrendered to the current, letting it take them both where it wanted to go.

CHAPTER TWENTY-ONE

One week to go until the grand opening of Bug's Bar, and Clay was starting to feel like he was driving a runaway train.

"Now remember"—Dottie Gallagher squinted at him through her bifocal glasses as she perched on one of his newly installed leather barstools—"I only told Mayor Horton I was all right with you getting your liquor license *with reservations*."

"I remember, ma'am."

"I go to bed at nine."

Right, just like June's guests. "We'll do our best to keep it down."

"You better." She jabbed a bony finger at him. "And remember—it's not only me you need to worry about. Business is so slow, everybody's grumpy."

Frowning, he glanced at the corner of the room where June was pretending not to listen while she worked on something on her laptop. She'd mentioned having money troubles the day they'd played hooky. She'd made out like it was no big deal, and there in the water on a beautiful day, he'd believed her. But ever since they'd returned to reality, she'd seemed stressed. Was that still what was bothering her?

"Thanks for the warning, Dottie."

"I mean it." Dottie dropped her hand to wrap it around the handle of her walker. Glancing out the window, she scowled. "That busybody Patty Boyd has a bull's-eye painted on your forehead in her mind."

Yup. Patty Boyd was definitely the busybody in this scenario. "I'll take it under advisement."

Dottie rambled a few more vague warnings at him, but they all boiled down to the same thing. We don't trust you, keep the noise down, Patty's going to kill you in your sleep, blah blah blah.

Ever since he'd finally gotten his liquor license sorted out, he'd thought he was done with fighting this town, but apparently it was gearing up to go another couple of rounds. In the run-up to the grand opening, a whole host of his neighbors had come out of the woodwork. Some like Bobbi showed up offering baked goods and support. Ella from the wine bar had mostly swung by to rib him and compare notes.

And then there was Dottie.

At long last, she wrapped it up. "Well, good luck to you, then, I suppose," she told him. "You're going to need it."

"Uh...thanks?"

Grumbling under her breath, she got her walker situated and slid off the barstool. He lurched ahead to open the door for her and ended up standing there like a dunce as she plodded her way over.

When the door swung shut behind her, he let out a sigh of relief. He could practically hear Bug laughing down at him, and he shot a silent glare at the sky in warning.

"I thought she'd never leave," June confided, getting up and stretching her arms over her head.

Clay nodded. "You and me both."

She wandered on over to join him as he sat back down at

the makeshift command center he'd set up on one side of the bar. Before Dottie had showed up out of the blue, the two of them had been hanging out, working, separate but together. She was doing some accounting stuff for the inn while he tried to get his own problems sorted out, and it was...Nice. Weird, but nice.

"Have a sec?" she asked.

"For you? All the time in the world."

She grinned and leaned in. "Charmer."

They shared a quick kiss, and his insides went all warm and funny.

Casual intimacy with a beautiful woman had become a regular part of his life. Who woulda thunk it?

The past couple of weeks since his buddies had left and he and June had gone on their little daytrip, the two of them had grown even closer. He was trying not to get too comfortable, though. People in his life didn't tend to stick around for long. At the moment, everything between them was hunky-dory. She was opening up to him more, and he felt like he could tell her just about anything. But he had this itching suspicion that there was more to her problems at the inn than she was letting on. And if she was keeping secrets about that, what else might she be choosing not to let him in on?

Bringing him back to reality, she laid her phone on the bar in front of him and tapped on an image. "It's a little something I whipped up when I got bored of crunching numbers."

Pulling the screen closer, he read aloud, "Sweetbriar Inn brunch special."

"Free drink with purchase of any brunch menu item," she continued. The text was laid over one of the promo graphics Lisa had done for him. The Sweetbriar Inn logo was tucked in the corner. They looked good together. "Just show a receipt from Bug's Bar. And that's not all." She flicked to the next image, which had the same branding. "We could do the same thing at the inn. Guests show their room key over here and get a couple of bucks off their bill. What do you think?"

"I think I need all the help I can get."

"Don't we all?" She laughed, but there was as much nervous energy to the sound as there was humor.

"It's a good idea. I like it."

June had been talking about a bunch of new marketing strategies, both for the inn and for his bar. Cross-promotion tie-in synergy hocus-pocus type stuff. He didn't pretend to understand it all. She seemed to know what she was doing, so he mostly stood back and left her to it.

If he occasionally heard AJ's voice in his head, telling him she was steamrolling him, well. He was pretty sure he had one hand firmly on the steering wheel, at least.

"I'll send them to the printers, and toss them up on social media."

Because she'd set up accounts for his bar on all those platforms, too.

He patted her hand. "Thanks, babe."

Apparently satisfied, she pressed a hard kiss to his cheek. He squeezed her fingers, and she stood and stretched.

"Find any good ones?" she asked, pointing at the stack of résumés he was attempting to sort through.

With a low groan, he scrubbed his hands over his face. "I don't know why I thought this would be the easy part."

June laughed and rubbed his shoulders.

Seriously, renovating a pink-on-pink-on-pink quilt shop into a good old-fashioned watering hole had seemed like the biggest obstacle to his plan, but finishing that had only been the beginning. Lately, he'd been running around like a chicken with his head cut off, sorting out all kinds of logistical crap he hadn't anticipated. Stuff he and Bug had never so much as thought about, nights they'd spent under the stars on watch, dreaming up this harebrained scheme. Now he had menus to create and staff to hire and suppliers to figure out deals with and bookkeeping software to learn, and at this rate, he was going to need ibuprofen for more than just his stupid knee.

"You doing more interviews tomorrow?" June asked.

"A couple."

He'd already gotten a cook and a few waitstaff, but most of those had been through word of mouth. Stephanie from the hardware store had a brother, and Tracy and Duke knew a guy, and June had even had a friend of a friend of a friend's cousin she'd been able to send his way. He was grateful for all of them, because practically everyone who'd responded to his ad in the *Chronicle* was wildly unqualified.

Seriously. Who put video game levels defeated on their résumé under "Relevant Experience"?

"Finding good people isn't easy," June reminded him, "but it's worth it."

As she was saying it, a quick knock sounded on the front door. Han strode in without waiting for so much as a holler in return.

"What's that about good people?" he asked, heading over and setting a cut-open liquor box full of takeout on the bar.

"That there aren't any," Clay complained. As he went around to the other side of the bar to get plates and silverware, he looked to Han. "Can you believe some kid interviewed for a busboy position thinking he was going to drive a bus?"

"Yup." Han didn't miss a beat. "You need a server or a hostess? My little sister Zoe might be looking for something."

"Yeah?" Clay narrowed his eyes. "Wait—why's she not working for you?"

Family restaurants were usually staffed by just that. Family. Right?

Han let out a sound of pure frustration. "She has, like, forever. But she just got home from college, and she and my mom are going to kill each other if they're cooped up at the restaurant together all day. Girl's good, but she needs to go somewhere else."

"College, huh?" That drove up the salary.

"She's 'trying to figure out what she wants to do with her life.'" Exasperation colored Han's tone. "She'll work for cheap, if that's what you need. But she also won't stay forever."

Clay could live with that. "Tell her to stop by tomorrow."

"Will do."

Clay set out plates for himself and June, then held up a third. "You wanna stay?"

Han checked his phone. "Maybe for a minute."

Clay put out a plate for Han next to his own on the bar. June started unpacking food when her phone went off. She put down the container of whatever pork dish she'd ordered from the secret "I can speak Mandarin" menu—her words, not his—and took out her phone.

Her eyes lit up. "Sorry, I have to take this."

Clay snatched the takeout carton from her. He might not speak Mandarin, but he knew good food when he smelled it. "Everything okay?"

"Yeah." She was already headed toward the rear exit, which was fine. She could have her privacy. "It's just my sister."

Excitement lifted her voice.

Han stood up. He opened his mouth, then closed it and sat back down.

Clay frowned at him. "What?"

"Nothing. Just." He shook his head. "May," he said by way of explanation, and oh right. His ex.

Without a word, Clay turned. He'd only gotten one tap set up so far, but that was enough. He grabbed a pint glass and filled it to the brim. He slid it across the bar to Han. Out of respect for his sad friend, he resisted the impulse to fist pump. He and Bug had always talked about how cool it would be to do that slick kind of move.

He leaned on the bar. "You wanna talk about it?"

Han caught the beer and drained a quarter of it in a go. Setting it down, he swiped his wrist across his mouth. "Not even a little."

"May, hi," June breathed into the phone. The back door to the bar swung closed behind her. The sounds of Clay and Han talking disappeared, replaced by the breeze and the rustling of the first autumn leaves.

She clutched the phone to her ear.

"Hey," her sister replied. Her voice crackled over the mediocre reception. People were talking in the background; she was probably on her way out of the office.

It didn't matter. June hadn't heard her sister's voice in ages, and the mere sound of it soothed something in her soul.

Growing up, May and June had been two peas in a pod. June was barely two years older. They'd been sisters, playmates, confidantes. There'd been a bigger gap between Elizabeth and May.

May and June...they understood each other. They were old enough to remember their father's unpredictable temper.

They were old enough to remember watching him walk out the door.

June may have become the second-in-command that day, but May was her lieutenant. June directed operations, and May executed her plans. Together, they took care of their mother, the apartment, the baby.

They took care of each other, after their mother uprooted them and brought them to this town where it felt like no one looked like them or sounded like them. Sure, there were the Leungs, but that was about it for Asian Americans in the area. While the Wu family was generally welcomed into the fold, those first couple of years were tough. May and June got each other through.

June thrived here. She fell in love with the rhythms of the place. She decided to stay and keep taking care of her mom and stepdad and Elizabeth and their inn.

While May...

May never fully settled in. She struggled socially. She may have had Han as her boyfriend, but she never found her Bobbi. Instead, she found bullies who made her life difficult at every turn.

When she chose to leave for college, June sent her off with hugs, kisses, and weekly care packages.

Only May never came back.

She visited for holidays when she could, of course. But she found her passion for writing about far-away, fantastical destinations. Her career took off.

June was proud of her little sister.

And sometimes she missed her so much it hurt.

"Hi," she said again, bumbling. She hadn't been prepared for this.

"Mom said you wanted to talk?"

"Yeah. I mean. I did. Yes." June covered her face with her hand. "Thanks."

"Sorry it took me so long." The background noise shifted from muffled voices to honking horns and New York traffic. "Things here have been ridiculous."

"Yeah?"

"New parent company. Again. You know how it is."

Barely, but June wasn't going to pick a fight today. "You think you're going to be okay?"

"Probably, but it's hard to say. I have half the budget and twice the number of articles to write, so yay."

"Ouch."

"Things okay there?" May had a way of asking that kind of question that made it sound less like an opportunity to catch up and more of a way of directing June to get to the point.

Which. Right, sure, of course. June had sicced their mother on May. This wasn't a purely social call.

June gripped the phone tighter. If only.

June had Clay and Mom and Elizabeth and Bobbi and so many people in her corner, but there was no one she could talk to about some of the things that were going on right now.

The dire financial situation she was in, for one.

The new bill she'd been made aware of a couple of weeks ago was a doozy. Every second she hadn't spent running the inn or midwifing the Pumpkin Festival or helping Clay with the bar she'd spent on the phone with medical billing departments, trying to figure out how the bill had been missed in the first place, or if she could roll it into the rest of the debt—or if she had any options at all.

It felt like the walls were closing in. If she couldn't get this sorted out soon, she didn't know what she was going to do.

"Things are okay," she said, hedging. She'd tell May all

about this when she came to visit. Maybe she'd have some ideas. "I just wanted to ask about when you were coming in for the Pumpkin Festival. I can't find an itinerary."

"Um."

June's heart sank into the floor. "May."

"I know, I know, but it's like I said. Things here are a mess. In another few months when things are sorted—"

"I don't have a few months," June snapped, and she wanted to grab the words and shove them right back into her mouth.

"What?"

"I mean." She paced over to the wall of the building and dropped her forehead to lean against the brick. "Pumpkin Festival won't be here in a few months."

"I know, but—"

"I really wanted you to see it. It's going to be great this year. We even got the guy who carves the big ugly faces on the giant pumpkins. Remember?"

"Of course."

"And we're dunking Principal Hardy and Officer Dwight." June was grasping at straws here.

May laughed. "Elizabeth must be thrilled."

"She's going to make the whole festival solvent, she's already bought so many tickets." June swallowed, turning around and putting her back to the wall. She stared up at the sky, desperate. "Please, May. Please come. You promised."

"I said I'd try."

June closed her eyes.

Okay. Okay, fine, May wasn't coming. There'd be no big article in some fancy magazine.

There'd be no hashing out how to fix the giant gaping hole June had put the inn at the very bottom of.

"I'll make it up to you," May swore.

June blinked. She swallowed down the petulance that wanted to rise into her voice. "You better."

"I will. I swear." May paused for a second. "Look, I have to go. We'll talk again soon, okay?"

"Sure."

"Okay." May hesitated. "Bye, June. I really am sorry."

"I know you are."

That was kind of the worst part.

They said their goodbyes, and May hung up.

She lowered the phone from her ear.

For a minute, she stood there, numb.

May wasn't coming to save her.

She wasn't going to write an article about Blue Cedar Falls or the Pumpkin Festival or Clay's bar or the inn.

It was like the highway opening all over again, cutting the town off. Only this time, June was the town. May hadn't been her last hope, but she had been her best one.

All those bills. This tourist town that was no longer on the way to anywhere, that no one had to go through for anything. Her mom.

They were her responsibility.

And no one was coming to help.

Digging her nails into the palms of her hands, she straightened her spine. She was not going to wallow in self-pity about this, no matter how tempting that might be.

Instead, she pocketed her phone and put on her game face. She headed back into Clay's bar with a tight smile. Han raised a brow at her, a nearly empty pint glass in front of him.

He frowned. "I was going to ask you how May's doing, but looking at your face, I'm pretty sure I know."

"She's fine," June said in a clipped voice. She fixed a plate for herself, banging the spoons too hard. "Chopsticks?"

Clay grabbed her a set from inside the box, and she tore the wrapper off.

"Fine-fine?" Han asked. "Or May-fine?"

"May-fine?" Clay crinkled his brow.

Han finished his beer in a final gulp. "Trust me, it's a thing."

"How about 'too busy with her own life to notice that the people around her need her' fine?" June said briskly.

Clay blinked. "Uh..."

"Yeah." Han's Adam's apple bobbed. "So May-fine, then."

A dark shadow colored his gaze, and for a second, June felt for him. She didn't know exactly what had happened between him and her sister all those years ago, but she knew it had been tough on both of them. May was her sister, so June would always be on her side, but Han had been the one to stay behind. The one who was duty-bound to take care of his family, no matter the cost.

So, yeah. June could kind of see his side, too.

Clay cleared his throat. "So...?"

"So nothing," June said firmly. She scooped up a bit of mushroom and rice with her chopsticks.

"Nothing," Clay said dryly.

"Nothing." June popped the bite into her mouth and chewed. She put her chopsticks down with intention.

May wasn't coming. Whether that was May-fine or fine-fine was beside the point. So were Han's feelings.

So were her own.

Nudging her plate aside, she reached for Clay's notepad.

Enough fun and games. Enough reminiscing about the past. *More* than enough hoping someone would come along and help her out.

She still didn't know how she was going to save the inn, much less Blue Cedar Falls.

So she threw herself into work she did know how to do.

"Now," she said. "What other ideas do we have to make sure this bar's opening is a huge success?"

CHAPTER TWENTY-TWO

❖ ❖ ❖ ❖ ❖ ❖ ❖ ❖ ❖ ❖ ❖ ❖

This was a terrible idea," Clay grumbled under his breath, hanging up the last poster on the wall.

"You can do it, boss." Zoe patted him on the back as she zipped by him, chipper as could be, and it didn't make him want to get in his truck and drive to Alaska. Nope, not at all.

He glared at her as she set out rolls of silverware at the half dozen tables scattered around the front room. Grudgingly, he had to admit that Han had been right. His little sister was a good worker, as annoyingly upbeat as she was. He hadn't had to train her at all. She just walked in in a jean skirt and a T-shirt and started setting the place up.

He was lucky to have her, honestly.

Because everything else was a freaking mess.

With less than an hour to go before Bug's Bar's grand opening party, he was down a keg of IPA, his dishwasher had called in sick, and the signature menu item of cheese fries with gravy was lacking *cheese*. June had ordered flipping flowers to put at the tables, and he didn't have anything to put them in. The flyers he'd been supposed to hand out on the north side of town had never come back from the printers.

Worse, he kept looking at the cerulean napkins and hearing his army buddies' comments in his ears. Would Bug actually like any of this?

He scrubbed his eyes until colors spread like fireworks across the insides of his lids. "What were we thinking, Bug?"

But Bug didn't answer, because of course he didn't.

Grinding his teeth together, he checked to make sure the poster was hung straight. All the physical therapy exercises in the world couldn't compete with how much trudging up and down stairs and ladders he'd done the past couple of days. His knee groaned, and he clenched his jaw harder.

The poster was good enough. Who even cared? No one was going to come. He'd eat his cheese-free cheese fries with his friend's little sister alone.

Okay, fine, June would come. Wild dogs couldn't keep her away. Maybe Han, too.

But that was it.

Zoe disappeared into the back again, doing who knew what, and Clay stalked toward the bar. He grabbed the bottle of ibuprofen he'd strategically stashed under there, shook out a couple, and swallowed them dry. His battle injury flaring up hadn't helped matters as he'd rushed around trying to get everything ready. He hadn't been sleeping right, a combination of nerves and pain, and even when he did pass out, he had nightmares about Bug, about blood, about June realizing what a mess he was and walking out on him, and it was all pushing him toward a brink.

Zoe returned with a full dish tub balanced between her hands. "What are you—?"

She set the tub down and produced an empty beer bottle, except it wasn't empty. She'd half-filled it with water and made a little bouquet out of the stupid flowers June had sent and some drink umbrellas and—was that a fork with a Bug's Bar coaster taped to its tines?

"What—"

"Oh come on, they're cute," she insisted, and she...

Was right.

"Fine, fine," Clay grumbled. That was one problem solved, he supposed.

The door swung open, and he turned toward it, ready to tell whoever it was to go away, but it was Han carrying a keg of IPA. "Got it," he grunted.

"How—"

"Called in a favor, now where do we get this hooked up?"

"Downstairs," Clay started.

But then more people came in after him.

A kid he didn't know—maybe eighteen at best. The kid grinned. "Hey, I'm Kenny, Marty's brother. He got a call from June and said you needed a dishwasher?"

"Uh..."

Bobbi and Caitlin strode in the back door. "Okay," Bobbi said, breathless, "we handed out the flyers all over town."

Clay frowned. "You what?"

"June got them from the printer an hour ago and told us you needed help," Caitlin said.

He couldn't even muster the energy to protest, he was so taken off guard. "Um. Thanks."

"So what do you say?" the Kenny kid asked. "You want me or not?"

June charged in the front door. She held up two shopping bags in triumph. "I found cheese!"

Because of course she had.

Clay looked around at all of them. These friends he'd made here in this town.

This woman who had rallied them together. Who'd shown up for him.

And who was staring at him like this hadn't been a hassle at all. Like she was happy to help, and he was so grateful, he could barely stand up straight. He gazed at her through eyes gone blurry, and she stared right back as if she could hear every ridiculous, sappy, idiotic thought floating through his brain. Especially the ones he couldn't say out loud.

"Okay," he managed. "Okay, yeah."

Nobody might show up. This whole thing might be exactly as much of a disaster as it had looked like five minutes ago. But if everything went pear-shaped, at least it wouldn't have been for a lack of trying.

He rubbed his hands together. "Let's do this."

Holy crap. They'd really done this.

June paused for a minute to take it all in.

The party at Bug's Bar was *raging*. Two hours in and new people were still arriving. Half of Blue Cedar Falls had shown out, not to mention a whole crew of folks she didn't know who must've driven in. Her and Clay's and all their friends' hard work had paid off.

Thank goodness.

She'd been running around like a chicken with her head cut off today, taking care of the usual business at the inn and getting an extension on the due date for her medical bills and trying to gather the troops and play whack-a-mole with Clay's whole series of preopening disasters. How many favors had she called in? How many friends had pitched in and helped out?

She gazed out over the sea of people, pride overwhelming

her. She'd told Clay this town came through for people. There
was no better place in the entire world to be than Blue Cedar
Falls, North Carolina.

She glanced over at him. Tending bar and smiling in
a way she'd only seen him smile with his army buddies
before, he was starting to look like he finally understood. He
poured beer and hollered orders to the kitchen and chatted
with everybody who came through like they were lifelong
friends.

Her throat went tight. Seeing him live out his dream touched
something deep inside her.

And to think. When he'd first arrived, he'd told her to her
face she wouldn't like him. She wouldn't like anything he was
trying to build. It wasn't for her.

She'd had her doubts, too. To some extent, she still did. A
dive bar on Main Street shouldn't work. The soundproofing
he'd installed was pretty good, but as the party grew, how
would her guests at the inn respond?

She supposed she'd find out.

For now, what mattered was that Clay had realized his
vision of the bar, blending the things Bug had told him with
the things that mattered to him and the things that mattered to
Main Street. She hoped he was as happy with the results as
she was. Sure, there were rough edges that needed refinement.
Kinks to be worked out; she wished he could have hired and
trained his staff earlier.

But this was a soft opening. Getting the mix perfect was
never going to happen on the first night. By the time the
Pumpkin Festival kicked off in a couple of weeks, everything
would be running smoothly.

Right?

As she stood there, nursing a glass of chardonnay she'd

managed to convince him to put on the menu, the crowd continued to grow. It had spilled onto the sidewalk and even into the street here and there.

Nervously, she glanced out the big front window. People on Main Street weren't used to loud parties.

An erratic mix of hair metal and twanging country music played on the jukebox. Groups sang along and danced, and the louder they got, the louder everyone else got just to be heard over them.

The last thing they needed were the neighbors who had looked down their noses at Clay when he'd made his case to the business association showing up and telling them to turn it down. Dottie Gallagher had come by to remind Clay about her "reservations" again yesterday, and who knew how Patty Boyd would react.

She chewed the inside of her lip. Maybe this whole thing had been *too* successful. They should have shot for a smaller opening. Fewer people. If the kitchen ran out of food or the taps dried up, no one was going to be happy.

"Why the long face?" Bobbi drawled, coming up behind June and slinging an arm around her shoulder.

June smiled and shook her head, looking at her friend fondly. "Just keeping an eye on things."

Caitlin stood on Bobbi's other side. She waved a hand, her body language almost as loose as Bobbi's. "Relax."

"Throwing a party this good takes a lot of work, you know."

"Work, work, work." Bobbi rolled her eyes and leaned her head on June's shoulder.

When June delicately shrugged Bobbi off, she rolled her head to the other side, letting it rest on Caitlin's shoulder, and Caitlin wrapped an arm around her. Instinctively, June glanced around, but nobody seemed to be looking.

The song on the jukebox changed to a real eighties head-banger. Straightening up, but not putting any distance between herself and Caitlin, Bobbi whooped and downed the rest of her cocktail. "I love this song!"

"You have the worst taste," Caitlin told her, but her eyes were shaped like hearts.

"Come on, June!" Bobbi grabbed June's hand and Caitlin's, too, dragging them toward the center of the room. "Remember those dances in junior high?"

"Despite all my best efforts to forget."

"Party pooper," Bobbi yelled.

Other people were getting into it, too. Funny Bobbi would bring up junior high school dances, because it was starting to look like one of those in here.

On a makeshift dance floor in the center of the bar, a whole crowd had gathered, some of them so many sheets to the wind, they made Bobbi look sober. Bobbi joined right in with them, hopping up and down and playing air guitar, her blond hair whipping around. Caitlin laughed and danced right up into her, and June bit her lip.

June reached for Bobbi to try to get her attention, remind her she was in public here, but she got a face full of hair for her trouble. She staggered back and bumped directly into Han and a couple of his friends.

"Oh hey, June." Han caught her by the shoulders to keep her from crashing into his buddy Devin.

"Hey. Sorry," she said to Devin, not that he seemed to notice. She followed his gaze to Han's little sister Zoe, who was carrying a platter of food out toward the front.

Han didn't seem to notice his buddy's wandering eyes, and June certainly wasn't going to draw attention to them. "Having fun?" she asked.

"Heck yeah, this is amazing."

"It's pretty great, right?" June agreed, though deep down, the worry in her gut was only growing.

Then someone at the pool table stepped back and right into Zoe. She yelped, and Devin stood up straight.

June rushed forward, pushing her way through the dance floor, past Bobbi and Caitlin who were still *way* too cozy.

The guy who'd accidentally knocked into Zoe apologized, shoving a napkin at her chest, but she batted him away.

"You okay?" June asked.

"Fine, fine." Zoe kept walking, taking her tray out the open door.

June followed her, ready to steer her toward the kitchen. Zoe's shirt was soaked in beer—did she even realize how it was clinging to her?

But outside, the crush was just as ridiculous.

"Zoe," she called, as the girl headed to a crew of people assembled under a tree. Was that one of the tables from Bobbi's bakery they'd commandeered?

Whoever's it was, Zoe passed out drinks and apps with a smile, collected money and made change from her apron without so much as breaking stride. She turned around with a couple of credit cards in hand.

But Han and Devin had apparently followed them both out, because they were right there.

"Come on, Zo." Han reached for her at the same time Devin did.

"I'm fine, you idiots," Zoe told them. "Let me work." She pushed her brother away, but when her hand grazed Devin's, she glanced away, her cheeks pink, and Devin's Adam's apple bobbed, and oh wow, this was going to be a thing.

Oblivious, Han tried to pull her away. "I've got an extra shirt in my truck."

"I told you, I'm fine."

"Hey," a familiar, raspy voice shouted. "Hey, can we get some service here?"

June turned to find Patty Boyd raising an empty margarita glass in the air.

One of her perfect, asymmetrical-haircut friends did likewise with a beer mug. Belching loudly, she shouted, "Beer me!"

June's eyebrows hit her hairline.

Zoe called, "Be right there."

Han tried to block her way, but she pushed past him, hissing something June couldn't hear.

She stalked away, and Han smacked his forehead, leaning into Devin. "Everyone can see my baby sister's boobs," he groaned.

Devin looked about ready to groan himself. He made to follow Zoe, but before he could get far, tires screeched as a car pulled up to the curb right in front of them.

June jumped back with a yelp. What idiot was driving?

The driver's side door swung open, revealing none other than Dottie Gallagher. Her husband got out behind her and went around to the trunk to get her walker. Two of her senior citizen friends shoved their way through the crowd like football linebackers, and June darted out of the way as alarm bells rang in her head. Where was Clay? Someone had to warn him.

She snuck her phone out of her pocket and sent him a quick SOS text.

"You people need to go home," Dottie shouted, grabbing her walker and using it to push people out of her way. "People are trying to sleep."

"Oh, shut up." Patty put herself right in Dottie's path. She was staggering, her face red and her makeup just short of perfect.

"Get out of my way, Boyd."

"Make me." Patty swung her hands to the side. Her margarita glass must not have been quite empty after all, because a splash of it went flying.

One of Dottie's friends shrieked and lurched backward, jostling Zoe again, who barely kept her feet.

"You kids and your loud music and your booze," Dottie yelled. "What's the matter with you?"

"Us?" Patty pointed to herself in absolute outrage. "What's the matter with *us*? You're the one who let this bar open in the first place. I'm just here enjoying it."

Dottie lifted the front legs of her walker menacingly. "I said I approved *with reservations*."

"Ooh." Patty mimicked Dottie. "'Reservations.' I'm sure that had everybody shaking in their boots."

"Used to be people respected their elders in this town."

"Hey, hey." Clay emerged at June's side. "What's all the fuss?"

What on earth was he grinning about? Didn't he see how close this was to spiraling out of control?

"Like you respected Uncle Ray back in 'ninety-nine?" Patty hurled.

Dottie bared her false teeth. "Don't you speak his name."

June whipped her gaze around, desperate for a solution, only she couldn't think of a way to tear these two apart, and Clay was just watching the show. "You have to do something," she implored him.

"Are you kidding?" He shook his head. "I've been waiting to see these two go at it since the first Busybody Association Meeting."

June gaped at him, but she didn't have time to concentrate on his callousness, as Bobbi and Caitlin appeared on the scene.

Bobbi tugged on June's sleeve. "What on earth is going on?"

"I have no idea," June muttered, faint.

"Whoa, watch out," Caitlin warned.

One of Patty's friends had grabbed one of Dottie's friends' canes. They wrestled with it, shouting at each other.

"You're the reason Main Street is *dying*," Dottie yelled at Patty. "Your stupid gallery."

"Like your flower shop brings anybody in."

Dottie swung her walker wildly toward Patty, who put her arms up in self-defense. Dottie geared up for another shot, pitching the contraption in the other direction. Clay was shouting something at Han, not paying attention. Before June could cry out to warn him, the tennis balls on the bottom of the walker caught him square in the leg, and he yowled, crumpling.

"Clay!" June dove for him, shoring him up. His face had gone pale.

"I'm fine," he choked out, staggering away, but he was limping.

"Your knee—"

"Had worse."

Patty grabbed Dottie's walker, but Dottie wasn't letting go of either it or their grudge.

As they grappled, Dottie swore, "The *Chronicle* says my flower shop is a gem!"

"Bobbi?" a shocked voice gasped.

June's breath caught.

Because right there on the sidewalk stood Tracy and Duke. Tracy had her hand over her mouth. Duke's gaze was thunderous.

Bobbi pulled away from Caitlin, who she'd apparently started kissing in the middle of all this chaos. "Mom?" Her voice trembled. "Daddy?"

"You—" Tracy sputtered. "She— How—"

"Mom, Dad, I—"

"Let's go, Tracy." Duke shot Bobbi a glare. "We'll see you at the house first thing in the morning, young lady." His jaw flexed. He shifted his gaze to Caitlin. "Alone."

Caitlin reached for Bobbi, but she pulled away.

"Look," June started, but Bobbi kept calling after her folks, and Caitlin who was usually so stoic looked like she was about to cry.

On June's other side, Dottie screeched, "Your gallery is crap."

Letting go of her walker, she picked up a full pitcher of margaritas and threw it at Patty.

Only Patty ducked, and the entire thing sloshed everywhere. June gasped as frigid liquid soaked the skirt of her dress.

"Enough!" Clay shouted. Finally taking this seriously, he reached for Dottie and Patty as they lunged at each other.

And that was when Officer Dwight showed up.

CHAPTER TWENTY-THREE

$\diamondsuit$ $\cdot$ $\diamondsuit$ $\cdot$ $\diamondsuit$ $\cdot$ $\diamondsuit$ $\cdot$ $\diamondsuit$ $\cdot$ $\diamondsuit$ $\cdot$ $\diamondsuit$ $\cdot$ $\diamondsuit$ $\cdot$ $\diamondsuit$

Have a good night, now, June." Officer Dwight closed up his notepad and stowed it in his pocket.

"Thanks. You, too." Numb, June turned away from him.

Lou Ellen Page from the *Blue Cedar Falls Chronicle* stood on the corner, her voice recorder pointed at Zoe, and it was all June could do not to run over there and tear it out of her hand. It was no use, though. The only thing that could make this evening worse was ending up on record assaulting a reporter.

A hysterical fit of laughter formed like soap bubbles in her mouth. She swallowed them down, and they were bitter, but they didn't leave her feeling any cleaner.

The past hour had been a nightmare. Officer Dwight showing up had set off all kinds of chaos. Half the crowd had tried to buy him a beer while the other half had seen his arrival as a sign to get out of Dodge, knocking over tables and chairs in their haste. After giving him an earful for taking so long to show up, Dottie had tried to get him to arrest Patty; she did that a few times a year anyway, so it wasn't anything new, but she came closer this time than most.

Officer Dwight had dispersed the crowd pretty fast after that. Among them, Bobbi and Caitlin. An echo roared in June's ears. She could still hear Bobbi calling her mom and dad after they'd turned from her, could see her face falling as Caitlin gathered her in her arms and steered her away.

June looked around, her vision blurring.

The front window of the bar had been shattered when Patty Boyd had tossed a chair—June was a little hazy on the details there, but Han swore he'd seen it with his own eyes. The big wooden sign Clay had carved had fallen and split in two. Everywhere, empty bottles and glasses and plates had been scattered. The sidewalk ran amber with beer. Cheese stains from an overturned pile of house special fries dripped down the fence, marring what had once been a perfect paint job.

How on earth had this all gone so wrong?

Or was it just that it had all gone exactly the way everyone on Main Street had told her it would?

From the minute Clay moved into this building, he'd been clear about who he was and what he wanted. He'd told her to her face she would hate his bar. When she'd raised her concerns, he hadn't seemed to care if his actions hurt every single business on Main Street.

Over the course of the past few months, she'd thought he'd changed his mind. Through his words and deeds, he'd shown her and everybody else that he was willing to expand his vision and really become a part of the community. But his indifference to tonight's party descending into chaos had rocked her. She wanted to believe the best of him. She wanted to believe that together they could fix this, but how?

Lou Ellen finished up with Zoe and traded her voice recorder for the camera hanging around her neck. She started snapping shots of the squad car, the overturned tables and spilled pitchers. Instead of showcasing the great job Clay had done rehabbing the place, all the pictures tomorrow would be of this mess. Compounding matters, the Sweetbriar Inn would be in the background of half the shots, and there was nothing June could do about it. If it was possible, her heart sank deeper.

Was it only a handful of weeks ago that June had pictured Clay's reenvisioned bar becoming a highlight of the story she was going to get May to write to drum up tourism for the town?

Ha. Forget a profile in a glossy travel magazine.

Instead, Clay's bar was going to be front and center on the first page of the morning news.

Lou Ellen got into her minivan and immediately started talking on the phone with someone. Through the open window, her voice carried. "Oh yeah, Frank, I got everything. You're not going to believe—"

She backed up, and June took a step forward.

The crunch of the van's rear bumper hitting the sign in front of the Sweetbriar Inn echoed across the street.

"Hey!" June shouted.

But Lou Ellen was still talking on the phone. She didn't hear. June jogged out to the curb, yelling at her, waving her arms as Lou Ellen drove off, one of June's mother's rosebushes dragging from the van's bumper. June took another step after her, but the blaring siren of Officer Dwight's cop car drowned her out. She jumped out of the way as the cruiser careened off into the night.

Once it was safe, June strode across the street, her vision blurring. She knelt on the ground and cursed beneath her breath. Splinters covered the walk. The roses hadn't been in bloom, but it didn't matter. Half a dozen branches had been ripped out. Tire tracks tore across the lawn.

The front door to the inn creaked as it swung open.

Two harried, middle-aged white people stormed out, suitcases in hand.

June's mother chased after them, dressed in a bathrobe, clutching at her cane. "We make it up to you," she called.

The man from the couple spat back, "You can make it up to us with a full refund."

"Honestly," his wife cried. "We came here for some peace and quiet, and we got this!"

She gestured all around, and June followed her gaze, taking in the mess. The ruined landscaping and the broken signs. The scattered groups of bar patrons still dispersing and the faint strains of music playing from across the street.

June started to go after them. That was what she should do. Her mother was great at managing the inn, but June was the customer service pro these days. She could try to smooth things over.

But could anything really make this right?

"Be sure to leave good review!" her mother shouted.

June covered her face with her hands. When she looked up again, it was to find her mom giving her the thumbs-up sign, and it was all she could do not to actually break down in tears.

Her mom headed back inside, thank goodness. June watched their departing guests lug their suitcases to the lot behind the inn. They hadn't been kidding about that refund, and if she didn't want them taking her mother up on her request that they leave a review, she was probably going to have to give it to them, too.

This fall had been make-or-break for the family business. She'd had one last chance to pay down enough of the new batch of medical debt to keep the collection agencies out of the picture.

What was she going to tell her family?

How much longer could she keep their impending disaster to herself?

How would her mom's and Ned's faces fall once they knew? If Elizabeth had pulled a stunt like this, maybe they could have written it off. But June? Who'd promised them that she'd take care of everything? The responsible one who all of them trusted?

Furious tears filled her eyes. Her chest tightened like bands of iron around her ribs.

It couldn't come to that. She wouldn't let it.

Across the street, shattered glass clinked. She jerked her gaze up and spotted Clay with a dustpan and a broom, whistling, *smiling*, and something threatened to crack inside her. Didn't he have any concept of how monumental of a catastrophe this had been?

Despair crashed over her, but fire flooded her veins in its wake.

This always happened. She let down her guard for one minute. She minded her place, stepped aside, and let somebody else handle all the details, and everything went off the rails.

Well, not anymore. She was going to have to take the wheel here.

And pray to anyone who was listening that she could steer this flaming wreckage back on track.

What a disaster. Clay whistled to himself as he swept up the shattered glass from the front window.

An amazing, fantastic disaster.

"Good grief, Bug," he muttered under his breath.

All night, Bug's Bar had been hopping. It had been like something out of his dreams, plucked straight from the stories he and Bug would tell themselves out in the desert. People had packed into the renovated storefront for beer and whiskey and fries. June had been right about putting a few cocktails on the menu, too. He'd had to send that busboy Kenny out to get more limes they had sold so many margaritas, and he couldn't complain about that.

Rock and roll music, good drinks and good food and a game playing on the one TV in the corner. The cash register had almost overheated, he'd stuffed so much green into it.

And when the whole place had erupted into chaos?

It had been beautiful. After the crap those holier-than-thou Main Street types had given him, acting like his bar was going to bring down property values just by existing. He'd pulled in a crowd, all right. The half dozen actual bikers who had shown up had been model citizens, while the Main Street folks who'd looked down their noses at him?

They'd been the loud, out-of-control idiots. They'd been the ones to start fighting with each other and breaking things. They'd been the ones to call the cops.

Bug would've loved it. Every messy, ridiculous, hypocritical minute of it. The wilder the night he and Bug had had back in the service, the better the stories they'd had the next day, and this one would've been one for the ages.

Sure, Clay could've done with less property damage, but he had insurance for that. He'd be all right. The bar would be, too—he was sure of it. You couldn't get better publicity than that many happy people shaking their rear ends to eighties metal. They'd be back, and they'd bring their friends. Heck, the bar would probably make the front page of the morning news. Zoe had even done an interview. What was it they said about all publicity being good publicity?

Dottie Gallagher had talked to the reporter who'd shown up, too—probably about her reservations, but he wasn't worried.

Clay chuckled to himself. Maybe he should offer a special just for senior citizens. Buy one get one free on your first drink order for ages sixty and up. That'd really get her goat.

He swept the last of the glass into the dustpan. His knee screamed as he knelt to scoop it up and headed for the trash can. The walker he'd taken to the patella had sucked, but even that had been worth it.

Because he could stand here all night, reliving the thrill of a wild night at his very own bar, imagining how much his dead best friend would've loved it. But really, the hot feeling in his chest right now was about more than that.

He'd built this bar as a place for people to come together, have a drink, and forget about their worries for a while. Thanks to June, he'd extended his plan beyond the folks this tourist town had left behind—though plenty of them had come out and had a grand old time. But he'd brought everybody together. People from every part of this random little dot on the map.

He was proud of it. Bug would've been deep-down proud about it, too.

And Clay owed it all to one person.

Good timing, then, that the person in question was barreling toward him. He dumped the glass and set down the broom and pan, then turned to meet June right outside the door. She was a beautiful mess, just like the rest of this, her dress soaked on one side and her perfect, gorgeous, silky hair flying around in wisps, her eye makeup smudged. She started to speak, but he hauled her up into his arms and planted a hard kiss on her mouth before she could get a word out.

Only for her to push him away.

"What—"

Then he got a better look at her. Her chest heaved, and not in a good way. He forced his gaze up to her narrowed eyes and her full, red lips. She pinched them together. Her shoulders rose, and her hands were clenched.

He frowned. "June? You okay?"

Because his opinion of this whole night would change if she'd gotten hurt and he hadn't realized it. He'd had a lot of things to juggle when the fecal matter hit the rotating blades, but he thought he'd kept a decent eye on her. She'd seemed to be holding her own.

Her knuckles went white, and when she spoke her voice was hard. "This was a disaster."

Phew. She was fine.

He grinned. "I know, right?"

He turned to go inside. She followed him and locked the door behind them.

But instead of sauntering forward and kissing him in private, she held her ground and seethed, "You have to shut this place down."

She might as well have slapped him.

He drew back. "What?"

"This." Flinging her arms out to the sides, she let out a ragged breath. "All of this...this...this *fiasco*—"

"Excuse you?"

"Clay, this can never happen again."

"Define 'this.'"

"Any of it," she practically shouted. "The cops got called."

"Always a sign of a good party," he said, trying to keep it light, but gears ground together inside him.

"Do you even care about how terrible this all is?"

He fought to keep his calm. "What? The glass? The sign? I can fix those."

"How about the sign at the inn, or the tire tracks on the lawn? My mother's rosebushes."

"They got the bushes?"

"That all costs money."

"Don't you have insurance?"

She barked out a laugh, and okay. Wow.

"June..."

"Don't 'June' me," she snapped. Just like that, the laughing part was over. Deadly serious, she stared him down. "I need you to take this seriously."

His attempts to do anything but finally failed him. "What? What exactly am I supposed to take seriously? We opened a bar together, June, and it was awesome."

"It was loud."

"Because it was awesome."

"People fought. You got hurt."

"I don't care."

"Your window got broken."

"I told you." Wasn't she hearing a thing he was trying to tell her? "I don't care."

"Well, I do." Tears formed in her eyes. "I can't afford this, Clay."

He worked to keep his voice even against the tide of confusion and panic. Where was all this emotion coming from? She'd mentioned having money troubles, but she'd played it off as no big deal. "The sign? The bushes?"

What was he not getting here?

"Any of it." The sheen to her eyes only got worse. "Guests left the inn."

"Good riddance."

"No. Not good riddance." She clawed at her hair, raking it out of her face, and it made her look wrecked and fierce. Dangerous, even.

And it was like the first few times they'd met, when their

arguments had lit a match inside of him. Only this time, her anger was leaving him cold.

"June..." He tried again. "Tonight was a huge success. People had fun." He gestured at the bar. "I made a ton of money. We're getting free coverage in the *Chronicle*."

"Because of the police."

"Because people had a good time."

She pinched the bridge of her nose. When she dropped her hand from her face, it was trembling. "We have to fix this, Clay."

Okay, he was done with this. Voice dropping, everything in him going still, he took a step forward. He loomed over her, looking down at her, trying to will her to freaking get it already. "There. Is. Nothing. To. Fix."

And he should have seen it coming. She was clearly on the edge of tears, but she was a fighter. Since day one, they'd butted heads. He'd yelled at her, and she'd yelled right back.

So her choking on a sob and pulling away caught him totally off guard.

She staggered back, and a knife twisted in his chest.

She was really mad.

She really hated his bar, the one they'd built together. She'd hated this—one of the best nights of his life.

"June..."

She retreated farther, her hand over her mouth as her whole body shook again. Her pretty brown eyes overflowed, and what was he supposed to do.

"I can't believe I was so *stupid*," she finally spat out.

"You—"

"To think this bar could help save us."

What? "Save—"

"I thought, if we could just get it right, it'd bring in enough people. Get enough publicity. May could use it in her article."

Clay's head spun. "Your sister?"

June laughed, the sound pained. "Don't worry, she's not coming."

Clay was so confused. "Wait—"

"What a waste of time." She gestured around wildly. "Making this some new gem of Main Street."

A cold realization settled on him.

All this time, he'd thought she was invested in him. Sure, this had started out as a business relationship, but it had grown into something more. Hadn't it?

Or had she just been using him?

Oblivious to the ice crackling his chest, she ranted on. "A bar. A *bar*. I should have known." She rounded on him. "I did know. From day one. You told me I would hate this place."

He jerked back. "That was a million years ago."

"But you were right. Everything this place stands for—it's the opposite of what my family tried to build."

He growled. "Now wait one—"

"How could I have put my faith in *you*."

Acid burned in his throat. He dropped his hand.

He didn't want to reach for her again. Not if that was the way she saw him.

He'd sworn, so many times, when they were together, that she'd seen past those awful first impressions he'd worked so hard to make, back when he was hurting and alone. But she hadn't, had she?

"Heck if I know, sweetheart." His tongue stuck in his throat, his mouth filled with ash.

"You ruined this town. Just like you said you would."

He'd thought this town had saved him. He'd thought this woman had. "What else did you expect?"

He was just some guy in a truck. Tatted up and broken, with nightmares and blood on his hands and a ghost in his head.

She'd looked at him like he was more. But not now.

Now, she looked as lost as he'd always felt. "I don't know."

"I never hid who I was." He hadn't. Not once. "I was honest about what I wanted."

"Right."

"You're the one who tried to turn me into something else." Righteous fury churned in his gut. The guys had warned him, and like an idiot, he hadn't listened. "You tried to turn this place into something else."

She laughed, and it sliced at his heart. "Well, I failed pretty spectacularly at that."

Was that what she thought?

She'd influenced every inch of this place. The paint and the lights and the stupid flowers on the tables, wilted as they were now.

But it still wasn't good enough for her, was it?

"Yeah." His voice creaked. "I guess you did."

"I don't know why I wasted so much time."

It felt like his ribs were crushing in.

The fury twisted and grew in his gut.

It came hurling out of him, but hot as it burned, it turned to ice when it came out of his mouth. "I do."

He advanced on her. Angry and mean, because it felt better than being angry and hating himself.

"You wasted your time because you can't stop yourself," he spat. "You knew what I was from the first minute, huh? Well, I knew who you were, too. Snobby, nosy, can't leave anything well enough alone."

Her eyes flew wide, her face going pale. "I'm not—"

"Trying to control everything." And he was talking too

loudly, too angrily. "You try to control me, my bar, my business. You talk your friend Bobbi into cockamamie schemes instead of actually helping her with her folks."

"I never—" She shook her head, backing away.

Clay didn't cede an inch. The fire inside of him was out of control. "Your whole family's terrified of you, aren't they? You ever let them so much as breathe without you giving them permission to? Or do you schedule that on your calendar, too?"

"They're not—"

"Your mom begs you to let her lift a finger and you say no," he spat, and the way she flinched at every word made him burn with self-loathing, but every word of it was true. "Elizabeth keeps trying to prove herself, but you won't have any of it, will you? They try to take care of you, but you won't let them."

She wouldn't let anybody.

For one second, he'd imagined she might let him take care of her. He'd imagined she felt the way he felt about her, but no. She'd never really trust him. She'd never really trust anyone.

Wetness gleamed at the corners of her eyes. "I'm not—"

"They must hate you," he gritted out, and heaven help him. He hated himself. That was too far. He knew it.

She did, too.

Her nostrils flared, her eyes flying wide as she staggered back and away from him. "They don't. They. No."

But he couldn't rein himself in. "Always ordering them around. Acting like you care, but you're just trying to make them do things your way."

Like she'd done with his bar. Like she'd done with him.

She sputtered, and he should shut his fool mouth, but he couldn't seem to figure out how.

Advancing on her again, he ground out, "Well, you don't need to waste any more of your time trying to fix me, because

I'm not broken." Lies. He sucked in a breath that burned like fire. "This bar is fine without you trying to turn it into something it's not. Little Miss Perfect." She was so perfect. Too perfect for him. "You can take all your perfect crap back home with you."

Her hands curled into fists, bright pink replacing the pale cast to her cheeks. "Seriously, you don't get it, do you?"

"Get what? What am I too stupid to understand?"

Finally, she shoved herself into his face. "I'm not perfect, Clay." Then she staggered back, and he was so flipping confused. "I'm the furthest thing from it."

"Ha-ha."

She turned black, shadowed eyes on him, and something inside him froze. "I can't save the inn, Clay."

He flinched. "What?"

"We're teetering on the edge of bankruptcy. Isn't it obvious?"

"June. I don't understand."

He didn't understand how her voice could waver like that, and how it could dig into the deepest parts of him. All that venom they'd just slung at each other, but one vulnerable word from her and he wanted to wrap her in his arms.

But she was bristling. Shaking and rattling with anger and loss.

"My mother was in the hospital for weeks. It wiped out everything we had. We're in debt up to our eyeballs, and it was my job to fix it."

He shook his head, but she held up a hand.

"I was supposed to figure it all out. They're relying on *me*. I didn't force them to do anything. I didn't terrorize or control them."

He was such a jerk. "I know—"

"I tried to save us all, but the highway cut Blue Cedar Falls

off. Everyone around here is suffocating, and yeah. Maybe I
thought your bar could help give us some air, so I tried to bend
the tube to get a breath. I'm sorry."

"No, no..."

"You say I butt in, but I butt in because I need to. You
don't know what it's like to have everyone depend on you."
She sagged, like the weight she'd been trying to carry suddenly
crushed her. "So I'm sorry I tried to help. I'm sorry you thought
I tried to change you. I just wanted to help. I wanted to help
everyone." She sucked in a breath, but it tapered into a sob.
"But I failed at that, too."

What was he supposed to say to that? "I had no idea."

"Of course you didn't." Her smile was so brittle it hurt. "We
were casual, right?"

More lies.

"I was the one who wanted us to be casual," she said. "Because I couldn't handle anything more. I couldn't tell you how
I was drowning, because no one wants to see that, do they?"

"I would have," he vowed.

How many times had he asked her what was going on? He'd
thought she was opening up to him, but there was always a part
that she kept hidden. And now it was too late.

"I thought I could have fun with you while trying to fix
everyone and save everything. But I was wrong." She gestured
at the wrecked room around them. The broken glasses and the
shattered edges of the window and the beer spilled on the floor.
"I stop working for one second. I let my guard down for one
instant and you see what happens?"

"A really great party?" he tried, but it was weak.

Fresh tears sprung to her eyes. "Everything falls apart."

He reached out for her, his head spinning and his heart
squeezing so hard he couldn't breathe. He didn't understand

anything, and he wanted to stop time. To go back and figure out what was going on.

But she slipped out of his grasp. She turned.

The door slammed behind her on her way out, leaving him alone, surrounded by the destruction of what had seemed like the first good thing he'd ever done.

Left behind by the one person he thought understood him.

Again.

CHAPTER TWENTY-FOUR

Y̶our mom is getting better at memes." Bobbi chuckled as she tapped at her phone.

June shoved another handful of popcorn in her mouth and washed it down with a sip of wine. "She couldn't have gotten much worse."

On the TV screen in the background, some sappy rom-com was playing, but no one was really paying attention. This impromptu girls' night at Bobbi's house was supposed to be about having fun and ignoring their problems, but some problems were too big to ignore.

Over the past week, Bobbi had been tight-lipped about her parents catching her and Caitlin together at Clay's bar. What little she'd said hadn't been good. They'd had it out exactly once, the morning after the opening, and "things had been said." Since then, her parents had made no effort to get in touch with her, and her one attempt at contacting them had been met with silence.

June had tried to reassure her that it would be all right. It was just a shock. They'd get over it.

Bobbi seemed convinced her worst nightmares about them rejecting her and cutting her out of their lives might be coming true.

At this point, June was fresh out of ideas for how to help, and goodness knew she wasn't going to try to rope her friend into any "cockamamie schemes." All she could do was be there for her.

The fact that she could use some consoling herself was immaterial.

With another snicker, Bobbi passed June her phone. On it was a picture of Sunny the cat, laid out dramatically on the couch, the tattered remains of a tissue box spread out around her, a carton of ice cream and an empty wine bottle on the side table. In big white letters with black outlines it said, "MY DAUGHTER AFTER BREAKUP."

Was there no loyalty in this world?

"Very funny," June ground out, dropping Bobbi's phone into her lap.

"I mean, it kind of is." Bobbi eyed her up and down. "You have to admit it's on point."

"I have literally never clawed a tissue box to death." June gulped down the rest of her wine. "And I'm not going through a breakup."

"Uh-huh."

She wasn't. She and Clay had had a huge fight, during which he'd refused to admit that his bar's opening had been a train wreck and called her a control freak whose family hated her. She'd barfed her problems all over him and told him the bar he'd built was a disaster and questioned how she could have ever put her faith in him.

Her stomach roiled as she flashed back to those awful things they'd said to each other. They'd both been hurting. She'd been desperate and angry and terrified, but that was no excuse. How could she have been so cruel?

They hadn't spoken since. That wasn't a breakup. That was a disaster.

"So how is Clay anyway?"

"Fine, I'm sure." Based on the glimpses she'd caught of him going about his business across the street, he seemed just dandy.

Bobbi arched a brow. "You consider talking to him, or you going to keep staring at him out the window like a creep?"

Good grief, didn't she have any allies here?

Grumbling, she set her empty glass down on a coaster. "Remind me why I'm here again?"

"Because your mom kicked you out of the house after you refused to leave it for a week," Caitlin said, emerging from the kitchen with brownies. She placed them on a trivet on the coffee table, then plopped down in the armchair on the other side of Bobbi.

Pouting, June snagged a brownie. It was annoyingly good.

"I left the house." To go work in the office behind the front desk of the inn, trying to find a way out of the mess she and her family were in. So no, she hadn't technically left the building, but it wasn't like she'd been moping around her room in her pajamas or anything.

Much.

Anyway, she was out now. Hanging with her best friend at her house, watching cheesy rom-coms and eating popcorn and brownies like a normal, well-socialized human being.

"Besides," she added, still grumpy about it, "she kicked me out because she was having a dinner party with some friends."

Which June hadn't tried to talk her out of at all. See? She wasn't a control freak who manipulated her family at every turn. Even when they were overexerting themselves.

Bobbi held out her hand expectantly. Realizing she still had her phone, June passed it over, making another stink eye at the meme.

"Where did you even find that?"

"On your mom's Facebook." Bobbi said it so matter-of-factly. "Duh."

Was June really the only person in the world who didn't have time for that stuff?

Bobbi flicked her thumb across the screen. She frowned. "Huh."

"What?"

"Nothing, just—"

Caitlin swooped in and snagged the phone out of her hand.

"Hey!"

Caitlin's eyes widened. "Oh."

"What?" June asked.

Ignoring Bobbi's efforts to grab it back, Caitlin turned the screen so June could see. It was a selfie her mom had taken of herself and Ned and...

June squinted. "What are your parents doing there?"

Bobbi's mouth flattened into a straight line. "I wouldn't know."

Right.

June chose her words carefully. "Have you talked to them at all?"

"Nope."

Caitlin met June's gaze over Bobbi's head, her expression grim. She passed Bobbi her phone and pressed a kiss to her temple.

"Well." Bobbi tossed her phone aside. "I guess it's good to know they're still alive."

"Bobbi..."

She ignored her and picked up the remote. "Is anybody actually watching this garbage?"

June glanced at the screen. The movie had mostly been on as background. She shrugged.

Taking that as the answer it was, Bobbi surfed to the menu and started scrolling for something else. June frowned at her. Should she press?

Before she could make up her mind, loud banging sounded on the door.

"Uh." Caitlin scrunched up her face. "Were we expecting any more depressed people?"

"Nope," Bobbi said, "just us."

"I'm not depressed," June protested.

"Sure." Caitlin rose from her seat and crossed the room. She checked the peephole. Blinking, she jerked away. "Uh..."

"Whoever it is, tell them go away," Bobbi told her, picking an action movie from her queue. Quite a change from rom-coms, but it wasn't like June really cared.

Caitlin shook her head. "Dude, it's your parents."

Bobbi jumped up, dropping the remote and half a bowl of popcorn. "What? No." She crouched to the floor. "Don't answer. We're not here."

"We can see you through the window," her mother's muffled voice came from outside.

June jerked her gaze up, and yeah, there was a big gap in the curtains, and there was Tracy Moore.

"I have a key," her dad bellowed.

"Oh crap." Bobbi swept up the wineglasses and ran them to the next room.

"Hey." June made grabby hands at the bottle, but it was no use.

"I'm just going to quick go change," Bobbi called.

Caitlin rolled her eyes. "Your parents have seen you in your pajamas before."

Bobbi stopped dead in the middle of the room. She bit her lip, and her eyes were wild. "We could sneak out the back. The airport's only a couple of hours away. I hear Hawaii's really nice this time of year."

All her panic bled into the room. June rose to stand beside her. She took her hand. "They're here, Bobbi."

"I know, that's why I'm freaking out."

"Don't you think you should listen to what they have to say?"

"I can still see you," Mrs. Moore said, knocking on the glass now.

"Oh, no." Bobbi pulled her hand away and covered her face with her palms. "This is like the zombie apocalypse, but instead of eating my brains, they're going to send me to conversion camp."

"They are *not* going to send you to conversion camp." Caitlin crossed her arms over her chest.

"You're a grown woman," June reminded her. "They can't do anything to you that you don't let them."

Bobbi's terrified eyes met hers. "They can tell me they never want to see me again."

June swallowed. "Yeah. They can." She looked past Bobbi to the window, where Mrs. Moore was staring in at them. Their gazes met, and the lump in June's throat finally started to shrink. She took Bobbi by the shoulders and turned her around. Keeping hold of her, she said, quietly, "But if that's what they were planning to do, do you think that they'd be staring at you like that?"

Bobbi peeked between her fingers. Her mother put her hands over her heart. Bobbi sucked in a rattling breath.

"Should I let them in?" Caitlin asked.

"Yeah." Bobbi exhaled, long and slow. "Yeah, I guess you better."

Caitlin opened the door, but she blocked the way in with her body. She stared Duke Moore down in a way June hadn't seen many people dare to in her life.

After a moment, Duke huffed out a breath. "Can we come in?"

Caitlin squared her jaw. She stepped out of the way and moved to go stand on Bobbi's other side. Bobbi took both Caitlin and June by the hand. She tipped her chin up. June squeezed her palm.

Bobbi's parents came rushing in.

"Oh, sweetie," her mom cried, her hands clasped over her mouth.

Bobbi trembled, but she stood strong.

Like she couldn't restrain herself a moment longer, her mother ran at her, her father not far behind. They stopped a scant foot away.

"I am *so* sorry," Mrs. Moore said.

Mr. Moore corrected. "We both are."

"Seeing you and your—your girlfriend." Mrs. Moore looked up at Caitlin, and her throat bobbed. "Seeing you together took us by surprise, and we should have reacted better. When you tried to explain it to us, we should have listened."

"We love you, pumpkin. No matter what." Her dad's eyes were glassy, the line of his mouth beneath that signature mustache of his fierce.

"And we should have made that clearer from the start."

Bobbi's whole body trembled. She dropped June's hand, and June stepped back.

"So you don't mind?"

"It'll take some getting used to," her mom warned. "But you're our baby girl. Always."

Mr. Moore nodded. "There's nothing you could tell us about yourself that could change that, okay, pumpkin?"

"I'm so sorry we ever let you doubt that," her mom said.

Bobbi melted. "I was so scared you'd hate me forever."

"Never," Mrs. Moore vowed. She pulled Bobbi into a fierce hug, and Bobbi wrapped an arm around her, too. Mr. Moore piled in, but Bobbi never let go of Caitlin's hand.

June's eyes misted over. She watched for a minute, but contrary to what Clay said, she *was* capable of keeping her nose out of other people's business. This was clearly a private moment.

Slinking away, she grabbed her purse and caught Caitlin's eye. "I'm gonna," she mouthed, and she mimed walking out the door.

Caitlin smiled and nodded.

Duke caught her before she could get out the door. "Tell your mother thank you for us, Juney."

June smiled. "I sure will."

Of course her mom would have been behind all this. The woman was stubborn and ridiculous, and she and June were going to have a Talk after that meme she'd posted about her.

But deep down, she was the most caring person in the world, and she was more than willing to take any wayward person by the ear and pull on it until they agreed to do the right thing for their family.

Maybe she should have pulled on June's ear more, these past nine months.

To think. June had almost tried to talk her mother out of hosting a dinner party tonight, worried as ever that she'd overtax herself. Clay's accusations about how controlling she was rang in her ears, and deep inside she simmered with shame.

June was lucky to have her mom exactly the way she was, stupid cat pictures and aggressive hostess instincts and all.

Just like Bobbi was lucky to have her parents. It might take them some time to get used to seeing their daughter in a new light, but they would get there. Bobbi would get to keep her parents. And with Caitlin, she'd get to have her happily ever after, too.

Who knew? Maybe June would get a chance to be better to the people in her family who cared about her, too.

Bruised as it might be, June's heart felt full. With a small smile, she slipped away and left them to it.

June let herself into her family's living area in the back of the inn. She passed Ned, who was doing the dishes from their little dinner party.

"Have a nice night, Juney?"

She came up beside him and gave him a kiss on the cheek. "Sure did."

"Glad to hear it."

"I can take care of these," she offered.

"Nah, thanks, though."

Shrugging, she headed into the living room where she found her mother spread out on the couch with the cat and a book. June couldn't read the characters on the cover, but the picture of a Chinese woman in a flowing robe, striking a martial arts pose, told her most of what she needed to know.

Her mother made a vague sound of acknowledgment while Sunny rolled farther into her chest. June shook her head at the cat. So possessive.

Coming to stand next to the couch, she leaned in and pressed her lips to her mom's brow. Her mother accepted it with a half smile.

"Thanks," June said.

"For what?"

"You know what."

Looking up from her book, June's mom waved her stronger hand dismissively. "It was nothing. I just give Tracy and Duke a little nudge in the right direction."

"Well, it worked. They showed up at Bobbi's crying and begging for forgiveness."

"Good." Her mom pretended to look at her book again, but she clearly wasn't done discussing her success. "Sometimes wrongheaded people just need a good slap in the face."

"I thought you 'nudged' them."

"Nudge, slap, all the same." Her mom raised her gaze. "Families stick together. Gay, straight, trans, whatever. You never turn your back on your child."

Something hot and uncomfortable turned over in June's gut.

She really hoped her mother meant that. Especially once she found out what a mess June had made, trying to juggle their family's debts. A part of her wanted to spill the beans now and get it over with, but she held it in. She had one or two last avenues to exhaust, first.

She took a step back. Her mom returned to her book, licking her finger to turn the page. "Anybody else you need me to nudge?" Her brows rose, even as she kept her gaze on the text. "Hot guy across street, maybe?"

That made a different kind of uneasiness spread through June. "No, Mom."

"Okay, but you let me know if you change your mind. I am very good at nudging."

June laughed, but there wasn't any humor in it. "Will do."

What would her mother "nudge" Clay about anyway? June had been nudging him herself for months, and apparently all it had done was convince him that she was a control freak. She could admit that there was a grain of truth to his assessment of her, but that didn't change the fact that he was a stubborn jerk who hadn't really changed at all. No one could talk any kind of sense into him. Not even her mom.

He could stay over there with his wild crowds at his rowdy bar. That was his dream, right? He didn't need her being a manipulative killjoy, ruining his good time. He didn't need anybody.

And June didn't need him, either. She didn't need his rare smiles that crinkled the corners of his eyes, or the gentle way he listened to her, like he was really hearing what she was saying. She didn't need the way he looked at her that made her feel like he didn't expect anything from her—like she didn't have to do anything to please him or prove her worth. She didn't need the quiet strength of his presence or the sun-dappled days off at the swimming hole or the freedom she felt to just relax and enjoy their time together. She didn't need his kiss or the way his touch made her skin come alive.

She didn't need any of it.

Setting her purse down, she tipped her head toward the door. "I'm going to go check on Elizabeth."

Her mother waved her off.

She shut the door to the office behind her on her way out to the front desk.

There she found Elizabeth, her purple-streaked hair done up in twin buns on top of her head. She sat in the chair, her back to the office door. June couldn't see what she was looking at, but whatever she was doing, she was sure engrossed.

"Hey," June called as she approached.

Elizabeth jerked her gaze up. She spun around.

June stopped cold.

Because her sister's eyes were red, her mouth hard. She held up a piece of paper.

And June's heart stilled in her chest.

"Tell me this isn't what I think it is," Elizabeth said. The latest overdue notice from the hospital crumpled in her hands.

"I can explain."

Elizabeth snorted. "Now this I've got to hear."

"I've got it under control."

"Really? Because it looks to me like the exact opposite."

June's feet finally came unstuck from the floor. "How did you even?"

Elizabeth snatched the paper back before June could grab it. "Silly me, thinking I'd help out a little. File some paperwork."

"It was locked."

"Please." Elizabeth rolled her eyes. "I copied all the keys like ten years ago."

"You *what*?"

"Not the point." Elizabeth rose to her feet as June closed the distance between them. "What is going on with these bills? Spill. Now."

June cast about, trying to come up with any sort of explanation.

But she was out of options. She might have been able to justify keeping the truth from her mother for a little bit longer, but her youngest sister had caught her dead to rights. The months-long sham was over. Everyone would know now.

Shame flooded her. Right on its heels, though, was an intense wave of relief.

Dropping into the other chair beside Elizabeth's, June beckoned her sister to sit. She did so warily, looking at June the whole time like she was about to eat her, but June didn't have the strength anymore to so much as raise her voice.

"It started as soon as Mom got out of the hospital," she admitted.

From there, the entire story came pouring out of her. The small bills and the big ones, and everything June had done to try to juggle them and make enough minimum payments to keep the collection agencies off their backs, only it had never been enough.

She'd tried everything. Payment plans and debt consolidation. Promotions at the inn and marketing.

She'd tried helping Clay open a bar across the street and asking May to come, and none of it had so much as made a dent. Even if the Pumpkin Festival was the smash success she'd worked so hard to shape it into, there wasn't time to turn this ship around. Forget her delusions of using Pumpkin Fest as a springboard for launching even more new ideas. The inn would be in foreclosure by then.

She was a failure. All her plans and efforts, all the meddling and controlling that Clay had accused her of, and none of it had helped even the tiniest little bit.

Elizabeth's eyes grew wider and wider. Finally, by the time it was all out there, her jaw was practically on the floor. "For Pete's sake, June."

"I know." June hid her face behind her hands.

"Like, *how.*"

"I said I know."

"But, like…" Her sister chewed her words for a minute. "Did it ever occur to you to ask for help?"

"I told you I talked to May about coming to visit."

"But did you tell her *why*?"

"I asked her three times. I said 'please.'" Wasn't that

enough? June never used to show that kind of vulnerability before. May must have known that if June was asking her to come, she needed her.

"Really pulling out the big guns there." Elizabeth rolled her eyes. "Did you tell her the rest of it?"

She'd tried, hadn't she?

Just not hard enough.

"May was busy. She's worried about her job. I didn't want to stress her out even more."

Out of nowhere, Elizabeth put her hand over June's. June jerked her head up, her breath catching.

It wasn't that she and her sister didn't love each other. They did. Their family just wasn't touchy-feely.

"I get it. Okay?" Elizabeth caught and held her gaze. "But what about me?"

All the reasons June had told herself for keeping this a secret faded away. They'd seemed solid enough, but they couldn't hold up to the scrutiny of being asked a direct question like this. "I didn't want to..."

Elizabeth's mouth tilted into a pained smile. "You didn't trust me."

"It's not that—"

Elizabeth waved her off. "It's fine. I told you, I'm used to it. I can't even blame you, entirely."

"Look. I mean—"

"I was a jerk in high school, June. I know that." Elizabeth sighed. "It wasn't easy trying to live up to you and May, so I didn't try."

"Nobody expected you to—"

"Please. You guys were supersmart, while I was just me, and I'm fine with that."

Guilt twisted June's stomach. Because they'd had this

conversation before, hadn't they? Something had changed, though. Maybe it was June screwing up so bad. It had broken down the walls between them. Instead of getting defensive, Elizabeth was laying it all out there so frankly.

And June had no desire to poke at old wounds.

Yes, Elizabeth had been irresponsible back in the day. But maybe that had clouded June's judgment. Kept her from seeing the person her sister had become.

"Look," Elizabeth said, "it's not easy being the screwup of the family. Having nobody trust you, no matter how hard you try to show them that they can—once you get your head on straight, that is." When June opened her mouth to interrupt, her sister held up a hand. "But sometimes I wonder if it wasn't harder being you."

That made June pause. "Me?"

Elizabeth narrowed her eyes at her. "Nobody's perfect all the time, June."

June's ears went hot.

Wasn't that what Clay had called her, too? Little Miss Perfect? She'd told him then, and she'd tell her sister now. "I never pretended—"

"Of course you did. All the time. Used to be, I even believed it." Elizabeth shook her head. "It's just. You don't have to keep doing that. Acting like you're always okay." She gestured at the bills spread out across the desk. "Or like you can handle everything on your own."

A full-body flush traveled from June's face to her toes and back again. What was she supposed to say to that?

All the same rationales and reasons she'd been telling herself this entire time flooded her, each more useless than the last, and hadn't Clay tried to tell her this, too?

When she'd broken down and confessed what a mess she'd

made of her family's finances after they'd been saddled with all that medical debt, he asked her why she hadn't told him the full story earlier.

"I didn't want to bother anyone," she tried.

Clay's hurt face flashed across her vision. He'd sworn he would've wanted to know. But who really, honestly wanted to know about her problems?

Elizabeth squeezed June's hand, returning her to the present. "It's not a bother." With a tired echo of a laugh, she let go and picked up one of the bills again. "Honestly, letting it get this bad is probably going to be way more of a bother."

Well, that was a punch to the gut. The worst part was, her sister was probably right. "I kept thinking I could figure it out. Spare everybody."

"Do me a favor, would you?"

"What's that?"

"Next time you want to spare me, don't."

Unexpected laughter snuck up on June. She dabbed at her eyes. "Yeah, okay."

"Hey." Elizabeth put the papers down again. "We're going to figure this out, okay? Together."

June cracked a watery smile. It was like this bubble of light-ness forming and expanding inside her lungs. Like maybe she could breathe for the first time in months.

She had nothing cynical to say. No armor left to pierce and no will to keep her sister at arm's length. Or to hide how deeply she'd been struggling. "Okay."

Her sister gazed at her softly. "We're all in this together. I know you like to do things yourself, but there are people in your life who are here for you and want to help you. You just have to let us in sometimes."

June's ribs squeezed so hard she could scarcely breathe. She

wanted to shake her head, but Elizabeth seemed so sincere—
even after all the ways June had doubted her over the years.
The bubble of lightness in her lungs couldn't compete with the
sudden, suffocating tightness.

How badly had the weight of responsibility been pulling at
her these last few months? The last years, since May had left
and June had taken over as much as she could?

Maybe even her whole life. Since their father had abandoned
them and June had taken it upon herself to get the whole
family through?

Elizabeth's offer of help seemed impossible, but June had
no option but to believe it.

So what about other offers?

What about Clay asking her what was going on a thousand
times? What about the way he'd looked at her, there, at the end,
after she'd confessed the whole entire mess she was in?

When he'd told her he would have listened. He would
have helped.

But she'd never let him.

She'd been more open with Clay than she had been with
just about anybody else in her life, but she'd still been too
scared to let him see her deepest flaws. She hadn't been the
only offender, of course. He'd kept her at bay in his own way.
Macho, manly stuff—like he wasn't dealing with the layers of
trauma he had suffered in his life. At the bar opening, when
they'd fought, the insults he'd hurled at her had been targeted
missiles. They were meant to hurt.

Because she'd hurt him first. She'd told him the bar he'd built
with his own two hands was a disaster. She'd questioned his
worth and her ability to put her trust in him. She'd lashed out
in painful, unforgivable ways.

So he'd pushed her away.

But could she blame him? She'd pushed him away at least as hard.

Even when she'd thought she was letting him in, deep down, she was keeping him at arm's length this entire time.

And now, when she'd been forced to accept help, when she could see all the things he'd done for her so clearly . . .

Now it was too late.

CHAPTER TWENTY-FIVE

You know that if you want to hang out with me, you can just hang out with me, right?" Han set a bag of food down on the bar. "You don't actually have to order takeout."

Clay looked up from the paper he hadn't been reading. "Shut up and give me my dumplings."

Han shoved the bag closer like a zookeeper tossing steak into a tiger's cage. It probably wasn't a bad comparison. Clay felt about that mean and hungry.

In the week since the bar opening had gone pear-shaped and June had told him she hated him, he'd mostly been licking his wounds. He'd kept the place open, exactly the way it was. Or at least the way it had been left. The front window was boarded up again, and he'd tossed the broken pieces of the sign in the back office. He was still finding shards of glass in the corners of the place, no matter how many times he'd swept.

Zoe and Kenny and the other couple of people who worked for him treated him with kid gloves, which was great. As long as they left him alone. His customers got their food and their beer. They listened to music on the jukebox and watched the game on the TV in the corner, and it was everything he and Bug had ever imagined it would be. So what if it wasn't quite what he'd thought he was building with June these past few months? She wasn't here, so what did he care?

Snagging the bag of food, he tore into it. He had half a dumpling in his mouth before Han cleared his throat.

"What?" Clay grunted.

"Nothing." Han took a seat, uninvited, but making himself comfortable, apparently. "Just wondering if this is how you got June to fall for you. Your infinite grace and charm."

Stab him with a knife.

He dropped the other half of the dumpling on the lid of the open container. "Get out."

Han reached over his arm and grabbed a dumpling of his own. "Think I better stay for a few."

"So you can eat my food?"

"That I cooked and you haven't paid me for yet, so."

Clay wiped his hand off on the bar towel slung over his shoulder before reaching into his wallet. He shoved a twenty at Han. "Keep the change."

"I definitely will."

Han didn't make any move to leave, though. Annoyance brewed deep in Clay's gut.

Higher up in his chest, there was a dim glow of warmth.

Man, what he would do to have Tuck and AJ and Riz in town again. They would've dragged him out of his hole days ago. Too bad he hadn't told them about the opening they said they'd love to come back for. Or reached out to stay in touch with them at all.

He glanced at Han out of the corner of his eye. The guy wasn't the kind of person Clay usually made friends with. He was too smart and too put together for starters. But he was here, despite all the signals Clay had given him that he didn't need to be.

That counted for something.

Begrudgingly, Clay nudged the whole container closer to Han. "You want a beer?"

"Wouldn't say no."

Clay hid his wince as he got up and went around to the other side of the bar and poured a couple of pints. His knee was in better shape after a week of mostly sitting on his butt, being a miserable jerk, and avoiding leaving the building, but it was never going to be really right. His new PT regime had helped, and he'd stuck with it, but only through sheer stubbornness.

"You okay?" Han asked, brows raised.

"Peachy." Clay set down Han's glass and slid it toward him. He took a deep pull at his own before returning with it to his seat.

"I can see that."

Then mercifully, he shut up. They drank and ate together in peace. It was…nice. Clay hadn't been isolated, exactly, since he and June had had their blowout. It was pretty hard to run a bar and be alone. Zoe needled him and Kenny gawked at him, and his customers tried to make small talk, and it was all well and good.

But Han knew him. Having his silent companionship, without him pressuring Clay to talk about any of the crap running around in his brain…It was different. It was exactly what Clay needed, and he was going to savor it.

He lasted all of two minutes.

"She just," Clay sputtered. "She. She wants to change everything about me."

"Okaaayyy…"

"From day one, it's been the same crap. What if you did this, or what if you tried this." Bitterness flooded the back of Clay's throat.

For a minute there, while they'd been sleeping together, he'd thought maybe she accepted him the way he was, but she'd never stopped needling at him. Trying to fix him, and why wouldn't she? He'd always known she was too good for him.

So why did it still hurt so much?

"She doesn't give a crap about me." The truth of it burned.

Han chewed slowly. He swallowed and took a sip of his beer to wash it down, his gaze on Clay the entire time. "How exactly do you figure that?"

"You taking her side?" Clay ground his teeth together.

"I'm not taking anybody's side. I'm just asking. Because I'm not sure you can have it both ways. She was trying to change you but she also didn't care?"

June's words from the night of the opening made the bruise on his heart throb. "It was the bar. That was all she cared about. She was using me, thinking it'd help her make some money for her stupid inn."

Han narrowed one eye, his tone dry. "So she slept with you because of your bar."

"Yes. No." Clay scrubbed a hand through his hair. "I don't know."

Why was Han making this so hard? Couldn't he let Clay gripe without poking holes in everything he said?

"I'm so glad you've got this all figured out."

"She wanted to change the bar," Clay flung out, because that was the crux of this. The thing no one could dispute. "Me and Bug, our idea for it wasn't good enough so she tried to twist it around."

She'd gotten him all twisted around in the process, too, making him think cloth napkins and cocktails were a good idea. He liked some of the changes well enough. He liked the lights and the designs Lisa had done up for him, but that didn't change the fact that none of it had been part of the plan.

"Oh no." Han's voice dripped sarcasm. "She tried to help your business."

"She tried to make it into something it wasn't." Clay's tongue got stuck, everything he'd been tossing and turning about for the last week tangling his thoughts up in a knot. "She used me."

Han stared at him for long minutes, doing that thing where he waited Clay out, and Clay freaking hated it.

Well, it wasn't going to work this time. Clay plunked his elbows down on the edge of the bar and opened the other carton of food. He dug into it, and it smelled delicious, but it didn't matter. Everything tasted like ash.

"That sucks, man," Han finally said.

"Sure does."

"She used you...how, again, exactly?"

Clay tossed his hands in the air. "She changed all my plans for the bar to help her own business, because—"

He swallowed the rest of what he'd been about to say. It wasn't his story to tell.

But why? Why not just spill all her secrets? The Wus were broke, and it wasn't even their fault.

The acid in his throat crawled down into his stomach.

She'd waited to fling that little piece of information in his face until the very last second. She'd kept it from him, even as he'd showed her so many ugly sides to himself and his past. She hadn't trusted him with it.

He picked up his beer and drank and drank, but it didn't help.

He'd thought she was opening up to him, was the thing. She'd shared all these little glimpses behind the curtain, and he'd really started to believe that he was seeing everything. The good, the bad, and the not-quite-eggshell-chiffon.

But at the end of the day, deep down, there was a part of her that didn't trust him—and why should she? He was a busted-up, cynical army washout, while she was beautiful and smart. It had never made any sense for her to stick with him. But had he guarded his heart?

No. He was such an idiot freaking sap.

Even after everything that had happened to him. The scars and the loss and the way every single person and institution in his life had left him behind...After he'd spent a year withdrawing and pushing everyone away, intent on never having to get cast aside like that again...

He'd let her in. He'd still had enough of a heart to care about her. He'd had enough of a heart for her to break.

"Because she did," he finally huffed out. "The paint color, the menu. She put flowers on the tables, for crying out loud."

"And that was the final straw? The flowers?" Han's disbelieving tone just rankled Clay further.

"No—"

"Because they were pretty cute."

"Zoe made them cute, shut up." Clay wanted to slap his hands over his ears. "June used me. She wanted to change me and my bar, because we weren't good enough, that's all that matters."

Han chewed on that for a second. When he spoke again, it was slow, like he was choosing his words carefully. Like maybe he finally realized how worked up Clay was getting. "To be fair—so far, the only thing you've made a real case for her changing is the interior decorating. How did she try to change *you*?"

"Look at me." Clay's voice went rough. Man, he was pathetic. "I'm this messed up vet, covered in tattoos and scars. I wear T-shirts and work clothes, and she's...she's..."

She was gorgeous. She talked fancy, with a college degree and a head for business. The clothes she wore always made her look so beautiful. She had the silkiest hair and the softest lips. Her body was a miracle he still couldn't believe she'd let him touch.

"Yeah," Han agreed after a long moment. "The Wu girls are like nobody else. I'll give you that, all right." Han's Adam's apple bobbed, and for a second, it felt like he was somewhere else. Wherever it was, he returned to reality fast. He finished his beer and set it down with a thunk. "Can I make a couple of observations?"

"Has this been you holding back?"

"You have no idea." Han sucked in a breath and let it out. "Look, I'm just an outside observer here, but sounds like maybe you could use one of those. And here's what I can say. I have known June Wu since she was in middle school. And yeah, she's a perfectionist. She can't help trying to fix everything around her. You think she's uptight now, you should have heard some of the stories May used to tell."

"Do you actually have a point?"

Han's dark eyes focused in on him, intensity gleaming in them. "My point is, I have never seen her as laid-back and happy as I've seen her with you."

"Oh." And what was Clay supposed to say to that?

"You think she tried to change you, but I think you changed her—and for the better. She relaxed when she was around you."

Clay struggled to hold on to the fire that had been building inside him. "Great for her."

"Great for you." Han finished his beer. "Because you know what else?"

"What?"

"Maybe she did change you. Maybe, somehow, with all her powers of manipulation, she helped you."

"Big help," Clay scoffed.

"I didn't know you before, okay? I don't know what things were like for you before you came to Blue Cedar Falls. I do know you like to put on this big act about being a grouchy vet, and that's fine. Your grumpy cat impression is hilarious."

"I'm so glad I entertain you."

"But underneath all that gruff macho crap, I think June made you happy. So if she changed you, then I say good."

"It's not good," Clay shouted, the force behind it surprising even him. He was suddenly shaking, standing up before he'd even decided to move.

Of course June had made him happy. Happier than he'd ever been, but it hadn't meant the same things to her. She'd tossed him aside. She'd told him he was worthless to her and that she hated everything he'd worked to build. Everything he'd thought he'd been building *with* her—and didn't that just prove his point?

He turned away, flexing his hands to keep himself from slamming a fist into his only friend's face.

"The beer is five dollars."

Han's barstool made a scraping noise against the floor as he pushed it back. He slid the same twenty Clay had given him across the bar toward him. "Keep the change."

Clay didn't look up as Han's footsteps echoed across the deserted room.

"For the record," Han said. Light flooded in as he opened the door. "I don't think June's the one who doesn't think you're good enough."

With that, he left, letting the door slam closed behind him, and great. That was just great.

Breath heaving, Clay turned to face the emptiness just waiting to stare back at him. His pulse roared in his ears, and it was all he could do not to shove his lunch off the bar, let it and the glasses all crash to the ground.

How dare Han. Waltzing in here, pretending to be Clay's friend. Spouting all that crap. He ran a takeout joint, not a shrink's office. He didn't know what he was talking about. June had made herself plenty clear. Han hadn't been there. He didn't understand.

Clay started pacing, his knee yelling at him to sit down and numb out again, the way he had been this entire week.

Maybe this entire year.

Ever since Bug had died and he'd gotten hurt and the army had kicked him out. He'd just wandered around, keeping to himself, and it had been fine.

A rough sound escaped his throat. No.

It had been the worst year of his life.

Then he'd come here. He'd met June and Han and all these other people. For the first time since his parents' crash, he'd had a place. Blue Cedar Falls had felt like home. Building something here, making friends...it had felt right.

And nothing had felt more right than being with June.

He pounded his fist against the bar.

But none of it had been what he'd thought it was. She'd had ulterior motives. She'd kept things from him. She'd judged him.

Right?

Damn Han for making him doubt himself. Clay's righteous anger had been building and building, but now that he'd stopped to think it through, it felt like it was teetering.

He stormed across the room and back again, but it wasn't enough space to get his frustrations out. He kept going down the hall and was set to head right through the door. Maybe into his truck. He could take off and drive and drive, exactly like he'd done for the awful, lonely year he'd spent after Bug had died and before he'd landed here. He could keep going forever.

He marched through the door to the office to grab his keys.

But he smacked the door open too hard. It slammed into the chair that had been left too close to it. The thing spun and crashed into the flimsy old folding table where he'd put—

"No—" He reached out, but the cracked pieces of the sign he'd planned to glue together went tumbling. More splinters of wood flew across the floor, and he swore a blue streak. He stooped to pick them up.

He held the two broken pieces in his hands and stared down at them.

Bug's Bar. That had been their dream. They'd sat there together in the desert, taking those few precious moments away from fighting and bloodshed and never knowing when the next threat was going to come around the corner and blindside them. They'd imagined a future for themselves.

Then Bug had died. Clay'd been left alone with nothing but that dream, and he'd held on to it so hard.

But Bug wasn't here anymore. It wasn't about his dream.

It was about Clay's.

A sudden ringing started in Clay's ears. His vision blurred.

He put down the broken pieces of the sign.

The same way he'd put down the broken pieces of his life.

This spring, on the one-year anniversary of Bug's death, he'd gotten a wake-up call. Time was slipping away from him, and all he'd been doing was wallowing, sitting in cheap motel rooms or camping under the stars. Not making any decisions. Even when he'd gotten off his butt, he'd passed the buck. He'd followed Bug's dream without even trying to think about whether or not that dream was his own, and he couldn't regret it.

All those non-choices had led him here. To what June had called the best small town in the world, and it killed him to admit, but she was right.

He'd picked this place, and this place had picked him. June had chosen to help him—no matter her reasons. She'd listened to him and shaped this bar into what it had become, and he loved it.

He loved *her*.

She'd been the one to kiss him.

And did he really believe for a second she'd done that because she didn't think he was good enough?

Those nights he spent with her, he felt like a king. Doubt had lingered, sure, but she'd made him feel special.

The words she'd spoken in anger after his out-of-control bar opening had cost her money she didn't have didn't erase everything they'd shared. She'd hurt him, yeah. So he'd hurt her in return. It was no wonder she'd run away.

Especially after she'd finally confided in him how badly her family was really struggling, and he'd barely reacted.

He'd spent a year keeping everyone in his life out of arm's reach. Tuck, AJ, Riz. Lisa and Hadley.

One argument with June, and he'd done the same with her. Not because she'd told him he wasn't good enough.

But because he believed that. Exactly like Han had said.

He laughed into the void that had opened beneath his feet.

Well, not anymore. He was done living other people's dreams. He was finished pushing everyone away, assuming the worst about what they thought of him.

It was time to take the broken pieces of the life that had been handed to him and to stop sitting there, cutting himself on the jagged edges.

It was time to use them to build something new. Something that would help the woman he loved and this random dot on a map that had somehow turned into his home.

Something that would maybe even help him help himself for once.

And he knew exactly where to start.

CHAPTER TWENTY-SIX

*D*ear *Clay,* June wrote, sitting behind the front desk at the inn, her pen scratching across yet another piece of paper she'd yanked out of the printer. *I'm so sorry I've been such an idiot—*

"Morning, June," a voice called out.

Instinctively shielding the paper she'd been writing on with her arm, she looked up. Mindy Dawes and one of her friends from the permit office waved on their way toward the dining room.

June smiled tightly. "Morning."

She looked down again at the letter she was trying—and failing—to write.

The front door swung open again. "Hey, there, June."

June frowned and said hello to a couple of women she knew from the farmers' market. "Can I help you?"

"Nah, just grabbing a quick bite."

"Okay. Enjoy."

As the women disappeared around the corner, she did some quick mental math.

The first day of the weekend-long Pumpkin Festival always drew a brisk business for the breakfast crowd, but considering bookings were down and everything was terrible, June had assumed today would be as much of a disappointment as every other.

She glanced out the window, but with the bright morning sun streaming in, it was hard to see exactly what was going on out there. When she'd been helping get booths and tents set up at six a.m., the streets had been quiet. She'd been hiding away behind the desk since then, though, and she hadn't had the heart to follow up any further. Advance logistics, marketing, and promotion had been her jobs; day of coordination was on Patty and the business association.

At this point, a decent number of people seemed to be milling around. That was probably good news.

Not good enough, of course. Breakfast crowds picking up would help, but sales in the dining room would be hard-pressed to offset the downturn in room revenue.

And none of it mattered, anyway, because it was too late. The giant surprise bill she'd gotten slammed with was due at the end of the month, and the Wu-Millers were broke. Main Street—and Blue Cedar Falls with it—was dying.

Even Clay's bar had been silent the past few nights. She hated being proven right about his business going bust after its disastrous opening.

She hated even more knowing how he must be hurting. That place had been his dream. He'd put everything into it.

But that was how life was, wasn't it? You put your all into the people and places that mattered to you, but there was no guarantee that it would be enough. Businesses failed. Debts added up.

People let you down.

June had to confront that truth. She'd let her family down. She'd let the town down. Elizabeth might have been sanguine about June messing up, but she was just the first of many June would have to confess to, and to be fair, Elizabeth had her own unique perspective on recovering after a disaster. June wanted to believe that she would be forgiven—that it could all really be as straightforward as her sister had made it out to be, but deep down, she was still working on confronting her shame.

And then there was the matter of how she'd let Clay down.

A painful pang fired off behind her ribs.

She'd been so unfair to him. Ever since she and Elizabeth had hashed it out a few days ago, she'd been circling around how she'd screwed up her relationship with Clay. She hadn't been open with him. She'd pushed him away. She'd put too much pressure on his bar to succeed and help her business and the businesses around it. She'd blamed him for her problems when the whole plan had all gone south.

She stared at the words she'd written, and her vision blurred. They seemed so inadequate. Tossing her pen aside, she crumpled up the sheet and threw it in the recycling with the rest of her previous attempts.

The bin was almost full.

How many times had she picked up the phone to call or text him, or slung her bag over her shoulder, ready to storm across the street and tell him how sorry she was? Every time, though, she'd chickened out. How could she put everything she felt into words?

The way he made her feel. The freedom of being with him.

How deeply she missed him.

There was no way. So here she was. Sequestered behind the desk, ignoring the festival going on outside, putting pen to paper in a desperate, hopeless effort to get this right.

And she was screwing that up, too.

"Morning, June."

Reaching over to grab a fresh sheet of paper, she waved hello to yet another group of people heading toward the breakfast room. She frowned. They were younger than the usual Friday morning crowd, and a couple of them were looking at her strangely.

They kept walking eventually. They passed another group who had gotten there earlier and were on their way out. June exchanged wishes for a nice day with them before bending her head to try to figure out how on earth to apologize to Clay again.

The door swung open again barely two minutes later. "Hey, June."

"Hey," she replied, only glancing up this time as she started to write.

Another half dozen interactions passed like that, leaving her roughly equal parts annoyed, happy, and concerned. They hadn't been prepared for such a crowd. She should really go see if Ned could use a hand. Or maybe text Elizabeth to see if she was free in case they needed even more help.

But before she could do any of that, one final, "Good morning, June," rang out.

She jerked her gaze up, startled to find Bobbi and Caitlin standing right in front of her.

"Oh, hi." She tucked her hair behind her ear, trying not to let on that they'd completely snuck up on her in her distraction. "Sorry, I can't really talk right now. We're slammed."

Bobbi grinned, almost bouncing. "I know, right?"

June pushed her chair back, glancing between the two of them. Caitlin held her cards close to her chest, but a knowing smirk flirted with the corners of her lips, and okay. Something was going on.

"Aren't you going to come out and see the festival?" Caitlin asked.

June waved a hand at two more folks heading through the lobby toward the dining room. "Kinda busy."

"Yeah, you really look it." Bobbi leaned over the desk and snagged the scribbled out, barely coherent half apology she'd been working on.

June leaped to her feet, her heart suddenly pounding. "Hey!"

Bobbi scanned the words and her eyes lit up. "Oh, perfect."

"Not funny."

Bobbi held the page out of reach. "Come out with us. You won't regret it."

"I have to go check on Ned. The breakfast crowd's been ridiculous."

"Ned is fine."

June whipped around to find her stepfather himself leaning on the desk, his apron on and a tired but genuinely happy smile on his face.

"What are you doing out here?" June asked.

"Spelling you for a bit."

June sputtered. "But breakfast."

"Is under control. I have help."

That was the first she'd heard about it. "Who?"

"Never you mind. Just run along with your friends, all right?"

"I can't 'just run along.' It's the middle of the day." Was he kidding?

"'Dear Clay,'" Bobbi read in an exaggerated voice.

"No," June shouted. "No, no, no, don't you dare."

Bobbi beamed, clutching the page to her chest. "Guess you'll have to stop me."

"I'm being ganged up on." June shot a glare at each of them in turn. Especially Ned. "You're in on this."

He shuffled past her and dropped into the chair. "Prove it."

"I'll do worse than that. I'll tell Mom."

"What makes you think your mother's not in on this, too?"

That brought June to a screeching halt. Where had her mother been all morning? With so many people coming and going, she hadn't even noticed, but now that she thought about it, her mom's usual gaggle of women of a certain age had failed to show.

"We are going to have words about this later."

"Oh believe me." Ned wiggled the mouse. "I know."

"Come *on*." Bobbi grabbed June's hand and dragged her out from behind the desk. "Unless you want me to start reading again."

June's cheeks flashed hot. "Absolutely not."

"We'll have her back before you know it, Mr. Miller," Caitlin promised.

"No rush." Ned leaned back in the chair, his hands behind his head.

"You know you can just put up the sign," June reminded him, even as Bobbi hauled her toward the door. "Did you turn all the burners off in the kitchen?"

"Have a nice morning," Ned called.

Caitlin got the door and Bobbi shoved June through it.

"Seriously." June tugged away from Bobbi's clutches. "What is going on?"

Bobbi took her by her upper arms and turned her around.

June's jaw dropped.

It wasn't even ten in the morning on the first day, and the Pumpkin Festival was the busiest June had ever seen it. Crowds of people stretched as far as the eye could see on both sides of Main Street.

"Morning, June," someone called, and June managed a faint, "Morning," in reply.

It wasn't just the usual folks that had come out, either. Where on earth had all these tourists come from?

"What..."

Bobbi lifted an arm to point across the street. June followed her direction, and her eyes practically bugged out of her skull.

"Is that—?"

Caitlin nodded. "It sure is."

A giant banner covered the brick facing on the side of Clay's bar. And on it was a picture of her mother's cat.

"I—" June tried to pick her jaw up off the floor and make her mouth form words, but it was hopeless. "What."

Beneath the huge photo was a sign. GET YOUR PICTURE TAKEN WITH THE INTERNET'S OWN SUNNY THE CAT.

Numb, June strode across the street. The crowd parted for her, revealing a booth with Sunny stretched out across a pillow, her favorite potted plant beside her and a whole pile of half-destroyed toy mice. A couple of teenagers posed in front of the cat, making peace signs as her mother snapped a picture.

"Mom?"

Her mom tapped a few buttons on the phone. "I tag you," she told the teenagers. Once they had gone, a middle-aged woman and her toddler took their place. June turned her head. At least another half dozen people stood in line, waiting their turn.

And every one of them was stuffing money in a box.

June's heart skipped. On the box was a picture of both her mom and Sunny, with a link to a fundraising website.

"Mom," June tried again, her voice rising.

"Guessing you didn't read the paper," her mom said dryly.

"The—"

Bobbi produced a copy seemingly out of nowhere. The headline read, LOCAL INTERNET CELEBRITY CAT RAISES FUNDS FOR OWNER'S MEDICAL BILLS.

June grabbed the paper and scanned the article, but the text blurred in front of her eyes. She looked to the photograph, the same one as was on the banner. The caption said the campaign, launched just the night before, had already raised ten thousand dollars.

"Ten *thousand*," June squeaked.

"Oh, sorry." Caitlin flashed her phone in front of June's face. "That went to the printer last night. It's a lot higher now."

June went dizzy, taking in the number. It was enough to pay off the bill coming due at the end of the month. Heck, it would make a decent dent in the ones she had the payment plan set up for.

"How?" June's throat clicked. Her chest was tight, at the same time it was expanding, a lightness she hadn't even imagined she could feel threatening to lift her right into the sky. "This—"

"Talk to your sister and your boyfriend," her mother said cheerily.

June looked past her mother, scarcely able to breathe.

Standing there, looking equal parts wary and smug, were Elizabeth and Clay.

With a wincing smile that made it look like she was bracing for impact, Elizabeth shrugged. "Surprise?"

"What." June blinked, snapping her gaze between the two of them. Then she took in the others who had gathered around them. Patty Boyd's scowl was sour, and Dottie Gallagher looked impatient to be off.

"You should have told us," Dottie said.

"Wouldn't be much of a tourist destination without an inn," Patty agreed.

"What," June repeated. Dottie, Patty, and their friends who had gathered for the big reveal wandered away, but that was fine. June looked again to Elizabeth, Clay, Han, Devin. Practically everybody she knew. "*How?*"

"Did we break her?" Caitlin asked.

"Give it a minute," Bobbi said.

Han shook his head. "I think you broke her." He lifted his phone and took a picture of her opening and closing her mouth like a fish.

"June?" Nerves shone in Clay's expression, too.

June replayed the last five minutes in her brain, but none of it made sense.

She jerked around, holding up a hand to Elizabeth and Clay as she addressed her mother. "Mom. The bills. You. I."

"Your sister told me."

"And you're not mad?"

Her mom turned away from the old man currently posing in front of Sunny. "Mad? I was furious."

June's heart sank. "Right."

Her mom waved her hand around. "Furious you didn't tell me."

"I can explain."

"You don't have to. Elizabeth tell me everything."

Oh, no. "Look—"

"You tried to handle everything, same way you always do." Her mother rolled her eyes. "It bit you in the butt. Happens to everybody."

"Wait—"

"You were only trying to protect me and take care of your family. Right?"

June felt faint again. "Of course."

"Then nothing else to be mad about. Next time there's a problem, you tell everyone. Let us help. Okay?"

June crinkled her brow. "I mean—"

"Okay?" her mom repeated pointedly.

"Okay."

"We're all good, then."

"But—"

Her mom got that same look on her face she'd had when she'd caught June sneaking in after spending the night with Clay for the first time—when June had expected to be read the riot act and instead received encouragement. Love.

"June." Her mother closed the space between them and took her hand, and June choked up all over again. "It's okay."

The words were the same, but the way her mother looked her in the eye and squeezed her palm made it different. She really, honestly wasn't mad.

And it couldn't possibly be that easy, could it? June had hidden the debt for months. Yes, it had been a mad gamble to try to protect her family and shelter them from the hardship of getting out from under this massive boulder that had fallen on them.

But shouldn't there be more to it now? She'd failed, *utterly*. And everybody seemed to think it was...fine.

Was it? If that number for the fundraiser was real, it was a miracle. They were on their way to solvency after all these months of hanging off the edge of a financial cliff.

So, what—all was well that ended well? It didn't seem possible. Just getting the money didn't change how much she'd screwed this up, but nobody seemed to care.

She spun around, taking in the crowds, the ever-increasing line of people waiting to get photographed with a cat. Her mother, Elizabeth, Han and Bobbi and Caitlin and Clay and...

None of them cared. In the best possible way.

They were still here for her. No one was yelling or disappointed—except maybe about the part where she had lived with this problem weighing on her shoulders for so long. Even that, they all seemed willing to let it go.

They seemed to love her anyway, and that was the most impossible part of all.

She'd spent her life taking care of everyone. Doing the right thing. She'd never dropped the ball before. Not once.

And this time she had. It would have left a crater in the ground, it was about to fall so hard, and it was *fine*.

It dawned on her, as tears formed in the corners of her eyes. Everything was going to be fine.

"How—?" She turned again toward Elizabeth and Clay.

Elizabeth smiled with fond exasperation.

"Are you sure we didn't break her?" Clay asked.

"I'm fine," June managed. She swabbed at her eyes. She felt weightless and free, and not just because the debt was going to be paid.

She'd screwed up, and nobody hated her.

The way they'd come out for her and solved this problem for her...It was incredible.

She threw herself at her sister first.

Elizabeth grunted as June flung her arms around her neck.

"Thank you."

Elizabeth patted her back gently. "Thank Mom for having a gazillion followers on Facebook and Instagram."

"Shut up, I'm thanking you right now."

"Yeah, if she's telling people to shut up already, she's going to be fine," Bobbi said.

June pulled away but didn't let go of her sister's arms.

Elizabeth squirmed under the scrutiny. "You're welcome?"

"I sold you short."

"It's fine." Elizabeth waved the apology off. "Everybody does."

"Not anymore."

"Told you you should have looped me in earlier."

She gazed at her baby sister, trying to figure out how she'd judged her so wrong.

Never again.

And her mom and sister weren't the only ones she'd under-estimated.

As if she could read her thoughts, Elizabeth looked to the side. "This was all Clay's idea anyway. Or at least mostly."

June let go of her sister. Clay cupped the back of his neck and suddenly seemed to find the cat photography really interesting.

Despair had gotten such a grip on June. She'd been so sure she'd ruined things with Clay.

But here he was. Rallying her family and her friends and—heck—the whole town and maybe half the state, it seemed.

"It was nothing," he grumbled.

"I don't believe that for one second." June stepped closer to him.

Elizabeth backed away. As if on cue, Han and Bobbi and Caitlin and everybody else did, too. They were still standing in the middle of a crowded street, in the middle of a town-wide festival, but it didn't seem to matter.

As her and Clay's gazes met for the first time in over a week, it felt as if everything and everyone around them disappeared.

"Thank you." She bridged the gap further, until there were only a couple of feet between them. Her insides tingled with awareness, a flare of that same attraction that had pulled at her from the moment they'd met, through their arguments, their partnership and beyond. Trying not to let it overwhelm her or send her jumping straight into his arms, she gestured at the crowd and the photo booth. "For all of this. It's amazing."

Clay scrubbed a hand through his hair. He was normally so proud and gruff. Seeing him stammering and unsure melted her heart even more. "Uh. You're welcome. But that's not all."

Her brows rose. "What—?"

He jerked a thumb at the building behind them.

She clasped a hand over her mouth.

Standing in front of the bar were three familiar faces. Decked out in Pumpkin Festival T-shirts, Tuck, AJ, and Riz waved at her.

"You guys—" she started.

"Our man Clay needed us." Tuck shot Clay a meaningful look, then smiled at June. "Had some work he wanted us to do."

Beside them was a woman she didn't know and a little girl she did, but only from a photo on the home screen of Clay's phone. June tipped her head to the side. "Hadley?"

"Uh-huh." Hadley beamed and bounced up and down. "I *love* your dress. Purple is *my favorite*."

"Told you," Clay muttered near June's ear, and June laughed.

"So you must be..." June turned to the woman.

She held out her hand. "Lisa. Bug's sister." As they shook hands, Lisa's lips curled up, and her eyes were bright. "When Clay told me the changes he wanted to make, I had to come see it all for myself."

She gestured at the bar, and June looked up, her heart in her throat.

Through the glass, she spotted the same familiar interior, only it was even better than before. All evidence of the bedlam from opening night had been swept away, the rough edges sanded smooth without losing any of their charm.

But where his walls used to display generic old posters, they were now decorated with vintage signs from all around town—ones for Sprinkles Ice Cream stand and Gracie's Café and Groovy Tunes Records. Black-and-white photos had been hung up, too, and it wasn't just the past that was alive and well in the town's brand-new watering hole.

An entire wall now proudly displayed a giant map of the United States, with a smaller one of the globe tacked up right beside it. Rainbow-colored pushpins invited travelers to record where they were from.

June's eyes misted over. He'd done it. He'd created an old-fashioned watering hole with a modern twist. A gem where locals and tourists alike could feel at home.

It was perfect.

Lisa squeezed June's hand. "Bug would've been real proud." She gazed past June, toward Clay. "And I for one love the new name."

Clay looked down and kicked a rock off the sidewalk. To June, he said, "I can change it again, if you don't like it."

Then June saw what else was new. She pressed her fingers to her lips harder, scarcely able to breathe. Her vision blurred.

"The Junebug," she read.

The new name of the bar was painted on the window and carved into a brand-new sign hung over the door.

"Like I said, if you don't like it…"

She dropped her hands and turned to him. The air between them crackled, and her heart felt full clear up to the brim. She reached for him, heat buzzing through her as she grasped his palm in hers.

"I love it." She faltered. "But you don't have to. You didn't have to. All the changes I was suggesting, it was about trying to help, but they were just suggestions." He tried to talk over her, but she kept going, her voice spiraling higher, but she had to get this out. "I'm sorry I got so mad at the opening.

I was upset and not thinking clearly. The bar was great the way it was."

He was great, exactly the way he was. No changes necessary.

His mouth spread into a soft smile that beamed into the tender center of her. "I didn't have to. I wanted to." He brought her hand to his lips and pressed a kiss to her knuckles that she felt all the way to her toes. "The bar I came here to build was Bug's idea, not mine. I followed it because I didn't have anything else. But then I came here. I met you and"—he waved his free hand around—"everybody else in this town, and you all got under my skin." If it was possible, his gaze went even softer. "You took the blinders off my eyes. The place I wanted to build was for Bug, sure, but more than that, it was a giant F you to the world, and that's not what I want to say anymore."

She squeezed his fingers tighter.

"I'm not so angry anymore, June. I don't want to keep the world away or drown my troubles. I want to let the world in. All of it." His throat bobbed. "I want to let you in. More than anything."

"I want that," she agreed. "So much." Her eyes were misty, and she didn't care. "I want to let you in, too. I don't want to hide when I'm hurting or struggling, and I'm—I'm going to work on that. I promise."

Because the people who loved her didn't care that she messed up sometimes. She could accept their love and their help, and it didn't make her flawed or unlovable.

"Good. And I'm going to work on it, too." He sucked in a breath. "I was hurt the other night, and I lashed out. I'm so sorry."

She shook her head. "Like I didn't do the same. The things I said...I can't tell you how terrible I feel. I want to make it up to you."

"You don't have to," he said, and it shouldn't be possible for him to sound that fond while basically agreeing she'd messed up, but apparently that was the theme for the day. "But you were trying to help everyone. Me, your family, this whole town."

She laughed at herself through blurry eyes. "Idiot."

"Nah." He released her hands to cup her face. His thumb rubbed a tear from the top of her cheek. "You try so hard and you do so much. Too much, sometimes, but nobody's perfect."

"I'm getting that."

"You tried to make the bar better, and you succeeded." A crack appeared in his voice. "You made me better."

Her eyes stung, and her heart squeezed. "You were both already pretty great."

He slid his hands down to rest at the place where her shoulders met her neck. "I'd given up. After the army and Bug and getting hurt." His green eyes gleamed. "But you showed me there's more out there. Even for a guy like me."

She laughed, watery and full of adoration for this man. "You sell yourself so short."

"I don't have a lot to offer you," he pressed on, determination burning in his gaze, but there was something else there, too. Something she wouldn't have dared to hope for before today.

But had it been there all along?

Had she ignored it the same way she'd ignored her friends' and her family's unconditional support?

Their love?

"Clay..."

"Let me get this out. I don't have anything more to offer you than myself, June. But if you want it—"

"I do," she rushed to tell him. "Clay, you have so much to offer." She blinked away the happy tears she couldn't seem to fight off any longer. "You're strong and brave and determined. If anyone should be giving out disclaimers here, it's me." She waved a hand across the street. "All I have is an old inn and a lot of opinions."

"So many," he agreed, but he smiled, bright and real.

"And I'm so sorry. I kept you at arm's length, too, and that wasn't fair. I was so scared to let anyone see the real me, like if they ever realized I was less than perfect, they'd walk away."

Chuckling, he tugged her closer and shook his head. "What part of me calling you a nosy, judgmental, overbearing snob did you think was me demanding you be perfect?"

"Oh, shut up." She swatted at him, but there wasn't any malice in it.

Her brain wasn't always logical. No one's was.

No one was perfect, least of all the two of them. But...

"We're perfect for each other," she told him.

"Yeah." Awe roughened his voice. "Yeah, we are, aren't we?"

"I just know you make me feel alive, and like I can let go in a way I've never been able to with anyone else, ever." She grabbed on to his wrists and held on tight. "I was so wrongheaded, acting like letting go around you was the problem, when it was probably the happiest I've ever been in my life. I can't tell you how sorry I am—"

Bobbi suddenly appeared at their side, practically vibrating. "But I can."

She thrust the letter she'd snatched from June's desk earlier in Clay's face.

"Bobbi, I swear to—" June tried to grab it back.

Clay took it and held it above her head, and she jumped, but it was no use. As he scanned it, she groaned and gave up, letting her head fall to rest against his firm, warm chest. He put a hand at the nape of her neck and held her there, and it was the best, most embarrassing moment of her life.

"I'm going to kill you," she vowed, glaring at Bobbi.

"No you're not," Bobbi and Clay both replied at once.

June shut her eyes and sighed.

Clay folded up the letter and tucked it in his pocket. "I'm keeping that for later."

"Please don't."

"I'm keeping it forever." He pulled her in against his chest, wrapping his big arms around her.

Mentally making a note to steal it back later, she melted into him. "Does that mean you're keeping me forever, too?"

"For as long as you'll have me."

He loosened his hold on her, and she leaned back to look up into his eyes. He tucked a bit of her hair behind her ear, his warm, calloused fingertips lingering on her cheek.

She pressed a kiss to his palm. "You really mean that, don't you?"

"I do." He swallowed. With wonder in his voice, he said, "I love you, June."

And what was there to say to that? This man who'd seen all her flaws, who'd seen her at her worst. This man who'd maybe even brought out her worst.

This man who'd changed his whole life plan for her and helped to save her family...

He loved her.

"I love you, too." Her heart glowed with the truth of it.

Taking her face between his hands again, he leaned down to kiss her as she lifted up onto her toes to do the same. They met in the middle, just like they always did.

Hoots and hollers went up from Clay's friends.

"Ew, get a room," her sister scolded.

Laughing, June pulled away, but she didn't go far. Their surroundings seeped back in, reminding her that they were in the middle of a crowded sidewalk next to a stall for an internet-famous cat.

Catching Clay's eye, she nodded her head to the side. "Come on, want to check out the festival with me?"

"I'd love to."

"Guess I'll go manage the inn," Elizabeth shouted after them.

June waved her appreciation. "Thanks!"

Arm in arm with Clay, she headed off down Main Street, past the shops she'd known her entire life and past the ones that had popped up over the last few years, too. People stopped to say hello, and she snuggled closer to Clay's side.

Blue Cedar Falls had always been the greatest small town in the world, but somehow, with him, it had become even better.

And she couldn't wait to keep watching it grow.

Together.

When May Wu returns to her hometown, all the changes in Blue Cedar Falls take her by surprise. But the biggest shock of all? The fierce attraction that still burns between her and her first love, Han Leung. Don't miss May and Han's swoon-worthy reunion!

Available Summer 2022

ABOUT THE AUTHOR

Jeannie Chin writes contemporary small-town romances. She draws on her experiences as a biracial Asian and Caucasian American to craft stories that speak to a uniquely American experience.

She is a former high school science teacher, wife to a geeky engineer, and mom to an extremely talkative preschooler. Her hobbies include crafting, reading, and running.

You can learn more at:
    JeannieChin.com
    Twitter @JeannieCWrites
    Facebook.com/JeannieCWrites

For a bonus story from another author that you'll love, please turn the page to read
Kiss Me at Sweetwater Springs by Annie Rains.

If Lacy Shaw could have one wish, it'd be that the past would stay in the past. And with her high school reunion coming up, she has no intention of reliving the worst four years of her life. Especially when all she has to show for the last decade is how the shy bookworm blossomed into...the shy town librarian. Ditching the event seems the best option until a blistering hot alternative roars into Lacy's life. Perhaps riding into the reunion on the back of Paris Montgomery's motorcycle will show her classmates how much she's really changed...

FOREVER

KISS ME IN SWEETWATER SPRINGS

A Sweetwater Springs Novella

ANNIE RAINS

FOREVER

New York Boston

CHAPTER ONE

Lacy Shaw looked around the Sweetwater Springs Library for the culprit of the noise, a "shhh" waiting on the tip of her tongue. There were several people reading quietly at the tables along the wall. A few patrons were wandering the aisles of books.

The high-pitched giggle broke through the silence again.

Lacy stood and walked out from behind her counter, going in the direction of the sound. She wasn't a stickler for quiet, but the giggling had been going on for at least ten minutes now, and a few of the college students studying in the far corner kept getting distracted and looking up. They'd come here to focus, and Lacy wanted them to keep coming.

She stopped when she was standing at the end of one of the nonfiction aisles where two little girls were seated on the floor with a large book about animals in their lap. The *shhh* finally tumbled off her lips. The sound made her feel even more like the stuffy librarian she tried not to be.

The girls looked up, their little smiles wilting.

Lacy stepped closer to see what was so funny about animals and saw a large picture of a donkey with the heading "Asses" at the top of the page. A small giggle tumbled off Lacy's lips as well. She quickly regained control of herself and offered a stern expression. "Girls, we need to be quiet in the library. People come here to read and study."

"That's why we're here," Abigail Fields, the girl with long, white-blond curls, said. They came in often with their nanny, Mrs. Townsend, who usually fell asleep in the back corner of the room. The woman was somewhere in her eighties and probably wasn't the best choice to be taking care of two energetic little girls.

"I have to write a paper on my favorite animal," Abigail said.

Lacy made a show of looking at the page. "And it's a donkey?"

"That's not what that says," Willow, Abigail's younger sister, said. "It says..."

"Whoa!" Lacy held up a hand. "I can read, but let's not say that word out loud, okay? Why don't you two take that book to a table and look at it quietly," she suggested.

The little girls got up, the older one lugging the large book with both hands.

Lacy watched them for a moment and then turned and headed back to her counter. She walked more slowly as she stared at the back of a man waiting for her. He wore dark jeans and a fitted black T-shirt that hugged muscles she didn't even have a name for. There was probably an anatomy book here that did. She wouldn't mind locating it and taking her time labeling each muscle, one by one.

She'd seen the man before at the local café, she realized, but never in here. And every time he'd walked into the café, she'd noticed him. He, of course, had never noticed her. He was too gorgeous and cool. There was also the fact that Lacy usually sat in the back corner reading a book or people-watching from behind her coffee cup.

What is he doing here?

The man shifted as he leaned against her counter, his messenger bag swinging softly at his lower hip. Then he glanced over his shoulder and met her gaze. He had blue crystalline eyes, inky black hair, and a heart-stopping smile that made her look away shyly—a nervous remnant of her high school years when the cool kids like him had picked on her because of the heavy back brace she wore.

The brace was gone. No one was going to laugh at her anymore, and even if they did, she was confident enough not to find the closest closet to cry in these days.

"Hey," he said. "Are you Lacy Shaw, the librarian here?"

She forced her feet to keep walking forward. "I am. And you are?"

He turned and held out a hand. "Paris." He suspended his hand in midair, waiting for her to take it. When she hesitated, his gaze flicked from her face to her hand and then back again.

She blinked, collected herself, and took his hand. "Nice to meet you. I'm Lacy Shaw."

Paris's dark brows dipped farther.

"Right," she giggled nervously. "You didn't need me to introduce myself. You just asked if that's who I was. Do you, um, need help with something? Finding a book maybe?"

"I'm actually here for the class," he said.

"The computer skills class?" She walked around the counter to stand behind her computer. "The course instructor hasn't arrived yet." She looked at the Apple Watch on her wrist. "It's still a little early though. You're not late until you're less than five minutes early. That's what my mom always says."

Lacy had been wanting to offer a computer skills class here for months. There was a roomful of laptops in the back just begging for people to use them. She'd gotten the computer skills teacher's name from one of her regular patrons here, and she'd practically begged Mr. Montgomery over the phone to take the job.

"The class runs from today to next Thursday. It's aimed toward people sixty-five and over," she told the man standing across from her, briefly meeting his eyes and then looking away. "But you're welcome to attend, of course." Although she doubted he'd fit in. He appeared to be in his early thirties, wore dark clothes, and looked like his idea of fun might be adding a tattoo to the impressive collection on his arms.

Paris cleared his throat. "Unless I'm mistaken, I *am* the instructor," he said. "Paris Montgomery at your service."

"Oh." She gave him another assessing look. She'd been expecting someone…different. Alice Hampton had been the one to recommend Paris. She was a sweet old lady who had sung the praises of the man who'd rented the room above her garage last year. Lacy never would've envisioned the likes of this man staying with Mrs. Hampton. "Oh, I'm sorry. Thank you for agreeing to offer some of your time to our senior citizens. A lot of them have expressed excitement over the class."

Paris gave a cursory glance around the room. "It's no problem. I'm self-employed, and as I told you on the phone, I had time between projects."

"You're a graphic designer, right?" she asked, remembering what Alice had told her. "You created the designs for the Sweetwater Bed and Breakfast."

"Guilty. And for a few other businesses in Sweetwater Springs."

Lacy remembered how much she'd loved the designs when she'd seen them. "I've been thinking about getting something done for the library," she found herself saying.

"Yeah? I'd be happy to talk it over with you when you're ready. I'm sure we can come up with something simple yet classy. Modern. Inviting."

"Inviting. Yes!" she agreed in a spurt of enthusiasm before quickly feeling embarrassed. But that was her whole goal for the library this year. She wanted the community to love coming in as much as she did. As a child growing up, the library had been her haven, especially during those years of being bullied. The smell of books had come to mean freedom to her. The sound of pages turning was music to her ears.

"Well, I guess I better go set up for class." Paris angled his body toward the computer room. "Five minutes early is bordering on late, right?" he asked, repeating her words and making her smile.

He was cool, gorgeous, *and* charming—a dangerous combination.

———

Paris still wasn't sure why he'd agreed to this proposition. It paid very little, and he doubted it would help with his graphic design business. The librarian had been so insistent on the phone that it'd been hard to say no to her. Was that the same woman who'd blushed and had a hard time making eye contact with him just now? She looked familiar, but he wasn't sure where or when they'd ever crossed paths.

He walked into the computer room in the back of the library and looked around at the laptops set up. How hard could it be to teach a group of older adults to turn on a computer, utilize the search engine, or set up an email account? It was only two weeks. He could handle that.

"You're the teacher?" a man's voice asked behind him.

Paris whirled to face him. The older man wore a ball cap and a plaid button-down shirt. In a way, he looked familiar. "Yes, sir. Are you here for the class?"

The man frowned. "Why else would I ask if you were the teacher?"

Paris ignored the attitude and gestured to the empty room. "You have your pick of seats right now, sir," Paris told him. Then he directed his attention to a few more seniors who strolled in behind the older man. Paris recognized a couple of them. Greta Merchant used a cane, but he knew she walked just fine. The cane was for show, and Paris had seen her beat it against someone's foot a couple of times. She waved and took a seat next to the frowning man.

"Paris!" Alice Hampton said, walking into the room.

He greeted her with a hug. After coming to town last winter and staying at the Sweetwater B&B for a week, he'd rented a room from Alice for a while. Now he had his own place, a little cabin that sat across the river.

All in all, he was happy these days, which is more than he could say when he lived in Florida. After his divorce, the Sunshine State had felt gloomy. He hadn't been able to shake the feeling, and then he'd remembered being a foster kid here in Sweetwater Springs, North Carolina. A charity event for bikers had given him an excuse to come back for a visit, and he'd never left. Not yet, at least.

"I told all my friends about this class," Alice said. "You're going to have a full and captive audience with us."

Nerves buzzed to life in his stomach. He didn't mind public speaking, but he hoped most were happy to be here, unlike the frowner in the corner.

More students piled in and took their seats, and then the timid librarian came to the door. She nibbled on her lower lip, her gaze skittering everywhere but to meet his directly. "Do you need anything?"

Paris shook his head. "No, we have plenty of computers. We'll just get acquainted with them and go from there."

She looked up at him now, a blush rising over her high cheekbones. She had light brown hair spilling out of a messy bun and curling softly around her jawline. She had a pretty face, made more beautiful by her rich brown eyes and rose-colored mouth. "Well, you know where I am if you do need something." She looked at the group. "Enjoy!"

"You hired a looker!" Greta Merchant hollered at Lacy. "And for that, there'll be cookies in your future, Ms. Lacy! I'll bring a plate next class!"

The blush on Lacy's cheeks deepened as her gaze jumped to meet his momentarily. "Well, I won't turn down your cookies, Ms. Greta," she said.

Paris watched her for a moment as she waved and headed back to her post.

"The ink in those tattoos going to your brain?" the frowner called to him. "It's time to get started. I don't have all day, you know."

Paris pulled his gaze from the librarian and faced the man. "Neither do I. Let's learn something new, shall we?"

An hour later, Paris had taught the class of eleven to turn on and turn off the laptops. It'd taken an excruciating amount of time to teach everyone to open a browser and use a search engine. Overall, it'd gone well, and the hour had flown by.

"Great job," Alice said to him approvingly. She patted a motherly hand on his back that made him feel warm and appreciated. That feeling quickly dissipated as the frowner headed out the door.

"I already knew most of what you taught," he said.

Who was this person, and why was he so grouchy?

"Well, then you probably didn't need this class," Paris pointed out politely. "Actually, you probably could've taught it yourself."

The frowner harrumphed. "Next time *teach* something."

Paris nodded. "Yes, sir. I'll do my best."

"Your best is the only acceptable thing," the man said before walking out.

Paris froze for a moment, reaching for the memory that the frowner had just stirred. *Your best is the only acceptable thing.* His foster dad here in Sweetwater Springs used to say that to him. That man had been nothing but encouraging. He'd taught Paris more about life in six months than anyone ever had before or since.

Paris hadn't even caught his student's name, and there was no roster for this computer skills class. People had walked in and attended without any kind of formal record.

Paris watched the frowner walk with slow, shuffled steps. He was old, and his back was rounded. A hat sat on his head, casting a shadow on his leathered face. All Paris had really seen of him was his deep, disapproving frown. It'd been nearly two decades since Paris had laid eyes on Mr. Jenson, but he remembered his former foster dad being taller. Then again, Paris had been just a child.

When Paris had returned to Sweetwater Springs last year, he'd decided to call. Mrs. Jenson had been the one to answer. She'd told him she didn't remember a boy named PJ, which is the name Paris had gone by back then. "Please, please, leave us alone! Don't call here again!" she'd pleaded on the line, much to Paris's horror. "Just leave us alone."

The memory made Paris's chest ache as he watched the older man turn the corner of the library and disappear. He resisted the urge to follow him and see if it really was Mr. Jenson. But the Jensons had given Paris so much growing up that he was willing to do whatever he could to repay their kindness—even if it meant staying away.

———

Lacy was checking out books for the Fields girls and their nanny when Paris walked by. She watched him leave. If you flipped to the word *suave* in the dictionary, his picture was probably there.

"I plan to bring the girls to your summer reader group in a couple weeks," Mrs. Townsend said.

Of course she did. That would be a convenient nap time for her.

"I always love to see the girls." Lacy smiled down at the children. Their father, Granger Fields, and his family owned Merry Mountain Farms in town where Lacy always got her blue spruce for the holidays.

Lacy waved as the little girls collected their bags of books and skipped out with Mrs. Townsend following behind them.

For the rest of the afternoon, Lacy worked on ongoing programs and plans for the summer and fall. At six p.m., she turned off the lights to the building and headed into the parking lot.

She was involved with the Ladies' Day Out group, a gaggle of women who regularly got together to hang out and have fun. Tonight, they were meeting at Lacy's house to discuss a book that she'd chosen for everyone to read. They were in no way a book club, but since it was her turn to decide what they did, Lacy had turned it into one this time.

Excitement brimmed as she drove home. When she pulled

up to her small one-bedroom house on Pine Cone Lane, she noticed two of her sisters' cars already parked in the driveway. Birdie and Rose had texted her during the day to see what they could do to help. Seeing the lights on inside Lacy's home, they'd evidently ignored Lacy's claims that she didn't need anything and had used her hideaway key under the flowerpot.

"Honey, I'm home!" Lacy called as she headed through the front door.

Birdie, her older sister by one year, turned to face her. "Hey, sis. Rose and I were just cleaning up for you."

"Great." Lacy set her purse down. "Now I don't have to."

"What is this?" Rose asked, stepping up beside Birdie. Rose was one year younger than Lacy. Their mom had been very busy those first three years of marriage.

Lacy looked at the small postcard that Rose held up.

"You were supposed to RSVP if you were going to your ten-year class reunion," Rose said. "You needed to send this postcard back."

"Only if I'm going," Lacy corrected.

"Of course you're going," Birdie said. "I went to my ten-year reunion last year, and it was amazing. I wish we had one every year. I wouldn't miss it."

Unlike Lacy, her sisters had been popular in school. They hadn't had to wear a bulky back brace that made them look like a box turtle in its shell. It had drawn nothing but negative attention during those long, tormenting years.

"It's not really a time in my life that I want to remember," Lacy pointed out as she passed them and headed into the kitchen for a glass of lemonade. Or perhaps she should go ahead and pour herself something stronger. She could tell she might need it tonight.

A knock on her front door made her turn. "Who is that?"

Lacy asked. "I scheduled the book discussion for seven. It's only six." Lacy set down the glass she'd pulled from the cabinet and went to follow her sisters to the door.

"About that," Birdie said a bit sheepishly. "We changed the plan at the last minute."

Lacy didn't like the sound of that. "What do you mean?"

"No one actually read the book you chose," Birdie said as Rose let the first arrivals in. "Instead, we're playing matchmaker tonight. What goes together better than summer and love?"

Lacy frowned. "If you wanted summer love, I could've chosen a romance novel to read instead."

Birdie gave her a disapproving look. Lacy doubted anyone was more disappointed about tonight's shift in festivities than her though.

CHAPTER TWO

Paris hadn't been able to fully concentrate for the last hour and a half as he sat in front of his computer working on a job for Peak Designs Architectural Firm. His mind was in other places. Primarily the library.

The Frowner, as he'd come to think of the old man in his class, was forefront in his mind. Was it possible that the Frowner was Mr. Jenson?

It couldn't be. Mr. Jenson had been a loving, caring guy, from what Paris remembered. Granted, loving and caring were subjective, and Paris hadn't had much to go on back then.

Mrs. Jenson had been the mother that Paris had always wished he had. She'd doted on him, offering affection and unconditional love. Even though Paris had been a boy who'd landed himself in the principal's office most afternoons, Mrs. Jenson had never raised her voice. And Mr. Jenson had always come home from his job and sat down with Paris, giving him a lecture that had proved to be more like a life lesson.

Paris had never forgotten those lessons. Or that man.

He blinked the memories away and returned his attention to the design he was working on. It was good, but he only did excellent jobs. *Your best is the only acceptable thing.*

He stared at the design for another moment and then decided to come back to it tomorrow when he wasn't so tired. Instead, he went to his Facebook page and searched Albert Jenson's name. He'd done so before, but no profiles under that name had popped up. This time, one did. The user had a profile picture of a rose instead of himself. Paris's old foster dad had loved his rose gardens. This must be him!

Paris scrolled down, reading the most recent posts. One read that Mr. Jenson had gone to the nursing home to visit his wife, Nancy.

Paris frowned at the news. The transition must have been recent because Mrs. Jenson had been home when he'd called late last year. She'd been the one to pretty much tell him to get lost.

He continued to scroll through more pictures of roses and paused at another post. This one read that Mr. Jenson had just signed up for a computer skills class at the Sweetwater Library.

So it was true. Mr. Jenson, the foster dad who'd taught him so much, was also the Frowner.

———

Lacy had decided to stick to just lemonade tonight since she was hosting the Ladies' Day Out group. But plans were meant to be changed, as evidenced by the fact that the book discussion she'd organized had turned into the women sitting around her living room, eyes on a laptop screen while perusing an online dating site.

"Oh, he's cute!" Alice Hampton said, sitting on the couch and leaning over Josie Kellum's shoulder as she tapped her fingers along the keys of Lacy's laptop. Not that anyone had asked to use her computer. The women had just helped themselves.

Lacy reached for the bottle of wine, poured herself a deep glass, and then headed over to see who they were looking at. "I know him," she said, standing between her sisters behind the couch. "He comes into the library all the time."

"Any interest?" Josie asked.

Lacy felt her face scrunch at the idea of anything romantic with her library patron. "Definitely not. I know what his reading interests are and frankly, they scare me. That's all I'll say on that."

She stepped away from her sisters and walked across the room to look out the window. The moon was full tonight. Her driveway was also full, with cars parked along the curb. She wasn't a social butterfly by any means, but she looked like one this evening and that made her feel strangely satisfied.

"So what are your hobbies, Lacy?" Josie asked. "Other than reading, of course."

"Well, I like to go for long walks," Lacy said, still watching out the window.

Josie tapped a few more keys. "Mmm-hmm. What's your favorite food?"

Lacy turned and looked back at the group. "Hot dogs," she said, earning her a look from the other women.

"Do you know what hot dogs are made out of?" Greta wanted to know.

"Yes, of course I do. Why do I feel like I'm being interviewed for one of your articles right now?"

"Not an article," Birdie said. "A dating profile."

"What?" Lacy nearly spilled her glass of wine as she moved to look over Josie's shoulder. "What are you doing? I don't want to be up on Fish In The Sea dot com. Stop that."

Birdie gave her a stern look. "You have a class reunion coming up, and you can't go alone."

"I'm not going period," Lacy reiterated.

"Not going to your class reunion?" Dawanda from the fudge shop asked. She was middle-aged with spiky, bright red hair. She tsked from across the room, where she sat in an old, worn recliner that Lacy had gotten from a garage sale during college.

Lacy finished off her wine and set the empty glass on the coffee table nearby. "I already told you, high school was a miserable time that I don't want to revisit."

"All the more reason you *should* go," Birdie insisted. Even though she was only a year older, Birdie acted like Lacy's mother sometimes.

"Why, so I can be traumatized all over again?" Lacy shook her head. "It took me years to get over all the pranks and ridicule. Returning to the scene of the crime could reverse all my progress."

"What progress?" Rose asked. "You never go out, and you never date."

Lacy furrowed her brow. "I go to the café all the time."

"Alone and you sit in the back," Birdie pointed out. "Your back brace is gone, but you're still hiding in the corner."

Lacy's jaw dropped. She wanted to argue but couldn't. Her sister was right.

"So we're making Lacy a dating profile," Josie continued, looking back down at the laptop's screen. "Twenty-eight years old, loves to read, and takes long walks in the park."

"I never said anything about the park," Lacy objected.

"It sounds more romantic that way." Josie didn't bother to look up. "Loves exotic fruit…"

"I said hot dogs."

This time Josie turned her head and looked at Lacy over her shoulder. "Hot dogs don't go on dating profiles...but cute, wagging dogs do." Her fingers started flying across the keyboard.

"I like cats." Lacy watched for another moment and then went to pour herself another glass of wine as the women created her profile at FishInTheSea.com.

After a few drinks, she relaxed a little and started feeding Josie more details about herself. She wasn't actually going to do this, of course. Online dating seemed so unromantic. She wanted to find Mr. Right the old-fashioned way, where fate introduced him into her life and sparks flew like a massive explosion of fireworks. Or at least like a sparkler.

———

An hour later, Lacy said goodbye to the group and sat on the couch. She gave the book she'd wanted to discuss a side-long glance, and then she reached for her laptop. The dating profile stared back at her, taking her by surprise. They'd used a profile picture from when she'd been a bridesmaid at a wedding last year. Her hair was swept up and she had a dipping neckline on her dress that showed off more skin than normal. Lacy read what Josie and her sisters had written. The truth was disregarded in favor of more interesting things.

Lacy was proud of who she was, but the women were right. She wasn't acting that way by shying away from her reunion. She was acting like the girl in the back brace, quietly sitting in the far corner of the room out of fear that others might do something nasty like stick a sign on her back that read KICK ME! I WON'T FEEL IT!

"Maybe I should go to the reunion," she said out loud. "Or maybe I should delete this profile and forget all about it."

The decision hummed through her body along with the effect of one too many glasses of wine. After a moment, she shut the laptop and went to bed. She could decide her profile's fate tomorrow.

———

The next morning, Paris woke with the birds outside his window. After a shower and a quick bite, he grabbed his laptop to work on the deck, which served as his office these days. Before getting started on the Peak Designs logo, he scrolled through email and social media. He clicked on Mr. Jenson's profile again, only to read a post that Paris probably didn't need first thing in the morning.

The computer skills class was a complete waste of time. Learned nothing. Either I'm a genius or the instructor is an idiot.

The muscles along the back of his neck tightened. At least he didn't need to wonder if Mr. Jenson would be back.

He read another post.

Went to see Nancy today. I think she misses her roses more than she misses me. She wants to come home, and this old house certainly isn't home without her.

Paris felt like he'd taken a fall from his bike, landing chest-first and having the breath knocked out of him. Why wasn't Mrs. Jenson home? What was wrong with her? And why was Mr. Jenson so different from the man he remembered?

Paris pushed those questions from his mind and began work

on some graphic designs. Several hours later, he'd achieved much more than he'd expected. He shoved his laptop into its bag, grabbed his keys, and rode his motorcycle to the library. As he walked inside, his gaze immediately went to the librarian. Her hair was pulled back with some kind of stick poking through it today. He studied her as she checked books into the system on her desktop.

She glanced up and offered a shy wave, which he returned as he headed toward the computer room. He would have expected Mr. Jenson not to return to class today based on his Facebook comments, but Mr. Jenson was already waiting for him when he walked in. All the other students from the previous day filed in within the next few minutes.

"Today I'm teaching you all to use Microsoft Word," he told the group.

"Why would I use Microsoft Word?" Alice Hampton asked. Her questions were presented in a curious manner rather than the questions that Mr. Jenson posed, which felt more like an attack.

"Well, let's say you want to write a report for some reason. Then you could do one here. Or if you wanted to get creative and write a novel, then this is the program you'd use."

"I've always wanted to write a book," Greta told Alice. "It's on my bucket list, and I'm running out of time."

"Are you sick?" Alice asked with concern, their conversation hijacking the class.

"No, I'm healthy as a buzzard. Just old, and I can't live forever," Greta told her.

"Love keeps you young," Edna Baker said from a few chairs down. She was the grandmother of the local police chief, Alex Baker. "Maybe you should join one of those online dating sites."

The group got excited suddenly and turned to Paris, who had leaned back against one of the counters, arms folded over his chest as he listened.

He lifted a brow. "What?"

"A dating site," Edna reiterated. "We helped Lacy Shaw join one last night in our Ladies' Day Out group."

"The librarian?" Paris asked, his interest piquing.

"Had to do it with her dragging and screaming, but we did it. I wouldn't mind making a profile of my own," Edna continued.

"Me too." Greta nodded along with a few other women.

"I'm married," Mr. Jenson said in his usual grumpy demeanor. "I have no reason to be on a dating site."

"Then leave, Albert," Greta called out.

Mr. Jenson didn't budge.

"We're here to learn about what interests us, right?" Edna asked Paris.

He shrugged. There was no official syllabus. He was just supposed to teach computer literacy for the seniors in town. "I guess so."

"Well, majority rules. We want to get on one of those dating sites. I think the one we were on last night was called Fish In The Sea dot com."

Paris unfolded his arms, debating if he was actually going to agree to this. He somehow doubted the Sweetwater Springs librarian would approve, even if she'd apparently been on the site herself.

"Fine, I'll get you started," Paris finally relented, "but tomorrow, we're learning about Microsoft Word."

"I don't want to write a report or a novel," Mr. Jenson said, his frown so deep it joined with the fold of his double chin.

"Again, don't come if you don't want to," Greta nearly shouted. "No one is forcing you."

Paris suspected that Mr. Jenson would be back regardless of his opinions. Maybe he was lonely. Or maybe, despite his demeanor, this was his idea of a good time.

After teaching the group how to use the search bar function and get to the Fish In the Sea website, Paris walked around to make sure everyone knew how to open an account. Some started making their own profiles while others watched their neighbors' screens.

"This is Lacy's profile," Alice said when he made his way to her.

Paris leaned in to take a closer look. "That's not the librarian here."

"Oh, it is. This photo was taken when she was a bridesmaid last year. Isn't she beautiful?"

For a moment, Paris couldn't pull his gaze away from the screen. If he were on the dating site, he'd be interested in her. "Likes to hike. Loves dogs. Favorite food is a hot dog. Looking for adventure," he read. "That isn't at all what I would have pegged Lacy as enjoying."

Alice gave him a look. "Maybe there's more to her than meets the eye. Would you like to sit down and create your own profile? Then you could give her a wink or a nibble or whatever the online dating lingo is."

He blinked, pulled his gaze from the screen, and narrowed his eyes at his former landlord. "You know I'm not interested in that kind of thing." He'd told Alice all about his past when he'd rented a room from her last year. After his messy marriage, the last thing he wanted was to jump into another relationship.

"Well, what I know is, you're young, and your heart can take a few more beatings if it comes to it. Mine, on the other hand, can't, which is why I'm not creating one of these profiles."

Paris chuckled. "Hate to disappoint, but I won't be either." Even if seeing Lacy's profile tempted him to do otherwise.

———

At the end of the hour, Paris was the last to leave his class, following behind Mr. Jenson, who had yet to hold a personal conversation with him or say a civilized thing in his direction.

He didn't recognize Paris, and why would he? Paris had been a boy back then. His hair had been long and had often hung in his eyes. His body had been scrawny from neglect and he hadn't gotten his growth spurt until well into his teen years. He hadn't even had the same last name back then. He'd gone by PJ Drake before his parents' divorce. Then there was a custody battle, which was the opposite of what one might think. Instead of fighting *for* him, his parents had fought over who *had* to take him.

"Mr. Jenson?" Paris called.

The older man turned to look at Paris with disdain.

"How was the class?"

"An utter waste of time."

Paris liked to think he had thick skin, but his former foster dad's words had sharp edges that penetrated deep. "Okay, well what computer skills would you like to learn?"

The skin between Mr. Jenson's eyes made a deep divot as he seemed to think. "I can't see my wife every day like I want to because I don't drive. It's hard for an old man like me to go so far. The nurses say they can set up Skype to talk to her, but I don't understand it. They didn't have that sort of thing when I was old enough to learn new tricks."

"Never too late," Paris said. "A great man once taught me that."

That great man was standing in front of him now, whether he knew it or not. And he needed his own pep talk of sorts. "Come back tomorrow, and we'll get you set up for that."

Mr. Jenson frowned back at him. "We'll see."

———

Lacy was trying not to panic.

A blue circle had started spinning on her laptop screen five minutes ago. Now there were pop-up boxes that she couldn't seem to get rid of. She'd restarted her computer, but the pop-up boxes were relentless. She sucked in a breath and blew it out audibly. Then another, bordering on hyperventilation.

"You okay?" a man's voice asked.

Her gaze lifted to meet Paris's. "Oh. Yeah." She shook her head.

"You're saying yes, but you're shaking your head no." His smile was the kind that made women swoon, and for a moment, she forgot that she was in panic mode.

"My computer seems to be possessed," she told him.

This made Paris chuckle—a sound that seemed to lessen the tension inside her. "Mind if I take a look?"

She needed to say no. He was gorgeous, charming, and cool. And those three qualities made her nervous. But without her computer, she wouldn't be able to pay her bills after work. Or delete that dating profile that the Ladies' Day Out group had made for her last night. *Why didn't I delete it right away?*

"Yes, please," she finally said.

Paris headed around the counter. "Did you restart it?" he asked when he was standing right next to her. So close that she could smell the woodsy scent coming off his body. She could also feel a wave of heat radiating off him, burning the superficial layer of her skin. He was gorgeous, charming, cool, *and* he smelled divine. What woman could resist?

"I've restarted it twice already," she told him.

"Hmm." He put his bag down on the floor at his feet and stood in front of her computer. She couldn't help a closer inspection of the tattoos that covered his biceps muscles. They were colorful and artistically drawn, but she could only see parts of them. She had to resist pulling back the fabric of his shirt to admire the artwork there. What was wrong with her?

Paris turned his head to look at her. "Is it okay if I close out all the programs you currently have running?"

"Of course."

He tapped his fingers along her keys, working for several long minutes while she drifted off in her own thoughts of his muscles and tattoos and the spicy scent of his aftershave. Then he straightened and turned back to her. "There you go, good as new."

"Wow. Really? That was fast."

He shrugged a nonchalant shoulder. "I just needed to reboot and run your virus software."

"You make it sound so easy."

"To me it is. I know computers. We have a kinship."

Lacy felt the same way about books. She reached for her cup of coffee that she'd purchased this morning, even though a jolt of caffeine was probably the last thing her nerves needed right now.

Paris pointed a finger at the cup. "That's where I know you from. You're the woman at the café. You always sit in the back with a book."

Her lips parted as she set her cup down. "You've noticed me?"

"Of course. Why wouldn't I?"

She shrugged and shook her head. "We've just never spoken." And she'd assumed she was invisible in the back corner, especially to someone like him. "Well, thank you for fixing my computer."

"Just a friend helping a friend." He met her gaze and held it for a long moment. Then he bent to pick up the strap of his bag, hung it over his shoulder, and headed around to the other side of the counter. "Be careful on those dating sites," he said, stopping as he passed in front of her. "Always meet at a safe location and don't give anyone your personal information until you know you can trust them."

"Hmm?" Lacy narrowed her eyes, and then her heart soared into her throat and her gaze dropped to her fixed computer. Up on the screen, first and foremost, was FishInTheSea.com. She giggled nervously as her body filled with mortification. "I didn't…I'm not…" Why wouldn't her mouth work? "This isn't what it looks like."

Paris grinned. "The women in my class told me about last night. Sounds like you were forced into it."

"Completely," she said with relief.

He shrugged. "I doubt you need a website to find a date. They created a really attractive profile for you though. It should get you a lot of nibbles from the fish in the sea."

She laughed because he'd made a joke, but there was no hope of making intelligible words right now. Instead she waved and watched him leave.

"See you tomorrow, Lace," he called over his shoulder.

———

That evening, Paris kicked his feet up on the railing of his back deck as he sat in an outdoor chair, laptop on his thighs, watching the fireflies that seemed to be sending him secret messages with their flashing lights. The message he needed right now was "get back to work."

Paris returned to looking at his laptop's screen. He'd worked on the graphic for Peak Designs Architectural Firm all evening, and he was finally happy with it. He sent it off to the owner and then began work on a new agenda for tomorrow's class. He'd be teaching his students how to Skype, and he'd make sure Mr. Jenson knew how to do it on his own before leaving.

Paris liked the thought of reuniting Mr. and Mrs. Jenson through technology. It was the least he could do for them. Technology shouldn't replace person-to-person contact, but it was a nice substitute when two people couldn't be together. Paris suspected one of the main reasons Mr. Jenson even came to the library was because it was one of the few places within walking distance from his house.

Creating an agenda for live communication technology took all of ten minutes. Then Paris gave in to his impulse to search FishInTheSea.com. He found himself looking at Lacy's profile again, staring at the beautiful picture on the screen. Her brown hair was down and spilling over one shoulder in soft curls. She had on makeup that accentuated her eyes, cheekbones, and lips. And even though she looked so different from the person he'd met, she also looked very much the same.

"Why am I on a dating site?" he muttered, his voice blending with the night sounds. And for that matter, why was he staring at Lacy's profile? Maybe he was just as lonely as Mr. Jenson.

CHAPTER THREE

I love the design," Pearson Matthews told Paris on Friday afternoon as Paris zipped down the gently winding mountain road on his bike. The pavement was still wet from the rain earlier this morning. Puddles splashed the legs of his jeans as he hit them.

He had earbuds in place under his helmet so he could ride hands-free and hold a conversation without the roar of the engine interfering. "I'm glad you like it, sir."

"Love. I said love," Pearson said. "And I plan to recommend you to everyone I know. I'm part of the Chamber of Commerce, so I have business connections. I'm going to make sure you have enough work to keep you in Sweetwater Springs for years to come."

Paris felt a curious kick in his heart. He loved this town and didn't like to think about leaving... but he had never been one to stick anywhere for long either. He credited the foster system for that. "Thank you."

"No need for thanks. You did a great job, and I want others to know about it. You're an asset here."

Paris resisted saying thank you a second time. "Well, please make sure anyone you send my way tells me that you referred them. I give referral perks."

Pearson was one of the richest men in the community, so he likely didn't need any perks. "Sounds good. I'll talk to you soon."

They hung up, and Paris continued down the road, slowing at the entrance to the local library. His heart gave another curious kick at the thought of Lacy for a reason he didn't want to investigate. He parked, got off his bike, and then walked inside with his laptop bag on his shoulder.

Lacy wasn't behind the counter when he walked in. His gaze roamed the room, finding her with two little girls that he'd seen here before. She was helping them locate a book. One little girl was squirming as she stood in place, and Paris thought maybe she needed to locate a restroom first.

"Here you go. I think you girls will like this one," he heard Lacy tell them. "Abby, do you need to use the bathroom?"

The girl bobbed her head emphatically.

"You know where it is. Go ahead." Lacy pointed to the bathroom near the front entrance's double doors, and both girls took off in a sprint. Lacy watched them for a moment and then turned back to her computer. She gasped softly when she saw Paris. "You're here early. Do you need something?" she asked.

Need something? Yeah, he needed an excuse for why he'd been standing here stupidly waiting to talk to her.

"A book maybe?" Lacy stepped closer and lowered her voice.

"Yeah," he said. "I'm looking for a book."

"Okay. What exactly are you looking for?" she asked.

He scanned the surrounding shelves before his gaze landed back on her. "Actually, do you have anything on roses?"

Lacy's perfectly pink lips parted.

Paris had been trying to think of something he could do for his former foster parents, and roses had come to mind. Albert

Jenson loved roses, but his wife, Nancy, adored the thorny beauties. "I was thinking about making a flower garden at the nursing home, but my thumbs are more black than green."

Lacy giggled softly. "Follow me." She led him to a wall of books in the nonfiction area and bent to inspect the titles.

Paris tried and failed not to admire her curves as she leaned forward in front of him. *Get it together, man.*

"Here you go. *The Dummie's Guide to Roses*." She straightened and held a book out to him.

"Dummie's Guide?"

Her cheeks flushed. "Don't take offense. I didn't title it."

Paris made a point of looking at the other titles that had sandwiched the book on the shelf. "No, but you didn't choose to give me the one titled *Everything There Is to Know About Roses* or *The Rose Lover's Handbook*." He returned to looking at her, fascinated by how easily he could make her blush. "Any luck on Fish In The Sea dot com?"

She looked away, pulling her hands to her midsection to fidget. "I've been meaning to cancel that. The ladies had good intentions when they signed me up, albeit misguided."

"Why did they choose you as their victim?"

Lacy shrugged. "I have this high school reunion coming up. They thought I'd be more likely to go if I had a date."

"You're not going to your own reunion?" Paris asked.

"I haven't decided yet," she said as she inched away and increased the distance between them.

Unable to help himself, Paris inched forward. He told himself it was because they had to whisper and he couldn't hear her otherwise.

"Have you gone to one of yours?" she asked.

"No." He shook his head. "I never stayed in one place long enough while I was growing up to be considered an official part of a class. If I had, I would." He looked at her. "You should go. I'm sure you could find a date, even without the dating site." Part of him was tempted to offer to take her himself. By nature, he was a helpful guy. He resisted offering though because there was another part of him that wanted to be her date for an entirely different reason.

He lifted *The Dummie's Guide to Roses*. "I'll just check this out and get set up for my class."

Lacy headed back behind the counter and held out her hand to him. "Library card, please."

"Library card?" he repeated.

"I need it to check you out."

He laid the book on the counter. "I, uh, I..."

"You don't have one?" she asked, grinning back at him.

"I do most of my reading on the computer. I guess it's been a while since I've checked a book out."

"No problem." She opened a drawer and pulled out a blank card. "I can make you one right now. Do you have a driver's license?"

He pulled out his wallet and laid his license on the counter. He watched as she grabbed it and got to work. Then she handed the card back to him, her fingers brushing his slightly in the handoff. Every nerve in his body responded to that one touch. If he wasn't mistaken, she seemed affected as well.

There was the real reason he hadn't offered to be her date for her class reunion. He was attracted to Lacy Shaw, and he *really* didn't want to be.

———

Lacy lifted her gaze to the computer room in the back of the library where Paris was teaching a class of unruly elders. From afar, he actually seemed to be enjoying himself. She'd called several people before Paris, trying to persuade them to teach a class here, and everyone had been too busy with their own lives. That made her wonder why a guy like Paris was able to accept her offer. Did he have any family? Close friends? A girlfriend?

She roped in her gaze and continued checking in books from the pile beside her. Paris Montgomery's personal life was none of her business.

"Ms. Shaw! Ms. Shaw!" Abigail and Willow Fields came running toward the checkout counter.

"What's wrong, girls?" Lacy sat up straighter, noting the panic in the sisters' voices.

"Mrs. Townsend won't wake up! We thought she was sleeping, but she won't wake up!"

Lacy took off running to the other side of the room where she'd known Mrs. Townsend was sleeping. Immediately, she recognized that the older woman was hunched over the table in an unnatural way. Her skin was a pale gray color that sent chills up Lacy's spine.

Panic gripped Lacy as she looked around at the small crowd of people who'd gathered. "Does anyone know CPR?" she called. There were at least a dozen books here on the subject, but she'd never learned.

Everyone gave her a blank stare. Lacy's gaze snagged on the young sisters huddled against the wall with tears spilling over their pale cheeks. If Mrs. Townsend died in front of them, they'd be devastated.

"Let's get her on the floor," a man's voice said, coming up behind Lacy.

She glanced back, surprised to find Paris in action.

He gently grabbed hold of Mrs. Townsend and laid her on

the floor, taking control of the situation. She was never more thankful for help in her life.

"Call 911!" Lacy shouted to the crowd, relieved to see a young woman run toward the library counter where there was a phone. A moment later, the woman headed back. "They're on their way."

Lacy nodded as she returned to watching Paris perform chest compressions. He seemed to know exactly what to do. Several long minutes later, sirens filled the parking lot, and paramedics placed Mrs. Townsend onto a gurney. They revived her just enough for Mrs. Townsend to moan and look at the girls, her face seeming to contort with concern.

"It's okay. I'll take care of them, Mrs. Townsend," Lacy told her. "Just worry about taking care of yourself right now."

Lacy hoped Mrs. Townsend heard and understood. A second later, the paramedics loaded the older woman in the back of the ambulance and sped away, sirens screaming as they tore down the street.

Lacy stood on wobbly legs and tried to catch her breath. She pressed a hand against her chest, feeling like she might collapse or dissolve into tears.

"You all right?" Paris asked, pinning his ocean-blue gaze on hers.

She looked at him and shook her head. "Yes."

"You're contradicting yourself again," he said with a slight lift at one corner of his mouth. Then his hand went to her shoulder and squeezed softly. "Why don't you go sit down?"

"The girls," Lacy said, suddenly remembering her promise. She turned to where the sisters were still huddled and hurried over to where they were. "Mrs. Townsend is going to get help at the hospital. They'll take good care of her there, I promise."

Abby looked up. "What's wrong with her?"

Lacy shook her head. "I'm not sure, honey. I'm sure everything will be okay. Right now, I'm going to call your dad to come get you."

"He's at work," Willow said. "That's why we were with Mrs. Townsend."

"I know, honey. But he won't mind leaving the farm for a little bit. Follow me to the counter. I have some cookies up there."

The girls' eyes lit up, even as tears dripped from their eyelashes.

"I can call Granger while you take care of the girls," Paris offered.

How did Paris know that these sweet little children belonged to Granger Fields? As if hearing her thoughts, he explained, "I did some graphic design work on the Merry Mountain Farms website recently."

"Of course. That would be great," Lacy said, her voice sounding shaky. And she'd do her best to calm down in the meantime too.

———

Thirty minutes later, Granger Fields left the library with his little girls in tow, and Lacy plopped down on her stool behind the counter. The other patrons had emptied out of the library as well, and it was two minutes until closing time.

"Eventful afternoon," Paris said.

Lacy startled as he walked into view. She hadn't realized he was still here. "You were great with the CPR. You might have a second career as a paramedic."

He shook his head. "I took a class in college, but I'll stick to computers, thanks."

"And I'll stick to books. My entire body is still trembling."

Paris's dark brows stitched together. "I can take you home if you're not up for driving."

"On your bike?" she asked. "I'm afraid that wouldn't help my nerves at all."

Paris chuckled. "Not a fan of motorcycles, huh?"

"I've never been on one, and I don't plan to start this evening. It's time to close, and my plans include calling the hospital to check on Mrs. Townsend and then going home, changing into my PJs, and soothing my nerves with ice cream."

Paris leaned against her counter. "While you were with the girls, I called a friend I know who works at Sweetwater Memorial. She checked on things for me and just texted me an update." He held up his cell phone. "Mrs. Townsend is stable but being admitted so they can watch her over the next forty-eight hours."

Lacy blew out a breath. "That's really good news. For a moment there, she looked like she might die. If we hadn't gone over to her when we did, she might have just passed away in her sleep." Lacy wasn't sure she would've felt as safe in her little library ever again if that had happened.

"Life is fragile," Paris said. "Something like this definitely puts things into perspective, doesn't it?"

"It really does." Her worries and fears suddenly seemed so silly and so small.

Paris straightened from the counter and tugged his bag higher on his shoulder. "See you tomorrow," he said as he headed out of the library.

She watched him go and then set about to turning off all the lights. She grabbed her things and locked up behind her as she left, noticing Paris and his motorcycle beside her car in the parking lot.

"If I didn't know you were a nice guy, I might be a little

scared by the fact that you're waiting beside my car in an empty parking lot."

"I'm harmless." He hugged his helmet against him. "You looked a little rattled in there. I wanted to make sure you got home safely. I'll follow you."

Lacy folded her arms over her chest. "Maybe I don't want you to know where I live."

"The end of Pine Cone Lane. This is a small town, and I get around with business."

"I see. Well, you don't need to follow me home. Really, I'm fine."

"I'd feel better if I did."

Lacy held out her arms. "Suit yourself. Good night, Paris." She stepped inside her vehicle, closed the door behind her, and cranked her engine. It rolled and flopped. She turned the key again. This time it didn't even roll. "Crap." This day just kept getting better.

After a few more attempts, Paris tapped on her driver's side window.

She opened the door. "The battery is dead. I think I left my lights on this morning." It'd been raining, and she'd had them on to navigate through the storm. She'd forgotten her umbrella, so she'd turned off her engine, gotten out of her car, and had darted toward the library. In her rush, she must've forgotten to turn off her lights.

"I'll call Jere's Shop. He can jump your battery or tow it back to your house," Paris said.

Lacy considered the plan. "I can just wait here for him and drive it back myself."

"Jere is dependable but slow. You don't need to be out here waiting for him all evening. Leave your keys in the ignition, and I'll take you home."

Lacy looked at the helmet that Paris now extended toward her, her brain searching for another option. She didn't want to be here all night. She could call one of her sisters, but they would then follow her inside, and she didn't want to deal with them after the day she'd had either.

She got out of the car and took the helmet. "Okay," she said, shaking her head no.

This made Paris laugh as he led her to his bike. "You are one big contradiction, Lacy Shaw."

———

Paris straddled his bike and waited for Lacy to take the seat behind him. He glanced over his shoulder as she wrung her hands nervously. She seemed to be giving herself a pep talk, and then she lunged, as if forcing herself, and straddled the seat behind him.

Paris grinned and waited for another long second. "You know, you're going to have to wrap your arms around my waist for the ride."

"Right," he heard her say in a muffled voice. Her arms embraced him, clinging more tightly as he put the motorcycle in motion. Before he was even down the road, Lacy's grasp on him was so tight that her head rested on his back. He kind of liked the feel of her body hugging his, even if it was because she was scared for her life.

He knew the way to her house, but at the last second, he decided to take a different route. Lacy didn't speak up, so he guessed her eyes were shut tightly, blocking out the streets that zipped past.

Instead of taking her home, he drove her to the park, where the hot spring was. There were hiking trails and a hot dog vendor too. On her profile, Lacy had said those were among her favorite things, and after this afternoon, she deserved a few guilty pleasures.

He pulled into the parking lot and cut the engine. Slowly, Lacy peeled her body away from him. He felt her shift as she looked around.

She removed her helmet. "Why are we at the park?"

Paris glanced back. "Surprise. I thought I'd take your mind off things before I took you home."

She stared at him, a dumbfounded expression creasing her brow. "Why the park?"

"Because you love to take long hikes. And hot dogs, so I thought we'd grab a couple afterward. I didn't wear my hiking boots, but these will work for a quick half mile down the trail. Your profile mentioned that you love the hot spring here."

Lacy blinked. "You read my dating profile?"

"Great late-night reading." He winked.

She drew her hand to her forehead and shook her head. Something told him this time the head shake wasn't a yes. "Most of the information on my profile was exaggerated by the ladies' group. Apparently, they didn't think the real Lacy Shaw was interesting enough."

"You don't like hiking?"

"I like leisurely walks."

"Dogs?" he asked.

"Cats are my preference."

Paris let his gaze roam around them briefly before looking back at her. "What *do* you like?"

"In general?" she asked.

"Let's start with food. I'm starving."

She gave him a hesitant look. "Well, the hot dog part was true, but only because I added that part after they left."

Paris grinned, finding her adorable and sexy at the same time. "I happen to love a good chili dog. And there's a stand at the far side of the park." He waited for her to get off the bike and then he climbed off as well. "Let's go eat, shall we?"

"Saving someone's life works up an appetite, I guess."

"I didn't save Mrs. Townsend's life," he said as they walked. "I just kept her alive so someone else could do that."

From the corner of his eye, he saw Lacy fidgeting.

He reached for her hand to stop the motion. "I brought you here to take your mind off that situation. Let's talk about something light."

"Like?"

"You? Why did you let the Ladies' Day Out group make you a dating profile if you don't want to be on the site?"

Lacy laughed softly as they stepped into a short line for hot dogs. "Have you met the Ladies' Day Out group? They are determined and persistent. When they want something, they don't take no for an answer."

"You're part of the LDO," he pointed out.

"Well, I don't share that same quality."

"You were persistent in getting me to agree to teach a class at the library."

"True. I guess when there's something I want, I go after it." They reached the front of the line and ordered two sodas and two hot dogs. One with chili for him and one without for her.

Lacy opened the flap of her purse, and Paris stopped her. "I brought you here. This is my treat."

"No, I couldn't—"

She started to argue, but he laid a ten-dollar bill in front of the vendor. "It's just sodas and hot dogs." He glanced over. "You can treat me next time."

Her lips parted. He was only teasing, but he saw the question in her eyes, and now it was in his mind too. Would there really be a next time? Would that be so bad?

After collecting the change, they carried their drinks and hot dogs to a nearby bench and sat down.

"I didn't think I'd like teaching, but it's actually kind of fun," Paris confessed.

"Even Mr. Jenson?" she asked before taking a huge bite of her hot dog.

"Even him. But he didn't show up today. Maybe he dropped out." Paris shrugged. "I changed the syllabus just for him. I was planning to teach the class to Skype this afternoon."

"You didn't?"

He shook his head. "I went back to the lesson on Microsoft Word just in case Mr. Jenson showed up next time."

"Maybe he didn't feel well. He's been to every other class this week, right?"

Paris shook his head. "But he's made no secret that he doesn't like my teaching. He's even blasted his opinions all over Facebook."

Lacy grimaced. "Oh my. He treats everyone that way. I wouldn't take it personally. It's just how he is."

"He wasn't always that way. He used to be really nice, if memory serves me correctly."

Lacy narrowed her eyes. "You knew him before the class?"

Paris looked down at his half-eaten hot dog. "He and Mrs. Jenson fostered me for a while, but he doesn't seem to remember me."

"You were in foster care?"

"Yep. The Jensons were my favorite family."

Her jaw dropped. "That's so interesting."

Paris angled his body toward her. "Do you know what's wrong with Mrs. Jenson?"

Lacy shrugged. "I'm not sure. All I know is she's forgetful. She gets confused a lot. I've seen her get pretty agitated with Mr. Jenson too. They used to come into the library together."

"Maybe that's why he's so bitter now," Paris said, thinking out loud. He lifted his hot dog to his mouth and took another bite.

"Perhaps Mr. Jenson just needs someone to help him."

Paris chewed and swallowed. "I'm not even sure how I could help Mr. Jenson. I've been reading up on how to make a rose garden, but that won't make his wife well again."

Lacy hummed thoughtfully. "I think Mr. Jenson just needs someone to treat him nicely, no matter how horrible he is. No matter what he says to me, I always offer him a big smile. I actually think he likes me, although he would never admit it." She giggled to herself.

Paris looked at her. "You seem to really understand people."

"I do a lot of people-watching. And I had years of being an outcast in school." She swiped at a drop of ketchup at the corner of her mouth. "When you're hiding in the back of the classroom, there's not much else to do but watch everyone else. You can learn a lot about a person when they think no one is paying attention."

"Why would you hide?" he asked, growing increasingly interested in Lacy Shaw.

She met his gaze, and he glimpsed something dark in her eyes for a moment. "Childhood scoliosis. I had to wear a back brace to straighten out my spine."

His gaze dropped to her back. It was long and smooth now.

"I don't wear it anymore," she told him. "My back is fixed. High school is when you want to be sporting the latest fashion though, not a heavy brace."

"I'm sure you were just as beautiful."

She looked away shyly, tucking a strand of brown hair behind her ear with one hand. "Anyway, I guess that's why I know human nature. Even the so-called nice kids were afraid to be associated with me. There were a handful of people who didn't care. I'm still close with them."

"Sounds like your childhood was less than desirable. Kind of like mine," he said. "That's something we have in common."

She looked up. "Who'd have thought? The librarian and the bad boy biker."

"Bad boy?" he repeated, finding this description humorous.

Her cheeks blossomed red just like the roses he'd studied in the library book. She didn't look away, and he couldn't, even if he wanted to. Despite himself, he felt the pull between them, the sexual tension winding around its gear, cranking tighter and tighter. "Perhaps we have a lot more in common."

"Like what?" she asked softly.

"Well, we both like hot dogs."

She smiled softly.

"And I want to kiss you right now. Not sure if you want to kiss me too but..." What was he doing? It was as if something else had taken control of his mind and mouth. He was saying exactly the opposite of what he intended.

Lacy's lips parted, her pupils dilated, and unless he was reading her wrong, she wanted to kiss him too.

Leaning forward, he dropped his mouth and brushed his lips to hers. A little sigh tumbled out of her, and after a moment, she kissed him back.

CHAPTER FOUR

Sparks, tingles, the whole nine yards.

That was what this kiss with Paris was. He was an amazing kisser. He had a firm hand on her thigh and the other gently curled around the back of her neck. This was the Cadillac of kisses, not that Lacy had much experience recently. It'd been a while since she'd kissed anyone. The last guy she'd briefly dated had run the library in the town of River Oaks. They'd shared a love of books, but not much else.

Paris pulled back slightly. "I'm sorry," he said. "I didn't mean to do that."

She blinked him into focus, a dreamlike feeling hanging over her.

"All I wanted to do tonight was take your mind off the afternoon."

"The afternoon?" she repeated.

"Mrs. Townsend?"

"Oh." She straightened a touch. Was that why he'd kissed her? Was he only taking her mind off the trauma of what happened at the library? "I definitely forgot about that for a moment."

"Good." Paris looked around the park. Then he stood and

offered her his hand. "Want to take a walk to the hot spring before we leave?"

She allowed him to pull her to standing. "Okay."

She followed him because he'd driven her here. Because he'd kissed her. Because she wasn't sure what to think, but one thing she knew for sure was that she liked being around Paris. He was easy to talk to, and he made her feel good about herself.

"Penny for your thoughts?" he asked a couple of minutes later, walking alongside her.

She could hear the subtle sound of water as they drew closer to the hot spring. "Oh, I was just thinking what a nice night it is."

Paris looked around. "I don't think there's a single season in this town that I don't like. The air is easier to breathe here for some reason." She watched him suck in a deep breath and shivered with her body's response.

"I've always wanted to get in a hot spring," Lacy admitted, turning her attention to the water that was now in view.

"You've never been in?" Paris asked.

Lacy shook her head. "No. That was another fabrication for the profile. I've read that a spring is supposed to help with so many things. Joint and muscle pain. Energy levels. Detoxification."

"Do you need those benefits?" he asked.

Lacy looked up at him. "Not really." All she really needed was to lean into him and press her lips to his once more.

Paris sighed as they walked. "So what should I do?"

A dozen thoughts rushed Lacy's mind. "Hmm?"

"I want to help Mr. Jenson somehow, like you suggested."

"Oh." She looked away as she swallowed. "Well, he didn't show up at today's class. Maybe you could stop by and see him. Tomorrow is Saturday, so there's no class anyway. You could check on him and make sure he's okay."

Paris stared at her. "I have to admit, that old man kind of scares me."

Lacy giggled softly. "Me too." She gasped as an idea rushed into her mind. She didn't give herself time to think before sharing it with Paris. "But I'll go with you. It's my day off."

He cocked his head. "You'd spend your day off helping me?"

"Yes, but there's a condition."

He raised a questioning brow. "What's that?"

"I'll go with you if you'll be my date to my class reunion." Seeing Mrs. Townsend at death's door this afternoon had shaken her up more than she'd realized. "I don't want to hide anymore. I want to go, have a blast, and show everyone who tried to break me that they didn't succeed." And for some reason, Paris made her feel more confident.

Paris grinned at her. "Are you asking me out, Lacy Shaw?"

She swallowed. "Yes. Kind of. I'm offering you a deal."

He shoved his hands in his pockets. "I guess Mr. Jenson might be less likely to slam the door on my face tomorrow if I have a beautiful woman by my side. You said he likes you, so..."

Her insides fluttered to life. "My old bullies might be less likely to pick on me if I have a hot graphic designer as my escort."

This made him laugh. Then Paris stuck out his hand. "Want to shake on it?"

She would prefer to kiss on it, but that first kiss had come with an apology from him. This deal wasn't romantic in nature. It was simply two people helping one another out.

———

Even though Paris worked for himself, he still loved a Saturday, especially this one. He and Lacy were spending the day together, and he hadn't looked forward to something like this in a while. He got out of bed with the energy of a man who'd already had his coffee and headed down the hall to brew a pot. Then he dressed in a pair of light-colored jeans and a favorite T-shirt for a local band he loved.

As he sipped his coffee, he thought about last evening and the kiss that probably had a lot to do with his mood this morning. He hadn't planned on kissing Lacy, but the feeling had engulfed him. And her signals were all a go, so he'd leaned in and gone for it.

Magic.

There'd be no kissing today though. He didn't like starting things he couldn't finish, and he wasn't in the market for a relationship. He'd traveled that path, and his marriage had been anything but the happy ending he'd envisioned. He couldn't do anything right for his ex, no matter how hard he'd tried. As soon as he'd realized she was having an affair, he'd left. He didn't stick around where he wasn't wanted.

Paris stood and grabbed his keys. Then he headed out the door to go get Lacy. He'd take his truck today so that he didn't need to torture himself with the feel of her arms around his waist.

A short drive later, he pulled into her driveway on Pine Cone Lane, walked up the steps, and knocked. She opened the door, and for a moment, he forgot to breathe. She wore her hair down, allowing it to spill softly over her shoulders just like in her profile picture. "You look, uh...well, you look nice," he finally said.

She lifted a hand and smoothed her hair on one side. "Thanks. At the library, it's easier to keep my hair pulled back," she explained. "But since I'm off today, I thought I'd let loose."

It was more than her hair. A touch of makeup accented her brown eyes, and she was wearing a soft pink top that brought out the colors in her skin. If he was a painter, he'd be running for his easel. If he was a writer, he'd grab a pen and paper, ignited by inspiration.

But he was just a guy who dabbled on computers. A guy who'd already decided he wasn't going to act on his attraction to the woman standing in front of him.

"I'm ready if you are," she said, stepping onto the porch and closing the front door behind her. She looked out into the driveway. "Oh, you drove something with four wheels today. I was ready for the bike, but I admit I'm kind of relieved."

"The bike grew on you a little bit?"

She shrugged one shoulder. "I could get used to it. My mother would probably kill you if she knew you put me on a motorcycle last night."

"I was rescuing you from being stranded in a dark parking lot," he pointed out.

"The lesser of two evils."

Paris jumped ahead to open her door, winning a curious look from her as well as a new blush on her cheeks—this one not due to makeup.

"Thanks."

He closed the door behind her and then jogged around to the driver's side. Once he was seated behind the steering wheel, he looked over. "Looks like Jere got your car back okay." He gestured toward her Honda Accord parked in front of a single-car garage.

"He left it and texted me afterward. No charge. He said he owed you." Lacy's brows subtly lifted.

"See, it pays to hang around me." Paris started the engine.

"I was thinking we could stop in and check on Mrs. Townsend first."

Lacy pointed a finger at him. "I love that idea, even though I'm onto you, Paris Montgomery. You're really just procrastinating because you're scared of Mr. Jenson."

He grimaced as he drove toward the Sweetwater hospital. "That's probably true."

They chatted easily as he drove, discussing all of Lacy's plans for the library this summer. She talked excitedly about her work, which he found all kinds of attractive. Then he pulled into the hospital parking lot, and they both got out.

"We shouldn't go see Mrs. Townsend empty-handed," Lacy said as they walked toward the main entrance.

"We can swing by the gift shop before we go up," he suggested.

"Good idea. She likes magazines, so I'll get her a couple. I hope Abby and Willow are okay. It had to be confusing for them, watching their nanny being taken away in an ambulance."

"The girls only have one parent?" he asked.

"Their mother isn't around," Lacy told him.

Paris slid his gaze over. He wasn't sure he wanted to know, but he asked anyway. "What happened to their mom?" He'd heard a lot of stories from his foster siblings growing up. There were so many reasons for a parent to slip out of the picture. His story was rather boring in comparison to some. His parents didn't like abiding by the law, which left him needing supplementary care at times. Then they'd decided that another thing they didn't like was taking care of him.

"Their mother left right after Willow was born. There was speculation that maybe she had postpartum depression."

Paris swallowed as they veered into the gift shop. "It's good that they have Granger. He seems like a good dad."

"I think so too. And what kid wouldn't want to grow up on a Christmas tree farm? I mean, that's so cool." Lacy beelined toward the magazine rack in the back of the shop, picking out three. They also grabbed some chocolates at the register.

Bag of presents in hand, they left the shop and took the elevator up to the third floor to Mrs. Townsend's room. Lacy knocked, and they waited for Mrs. Townsend's voice to answer back, telling them to "come in."

"Oh, Lacy! You didn't have to spend your Saturday coming to see me," Mrs. Townsend said as they entered her room. "And you brought a friend."

"Mrs. Townsend, this is Paris Montgomery. He did CPR on you in the library yesterday."

Mrs. Townsend's eyes widened. "I didn't even know I needed CPR. How embarrassing. But thank you," she told Paris. "I guess you were instrumental in saving my life."

"It was no big deal," he said.

"To the woman who's still alive today it is." Mrs. Townsend looked at Lacy again, her gaze dropping to the bag in her hand. "What do you have?"

"Oh, yes." Lacy pulled the magazines out and offered them to Mrs. Townsend, along with the chocolates.

Mrs. Townsend looked delighted by the gifts. "Oh my goodness. Thank you so much."

"Are you doing okay?" Lacy asked.

Mrs. Townsend waved a hand. "The doctors here have been taking good care of me. They tell me I can go home tomorrow."

Lacy smiled. "That's good news."

"Yes, it is. And I'll be caring for the girls again on Monday. A little flutter in the heart won't keep me from doing what I love."

Lacy's gaze slid to meet Paris's as worry creased her brow. He resisted reaching for her hand in a calming gesture. His intentions would be innocent, but they could also confuse things. He and Lacy were only out today as friends. Nothing more.

They stayed and chatted a while longer and then left, riding down the elevator in silence. Paris and Lacy walked side by side back to his truck. He opened the passenger side door for her again and then got into the driver's seat.

"I'm glad Mrs. Townsend is okay," Lacy said as they pulled back onto the main road and drove toward Blueberry Creek Road, where Albert Jenson lived.

"Me too," Paris told her.

"But what happens next time?"

"Hopefully there won't be a next time."

"And if there is, hopefully you'll be around," Lacy said. Something about her tone made him wonder if she wanted to keep him around for herself too.

A few minutes later, he turned onto Mr. Jenson's street and traveled alongside Blueberry Creek. His heart quickened as he pulled into Mr. Jenson's driveway.

"I can't believe he walks from here to the library," Lacy said as he cut the engine. "That has to be at least a mile."

"He's always loved to walk." Paris let his gaze roam over the house. It was smaller than he remembered and in need of new paint. The rosebushes that the Jensons loved so much were unruly and unkempt. He was in his seventies now though. The man Paris knew as a child had been middle-aged and full of energy. Things changed. He looked over. "All right. Let's get this over with. If he yells at us, we'll know he's okay. The buddy system, right?"

"Right."

Except with each passing second spent with Lacy, the harder it was for him to think of her as just a buddy.

———

Lacy had never been to Mr. Jenson's home before. She'd known that the Jensons kept foster children once upon a time, but it surprised her that one of them was Paris.

"Strange, but this place feels like home to me," Paris said as he stood at the front door.

"How long did you live here with the Jensons?"

"About six months, which was longer than I lived with most."

"Makes sense why you'd think of this place fondly then." She wanted to ask more about his parents, but it wasn't the time. "Are you going to ring the doorbell?" she asked instead.

"Oh. I guess that would help." Paris pushed the button for the doorbell with his index finger and let his hands clasp back together in front of him.

"If I didn't know better, I'd think Mr. Cool was nervous," she commented.

"Mr. Cool?" He glanced over. "Any relation to Mr. Clean?"

This made her giggle until the front door opened and Mr. Jenson frowned back at them.

Lacy straightened. From the corner of her eye, she saw Paris stand more upright as well.

"Mr. Jenson," Paris said. "Good morning, sir."

"What are you doing here?" the old man barked through the screen door.

"Just checking on you. You missed a class that I put together just for you."

"I hear you were trying to kill people at the library yesterday," Mr. Jenson said, his frown steadfast. "Good thing I stayed home."

"Mrs. Townsend is fine," Paris informed him. "We just checked on her at Sweetwater Memorial."

"And now you're checking on me?" Mr. Jenson shook his head, casting a suspicious glare. "Why?"

Paris held up his hands. "Like I said, I missed you in yesterday's class."

Mr. Jenson looked surprised for a moment, and maybe even a little happy with this information. Then his grumpy demeanor returned. "I decided it wasn't worth my time."

Lacy noticed Paris tense beside her. "Actually, the class is free and taught by a professional," she said, jumping in to help. "We're lucky to have Mr. Montgomery teaching at Sweetwater Library."

Mr. Jenson gave her a long, hard look. She was prepared for him to take a jab at her too, but instead he shrugged his frail shoulders. "It's a long walk, and my legs hurt yesterday, okay? You happy? I'm not a spring chicken anymore, but I'm fine, and I'll be back on Monday. If for no other reason than to keep you two off my front porch." Mr. Jenson looked between them, and then he harrumphed and promptly slammed the door in their faces.

Lacy turned to look at Paris. "Are you sure you're remembering him correctly? I can't imagine that man was ever very nice."

"Did you see him smile at me before he slammed that door though? I think he's softening up."

Lacy laughed, reaching her arm out and grabbing Paris momentarily to brace her body as it shook with amusement. Once she'd realized what she'd done, she removed her hand and cleared her throat. "Okay, our well-check visits are complete. Mrs. Townsend and Mr. Jenson are both alive and kicking."

"I guess it's time for me to keep my end of the deal now," Paris said, leading her back to his truck.

Lacy narrowed her eyes. "But my reunion isn't until next Saturday."

"Yes, but I'm guessing you need to go shopping for something new to wear, right? And I can't wear jeans and an old T-shirt." He opened the passenger door for her.

"You can wear whatever you want," she told him as she stepped inside. Then she turned to look at him as he stood in her doorway.

"I want to look my best when I'm standing beside you. And I hear that Sophie's Boutique is the place to go if you want to dress to impress." He closed the door behind her and walked around to get in the driver's seat.

"Are you seriously offering to go dress shopping with me right now?" she asked once he was seated. "Because guys usually hate that kind of thing."

Paris grinned as he cranked the truck. "Sitting back and watching you come in and out of a dressing room, modeling beautiful clothes, sounds like a fun way to spend an afternoon to me." He winked before backing out of the driveway.

For a moment, Lacy was at a complete loss for words. "I mean, I'm sure you have other things to do with your Saturday afternoon."

He glanced over. "None as fun as hanging out with you."

She melted into the passenger seat. No one in her life had made her feel quite as interesting as Paris had managed to do last night and today. Just the opposite, the Ladies' Day Out group, while well-meaning, had made her feel boring by elaborating on the truth.

Paris made her feel other things as well. Things that were too soon to even contemplate.

CHAPTER FIVE

Every time Lacy walked out of the dressing room, Paris felt his heart kick a little harder. The dresses in Sophie's Boutique were gorgeous, but they paled in comparison to Lacy.

"You're staring at me," she said after twirling in a lavender knee-length dress with small navy blue polka dots. "Do you like this one or not?" She looked down. "I kind of love it. It's fun, and that's what I want for my reunion." She was grinning when she looked back up at him. "I want to dance and eat all the foods that will make this dress just a little too tight the next morning." A laugh tumbled off her lips.

Paris swallowed, looking for words, but they all got stuck in his throat. His feelings for Lacy were snowballing with every passing second—and it scared him more than Mr. Jenson did.

"Well?" she said again.

"That's the one for sure." He tore his gaze from her, pushing away all the thoughts of things he wanted to do to her in that dress. He wanted to spin her around on the dance floor, hold her close, and kiss her without apology next time.

Next time?

"Oh, wow! You look so beautiful!" Sophie Daniels, the

boutique's owner, walked over and admired Lacy in the dress. "Is that the one?"

Lacy was practically glowing. "I think so, yeah."

Sophie turned to look at Paris. He'd met Sophie before, and she'd flirted mildly with him. He hadn't returned the flirting though because, beautiful as she was, he wasn't interested.

But he couldn't deny his interest in Lacy.

"Now it's your turn," Lacy said.

Sophie gestured to the other side of the store. "I have a rack of men's clothing in the back. Let's get you something that will complement what Lacy is wearing but not steal her show."

"As if I could steal the attention away from her," he said while standing.

Sophie's mouth dropped open. With a knowing look in her eyes, she tipped her head, signaling for him to follow her while Lacy returned to the dressing room to change.

"You seem like a nice guy, Paris, and Lacy deserves someone who will treat her well," Sophie said to him over her shoulder as she led the way.

"It's not like that between us." He swiped a hand through his hair. "I mean, Lacy is terrific, but the two of us don't make sense."

Sophie started sifting through the men's clothes on the rack. "Why not? You're both single and attractive. She avoids the spotlight, and you kind of grab people's attention wherever you go."

"I do?" he asked.

Sophie stopped looking through the clothes to give him another knowing look. "Opposites attract is a real thing, and it makes perfect sense." She pulled out a dark purple button-down shirt that would match Lacy's dress. "Do you have black pants?"

"I have black jeans," he told her.

She seemed to think about this. "Yes, black jeans will work. You just need to dress up a little bit. You're a jeans and T-shirt kind of guy, so let's keep the jeans." She nodded as if making the decision. "You, but different."

"Me, but different," he agreed, taking the shirt from her. That's how he felt with Lacy. He was still him but more grounded. And Lacy was still reserved but also coming out of her shell, and he loved watching it happen. "Do you have any bathing suits?" he asked on a whim. "One for me and one for Lacy?"

Sophie's eyes lit up, a smile lifting at the corners of her mouth. "Of course I do."

"I'll take one for each of us then. And this shirt for the reunion," Paris said.

Sophie gave him a conspiratorial wink. "I'll take care of it."

————

Lacy felt like Julia Roberts in *Pretty Woman*. She loved the dress she'd picked out, and she'd enjoyed the way Paris had stared at her as she'd modeled each one before it.

They left the boutique and walked back to Paris's truck. He opened her door, and she got in, tucking her bag in the floorboard at her feet. "That was so much fun. Thank you."

He stood in the open doorway of his truck, watching her. His gaze was so intense, and for a moment, her heart sped up. Was he going to kiss her again?

"I want to take you somewhere else," he said.

She furrowed her brow. They'd already spent nearly the entire day together, not that she minded. "Where?"

He placed a second bag in her lap and winked before shutting the door behind her and walking around the truck.

Lacy peeked inside the bag and gasped as he opened his own door and got behind the wheel. "This is a bathing suit."

"You said you always wanted to go to the hot spring. You and I are on one big adventure today, so I thought it'd be fitting to end our expedition by doing something on your bucket list."

"I don't actually have a bucket list," she noted, looking down at the bathing suit again, "but if I did, this would be on it. I can't believe you got me a bathing suit." Underneath her bright pink suit in the bag was a pair of men's board shorts. "Are we really going to do this?"

Paris looked over. "Only if you agree. Will you go on a date with me to the hot spring?"

A date? Had he meant that the way it'd sounded? Because a date implied that they were more than friends, and that's the way she felt about him right now.

———

The night was alive with sounds of nature. In the past hour, the sun had gone down behind the mountains, and stars had begun to shimmer above as darkness fell.

Lacy came out of the changing room with her bathing suit on and a towel wrapped around her waist. Paris was waiting on a bench for her, bare chested and in a pair of swim shorts.

Her mouth went dry. This wasn't her. She didn't visit hot springs with gorgeous men. Her idea of fun on a Saturday night was curling up on her front porch swing with a good book. This was a nice change of pace though, and with Paris beside her, she didn't mind trying something new.

"Ready?" he asked, standing and walking toward her. He reached for her hand and took it. The touch zinged from her heart to her toes, bouncing back up through her body like a ball in a pinball machine.

The sound of water grew louder as they approached the hot spring. They were the only ones here so far this evening, which she found odd and exciting.

Paris stood at the steps and looked at Lacy. "You're going to have to drop that towel," he said, his gaze trailing from her face and down her body toward her hips.

"Right." She swallowed and let go of his hand. She was about to remove her towel, but he reached out for her and did the honors. There was something so intimate about the gesture that her knees weakened. The towel fell in his hand, leaving her standing there in just her suit. She felt exposed and so alive.

He met her gaze for a long moment and then folded the towel and left it on a bench. Turning back to her, he reached for her hand again. "Careful," he said quietly, leading her down the steps and into the water.

She moaned softly as the hot water lapped against her skin. "This is heavenly," she finally said once she'd taken a seat inside. He was still holding her hand, and that was heavenly as well. They leaned back against the spring's wall, and both of them looked up at the stars.

"Anywhere I've been in my life," Paris whispered after a moment, "I've always been under these same stars. I've always wished I was somewhere different when I looked up, but tonight, there's nowhere else I'd rather be." He looked over, his face dangerously close to hers.

She swallowed. "Are you going to kiss me again?"

His blue eyes narrowed. "Do you want me to kiss you again?"

"Ever since that first kiss."

His eyes dropped to her mouth. Her lips parted for him. Then he leaned just a fraction, and his lips brushed against hers. He stayed there, offering small kisses that evolved into something deeper and bigger. One of his hands slid up her thigh, anchoring midway. The touch completely undid her, and if they weren't in a public setting, she might have wiggled until his hand slid higher.

"Are you going to apologize again?" she asked once he'd pulled away.

He shook his head. "I'm not sorry."

"Me neither," she whispered. Then she leaned in and kissed him this time. Who was she these days? This wasn't like her at all.

They didn't stop kissing until voices approached the hot spring. Lacy pulled back from Paris. Another couple appeared and headed toward the spring. They stepped in and sat across from Lacy and Paris.

"We have to behave now," Paris whispered in Lacy's ear.

"Easier said than done." She grinned at him.

"And I'm not leaving until this little problem I have has gone down."

"What problem?" she asked, looking down through the clear bubbles. Then she realized what he was referring to, and her body grew impossibly hotter.

They returned to looking at the stars and talking in whispers, sharing even more details about themselves. Lacy could've stayed and talked all night, but the hot spring closed at ten p.m. When she finally stepped out of the water, the cool air was a harsh contrast.

After toweling off and changing in the dressing room, Lacy met Paris outside and got into his truck. He drove slowly as he took her home, their conversation touching various subjects. And the more she learned about Paris, the more she wanted to know.

Finally, he pulled into her driveway and looked at her.

"I'm not sure you should walk me to my door," Lacy said. "I'd probably end up asking you if you wanted to come inside." She nibbled softly on her lower lip. "And, well, that's probably not the best idea."

"I understand." He reached for her hand. "Thank you for the best day that I can remember."

She leaned toward him. "And the best night."

She gave him a brief kiss because there was still the risk that she might invite him inside. She was doing things that were surprising even herself. "The library is closed tomorrow. I can make lunch if you want to come over."

He hesitated.

"I mean, you don't have to, if you have something else to do."

He grinned. "I have work to do tomorrow, but a man has to eat, right? Lunch sounds nice. I'll be here."

"Perfect." She pushed the truck door open before her hormones took over and she climbed over to his side of the truck instead. "Good night, Paris."

"Good night, Lace."

CHAPTER SIX

Lacy wasn't thinking straight last night. Otherwise, she would've remembered that a few members of the Ladies' Day Out group were coming over for lunch after church. No doubt they wanted to nag her about one thing or another. Today's topics were most likely the dating site and her reunion.

Then again, that was all the more reason for Paris to join them for lunch. His presence would kill two birds with one stone. She didn't need a dating site. And she and Paris were going to have an amazing time at her reunion next weekend.

She heard his motorcycle rumble into her driveway first. She waited for him to ring the doorbell, and then she went to answer. Butterflies fluttered low in her belly at the sight of him.

"Come in." She led him inside the two-bedroom house that she'd purchased a couple of years ago. "It's not much, but it's home."

"Well, sounds cliché, but I've learned that home really is where the heart is," he said.

She turned to look at him, standing close enough that she could reach out and touch him again. Maybe pull him toward her, go up on her tiptoes, and press her lips to his. "By cliché, you mean cheesy?"

Paris pretended to push a stake through his heart. "When you get comfortable with someone, your feisty side is unleashed. I like it." He leaned in just a fraction, and Lacy decided to take a step forward, giving him the not-so-subtle green light for another kiss. He was right. She was feisty when she was with him, and she liked this side of her too.

The sound of another motor pulling into her driveway got her attention. She turned toward her door.

"Are you expecting someone else?" Paris asked, following her gaze.

"Yes, sorry. I didn't remember when I invited you last night, but I have company coming over today."

"Who?" Paris asked.

"My mom."

He nodded. "Okay."

"And my two sisters, Birdie and Rose," Lacy added. "*And* my aunt Pam."

Paris started to look panicked. "Anyone else?"

"Yeah. Um, Dawanda from the fudge shop. They're all part of the Ladies' Day Out group. I got a text earlier in the week telling me they were bringing lunch."

"Well, I'll get out of your guys' hair," he said, backpedaling toward the door.

She grabbed his hand, holding it until he met her gaze. "Wait. You don't need to leave. I want you here."

Paris grimaced. "Family mealtime has never really been my strong point."

Lacy continued to hold his hand. She wanted to show the women outside that she could find a guy on her own. She didn't need FishInTheSea.com. She also wanted to show them this new side of herself that seemed to take hold when she was with Paris. "They're harmless, I promise. Please stay."

Paris shifted on his feet, and she was pretty sure he was going to turn down the invitation. "You didn't take no for an answer when you wanted me to teach the computer class at the library," he finally said. "I'm guessing the same would be true now, huh?"

She grinned. "That's right."

"You're a hard woman to resist."

"Then stop trying," she said, going to answer the door.

———

The spread on Lacy's table was fit for a Thanksgiving dinner by Paris's standards. Not that he had much experience with holidays and family gatherings. He'd had many a holiday meal with a fast-food bag containing a burger, fries, and a small toy.

"I would've brought Denny if I'd known that men were allowed at lunch today," Mrs. Shaw said, speaking of her husband. She seemed friendly enough, but Paris also didn't miss the scrutinizing looks she was giving him when she thought he wasn't looking. He was dressed in dark colors and had tattoos on both arms. He also had a motorcycle parked in the driveway. He probably wasn't the kind of guy Mrs. Shaw would have imagined her sweet librarian daughter with.

"Good thing you didn't bring Dad," Lacy's sister Birdie said. "He would've grilled Paris mercilessly."

"Paris and I aren't dating," Lacy reiterated for the tenth time since she'd welcomed the women into her home. She slid her gaze to look at Paris, and he saw the question in her eyes. *Are we?* When the ladies had come through the front door, they'd all immediately began calling him Lacy's secret boyfriend.

"Sounds like I'd be in trouble if you and I did get together," Paris said. "Your dad sounds strict."

Lacy laughed softly. "Notice that my sisters and I are all still single. There's a reason for that."

Lacy's other sister, Rose, snorted. "Dad crashed my high school prom when I didn't come home by curfew. Who has a curfew on prom night?" Rose slid her fork into a pile of macaroni and cheese. "I thought I'd never forgive Dad for that. I liked that guy too."

"What was his name again?" Mrs. Shaw asked.

Rose looked up, her eyes squinting as she seemed to think. "I can't remember. Brent maybe. Bryce? Could've been Bryan."

"You couldn't have liked him too much if you can't remember his name," Mrs. Shaw pointed out.

Everyone at the table laughed.

"Don't you worry, Rose," Dawanda said, seated beside Mrs. Shaw. "I've read your cappuccino, and you have someone very special coming your way. I saw it in the foam."

"Well, I'll be sure to keep him away from my dad until the wedding," Rose said sarcastically, making everyone chuckle again.

Whereas some read tea leaves, Dawanda read images formed in the foam of a cappuccino. She'd done a reading for Paris last Christmas. Oddly enough, Dawanda had told him he was the only one whose fortune she couldn't read. Dawanda had assured him it wasn't that he was going to fall off a cliff or anything. His future was just up in the air. He had shut his heart off to dreaming of a life anywhere or with anyone.

He didn't exactly believe in fortune-telling, but she was spot-on with that. Some people just weren't cut out for forever homes and families. He guessed he was one of them.

"Dad's first question any time he meets any of our dates is 'What are your intentions with my girl?'" Rose said, impersonating a man's deep voice.

"He actually said that while sharpening his pocketknife for a date I brought home in college," Birdie said. "I didn't mind because I didn't like the guy too much, but what if I had?"

"Then you would've been out of luck," Lacy said on a laugh.

The conversation continued, and then Mrs. Shaw looked across the table at Paris. "So, Paris," she said, her eyes narrowing, "tell us about yourself. Did you grow up around here?"

Paris looked up from his lunch. "I spent a little time in Sweetwater Springs growing up. Some in Wild Blossom Bluffs. My parents moved around a lot."

"Oh? For their jobs? Military maybe?" she asked.

Paris shifted. Ex-felons weren't allowed to join the military. "Not exactly. I was in foster care here for a while."

"Foster care?" Mrs. Shaw's lips rounded in a little O. "That must've been hard for a young child."

Paris focused his attention back on his food. "I guess I didn't really know any different. Most of the places I landed were nice enough." And there'd been somewhere he'd wished he could stay. Six months with the Jenson family was the longest amount of time he'd ever gotten to stay. It was just enough time to bond with his foster parents and to feel the loss of them to his core when he was placed back with his real parents.

He picked up his fork and stabbed at a piece of chicken.

"And what brought you back to Sweetwater Springs? If I recall, you moved here last year, right?" Dawanda asked. "You came into my shop while you were staying at the Sweetwater Bed and Breakfast."

Paris swallowed past the sudden tightness in his throat. He didn't really want to answer that question either. He looked around the table, his gaze finally landing on Lacy. "Well, I guess I decided to come back here after my divorce."

Lacy's lips parted.

Had he forgotten to mention that little detail to her? When he was with Lacy, he forgot all about those lonely years in Florida. All he could think about was the moment he was in, and the ones that would follow.

"That sounds rough as well," Mrs. Shaw said.

Paris shrugged, feeling weighed down by the truth. "Well, those things are in the rearview mirror now." He tried to offer a lighter tone of voice, but all the women looked crestfallen. Mrs. Shaw had already seemed wary of him, but now she appeared even more so.

"And since my husband isn't here to ask"—Mrs. Shaw folded her hands in front of her on the table—"what are your intentions with my daughter?"

"Mom!" Lacy set her fork down. "Paris and I aren't even dating." She looked over at him. "I mean, we went on a date last night. Two if you count that night at the park."

"Last night?" Birdie asked.

All the women's eyes widened.

"It wasn't like that." Lacy looked flustered. "We didn't spend the night together."

Mrs. Shaw's jaw dropped open, and Lacy's face turned a deep crimson.

Guilt curled in Paris's stomach. Lacy was trying her best to prove herself to everyone around her. Now her family and Dawanda were gawking at her like she'd lost her mind. It was crazy to think that she and Paris would be dating. Sophie

Daniels had told him at the boutique that opposites attract, but he and Lacy had led very different lives.

"Sounds like you're dating to me. Are you going to go out again?" Rose asked.

"Well, Paris offered to go with me to my reunion," Lacy said.

Mrs. Shaw's smile returned. "Oh, I'm so glad you decided to go! That's wonderful, dear. I want all those bullies to see that you are strong and beautiful, smart and funny, interesting—"

"Mom," Lacy said, cutting her off, "you might be a little partial."

"But she's right," Paris said, unable to help himself.

Lacy turned to look at him, and something pinched in his chest. He'd tried to keep things strictly friendly with her, but he'd failed miserably. What was he going to do now? He didn't want a relationship, but if they continued to spend time together, she would.

"So, Paris, how did you get our Lacy to agree to go to this reunion of hers?" Mrs. Shaw asked. "She was so dead set on not attending."

"Actually, Lace made that decision on her own," he said.

"Lace?" Both Birdie and Rose asked in unison.

The nickname had just rolled off his tongue, but it fit. Lace was delicate and beautiful, accentuated by holes that one might think made it more fragile. It was strong, just like the woman sitting next to him. She was stronger than she even knew.

"Well, I'm glad she's changed her mind. High school was such a rough time for our Lacy," Mrs. Shaw said. "I want her to go and have a good time and show those bullies who treated her so badly that they didn't break her."

Paris glanced over at Lacy. He wanted her old classmates to see the same thing.

Mrs. Shaw pointed a finger at Paris, gaining his attention. "But if you take her, it won't be on the back of that motorcycle in the driveway. Lacy doesn't ride those things."

"Actually, Mom, I rode on the back of it with Paris two days ago."

Mrs. Shaw looked horrified.

"Maybe he'll let me drive it next time," Lacy added, making all the women at the table look surprised.

"Lacy rode on the back of your bike?" Birdie asked Paris. "This is not our sister. What have you done with the real Lacy Shaw?"

He looked over at the woman in question. The real Lacy was sitting right beside him. He saw her, even if no one else did. And the last thing he wanted to do was walk away from her, which was why he needed to do just that.

————

An hour later, Lacy closed her front door as her guests left and leaned against it, exhaling softly.

"Your mom and sisters are great," Paris said, standing a couple of feet away from her. "Your aunt too."

She lifted her gaze to his. "You almost sound serious about that."

"Well, I'm not going to lie. They were a little overwhelming."

"A little?" Lacy grinned. "And they were subdued today. They're usually worse."

Paris shoved his hands in his pockets. "They love you. Can't fault them for that."

The way he was looking at her made her breath catch. Was he going to kiss her again?

"I guess not."

"They want what's best for you," he continued. Then he looked away. "And, uh, I'm not sure that's me, Lace."

She straightened at the sudden shift in his tone of voice. "What?"

He ran a hand over his hair. "When we were eating just now, I realized that being your date might not be doing you any favors. Or me."

"Wait, you're not going to the reunion with me anymore?" she asked.

He shook his head. "I just think it'd be better if you went with someone else."

"I don't have anyone else," she protested, her heart beating fast. "The reunion is in less than a week. I have my dress, and you have a matching shirt. And you're the one I want to go with. I don't even care about the reunion. I just want to be with you."

He looked down for a moment. "You heard me talking to your family. I've lived a different life than you. I'm an ex-foster kid. My parents are felons." He shrugged. "I couldn't even make a marriage work."

"Those things are in the past, Paris. I don't care about any of that."

He met her gaze again. "But I do. Call me selfish, but I don't want to want you. I don't want to want things that I know I'll never have. It's not in the cappuccino for me, Lacy." His expression was pained. "I really want you to believe me when I say it's not you, it's me."

Her eyes and throat burned, and she wondered if she felt worse for herself or for him. He obviously had issues, but who didn't? One thing she'd learned since high school was that no one's life was perfect. Her flaws were just obvious back then because of the back brace.

She'd also learned that you couldn't make someone feel differently than they did. The only feelings you could control were your own. The old Lacy never stood up for herself. She let people trample on her and her feelings. But she'd changed. She was the new Lacy now.

She lifted her eyes to meet Paris's and swallowed past the growing lump in her throat. "If that's the way you feel, then I think you should go."

CHAPTER SEVEN

On Monday afternoon, Paris looked out over the roomful of students. Everyone had their eyes on their screens and were learning to Skype. But his attention was on the librarian on the other side of the building.

When he'd driven to the library, he'd lectured himself on why he needed to back away from Lacy Shaw. Sunday's lunch had made that crystal clear in his mind. She was smart and beautiful, the kind of woman who valued family. Paris had no idea what it even meant to have a family. He couldn't be the kind of guy she needed.

Luckily, Lacy hadn't even been at the counter when he'd walked in and continued toward the computer room. She was probably hell-bent on avoiding him. For the best.

"Does everyone think they can go home and Skype now?" Paris asked the class.

"I can, but no one I know will know how to Skype with me," Greta said.

Janice Murphy nodded beside her.

"Well, you could all exchange information and Skype with each other," Paris suggested.

"Can we Skype with you?" Alice asked.

Warmness spread through his chest. "Anytime, Alice."

"Can I Skype you if my wife doesn't want to talk to me?" Mr. Jenson asked. "To practice so I'm ready when she does?"

Paris felt a little sad for the older man. When Paris had been a boy in their home, they'd been the happiest of couples. "Of course. If I'm home and free, I'll always make time to Skype with any one of you," he told the group, meaning it. They'd had only a few classes, but he loved the eclectic bunch in this room.

When class was over, he walked over to Mr. Jenson. "I can give you a ride home if you want."

Mr. Jenson gave him an assessing stare. "If you think I'm climbing on the back of that bike of yours, you're crazy."

Paris chuckled. "I drove my truck today. It'll save you a walk. I have the afternoon free too. I can take you by the nursing home facility to see Mrs. Jenson if you want. I'm sure she'd be happy to see you."

Mr. Jenson continued to stare at him. "Why would you do that? I know I'm not that fun to be around."

Paris clapped a gentle hand on Mr. Jenson's back. "That's not true. I kind of like being around you." He always had. "And I could use some company today. Agreeing would actually be doing me a favor."

"I don't do favors," the older man said. "But my legs are kind of hurting, thanks to the chairs in there. So walking home would be a pain."

Paris felt relieved as Mr. Jenson relented. "What about visiting Mrs. Jenson? I'll stay in the truck while you go in, and take as long as you like." Paris patted his laptop bag. "I have my computer, so I can work while I wait."

Mr. Jenson begrudgingly agreed and even smiled a little bit. "Thank you."

Paris led Mr. Jenson into his truck and started the short drive toward Sweetwater Nursing Facility.

"She sometimes tells me to leave as soon as I get there," Mr. Jenson said as they drove.

"Why is that?"

Mr. Jenson shrugged. "She says she doesn't want me to see her that way."

Paris still wasn't quite sure what was wrong with Mrs. Jenson. "What way?"

"Oh, you know. Her emotions are as unstable as her walking these days. That's why she's not home with me. She's not the same Nancy I fell in love with, but she's still the woman I love. I'll always love her, no matter how things change."

"That's what love is, isn't it?" Paris asked.

Mr. Jenson turned to look out the passenger side window as they rode. "We never had any kids of our own. We fostered a few, and that was as close as we ever got to having a family."

Paris swallowed painfully.

"There was one boy who was different. We would've kept him. We bonded and loved him as our own."

Paris glanced over. Was Mr. Jenson talking about him? Probably not, but Paris couldn't help hoping that he was. "What happened?"

"We wanted to raise him as part of our family, but it didn't work out that way. He went back to his real parents, which I suppose is always best. I lost him, and now, most days, I've lost my wife too. That's what love is. Painful."

Paris parked and looked over. "Well, maybe today will be different. Whatever happens, I'll be in the truck waiting for you."

Mr. Jenson looked over and chuckled, but Paris could tell

by the gleam in his eyes that he appreciated the sentiment. He stepped out of the truck and dipped his head to look at Paris in the driver's seat. "Some consolation prize."

———

Two nights later, Lacy sat in her living room with a handful of the Ladies' Day Out members. They'd been waiting for her in the driveway when she'd gotten home from the library and were here for an intervention of sorts.

"Sandwiches?" Greta asked, her face twisting with displeasure.

"Well, when you don't tell someone that you're coming, you get PB&J." Lacy plopped onto the couch beside Birdie, who had no doubt called everyone here.

"You took your online profile down," Birdie said, reaching for her own sandwich.

"Of course I did. I'm not interested in dating right now."

"You sure looked interested in Paris Montgomery," Dawanda said, sitting across from them. "And you two looked so good together. What happened?"

All the women turned to face Lacy.

She shrugged. "My family happened. No offense. You all behaved—mostly," she told her mom and sisters. "We just decided it'd be best to part ways sooner rather than later."

Birdie placed her sandwich down. "I thought you were the smart one in the family."

Rose raised her hand. "No, that was always me." A wide grin spread on her face. "Just kidding. It's you, Lacy."

Birdie frowned. "I was there last weekend. I saw how you two were together. There's relationship potential there," she said.

Lacy sighed. "Maybe, but he doesn't want another relationship. He's been hurt and…" She shrugged. "I guess he just doesn't think it's worth trying again." That was her old insecurities though so she stopped them all in their tracks. "Actually, something good came out of me going out with him a few times."

"Oh?" Birdie asked. "What's that?"

"I'm not afraid to go to my reunion, even if I have to go on my own."

"Maybe you'll meet someone there. Maybe you'll find 'the one,'" Rose said.

"Maybe." But Lacy was pretty sure she wouldn't find the *one* she wanted. He'd already been found and lost.

"I'll go with you if you need me to," Josie offered. She wasn't sitting on the couch with Lacy's laptop this time. Instead, she held a glass of wine tonight, looking relaxed in the recliner across the room.

"I wonder what people would think about that," Birdie said.

Lacy shrugged. "You know what, I've decided that I don't care what the people who don't know me think. I care about what I think. And what you all think, of course."

"And Paris?" Dawanda asked.

Lacy shook her head, but she meant yes. Paris was right. Her gestures often contradicted what she really meant. "Paris thinks that we should just be friends, and I have to respect that."

Even if she didn't like it.

CHAPTER EIGHT

Paris was spending his Saturday night in Mr. Jenson's rosebushes—not at Lacy's class reunion as he'd planned. He'd clipped the bushes back, pruning the dead ends so that they'd come back stronger.

Over the last couple of days, he'd kept himself super busy with work and taking Mr. Jenson to and from the nursing facility. He'd read up on how to care for rosebushes, but that hadn't been necessary because Mr. Jenson stayed on the porch barking out instructions like a drill sergeant. Paris didn't mind. He loved the old man.

"Don't clip too much off!" Mr. Jenson warned. "Just what's needed."

"Got it." Paris squeezed the clippers again and again, until the muscles of his hand were cramping.

Despite his best efforts, he hadn't kept himself busy enough to keep from thinking about Lacy. She'd waved and said hi to him when he'd gone in and out of the library, but that was all. It wasn't enough.

He missed her. A lot. Hopefully she was still going to her reunion tonight. He hoped she danced. And maybe there'd be a nice guy there who would dance with her.

Guilt and jealousy curled around Paris's ribs like the roses on the lattice. He still wanted to be that guy who held her close tonight and watched her shine.

"Done yet?" Mr. Jenson asked gruffly.

Paris wiped his brow and straightened. "All done."

Mr. Jenson nodded approvingly. "It looks good, son."

Mr. Jenson didn't mean anything by calling him son, but it still tugged on Paris's heartstrings. "Thanks. I'll come by next week and take you to see Mrs. Jenson."

"Just don't expect me to get on that bike of yours," the older man said for the hundredth time.

"Wouldn't dream of it." As Paris started to walk away, Mr. Jenson called out to him.

"PJ?"

Paris froze. He hadn't heard that name in a long time, but it still stopped him in his tracks. He turned back to face Mr. Jenson. "You know?"

Mr. Jenson chuckled. "I'm old, not blind. I've known since that first computer class."

"But you didn't say anything." Paris took a few steps, walking back toward Mr. Jenson on the porch. "Why?"

"I could ask you the same. You didn't say anything either."

Paris held his hands out to his sides. "I called last year. Mrs. Jenson answered and told me to never call again."

Mr. Jenson shook his head as he listened. "I didn't know that, but it sounds about right. She tells me the same thing when I call her. Don't take it personally."

Paris pulled in a deep breath and everything he'd thought about the situation shifted and became something very different. They hadn't turned him away. Mr. Jenson hadn't even known he'd tried to reconnect.

Mr. Jenson shoved his hands in the pockets of his pants. "I

loved PJ. It was hard to lose him… You." Mr. Jenson cleared his throat and looked off into the distance. "It's been hard to lose Nancy, memory by memory, too. I guess some part of me didn't say anything when I realized who you were because I was just plain tired of losing. Sometimes it's easier not to feel anything. Then it doesn't hurt so much when it's gone." He looked back at Paris. "But I can't seem to lose you even if I wanted to, so maybe I'll just stop trying."

Paris's eyes burned. He blinked and looked down at his feet for a moment and then back up at the old man. He was pretty sure Mr. Jenson didn't want to be hugged, but Paris was going to anyway. He climbed the steps and wrapped his arms around his foster dad for a brief time. Then he pulled away. "Like I said, I'll be back next week, and I'll take you to go see Mrs. Jenson."

"See. Can't push you away. Might as well take you inside with me when I go see Nancy next time. She'll probably tell you to go away and never come back."

"I won't listen," Paris promised.

"Good." Mr. Jenson looked relieved somehow. His body posture was more relaxed. "Well, you best get on with your night. I'm sure you have things to do. Maybe go see that pretty librarian."

Paris's heart rate picked up. He was supposed to be at Lacy's side tonight, but while she was bravely facing her fears, he'd let his keep him away. His parents were supposed to love him and stand by him, but they hadn't. His ex-wife had abandoned him too. He guessed he'd gotten tired of losing just like Mr. Jenson. It was easier to push people away before they pushed him.

But the Jensons had never turned their back on him. They'd wanted him and he wished things had gone differently.

Regardless of what happened in the past, it wasn't too late to reconnect and have what could've been now.

As he headed back to his bike, Paris pulled his cell phone out of his pocket and checked the time. Hopefully, it wasn't too late for him and Lacy either.

———

Lacy looked at her reflection in the long mirror in her bedroom. She loved the dress she'd found at Sophie's Boutique. She had a matching pair of shoes that complemented it perfectly. Her hair was also done up, and she'd put on just a little bit of makeup.

She flashed a confident smile. "I can do this."

She took another deep breath and then hurried to get her purse and keys. The reunion would be starting soon, and she needed to leave before she changed her mind. The nerves were temporary, but the memories from tonight would last. And despite her worries, she was sure they'd be good memories.

She grabbed her things and drove to Sweetwater Springs High School where the class reunion was taking place. When she was parked, she sat for a moment, watching her former classmates head inside. They all had someone on their arm. No one was going in alone. Except her.

She imagined walking inside and everyone stopping to stare at her. The mean girls from her past pointing and laughing and whispering among each other. That was the worst-case scenario and probably wasn't going to happen. But if it did, she'd get through it. She wasn't a shy kid anymore. She was strong and confident, and yeah, she'd rather have Paris holding her hand, but she didn't need him to. "I can do this," she said again.

She pushed her car door open, locked it up, and headed inside. She opened the door to the gymnasium, accosted by the music and sounds of laughter. It wasn't directed at her. No one was even looking at her. She exhaled softly, scanning the room for familiar faces. When she saw Claire Donovan, the coordinator of the event, standing with Halona Locklear and Brenna McConnell, she headed in that direction. They were always nice to her.

"Lacy!" Brenna exclaimed when she saw her walking over. "It's so good to see you." She gave her a big hug, and Lacy relaxed a little more. "Even though we all see each other on a regular basis," she said once they'd pulled apart.

Lacy hugged the other women as well.

"So you came alone too?" Lacy asked Halona.

"Afraid so. My mom is watching Theo for a few hours. I told her I really didn't need to come, but she insisted."

Brenna nodded as she listened to the conversation. "Sounds familiar. Everyone told me that you can't skip your high school reunion."

"This is a small town. It's not like we don't know where everyone ended up," Halona said. "Most everyone anyway."

"Don't look now," Summer Rodriquez said, also joining the conversation, "but Carmen Daly is veering this way."

Lacy's heart sank. Carmen was the leader of her little pack of mean girls. How many times had Lacy cried in the girls' bathroom over something Carmen had said or done to make her life miserable?

Lacy subtly stood a little straighter. Her brace was gone, and whatever Carmen dished out, she intended to return.

"Hi, ladies," Carmen said, looking between them. She was just as beautiful as ever. Lacy knew Carmen didn't live in Sweetwater Springs anymore. From what Lacy had heard,

Carmen had married a doctor and lived a few hours east from here. Her vibrant smile grew sheepish as she looked at Lacy. "Hi, Lacy."

Every muscle in Lacy's body tensed. "Hi, Carmen."

Then Carmen surprised her by stepping forward to give her a hug. For a moment, Lacy wondered if she was sticking a sign on her back like she'd done so long ago. KICK ME. I WON'T FEEL IT.

Carmen pulled back and looked Lacy in the eye while her friends watched. "Lacy, I've thought about you so many times over the years. I'm so glad you're here tonight."

Lacy swallowed. "Oh?"

"I want to tell you that I'm sorry. For everything. I'm ashamed of the person I was and how I acted toward you. So many times I've thought about messaging you on Facebook or emailing you, but this is something that really needs to be done in person." Carmen's eyes grew shiny. "Lacy, I'm so sorry. I mean it."

Lacy's mouth dropped open. Of all the things she'd imagined about tonight, this wasn't one of them. She turned to look at Summer, Brenna, and Halona, whose lips were also parted in shock, and then she looked back at Carmen.

"I've tried to be a better person, but the way I behaved in high school has haunted me for the last ten years."

Lacy reached for Carmen's hand and gave it a squeeze. "Thank you. Looks like we've both changed."

"We grew up." Carmen shrugged. "Can you ever forgive me?"

"Definitely."

Carmen seemed to relax. "Maybe we can be friends on Facebook," she said. "And in real life. Maybe a coffee date next time I come home."

"I'd like that." Lacy's eyes burned as she hugged Carmen

again and watched her walk over to her husband. Then Lacy turned her back to her friends. "Is there a sign on my back?"

"Nope," Brenna said. "I think that was sincere."

Lacy faced them again. "Me too. It was worth coming here tonight just for that." Someone tapped her shoulder and she spun again, this time coming face-to-face with Paris.

"Sorry to interrupt," he said, looking just as sheepish as Carmen had a few minutes earlier.

She noticed that he was dressed in the shirt he purchased from Sophie's Boutique. "Paris, what are you doing here?"

"Hoping to get a dance with you?" He looked at the dance floor, where a few couples were swaying.

"I... I don't know," she said.

Summer put a hand on her back and gave her a gentle push. "No more sitting on the sidelines, Lacy. When a boy asks you to dance, you say yes."

Lacy took a few hesitant steps, following Paris. Then they stopped and turned to face each other, the music wrapping around them. "Paris"—she shook her head—"you didn't have to come. As you can see, I didn't chicken out. I'm here and actually having a great time. I don't need you to hold my hand."

He reached for her hand anyway, pulling her body toward his. The touch made her grow warm all over. "You never needed me. But I'm hoping you still want me."

Lacy swallowed. *Yeah*, she definitely still wanted him. She looked at his arms looped around her waist. They fit together so nicely. Then she looked back up at him. "I lied when I said that we could still be friends, Paris. I can't. I want things when I'm with you. Things I shouldn't want, but I can't help it."

"Such as?" he asked.

Lacy took a breath. She might as well be honest and scare him off for good. "I want a relationship. I want to fall in love. I want it all. And I just think it would be too hard—"

Paris dropped his mouth to hers and stopped her words with a soft kiss.

"What are you doing?" she asked when he pulled back away.

"I want things when I'm with you too," he said, leaning in closer so she could hear him over the music. "I want to kiss you. Hold your hand. Be the guy you want a relationship with. To be in love with."

Lacy's lips parted. Since they were being honest…"You already are that guy. I mean, not the love part. We haven't known each other very long, so it's too soon for that. That would be crazy."

"Maybe, but I understand exactly what you mean," he said.

She narrowed her eyes. "Then why are you smiling? You said you didn't want those things."

"Correction. I said I didn't *want* to want those things." He tightened his hold on her as they danced. "But it appears it's already too late, and you're worth the risk."

"So you're my date to this reunion tonight," Lacy said. "Then what?"

"Then tomorrow or the next day, I was thinking I'd go to your family's house for dinner and win over your dad."

Lacy grimaced. "That won't be easy. He'll want to know what your intentions are with his daughter."

Paris grinned. "My intention is to put you on the back of my bike and ride off into the sunset. What do you think he'll say to that?"

She grinned. "I think he'll hate that response. But if you're asking what I think…"

"Tell me," Paris whispered, continuing to sway with her, face-to-face, body-to-body.

"I love it." Then Lacy lifted up on her toes and kissed him for the entire world to see, even though in the moment, no one else existed except him and her.

About the Author

Annie Rains is a *USA Today* bestselling author of small-town contemporary romances full of hope and heart. After years of dreaming about becoming an author, Annie published her first book in 2015 and has been creating happy-ever-afters for her characters ever since. When she isn't writing, Annie is usually spending time with her family, bingeing Netflix, or reading a book by one of her favorite authors. Annie also enjoys spending time with her two rescue pets, a mischievous Chihuahua mix and an attention-hungry cat, who inspire the lovable pets in her books.

You can learn more at:
   AnnieRains.com
   Twitter @AnnieRainsBooks
   Facebook.com/AnnieRainsBooks

FALL IN LOVE WITH MORE HEARTWARMING ROMANCES BY ANNIE RAINS!

Somerset Lake

Sweetwater Springs

 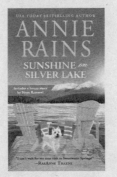 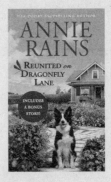

Can't get enough of that small-town charm?
Forever has you covered with these
heartwarming contemporary romances!

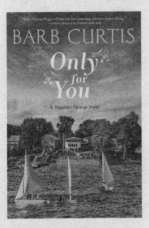

ONLY FOR YOU
by Barb Curtis

After Emily Holland's friend gets his heart broken on national TV, he proposes a plan to stop town gossip: a fake relationship with *her*. Emily has secretly wanted Tim Fraser for years, but pretending her feelings are only for show never factored into her fantasy. Still, her long-standing crush makes it impossible to say no. But with each date, the lines between pretend and reality blur, giving Tim and Emily a tantalizing taste of life outside the friend zone...Can they find the courage to give *real* love a real chance?

THE HOUSE ON SUNSHINE CORNER
by Phoebe Mills

Abby Engel has a great life. She's the owner of Sunshine Corner, the daycare she runs with her girlfriends; she has the most adoring grandmother (aka the Baby Whisperer); and she lives in a hidden gem of a town. All that's missing is love. Then her ex returns home to win back the one woman he's never been able to forget. But after breaking her heart years ago, can Carter convince Abby that he's her happily-ever-after?

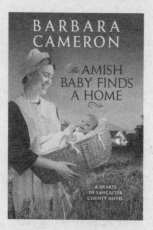

THE AMISH BABY FINDS A HOME
by Barbara Cameron

Amish woodworker Gideon Troyer is ready to share his full life with someone special. And his friendship with Hannah Stoltzfus, the lovely owner of a quilt shop, is growing into something deeper. But before Gideon can tell Hannah how he feels, she makes a discovery in his shop: a baby...one sharing an unmistakable Troyer family resemblance. As they care for the sweet abandoned *boppli* and search for his family, will they find they're ready for a *familye* of their own?

NO ORDINARY CHRISTMAS
by Belle Calhoune

Mistletoe, Maine, is buzzing, and not just because Christmas is near! Dante West, local cutie turned Hollywood hunk, is returning home to make his next movie. Everyone in town is excited except librarian Lucy Marshall, whose heart was broken when Dante took off for LA. But Dante makes an offer Lucy's struggling library can't refuse: a major donation in exchange for allowing them to film on site. Will this holiday season give their first love a second chance?

Discover bonus content and more on
read-forever.com

A STROKE OF LUCK
(2-IN-1 EDITION)
by Jill Shalvis

Get swept off your feet with two Lucky Harbor novels! In *At Last*, a weekend hike for Amy Michaels accidentally gets her up close and personal with forest ranger Matt Bowers. Will Matt be able to convince Amy that they can build a future together? In *Forever and a Day*, single dad and ER doctor Josh Scott has no time for anything outside of his clinic and son—until the beautiful Grace Brooks arrives in town and becomes his new nanny. And in a town like Lucky Harbor, a lifetime of love can start with just one kiss.

DREAM KEEPER
by Kristen Ashley

Single mom Pepper Hannigan has sworn off romance because she refuses to put the heart of her daughter, Juno, at risk. Only Juno thinks her mom and August Hero are meant to be. Despite his name, the serious, stern commando is anything *but* a knight in shining armor. However, he can't deny how much he wants to take care of Pepper and her little girl. And when Juno's matchmaking brings danger close to home, August will need to save both Pepper and Juno to prove that happy endings aren't just for fairy tales.